A SIRENS OF

OF SONG AND SCEPTER

LIESL WEST

OF SONG AND SCEPTER

Copyright © 2024 by Liesl West. All rights reserved. Published in the United States of America.

First Edition.

Publication date: July 2, 2024

www.lieslwest.com

No part of this publication may be reproduced, distributed, or transmitted in any form or by any means, including photocopying, recording, or other electronic or mechanical methods, without the prior written permission of the author, except as permitted by U.S. copyright law. For permission requests, please contact the author via email: author@lieslwest.com.

This book is a work of fiction. Names, characters, places, and events portrayed are products of the author's imagination. Any resemblance to actual persons living or deceased, places, buildings, and products is coincidental.

Identifiers: ISBN 979-8-9900482-1-8 (paperback) | ISBN 979-8-9900482-2-5 (hardcover) | ISBN 979-8-9900482-0-1 (ebook) | Kindle ASIN B0CWWH156Y

Cover design by Miblart.com
Map illustration by Rachael Ward at cartographybird.com
Developmental Editing by Clever Editors; Line Editing by The Blue Couch Edits; Proofreading by L.A.PS Studio

To the original little mermaid. You should've picked the knife.

CONTENT WARNING

THIS BOOK IS INTENDED for mature audiences and contains sensitive content not recommended for readers under the age of 18. Find a full list of content notes on the last page of this book or visit the author's website: www.lieslwest.com. For a list of spicy scenes and where to find or avoid them, reference the index titled *The Octopussy's Garden* at the back of this book.

www.lieslwest.com/content-notes

PRONUNCIATION GUIDE

Characters
Almar: ALE-mar
Aris: AIR-iss
Clio: CLEE-oh
Enna: EH-nuh
Hugo: HYOO-go
Myrrh: MER
Nara: NAR-uh
Odissa: oh-DISS-uh
Ruven: ROO-ven
Soren: SOAR-en
Tephra: TEFF-ruh
Varik: VAIR-ick

Places
Adria: AY-dree-uh
Aquisa: uh-KEY-suh
Vespyr: VES-per

PLAYLIST

Black Sea – Natasha Blume
Siren – Kailee Morgue
Killer – Valerie Broussard
Breakfast – Dove Cameron
You've Created a Monster – Bohnes
you should see me in a crown – Billie Eilish
Horns – Bryce Fox
A Little Wicked – Valerie Broussard
Blood // Water – Henri Werner, Salvo
FANGS – Neoni
Undone – SINA
Love into a Weapon – Madalen Duke
Mermaids – Florence + The Machine
Impostor – Henri Werner
Can't Help Falling in Love (DARK) – Tommee Profitt
Wicked as They Come – CRMNL
If I Killed Someone For You – Alec Benjamin
Deep End – Ruelle

Listen to the full playlist: https://lieslwest.com/links

Three may keep a secret, if two of them are dead.
———— Benjamin Franklin

Chapter One

ENNA

I count my life in kills.

My first was the hardest: a male siren with a scowling face. My knife didn't cut deep enough, and the poor fucker clung to his life. It took me until my twenty-third kill to perfect the flick and slice of my blade. I've killed 2,735 since him, and now I know better. I have learned how to make it painless, as easy as blinking.

I'm a death-dealer. A monster. But like Odissa says, there are worse things to be than deadly—dead is one of them.

Soon, I'll be thirteen kills older. Already, my blood warms with the anticipation of my task, hot against the cold, black water.

Twelve merman soldiers swim in single file above me, pumping their tails in a quick but labored rhythm. Each carries a darksteel trident strapped to their backs; the metal clinks against their scales.

These are royal soldiers. Their fear is palpable. I can smell it from down here, thick and uneasy. They're deep in the Drink—the home of monsters far more wicked than a death-dealer like me. In these abyssal plains, dredgebeasts make a quick snack of anyone stupid enough to cross their waters.

But I'm no one's snack.

Like a death sentence, I approach from beneath, rising through the black water. As mermen, they lack the advantage of heightened siren senses. Their noses are flat, their eyes beady and small.

Lesser beings. My father's disdainful voice filters through my memory, but I shove it away. I have no use for his sentiments here.

Mermaid or magic-wielder, we bleed the same. I angle for the back of the formation, where the soldiers swim with less confidence. *Easy targets.* The first soldier dies to my knife: one cut to his throat, across the gills, and the merman falls limp. His blood blurs my dark vision. I push his body into the blackness to mask his scent. I have less than a minute now to dispose of the formation before their blood attracts a feeding frenzy.

The next soldier goes the way of the first. One by one, I slit their throats, easing into my rhythm. At the center of the formation, the Abyssal Princess swims, oblivious to her approaching fate, the glint of her siren tail reflecting the dim light of the glowmites.

Killing the princess is Odissa's ticket out of the Drink, she said when she gave me the order. And if all goes well with this deal, she will release me from her service.

My knife cuts through withered skin. *That's 2,743 kills for Odissa.* And after each kill, she promises to grant me freedom from our blood oath. How many more kills after this hit? When will my work finally be enough to appease her?

2,744. With the blood of eight soldiers flooding the water, I'm out of time. Their bodies sink toward the abyssal plain below, where the dredgebeasts lie in wait. I grab the nearest bleeding neck and focus, stirring the magic in my belly. I run my fingers over the hot line of my cut. A quick, short hum of my siren Voice, and lightning zaps beneath my fingertips, cauterizing the wound. The purple light slices through the dark.

The princess screams, and the four remaining soldiers stir into action, fumbling for their weapons.

Time's up.

I dive deep, locating each sinking corpse before they escape. With a few more zaps of my magic, my job is nearly done.

Water rushes in my ear, stirring the glowmites into movement. A trident narrowly misses my head as I twist out of its path. I grab the staff and yank the guard off his balance. Smacking my tail, I send a fury of bubbles into his face, and he grunts before my knife finds its mark. *Zap.*

Three more soldiers, then the princess.

I can almost taste my freedom. Will she be the last siren I kill? The final price to pay for the life I want? Visions of warm beaches and sunlit tidal pools flood my brain. Rumors of these things come from merchants, though I've never confirmed the existence of the sun. I've always imagined it would be green, like a massive ball of glowmites suspended from the sea of air that gathers above the surface.

I barely dodge the jab of the next trident, growling in frustration as it slices my arm. Its darksteel edge leaves a stinging trail.

Dammit, Enna. Focus.

I turn on him, grasping his weapon. But the male is stronger than the others, unfazed by my attempt to unbalance him. In the light of the glowmites, I find his eyes—small, black orbs set in a flat, gray face. He bares his teeth, revealing a double row of sharpened bones.

We grapple for control of his weapon, our tails slapping together. The closer I keep my body to his, the less capable he is of making the shot with the trident. Where he is large and muscular, I am small and lithe, and my knives fit easily in tight spaces. I lift my knife through the opening beneath his arm, angling for his gills.

From out of the deep, a streak of turquoise light barrels toward us. The gel globe of the creature's head pushes through a cloud of glowmites, which illuminates at her touch. Glowing streamers dangle from her body. Out here, Odissa is conspicuous.

And she's going to ruin our score.

The princess shrieks again, whirling helplessly in the water and pointing at the oncoming attacker. The two remaining soldiers, previously scrambling to find me in the darkness, spot Odissa immediately and take aim. Maybe I should have killed the princess first.

The soldier I'm fighting takes advantage of my distraction and rips his trident out of my hands, sending me into a head-over-tail spiral. I lose my grip on my knife, and it sinks, lost, to the deep.

Fuck. That was my favorite one.

The soldier thrusts his trident at me. Unable to draw another dagger, I sink my claws into his face. His jaw works furiously, snapping those teeth. My magic stirs, and I let out a long, low note of my Voice. Lightning courses through my hands, illuminating each bone in him with crackling purple light. His eyes glow under my touch, and his body writhes, until I release his corpse into the Drink. My energy drains, and I curse.

Above me, Odissa has the princess bound in the tight web of her tentacles, leering as the siren wiggles.

A dead soldier sinks past me, the flesh of his face feathered and torn by Odissa's raging claws. A messy kill. Annoyed, I snatch him and suture the wounds best I can, but there's already too much blood in the water.

The princess screams again, so Odissa clamps her hand over the siren's mouth to stop her.

"Nobody can hear you scream out here, princess," she snarls. "Nobody but me and the dredgebeasts. And we don't want to wake them up, do we?"

"My brother will have you killed for this. Unhand me." The princess's voice comes out weak and shaking. The glowing light of Odissa's skin casts angry shadows over the planes of the royal's soft face.

With a long, sharp finger, Odissa traces the length of the princess's arm—pale, flawless, the skin of a siren. Not a mermaid's claw or tentacle in sight. "So beautiful." She snatches a strand of floating, silver hair, drawing it out of the restless tresses. "So fragile. But you know that already."

The princess's eyes widen, pale blue and round, reflecting the light of Odissa's translucent skin. "I have an appointment with the Kingdom of Coral. I will be missed, and they will come hunting, trench-scum."

I inhale through my mouth, scenting the water for signs of a dredgebeast. The soldiers' blood hangs in a thick, warm cloud. We should move.

"Odissa, let's go," I hiss.

The mermaid ignores my warning. "And what does their prince see in you? Princess Aris." The youngest sibling of the Abyssal King, but even that is debatable. Rumors of mermaids in the parents' royal bedchamber. Kings like their females high-born, or did you forget?" Odissa grabs a handful of hair, fingers twining tight against Aris's scalp. "You pass as a siren, at least. And you have the Voice?"

"Don't touch me," Aris whispers.

Pathetic, soft female. The princess reminds me of a younger version of myself—steeped in nobility, weakened by comfort. I almost feel bad for her, the way her wide stare searches for a hero who will never come. Hope fades into sad, resolute acceptance of her own death. Not a shred of fight left in her. Had I been this pathetic when Odissa found me that day, 2,746 kills ago?

"It's not nice to play with the target, Odissa," I snap. "Be done with it." I hate when I go soft, but I cannot stand to watch her suffer any longer. I've spent enough time burying my own regrets beneath a steel shell in my stomach, and I'm not about to dredge them up over a crying royal. Not with my life on the line.

I unsheathe another dagger, swimming closer. At the sight of my knife, the princess blubbers a stream of bargains as she finally fights for her life; too little, too late.

"Go ahead then," Odissa grunts, finally moving her hands to give me a clear shot at the neck. But as I aim the tip of my knife, she grabs my wrist.

"Wait," she snaps. "Not there. Cut her lower, between the ribs. Somewhere inconspicuous."

Aris writhes, her whines of protest loud and unrelenting. I glare at Odissa, irritated by her indecision. This mission has been anything but efficient—a bloody, botched mess, thanks to her.

The princess will die painfully. I'll crack her bones, puncture her lung. She'll die in a few minutes, gasping and gurgling, loathing me all the while. I angle my knife once more toward her neck, where it will be quicker.

A familiar cold grip of magic wraps around my wrist, halting my hand. I swore an oath to help Odissa succeed in every way—bound in blood until the day she frees me. I press against the magic, and the resistance tightens. It's a pointless fight. Either I do as she commanded, or I die defending this final shred of my morality.

What does it matter how she dies if I must kill her either way?

The grip of magic eases around my wrist. My knife slips between the ribs, and the princess's whine cuts off with a gurgle. She glares at me with unfocused eyes as life slowly drains from her face.

2,747.

I suture the wound, ears pricked and mouth scenting for the sounds of a dredgebeast.

Instead, I hear the clinking darksteel and stirring water. A lone wounded soldier pumps his tail, his trident reflecting the light from Odissa's skin.

Fuck. I missed one.

Chapter Two

ENNA

I'M NOT A SLOPPY killer. I take my job as a death-dealer seriously—I kill quietly, precisely, and I clean up the mess afterward.

Never have I let a target get away. The wounded soldier dives into the current that leads to the royal city, and I pursue him, leaving Odissa to harness and tether the princess's corpse.

My tail slices with swift precision. I track the male by the iron scent of his wounds. Odissa's blue light dims the farther I swim from her. My pulse races through my body in a thudding rhythm as fear creeps in. Sloppiness in the Drink is a death wish.

This was supposed to be a solo mission. Odissa would wait at the Hissing Bloodfish, connect with the client, and I'd deliver the body. Instead, my master showed up mid-mission, lit up the water with her glowing globe of a head, and distracted me enough to let a soldier slip through my fingers. Just so she could taunt the poor thing before I killed her?

Odissa isn't a strong swimmer. Her gelatinous body is soft, with the exception of her torso, arms, and face. Where my hair sprouts from my scalp, Odissa has four oral arms and a jelly bell. Where I have a sleek tail, her torso fades into strings of wispy tentacles. I can control my bioluminescence with a flick of my magic; her skin glows ceaselessly, a beacon in the darkness. Her talents as a death-dealer are advantageous in long-game missions, in complex schemes with moving targets.

She observes. She analyzes.

I kill.

It's the way we've operated since she found me in the royal city of Dredgemaw. Magic-wielders don't usually mix with mermaids; not in the Abyss. The sirens are glad of the divide the Drink creates between us. But I'm a half-breed, so I belong nowhere.

Odissa sees potential in me. From a distance, I look full siren, and with my Voice and high-born upbringing, I can blend in at the royal court. Her appearance would raise questions.

We make a good team—when we stick to our expertise. When we don't, shit like this happens. And I'm the one who has to clean it up.

Odissa calls out to me, the panic in her voice diluted by the water stretching between us. "Let him go, Enna!"

The soldier's tail is almost within my grasp. I fight to swim through his current, reaching up with both hands. My core burns with exertion. Blood roars in my head, matching the heat of my fury.

He will not escape me. Not this time.

"Enna! Let's go!"

A rumble sounds in the deep, low and grating. Then comes the clicking, echoing across the Drink—a dredgebeast seeking its prey.

My claws graze the slippery edge of the merman's tail.

"ENNA!" Odissa's shriek is desperate. She treads in a cloud of the soldiers' blood, tethering a fresh corpse, with no hope of outswimming the beast.

Another boom. The sound ripples through the water, pushing me off course. The merman dives out of my reach. If I let the witness go, the whole mission could fail. He'll report us to the Abyssal King, and we'll be dead in two sleeps' time.

The beast draws closer, its clicking tongue growing louder. Gritting my teeth, I pull up short. The soldier is bleeding. Odds are, the beast eats him, too.

"ENNA!"

I dive deep, following the light of Odissa's skin until I find her fumbling with the tether rope. I check her knot around the princess's waist, make an adjustment, and loop the cord through my harness. One final cinch, and the corpse snugs against my back like a rucksack.

"Let's go!" I kick my tail without waiting for her response. The corpse is heavy but not unmanageable. As long as I don't dive or twist too much, the body should stay in the proper state for delivery to the client waiting for us in Vespyr. With the extra weight, however, I cannot reach my usual speed. I pray to Tephra below that the dredgebeast goes for the wounded soldier.

Odissa undulates behind me, her tentacles contracting as she propels through the water. Her glowing skin is a moving target, the only light between here and our destination.

The clicking noises of the beast grow closer. Odissa's hands grasp my tail, hitching on for a ride. I struggle to cut through the water, anchored by not one but two dead weights.

"You just had to come out here, didn't you?" I scold her. "I had it under control!"

"Clearly not. That soldier should be dead."

She pulls herself up the length of my tail, twisting to latch onto my belly. Her wispy tentacles thread beneath my harness, and she clutches me tightly. The soft, gel globe of her head nestles beneath my chin.

I growl, knowing she can feel it rumble through my body. "And he would be dead if you had stayed in Vespyr and let me handle it."

"You would have sliced her neck."

"That's my protocol."

"Then you should be thanking me. The client needs the body in perfect condition."

Behind me, the dredgebeast increases its clicking. The water around us ripples as the beast's large, scaly form forces through. I can't see its paddle-like fins, but I can sense them—churning the deep.

If I can't outswim this dredgebeast, it won't matter what condition the body is in.

The clicking stops. An ominous silence settles in, the only sounds my fin's labored push through the water.

The dredgebeast is within attacking distance. *Fuck. Fuck. Fuck.* I squint into the darkness ahead of me, searching for the pinprick of light emanating from Vespyr.

There. A bright blue dot pierces the blackness like a beacon of safety—still out of reach. If we want to make it to the city alive, I'll have to fight off the beast.

"Odissa, let go," I whisper.

Her tentacles slither away from my body, releasing me from the burden of her weight and swimming toward the light of Vespyr. There's nothing to be done about the corpse, no time to transfer the tether. With a flick of my tail, I twist to face my adversary.

In the dim light of Odissa's retreating glow, I can only make out the outline of the beast's snout, each nare twice my length. The water stirs as the beast inhales, scenting my position.

The beast lunges. With a snick of its bones, the jaw unhinges in a woosh of water. I follow the current, floating closer to its face. Claws extended, I collide with its snout and begin to climb. The jaws snap shut, jolting me. My hold slips. The princess's corpse shifts, and I dig deeper, sinking my claws behind a thick scale into the soft flesh beneath.

The beast screeches, sending shockwaves. The reverberation shakes my skull, and my teeth clatter. Its head whips and bucks. Those slit nares flare as it tries to locate me by scent. But I'm too close. I claw my way on its nose, resting on the long surface between its eyes.

With what remains of my energy, I stir the magic in my belly. I could fight it with my knives, but I have extra cargo today—precious cargo I can't afford to damage in a bloody scuffle.

My Voice is off-pitch and urgent. Lightning splits the dark. Along the beast's head, a row of scales illuminates, running the length of its large body—one stripe down the middle means this is a male.

The males are smaller than their females, but they make up for it in aggression. He won't give up easily. With another shriek, he shakes his massive head, trying to dislodge me. But my claws anchor me in place. I draw my head close enough to sink my fangs into his scales, too.

I deepen my Voice. Lightning crackles from my hands and mouth. The magic burns in my eyes.

My stomach churns, rapidly depleting its energy stores. If the beast doesn't go numb soon, I will die from exertion. To kill a dredgebeast of his size will take everything I have.

The purple glow of my magic travels from his skull to the tip of his long, thrashing tail, caressing each of his bones.

But my magic is running dry, yet still, he moves.

I pry one hand from his skin and stretch for his great, black eye. Growling, I slice into the soft flesh—a straight shot to his brain. His body twitches, writhing, as my magic courses through him. His screech cuts short, and the mighty dredgebeast goes limp, tilting toward the abyssal plains below. I release his body with numb hands.

The energy tax of my magic squeezes. My brain fogs. My body turns to ice. The last thing I see is the distant speck of Vespyr, still out of reach.

The beast will awaken soon, and I pray to Tephra that he kills the wounded soldier after he finishes devouring me.

Chapter Three

SOREN

I AM THE PARAGON of power, sweating in a pair of linen pants.

The seat of my mother's throne grows harder against my ass with every passing minute. I shift, trying to find a better position. My stiff muscles protest, forced to assume a formal posture when I should be slicing a trident through the water in the reef's training ring right now. This duty belongs to my mother, the queen. But she's not here, and the throne cannot remain empty on the day of supplication. I will not allow it.

So I sit here, drenched in sweat. Like the rest of the palace, the Coral throne room is hot and humid—the most egregious downside of perching a palace atop the sandbar instead of beneath it. As I question the decisions of my ancestors, I survey the large, gilded door of the chamber and wait for the next supplicant to enter and state their complaint.

A dull ache forms at my temple. I rub the spot and groan, leaning against the back of my seat. The vaulted ceiling arches above, the sloping arcs of gold meeting in a domed center. A gilded frieze depicts scenes of my ancestors conquering the reef territory generations ago. Each figure is lined in gold paint, reflecting the light of the room. The prevalence of fangs and claws in the figures gradually lessens in their procession to the epicenter, showing the path of my lineage from vicious conquerors to reigning monarchs as we earned the civilized seat of power.

One image always catches my eye—the lead couple from the first generation. A strong, dark king wields his magic to seduce and subdue the terrain, while his warrior female mate brandishes a crooked knife. The female, Amura, is terrifying and cunning, whisking through the battlefield like a wraith, leaving fallen enemies in her wake, while the male, Eero, leads the charge against the dredgebeasts of the reef with a single trident and a brave heart.

They're like midnight and morning; opposite, complements that would not exist if not for the other.

Annoyance scratches the edges of my mind, as it does every time I study this painting. Eero and Amura's example of unity is the very reason I must marry before I can take the Coral Throne. The crown is stronger when two rule as one.

But the odds are slim of finding a female who meets my standards. In my three and a half decades, I've yet to find one who even comes close. It shouldn't be this difficult. All I want is someone who balances my power without hungering for more—equally intellectual, humorous, and passionate. And as much as I desire a mate who will love me for me and not for the throne I sit upon, I drowned that hope long ago.

The longer I procrastinate my selection, the less choice I'll have in the matter. With each roll of the tide, my mother grows more anxious to pass the throne. One of these days, she will appear with one final candidate in tow and put the whole thing to rest.

I swallow the thought with a frown, then tuck one ankle under the other and lean on the armrest. The soft fabric of my pants slides over my skin, wicking the sweat beneath my thighs.

Beside me, my late father's attendant—now mine—tuts his disapproval. The familiar sound conveys his reprimand for unfit posture of a future king. He pinches his long, thin nose.

I'm here only because my kingdom requires it of me. I've been trained from the day I hatched to fill this seat, doing my duty with a practiced smile.

To save Hugo and I both the argument, I stiffen into the proper position and raise my hand for the next supplicant.

The royal treasurer bows when he reaches the steps. "Ah, Your Highness," Lord Varik says, greeting me before I greet him. The treasurer has never respected my authority. His eyebrows knit in feigned confusion. "I was expecting—"

"My mother?"

"My business is with the queen." His voice is slippery as an eel.

"I am hearing the requests today." I focus my stare, unblinking, as if I could dissolve him with a mere look. He has distinct eyes—yellow, with thin black slits—and a round, dark green face. His smooth siren ears signal magical blood in generations past, but he is no magic-wielder.

"She's dealing with matters of state," I say. "Lord Varik, state your business with the crown."

"Yes. Well. This eliminates the middleman, doesn't it?"

"Speak plainly, Lord Varik. You waste the crown's time."

He bows his head, then flashes a devilish smile. "Your Highness, I hear you are still in need of a wife."

I drum my fingers on the armrest. "I am. But certainly not from one of your caves, my lord." The treasurer oversees many financial sectors, most prominently the underbelly of the reef.

"She's not from my caves, Your Highness."

Hugo eyes my twitching fingers, and I force them to lay flat against the marble.

"Your Highness, I'd like to introduce you to an eligible young lady for your consideration."

It was not a question of permission, but I once again ignore his slip in decorum and nod my assent.

He gestures to the gilded door behind him, and a tall female walks through.

I lean forward and press my fingertips together. She's young, not more than two decades old. The female is pretty, her youthful skin a glowing spring green. Curly brown hair styled in an exquisite Coral fashion. Bits of shell and pearl weave in elaborate patterns. A stray curl has worked its way out of the knot and dangles over her forehead, much like my own curls. I smile at that.

When my assessment reaches her eyes, yellow with rounded irises, the resemblance to Lord Varik is undeniable. The female appraises me with admiration, lingering on the lines of my physique. She flicks her gaze to the floor, but not before I catch the flash of ambition there, a burning lust I've seen all too often.

Lust not only for me, but for the throne.

Disappointment twists in my gut. It's a pity I must reject her—she has the natural poise of a queen.

"Your Highness," Lord Varik continues. "May I present to you my daughter, Miss Francesca Varik."

Miss Varik steps forward and curtsies. She holds her posture, waiting for my response.

I need a wife. I cannot claim my right to the throne without one. But here stands yet another female, ready to sink her fingers into my power.

"Miss Varik," I say. "How lovely to meet you." At that, she straightens and flashes her perfect teeth. Her eyes shine with triumph.

"Thank you for your generous offer, Lord Varik," I say. "I decline."

Francesca's nostrils flare. The smile dissipates, her mouth contorting into a snarl to match her father's.

Lord Varik clenches his jaw. "Your Highness—"

I hold up my hand. "You are dismissed."

"Your Highness, please. If you'll schedule me an appointment with the queen directly, I'm sure she'll hear my—"

"You are dismissed," I repeat, waving him away. The guards lurch forward, grasping Lord Varik and escorting him from the chamber.

Miss Varik raises her chin with a jerk and follows him out.

Hugo scribbles in his notes.

I slump into my seat. "How many more, Hugo?"

He checks his list. "Fifty, Your Highness."

My subjects bear the same requests every time I hear them: higher salary for the harvesters, more restrictions for careless magic-wielders, more parties for the notoriously drunk. No more marriage proposals, thank the gods. I drum my fingers on the armrest with each passing one, impatiently waiting for the line to dwindle. And yet the requests kept pouring through the door.

Between supplicants, I motion for Hugo. He bends down so I can reach his ear. "Make a note for me."

He readies his bone quill.

"My mother will be pleased to hear she's relieved of her duty. I will hear our subjects more often."

He hesitates with his quill in the air, considering my request. My lips twitch. He tucks the pad back into his robe.

"Very funny, Your Highness," he says. "Her Majesty would disapprove. You're not king yet."

"Her Majesty isn't here to laugh at my jokes. Her absence is the reason I'm doing this at all."

"Only a handful more until low tide, and then you can kick them out."

Sighing, I motion for the next request, the ache in my temple now pounding in a steady rhythm.

Five minutes before low tide, as if summoned by my irritation with her, the chamber doors swing open unannounced, and my mother breezes through.

The queen marches down the aisle. Her thick silver hair is knotted atop her head in a towering display. Her soft pink skirts hiss over the floor. The chained weave of her whitesteel chest piece softly clinks with every step, adorned with shells and colored glass that complement the glowing deep tan of her skin. Firm jaw, flashing eyes. At her sides, her hands flex open and closed. The room grows silent and still.

"Out," she says. The guards file out of the room.

"I've found you a queen," she announces.

"Hello, Mother," I say, rising from her throne. "How go the matters of state?"

She ignores me. "Since you've been so slow to secure a suitable bride, I've made the decision for you."

"Slow? Why, I heard a proposal just this morning."

This catches her off guard. "And?"

"Unworthy of your appraisal, Mother. I dismissed Miss Varik."

"No matter. The Abyss has offered a match. Their youngest princess, Aris."

My eyebrows twitch. From what I've known, the reclusive dark-dwellers don't deal with the surface kingdoms often, preferring to stew in their murk and nurse a centuries-long grudge against us for chasing the dredgebeasts into their territory.

"The princess arrives within the week. You'll court her, and we'll hold the wedding at the end of this moon. You'll be king, and I'll be in Cresway, sunning myself on the beach and enjoying my long-earned retirement."

I swallow past the tightness in my throat. "Just one moon?"

My mother massages her temples and closes her eyes. "Yes, Soren. Do keep up."

My fingernails dig into my palm, and I force my fist to uncurl. If she only knew how much I *keep up* with the mess she's leaving me, she wouldn't be making demands.

"Clio." She snaps her fingers, and her quiet attendant rushes forth, carrying a notepad. "We need to arrange for the escort, lodging, wardrobe, meals, royal balls..."

Clio's bone quill scratches, and I slump into my chair. I knew this day would come eventually—my mother would tire of my hesitation; I would be forced into an arranged marriage—but I wasn't prepared to face it quite so soon.

I didn't expect to feel this way when it happened. Empty. Like the vast chaos of my future has punched a hole into my stomach and sucked me into it.

I clench my teeth, fists, and toes—anything to keep me grounded in this room. There are things to be done; a kingdom to run. And, hell, I don't even know if I will like this Abyssal Princess. What if she has a third eye? What if she, like Miss Varik and the rest, only wants me for the power I represent?

"No," I declare.

The whine of my mother's voice cuts off, and she blinks at me. "Yes."

Clio stops scribbling.

I shake my head. "If I'm going to marry this princess, it'll be because *I* find her worthy. Not because you're telling me to. I'm not merely your subject to command, Mother. I'm your son."

She blinks again, as if I'm speaking to her in screamerfish. "This is not open for discussion."

"Hugo, what time is it?" I ask.

"Low tide, Your Highness."

"Good." I step toward the door. "I'm late for the practice ring."

Mother crosses her arms, and a low hum of magic fills the air. When she speaks, her Voice stirs the room, thick with persuasion. The strength of her magic tests the defenses of my mind. My thoughts soften and lift. A foreign willingness prickles at the back of my mind. "Soren, you will do what's best for the kingdom."

Her magic tugs me, but I cut it off with a short bark of my own Voice, slicing through the spell's mental chains. I push past her. The ache in my head roars now, loud as crashing waves.

"If you want *your* word to mean something," she thunders after me, "then marry the princess and earn your spot on that throne."

As if I haven't been trying.

Chapter Four

ENNA

My tail is burning. Scraping, more like. As if my scales are dragging across scorching, rough pumice.

My eyes fling open, greeted by the black stone streets of Vespyr, inches away from scraping off my nose. A rough rope threads through my vision, tethered to my harness, where I secured the Abyssal Princess in transit. But the weight of her corpse is gone.

The princess.

I've lost the fucking princess in Vespyr—the vile, malicious city that has been home to the scum of Adria since Goddess Tephra inhabited the sea. The city drowns in poverty, and a catch like mine will draw attention. Bounty hunters. Death-dealers. Starved guppies looking for easy meat. That corpse could be anywhere.

I thrash my tail, lifting myself in a fury. If some motherfucker is after my bountihead, I won't be dragged through the streets without a fight. I grab the rope and yank, bringing me closer to my kidnapper.

Odissa barrels into me with a grunt. Her tentacles tangle around me, ruffled with a cutting edge. "This is the thanks you give me after I dragged your ungrateful ass to safety?"

Then the princess's corpse bobs into me, attached to a second tether rope, also threaded through Odissa's harness.

"How did you...?" Odissa is weak. There's no way she completed the journey alone.

"Very slowly."

"And the dredgebeast?"

"Never returned. You zapped him good."

We don't mention the wounded soldier. I know I failed; Odissa will not set me free.

I grunt, making quick work of her tether knot. My body is sore, my magic barely beginning to refill in my gut. The thermal waters of Vespyr thaw my frozen fingers. "And the rendezvous?"

"Not much farther." She struggles to swim under the weight of the princess's corpse but seems to be managing well enough, so I let her keep it. Less work for me.

I scan the street for familiar landmarks. But every lamppost, glowing with green glowmites, looks the same in this goddessdamn city, and the abodes are too similar to distinguish. The dwellings carve into the face of a rocky column, the dark spaces within hollowed out as if by the goddess's spoon.

The city of Vespyr clings to the side of a vertical tower of pumice, warmed by the flowing lava within—the only source of life this far into the Drink. Sprouting from the sprawling desert of lifeless sea-rock and sand that covers the rest of the Drink, Vespyr's rockface stretches toward the surface, leagues above, disappearing at the edge of sight. I've swum to its peak once in my life, where the black water fades to gray, then blue. There's nothing but wide, open sea, and the stretching terror of it nearly stopped my heart.

Down here, the black water clutters with debris. Vespyr has been a dump for as long as I can remember. I weave through the dross as I follow Odissa through the street channel. If this is the last time I swim this route, it won't be a moment too soon.

We pass groups of mermaids huddled in their caves. A few are out swimming like me, but most have extinguished their lanterns and settled in for rest. As I pass, they glare up at us, their bulging eyes glowing faintly. They track my movements, round lips peeling back over sharp fangs.

As if I haven't spent most of my life scrambling in the darkness, just like the lot of them. Death-dealing is a respectable trade in Vespyr—one of the best sources of income among a cutthroat group of mermaids—but I'm the only death-dealer with magic.

And that means I can't be trusted. I'm one of *them*, a siren blessed with Voice. At any moment, I might force them to submit to the mercy of my magic.

I'm used to the wary looks. Sirens don't belong here unless they're dead and dragged through the street. I look like my siren father, with my smooth white skin and angelic black tail, features softened by magic. My mother's mermaid blood gave me fangs, spines, and the poison that runs in my veins. By Vespyr's judgment, I shouldn't be here. I should be cushioned and cozy in a water-tight mansion in the royal city. Warmed by magic. Ignorant of the realities across the Drink.

Vespyr would kill me in my sleep, if I weren't Odissa's weapon, bound to her by oath and magic far stronger than my own.

As I slip further down the rockface, the pockets of dwellings disperse, giving way for more of the rough, black stone and signaling the trade district. Soon, the Hissing Bloodfish, the small tavern where I conduct most of my transactions, comes into view. Relief spreads through my chest at the sight of its creaking metal sign picketed to the stone. Almost there.

Deliver the princess. Collect the bounty.

It should have been simple. But Odissa doesn't make the dive into the Hissing Bloodfish; instead she swims on, passing into the lower reaches of Vespyr. The glowmite lamps gradually lessen in number, and the pumice column grows warmer the closer we swim to the sea floor.

"Something you forgot to mention, Odissa?" I snarl. Mermaids poke their heads out of their caves as we pass. Their necks crane to get a better look at our obviously expensive cargo. Even in the darkness, I can sense their gazes assessing me.

"Not much farther," Odissa says. "Keep up."

"Who's the client, Odissa?" I rack my brain for our usual customers, skipping through the dour faces.

She doesn't answer.

My stomach skirts another dwelling, and I barely evade the mermaid hiding inside. Long, wiry hands writhe out of the hole, grabbing for the princess. Hissing, I unsheathe a knife and slice the mermaid's grasping fingertips. With a piercing howl, the hands retreat. *Motherfucker.*

The mermaid's wailing echoes after us until finally, Odissa dives for an opening in the rock. I recognize the entrance instantly: the jagged outline of its signature protruding edge. Like rows of teeth in black stone gums, the Jaws are aptly named.

Odissa disappears between the Jaws, entering the home of the Eater of Souls. And I have no choice but to follow her inside.

Chapter Five

ENNA

"Have you lost your *fucking* mind?" My voice reverberates down the long, rocky channel, awakening the glowmites.

Odissa smiles over her shoulder—her mouth too wide, her smile too forced. The glint in her eyes is too bright. "Something like that," she says, as though it's the simplest thing in the world. Like she's not swimming deep into the heart of Vespyr's rocky core, straight for the lair of the death goddess herself.

The water is thick and metallic, tinged with a subtle green glow of the glowmites. I inhale, taking in the strong metallic scent. In the bottom dredges of the channel, amidst curling and coiling poisonous plants, rests the skeletons of merfolk stupid enough to try and bargain with death. Tail bones jut out of a crevice, their wide fanning bones stripped clean of all flesh. Skulls sit in the porous holes of the channel, peering at us with black, gaping eyes. Their fangs eroded by years of soaking in saltwater. A thin film of bacteria coats the bones, giving them a clouded, fuzzy softness.

The temperature rises the further we swim, until the channel is unbearably hot. My gills flutter at my neck, laboring to draw in oxygen from the water.

The channel opens into a large cavern. Blood hangs in thick curtains, barely stirring in the lack of current. A few stray fish swim through, nibbling at the algae clinging to the walls. The chamber is empty, albeit well-lit. I scan the walls, the ceiling, the floor—anything for signs of life.

There's nothing here, save a layer of bones so thick I could walk on it two-legged and not touch the ground beneath.

"I don't think she's here, Odissa," I whisper. "Let's get out of here before—"

Odissa whirls and snaps her teeth at me, silencing my protest. "Don't you get it? Tephra *is* the client, Enna. We made a deal. She's here." She then glides into the chamber without hesitation, hefting the corpse.

I cough, spraying bubbles. It all makes sense: Odissa's refusal to reveal the client, the high cost of the bountihead, the sudden change of plans in the Drink. Had the original client fallen through, forcing Odissa into a deal with the devil?

"Who backed out of your deal, Odissa? I'll kill him with my bare hands. Tell me who. We'll hunt him down, force him to pay, and forget all about this goddess shit."

She centers herself in the room, untethering the corpse and arranging her neatly atop the pile of bones. The princess's silver hair—now soaking in blood—fans out across the lifeless faces.

"There's no time," she says. "That soldier will reach Dredgemaw, and her king brother will be after us soon enough. You want a way out of the Drink? This is it, Enna. There's no turning back." Hope flutters in my stomach. She might take me with her at least, if she doesn't plan to free me.

She cups the princess's cheek, smoothing her thumb over the jaw. "Besides, you made an oath. Or don't you remember?"

The first time I met her, Odissa held me at knife point. I vividly remember the cut of cold steel against my soft guppy throat, the tangle of her fingers in my hair as she held me against the wall in the dark corridors of my father's house. She smelled of ash and iron. Her sharp teeth glinted with blood. She did not kill me then, which is as good as saving my life. And when someone saves your life in Vespyr, you owe them a lifetime of service.

I touch the pit of my palm, where we'd dragged our blades until the blood ran thick, muttering our promises to the goddess of death—keeper of all bargains, Eater of Souls. A promise Odissa has never let me forget: *I will do everything in my power to help her succeed in every endeavor.* Seemed harmless to a guppy. But now?

"I remember," I mutter through gritted teeth. Would I have made it in this sea, had she not found me? Had she not cultivated me—me, a soft-bellied court shrimp—into a ruthless killer? I'll never know. She's the closest thing to family I have.

"Good," Odissa snaps, then unsheathes a blade and slides it across her palm. She lifts her bleeding hand and begins to chant. "*Dark is the water, thick is the mud. Come to your daughter, great goddess of blood.*"

The water stirs, a slow, cyclone current lifting the blood. Fish fall into the swirling current, struggling with useless fins to escape. From the top of the cave, a deep chuckle vibrates—grating and rough as the pumice of Vespyr. Louder. Louder. The goddess's voice trembles through my bones, and my gills grow still even as my heart thrums in my chest. I cling to the mouth of the channel, watching from a distance that no longer provides a sense of safety.

Then a shadowy figure descends, spinning with the current in a purple-suckered vortex. Eight thick tentacles fan out, each one as thick around as three of me. The metallic scent grows unbearably strong. The rumbling laughter intensifies until I can hear no other sound.

She lands on a writhing mass of tentacles, each limb slithering out with a mind of its own. Bones crack beneath her colossal weight. The goddess, Tephra, is huge; her smallest finger is the size of me. Like me, she wears the pale skin of an Abyssal siren, but her face is sharper, her teeth longer. Instead of rounded siren ears, hers fan out like fins, lazily paddling the water. Her lips are black as her tentacles, a sharp contrast to her almost translucent skin. Her dark eyes inspect the blood and the corpse Odissa offers, and that mouth curls into a wicked smile.

"Back so soon, little fish?" Tephra says, her voice as cold and deep as the Drink.

Odissa lifts her chin but does not meet the goddess's gaze. "I have sacrificed greatly for you, mighty Dark One. Please accept this life in exchange for completing my bargain."

The goddess bends at the waist, tentacles shifting, and she licks the blood from Odissa's hand, catching the last remnants of juice. For a moment, the goddess's gaze lands on me, assessing me with curiosity.

Then, with a twisting tentacle, Tephra caresses Odissa's cheek. "Tell me, little fish, which siren's body are you donating for the exchange? It seems you've brought two. And this one's still alive. I do enjoy a live sacrifice."

Every cell in my body unravels. My gills splutter against my neck as I draw shattered pulls. But I stay frozen to the skeleton floor, my blood oath clamping my free will in its icy grasp. *Help her succeed in everything she does.*

Even if it means making a deal with the devil. But if Odissa aims to *feed* me to the soul-eater, all oaths are off. I will not go down that easily.

Odissa smiles. "That one is not part of the exchange. Just the princess."

The goddess flicks her gaze to me once more. I meet her gaze squarely and lift my chin.

Tephra's smile only widens, wickedly so. "A blood bargainer, I see." A chill races through my body as her gaze travels from my scalp to the tip of my tail. "You sure you want to be here, pet? We could make a deal of our own."

My pulse flutters, missing a beat. The dark magic of my oath curls around my neck, my arms, tightening its grip. What is the goddess offering me? A way out? I narrow my eyes. That's not possible.

When I don't answer, Tephra blinks. "Very well," she says, returning her gaze to Odissa, and only then do I allow myself to relax.

Tephra's tentacle curls around the princess's limp tail, lifting it. Silver hair hangs like fine strands of kelp from Aris's scalp. "Ah, yes. The cost is great indeed, worthy of a great wish." She spins the body, inspecting every inch. "These scars will not come out, you know.

Wicked suture, that." The forming scar tissue on the corpse's chest where I stabbed her in the Drink is jagged and rough.

Odissa shoots me a look. "I know."

Tephra cocks her head, studying Odissa carefully. Odissa holds her posture under the goddess's scrutinizing gaze, and I wait for her to crack. But where many bargainers may have quivered and fled, Odissa stays erect. Focused.

The goddess finally blinks, breaking the tension. "You're after the Coral Prince, you said?"

"Yes, the princess is due to meet him for an arranged marriage. I expect to take her place and win his throne myself."

The goddess throws back her head, and that dark laughter ripples once more through the water. "Oh, this will be delightful. Truly. I love a good courtship scheme, and it's been far too long since those sun-drenchers got what's coming to them, don't you think?"

Odissa smiles. "Yes, that sounds quite—"

Tephra snaps her fingers, and Odissa falls silent. "I'm inclined to make a few tweaks to your initial request. That Coral Prince is a slippery fish to catch. I'm a woman of business, and for bargains like this, I require *proof*. Say, a wedding? You have until the end of the moon to secure your royal marriage. He must vow in my name to love you till the day he dissolves."

"You said all I needed to do was win his heart." Odissa's tentacles quiver, betraying her nerves. "Win it. As in, I get him to fall in love with me."

"Yes, well. Plans change. And what is love if nothing but a game? I need something a little more... substantial."

"But—"

Tephra raises a tentacle. "Pray you remember your place, little fish. I'm in a good mood."

Odissa's expression hardens, and she bows her head. "Thank you, you are most generous."

"Do we have a bargain?" The goddess leers, fixing Odissa with her perfectly off smile.

This deal weighs heavily in the goddess's favor. How Odissa expects to impersonate a royal, I have no idea. Not to mention, pulling off the ruse in another kingdom, and a surface kingdom at that. Princess Aris, trained from hatching to be a royal, would likely have struggled with the match. Odissa is a death-dealer from Vespyr with no Voice training. She will not survive this bargain. And when Odissa fails, I'll be left to clean up her mess.

What the *fuck* is she thinking?

This is unlike any of Odissa's previous schemes—it's rash, dangerous, and by the sound of it, half-improvised. And there's no kill at the end. Does she expect me to help her with this deadly love game? I'm notoriously bad at feelings. Sex, I can do. But the heart-pumping, gut-twisting romantic shit? I'd much rather knife a prince.

Odissa extends her hand. "It's a deal. And I never disappoint."

Tephra laughs, snatching her wrist between two fingers. With her fingernail, she cuts the flesh of Odissa's palm, flooding the water with her blood. Tephra presses her finger into the wound.

Odissa groans, her face contorting in pain. She gasps and clutches her wrist. The goddess lifts her finger to her mouth, sucking in a wispy trail of Odissa's blood, then licks her lips.

"Excellent," the goddess says, her voice taking on a musical quality. Tephra's song begins low—a deep, solemn note. Her hands glow white, channeling her spell. She releases Odissa's arm, and the death-dealer spins, sinking against the skeleton floor with a crackle of bone.

Tephra stirs the water into a circular current, sucking Odissa and the dead princess into a spinning vortex. The tendrils of Tephra's magic weave into the current, carrying the sound of her dark Voice. Odissa floats higher, her hands splayed out, her pink tentacles twisting out in a jumble. Shadows encircle her body, writhing over her and the corpse until only blackness remains. Odissa screams.

Tephra's song morphs, dissonant. Her mouth opens in a wry smile. She closes her eyes, tilts her head, and then, after what feels like an eternity, the goddess cuts her spell. Finally, Odissa's body drops to the floor, a lifeless carcass. The princess, dead moments prior, twitches with new life. The fluttering silver tail moves, slowing her descent to the floor. The arms raise. The eyes open—bright and blue—and the head turns to glare at the goddess with Odissa's signature scowl.

Tephra snatches Odissa's old body, dangling it before her mouth.

"Wait!" Odissa calls out in a light, melodic voice. Nothing at all like her graveling sneer. She lifts a dainty hand.

Tephra smiles, eyes alight with mischief. "That body is yours to keep for the remainder of its lifetime," she says. "If you succeed."

Odissa's new fins quiver. She presses her hand to her scarred chest, tracing the line of my suture. "And if I fail?"

Tephra's gaze flicks from Odissa to me and back again. "Then you'll be my dessert."

Chapter Six

SOREN

I TWIRL THE TRIDENT in my hand, savoring the familiar shift of its weight as it slices through the water. Muted light catches its three whitesteel tips. The sun filters from the surface above, casting a dance of light across the sandy seabed. The coral walls of the training arena curve up, forming a bowl in the sharp barrier.

Ten pairs of mermen square off in the arena. Their muscled tails stir the water as they hover in place, assessing each other, weapons poised. At the bark of a commanding officer, they charge one another. The clang of metal weapons weaves a steady rhythm, lulling me into a sense of calm. I relax my gills and tighten my grip on my own trident.

"Are you ready, Your Highness, or are we going to admire your fancy fork all evening?" Nara says.

I laugh, gripping the trident more tightly. "It is rather beautiful, is it not?"

The mermaid smirks, angling her own trident with the practiced ease of the kingdom's best military captain. "I've seen better."

If any other subject spoke to me that way, they'd lose their tongue. But Nara is different—a lifelong friend, and the closest I'll ever have to a sibling. We've known each other since we were mewling guppies exploring the reef—her sneaking into places she shouldn't be, me sneaking out of places I shouldn't leave, and the both of us getting into too much trouble for my mother's liking.

Nara stirs the water with her tail, her white-tipped tendrils disturbing a crowd of bubbles. The pattern of white and maroon stripes continues up her tail to cover every inch of her skin, wrapping around her stomach, the bulge of her muscled arms, the thick strands of her neck. Her red hair ties in a tight, efficient knot on top of her head. Nara watches me with large, round eyes, unblinking. The maroon irises focus with intensity, no doubt analyzing every twitch of my muscles and shift of my scales, just as I do for her.

With a flick of my tail, I attack, swinging my trident. Nara lifts hers to meet mine with a dull clash. She presses against my weapon, knocking me off balance. I swim back a pace, adjusting my grip and refocusing my aim. But Nara is quick. She wastes no time, stabbing at my open side. When the tines brush the bare skin of my chest, she withdraws.

"Contact," she says. "Your Highness is off his game this evening."

My gills flutter in irritation. "Again." I lift my trident and reassume my position. My mind is restless—too restless. I'm eager to find the sweet rhythm of exertion, swinging my trident again and again. The more we stop to talk, the longer it'll take to get me out of my head.

She quirks her mouth knowingly. "Eager to meet your new queenie?"

I roll my shoulders, and the tension eases for a moment. My body is wound tight like a lyre, ready to snap.

"Something like that," I say.

"You have a few days yet to cry about it. My squadron leaves bright and early tomorrow morning, and it'll be three days before we bring her home."

"Do me a favor? If she's a complete nightmare, just leave her there."

Nara laughs. The practicing soldiers turn to look in her direction, their faces bewildered and longing. As if the males could change her gender preference with an intense enough ogle.

"Oy!" I shout at them, and they avert their eyes.

She smirks. "Can't leave her, sorry. Orders from the queen and all."

"A prince can dream." I point my trident at her. "Again."

She wiggles her eyebrows, ignoring my request. "If you don't like her, be sure to introduce her to me personally before you send her back to the Abyss. I've heard the dark-dwellers are a prickly lot, and I wouldn't mind expanding my repertoire."

"She's a magic-wielding royal. She won't be prickly."

She frowns, running a hand over her hair. "That's a shame."

Taking advantage of her distraction, I bring my trident down. Nara lifts hers without flinching.

"You think you have a choice?" she chides. "Even if she does have spines?"

We take turns striking, and I push my advantage, backing her toward the crowd of fighting pairs behind us. The sounds of our spar blend with the clash of metal from the other soldiers, the noise ricocheting off the curved walls of the arena.

"This is my choice. I need to secure a queen."

She ducks my hit, then darts around me. Before I can twist to face her, her trident's tines graze the skin of my back.

"Contact. And you're a terrible liar."

"This is my choice," I repeat, louder, as if raising my voice might make it true. The words seem hollow, regardless of how many times I utter them. Nara lifts an eyebrow. "Again," I growl, launching into another attack.

The clash of whitesteel ripples through the water, and we fall into our easy rhythm at last. My muscles heat and my body slowly begins to unwind, settling into the comfortable pattern of movement. Even then, she easily overpowers me. With her decades of practice in body-movement fighting, I'm still burdened by my habitual reliance on magic. Most magic-wielders don't train in the arts of hand-to-fin combat, relying solely on their control of the Voice. But as the crown prince and sole heir to the Coral Throne, it's my duty to be better. To master myself in every way possible. I will be worthy of the throne when it's mine. I've worked my entire life to make sure of it.

But when Nara lands the tenth hit, I lose my resolve. She swings at me, and I tap into the energy that swirls in my gut, letting out a quiet tune. Dark green magic bursts from my lips, and I grasp Nara's trident with my tendrils of sound, yanking her off balance to land a hit to her stomach.

"Contact," I say.

"Where's your honor?" She shakes her head, the corner of her mouth curling in a smile.

"I have none," I say, mirroring her smirk.

"That's your worst lie yet today." She sheathes her trident in the holster between her shoulder blades and crosses her arms. "Hey, you okay?"

"Have to be."

She grimaces. "Well, you know where to find me."

"Good trip tomorrow? I hope the Intercurrent doesn't give you too much trouble."

"Nothing I haven't dealt with before." She jerks a thumb over her shoulder, indicating a crowd of guards sparring in the fighting rings. "I've gotta get back. Try not to shrivel up in your sandcastle till I get back, eh? Touch some water once or twice." Humor sparkles in her eyes.

I dip my head. Already, my mind feels clearer. Sharper. My muscles are smooth and warm, the soreness of the day leaking out slowly into the water. "Aye aye, Captain."

Chapter Seven

ENNA

"Still need to think this through?"

I stare at the Abyssal Princess's lips, fascinated by the way my master's caustic essence can still come through, despite her royal glamor.

I bare my teeth. "I was debating just killing you now, saving myself the trouble."

She sneers. "Fine. Send my condolences to the Abyssal King."

The Kingdom of Coral is a three-day swim to the west if we take the Intercurrent. According to Odissa's intel, Princess Aris is expected to meet the Coral escort at the Abyss entrance to the Intercurrent soon. We'll accept the escort in her stead, me in the place of a beloved handmaiden whom Aris would never abandon. And, if the Coral escort doesn't sniff out our lies by then, we'll follow them into the royal city of Aquisa and take things one step at a time. Odissa woos the prince. They marry. And she'll release me of my blood oath, never to ask for my help again.

Or so she says. But I have a good feeling about this job. It *will* be my last. One more headache for a life of freedom? It's a risk I'm willing to take.

Soon the lights of Vespyr disappear beneath us, and we swim, suspended in the darkness.

After a while, Odissa groans. "I can't see."

"Is that a request for assistance, Your Highness?" I ask, sarcastically.

She grunts, continuing to swim.

Then she slams into the pumice, her skin scraping along the rough rock. "These eyes are useless. How do sirens live like this?"

Feeling smug, I smile. If she thinks the double eyelids are weird, I cannot wait for her to discover the rest of her body's quirks. Her round, smooth teeth will struggle to cut raw meat, for one. And if Coral is anything like the Abyssal siren courts, she'll likely spend a lot of time in her two-legged form.

"Lower the inner lid. That's your dark vision. Your old body didn't have that."

Her eyelids *snick* into place. A moment passes. "I still can't see."

"Use your shiny new siren Voice, chum-brain. Make a little light for yourself."

Odissa concentrates, generating a gravely purr. She adjusts the pitch higher, then lower, but nothing happens.

"Voice-box broken?" My joke falls flat. Anxiety sinks its claws into my neck. If Odissa doesn't have the Voice, how the fuck is she going to convince these foreign royals she's a worthy suitor? Her charming personality?

She slaps on her chest, clears her throat, and tries again. The same grating purr. No lightning.

"It's a feeling in your gut. Tap into it. Do you sense the energy pooling there?"

Odissa screeches in frustration. "This body's a fucking half-breed. I knew there was a risk, but I thought, maybe..."

I brush off her implications. I know I'm part of a lucky few. Most half-breeds don't inherit the Voice. Maybe this princess was Voiceless. When I attacked her troop in the Drink, she hadn't fought, hadn't assailed me with her own magic.

"Fuck." Panic leaks out of her voice.

Sighing, I clench my muscles, emitting a soft purple glow from the stippled patterns beneath my skin. Odissa straightens her path but says nothing. Her arms flail as she pumps her tail, struggling to adjust to her new fins. Her blue eyes widen with desperation, but she sets her jaw and pumps harder.

"We'll figure something out," I say. I can see it now—my freedom slowly slipping away. Failing this assignment is not an option. "We'll have to."

Gradually, the blackness of the deep fades to gray, then to deep blue, as we draw nearer to the surface. We crest the rock column, passing into open waters. My eyelids click, the dark-vision layer lifting to adjust to the light. Though the pressure of the ocean has eased in our ascent, the pressure in my chest only squeezes harder. I survey the endless stretch of blue—wide and menacing.

Finally, a faint line of light appears above us, stretching across the ocean. A dark group of merfolk cluster near the Intercurrent's entrance, awaiting our arrival.

I nod toward them. "You ready for this?"

Odissa rolls her eyes. "Of course, dimwit," she says. "I've been studying. Follow my lead and stay quiet. You are a handmaid, remember, so act like one."

As we swim closer to the Intercurrent, my pulse quickens. I concentrate on the speed of my gills, forcing them to slow their pace. I've faced dredgebeasts in the Drink. A little fast water and social trauma is nothing compared to that.

The Coral escort comprises ten stern-looking, mermaid guards—nine males, one female. The array of colors represented in their scales alone surpasses the amount of color I've seen on any mermaid in my life. While the mermaids in the Abyss are mostly muted shades of gray or blue, these mermaids are pink and yellow and green and orange, all displayed in varying striped or spotted patterns. They're beautiful. Angelic, graceful, and soft.

Around their chests, they wear matching whitesteel armor, emblazoned with the curly crest of their court. They each hold whitesteel tridents. The female swims forward. Red and white stripes curl around her limbs and face. Her red hair is slicked into a tight bun. Her appearance is sharper than the rest, more menacing despite her smaller size. She carries a long knife belted to her waist, which she grasps lightly, as she angles her tail and bows in greeting.

"Your Highness. Captain Nara at your service," she says.

Odissa extends her hand, and the captain grasps it lightly, bowing to kiss her knuckles. "Pleased to make your acquaintance, Captain." Odissa's voice is smooth confidence, void of any trace of her usual disdain for the world at large. "I pray you have not been waiting long."

"It's a long journey from the deep," Nara says. The captain pauses, raking her eyes over Odissa as if searching for errors. My gills slow as my panic rises. Can this female's astute gaze sense our ruse?

At last, she smiles and nods. "We are pleased to see you arrive safely, Your Highness. Come." She gestures to the rushing stream of water. "We have arranged a transport for you."

Nara's mouth settles in a hard line, flat and unreadable. Her brow is equally unflustered. She raises her hand, and a fleetwhale exits the current. The great blue fish's head parts the roaring water, slipping out with a pump of its flat, wide tail. It backpedals its fins, slowing its speed and rearing its head as the driver perched atop its head pulls hard on its harness tethers.

The fleetwhale stops so that I am level with its large, black eye. Its eyelid clicks shut once, before reopening, fixed on me. In the inky depths of its eye, I find an intelligent soul, searching me just as I am observing it. I offer the creature a small smile, and it blinks again.

"Enna, darling," the princess's voice calls. I turn to see Odissa perched on the whale, as one of the guards attaches her harness to one of the many straps running in circumferent stripes down the creature's back.

Captain Nara stares at me, gesturing for me to join. I kick my tail, propelling toward the whale. A male soldier with a soft, spotted face catches my harness and pulls me to an attachment point. His hands brush my hips lightly.

My spines rise from their sheaths. My fangs lengthen at the threat. Rigidness seizes my posture, and a hiss escapes through my lips.

The soldier freezes, removing his fingers from my skin. "Apologies, my lady," he says. "I only mean to connect the tether."

A cloud of bubbles floats between us as my tail stirs the water. "I can knot my own tether, thank you," I manage through clenched teeth.

"Are you sure, my lady? It's my duty to be of assistance."

I twist to face him, and he backpedals. His eyes are calm and steady, seemingly unaffected by my outburst. He raises his hands in innocence, like he didn't just invade my personal space. Like I'm the one at fault here.

Over his shoulder, I can see Odissa, whose eyes are dark and commanding, as if she's trying to bend me to her will with only her thoughts. Her message is clear—a handmaiden shouldn't be acting like this. I am jeopardizing the mission.

I close my eyes, but even the shutter of my eyelids is not enough to soothe my nerves. Slowly, I force my gills to still through sheer will. I open my eyes and give a curt nod to the soldier.

"Certainly," I say. With quick hands, he tethers me in, careful to avoid touching my skin. Then, he secures himself to the attachment in front of me, giving me a view of the back of his shaved, red head.

The female captain ties herself in front of Odissa, giving me a curious sideways glance. "On your mark, driver," she shouts. The driver barks a command. Then, with a lurch, the fleetwhale dives into the rushing current.

The water tugs us forward with a speed that propels my heart. The fish lets out a low whine, pumping its tail. My tether shifts with its movements, but I am otherwise secured. We hang suspended in the tube-like current, the fish paddling calmly as the water whisks us forward at a velocity I never thought possible. Around us, more fleetwhales swim, each carrying their own loads. Little paddledrakes dart in and out of the current, maneuvering their broad, hard shells to weave between the larger fish.

Meanwhile, the ocean passes around us, leaving behind everything I once knew. A knot forms in my stomach as I stare down, straining my eyes as if I might see the dark expanse of the Drink below. But there's nothing but clear blue water in any direction, every particle and plankton highlighted by the sunlight streaming down from the surface. I'm exposed and vulnerable, even under the protection of the large fleetwhale. The water is too thin. The pressure, too soft. The light, too bright.

The only thing interesting to look at is the back of the soldier's head. I count the blue dots on his shaved scalp, making pictures and patterns from the chaotic arrangements. At one point, he grinds his teeth, and a blood-vessel pops out along his skull, like a rope running its length.

We float in silence long enough for the waters to darken, then lighten again. The rhythmic swish and flex of the fleetwhale's muscles lulls me into a shallow sleep filled with disorienting dreams.

***

Captain Nara clears her throat, stirring me from my restless reverie. "Welcome to Coral, Your Highness," she says, smiling over her shoulder at Odissa.

The water has brightened into a pure shade of turquoise, uncomfortably warm. Dread pools in my stomach. We are not trained for court. I know too little of its customs to fit in properly here. Of all the tasks Odissa has given me, this is the worst. This is a fool's errand, and I am no fool.

I could stay in the current, cut my tether and follow it to the Kingdom of Frost, or to Estuary. Seek out the nomadic group of the Brine. Make a life for myself from scratch. I could leave Odissa to her doomed love mission, never to see or hear from her again. I wrap my hand around the knot, poised for the move that would set me free. I locate the easiest tear point, just beneath the knot. I dig one claw into the fibers, then stop as the familiar restraint of my blood oath rushes through my veins.

I cannot do this. I cannot help her succeed.

But the magic doesn't listen, because it knows I'm lying. I may be the only person in the sea who can help her now. Like cold hands, the dark magic wraps around my wrist, releasing my grip from the rope.

The fish veers to the left. The exit comes, and the fleetwhale dives through it, severing my escape route with a flourish of bubbles.

Chapter Eight

SOREN

Afternoon low tide is my favorite time to run on the beach. In a few hours, the waves will nearly reach the walls of the keep, but for now, the exposed sandbar stretches in wide circumference around Aquisa's proud sprawl, leaving room for wandering thoughts. I settle into a rhythm quickly, keeping the wall to my right as I head north. I relish the way my muscles flex and burn in the heat. One foot after the other, digging into the warm sand.

My headache is worse today. Two days ago, I woke in blissful ignorance of my mother's dealings with the Abyss. Since her announcement and the departure of Captain Nara's escort, my time has been consumed by the plans for the princess's arrival this evening. The housekeeper, Clio, has whipped the staff into shape, preparing everything we requested on short notice.

I should be thrilled. All the pieces are falling into place, and I've hardly needed to lift a finger or make a decision.

The throbbing at my temple synchronizes with the rhythm of my feet. Nearer to the shoreline, merfolk lounge lazily, tanning their bronze legs and drinking rum, gossiping about the latest court drama. My name passes among them in whispers, paired with *Abyssal* and *invitation to the royal wedding,* and occasionally *about godsdamn time.* As I pass each group, they hush and touch their hidden gills in a sign of respect.

Set above, set apart—such is the life of a royal. I'm destined for loneliness and greatness all at once. I've carried this burden since my father's accident three years ago. With no possibility of continuing the royal line herself, my mother wasted no time lining up my suitors ever since.

Since the day I hatched, an endless stream of tutors drilled me in my studies, and mentors fine-tuned my skills in magic, weaponry, ancient language, and more. I've learned how to walk stick-straight, speak with authority, and hold my body in a manner that commands attention and exudes the confidence of a male nurturing a seat of power held for a millennium. I am just as sculpted as the statues that line the great hall, and someday soon, my own likeness will stand next to my father's.

I round the east side of the keep, where a few large boulders decorate the beach, creating a naturally secluded maze. Between the rocks, unseen bodies shuffle, voices moan, the sounds of a couple in the throes of orgasmic bliss. I lope past the rocks, pushing down the lump in my throat. By the night of the full moon, I'll be bedding a complete stranger.

Stumbling, I nearly miss a step. I round the south side, welcoming the sight of the long, empty beach. No one likes to lounge on this side of the keep due to the extremity of the sun, providing me solitude with my thoughts.

Thoughts of my destiny, slowly narrowing like a vise. The sun is suddenly too hot, too glaring, like a giant golden eye watching my every move. My stomach sours. I slow to a jog, then a walk. I make it only a few more paces before I lean onto my knees and vomit what's left of my lunch. I heave again and gag on dry air. Blackness teases the edge of my vision.

Pull it together.

I rise on shaking knees, kicking sand over my mess. The southern gate is not too far from here. I'll cut my run short. I'll go inside and lose myself in a steam bath—enjoy my last moments of freedom before my future washes up on this beach. I've been trying to outrun this moment for my entire life, and it's time to give up the game.

As I turn toward the gate, movement catches my eye. A lone figure walks along the beach. I squint. Not walking. *Hopping.*

She's undoubtedly female, with the smooth features of a magic-wielder, though she's no siren I've seen around my court before. Her skin is pale white, nearly the same color as the sand. If it wasn't for the black cloth dangling between her legs and the mess of black hair on her head, I might not have noticed her at all. Her short hair sticks up at odd angles. She moves in a sort of dance, hopping on one foot then the next and making wide arcing paths in no set direction that I can see. Like she's out here purely for the joy of dancing in the sand. She wears no chest piece, her breasts bare and bouncing with each step. For all I know, this strange, beautiful female could be my princess from the deep.

Then where is her escort?

I scan the beach, finding no sign of Captain Nara. Confused, I march toward the female. A deep tugging sensation propels me toward the little lonely dancer, like I've been hooked through the belly with a sudden, sharp need to protect her.

She looks Abyssal. There's no ignoring the pale white skin of her kingdom, likely to have never seen the light of the sun.

The female continues her hopping toward the gates of the keep. She pauses, spins in a circle, then cuts a path left away from the gate. Definitely lost.

The captain has some explaining to do. My concern threatens to burst out of me as I break into a run toward the helpless, wandering female with a ridiculous gait.

Chapter Nine

ENNA

I NEVER KNEW SAND could be this hot. The white grains—*not black!*—spread out in every direction on this damned beach, forming fluffy little piles from hell, and I swear my feet are about to combust into flames. The only way I can relieve the pain is by hopping from one foot to the other in an awkward dance, one so embarrassing to watch that Odissa ordered the Coral escort to carry her to the keep's gate, leaving me behind to flounder on my land legs. *That bitch.*

I've managed the two-legged transformation many times before. The pain of my bones cracking and rearranging within seconds, while once incredibly sharp, had become a reluctant routine in my frequent missions to the siren courts in Dredgemaw.

I know how to use my own damn pair of legs. The issue isn't me. It's this thin air, the trudging sand—all making it impossible to breathe, to balance, to *exist* without an immense amount of effort. If it weren't for that *fucking* blood oath, I would have turned around after my first step into this blasted kingdom.

The sun isn't anything like I expected. Its harsh light blinds me, reflecting off every surface in sight—the expanse of turquoise water that whispers behind me, the glitter that somehow *is* the sand, the white marble palace sitting proudly on the other side of this beach, and, *fuck,* the whiteness of my own skin. I can't even look at the back of my hands without squinting, eyes brimming with tears. And the *heat.* My skin feels like it's bubbling, boiling me from the outside in.

I hunch my shoulders and keep my face down, blinking rapidly and willing my eyes to focus and adapt. I drag in a shaking breath to steady my beating heart, pushing panic deep into my stomach. But the air is choking, full of heat and dust, nothing like the clean, cool, and sterile air in the siren sector back home. I cough, taking back everything I ever said about wanting to live in the tropics. This place isn't paradise. It's my personal living hell.

I scan the blurry horizon for the escort. They walked straight ahead, I think. Or was it to my right? The white world blurs around me. I grit my teeth, placing one stinging foot in front of the other, and march through the burning sand.

Damn this fucking court. Damn this climate. Damn this sand.

Run, I order, with a mental push on my legs. They, surprisingly, move with more speed than before, and I'm lumbering over the dunes.

Next thing I know, I smack into a rock. Pain explodes through my nose. Stars twinkle across my vision. I blink, forcing my eyes to focus on the rock. Or the chest, I realize, as I take in an impressive display of muscle that is undoubtedly male. Sweat beads on his rich brown skin, and his breath comes out in huffs. Dark emerald scales kiss the valley between his pectorals and gather around his belly button, trailing down, down, in a glittering path into—

"Seen enough, princess?" a deep voice purrs.

—into a pair of linen shorts, which cling to sculpted thighs.

"Princess," I repeat, its meaning suddenly lost to me.

I remember then that this rock of a body belongs to somebody, and I put up my hand, shoving hard on his chest to move him—or me—away as quickly as possible. He, as the rock, does not budge, and my shove only sends me plopping onto my ass. My bare, covered by only my loincloth, ass. I leap onto my feet with a yelp, crouching low. In the Drink, I kept this cloth folded in a pouch on my belt, large enough to protect the softer parts between my legs, yet small enough to pack away easily when I transitioned back into my tail. For the first time in my life, I see the downside of wearing as little clothing as possible. Here, it might just be the only barrier between this scalding sand and losing my sanity.

My feet burn beneath me, but I ignore them. Something tells me my skip-hop routine isn't local behavior. The male doesn't seem to mind the heat. I glare up at him, shielding my eyes against the sun with my arm.

His face is shadowed, backlit by the sun. But I can make out the hard lines of his jaw, the curtain of long black hair framing his face, the rounded edge of his siren ears, and the perfect slant of his nose. Above his nose, I find a pair of shimmering green eyes, which focus on me, deep and chaotic yet soft and kind, the eyes of a male who's never had to kill. They sparkle with mischief, roaming over my form as I squat in the sand and gape at him.

"Seen enough, my lord?" I say, smiling at my own wit.

His lips twitch at the corners. "Hard to tell," he says. "You blend in perfectly. I can hardly see you down there."

I don't like this tone of voice—teasing, playful, cocky. My eyes dart to his shorts again. The fabric is pleasantly tight, and I decide *cocky* is the right word for this male. And that smile? I know an entitled high-born when I see one; they look the same in every court.

He extends a hand to me. "Let's get you inside."

I stare at it, noting the smooth roundness of his fingernails, the rich, pretty color of his brown skin, and then I bare my fangs, waiting for the trick. There's always a trick with sirens. No magic-wielder has ever willingly helped me from the goodness of their heart.

"Feisty," he says, smiling wider. "Did our escort leave you to wander, or did you eat the captain in transit?"

I stand up, avoiding his outstretched hand. "Your captain is delicious, but unfortunately, she's not my type."

"And what is your type?"

I allow myself a moment of luxury, taking in the impressive male before me once again. He's prettier than any male I've seen in the Drink, even prettier than a few of the nobles I've killed. Maybe it's because he's a living, breathing male, or because he isn't actively trying to murder me before I can murder him, but I cannot seem to take my eyes off him. This Coral siren exceeds anything I envisioned from the merchants' stories back home. He's smarter, taller, broader—a sarcastic tower of muscle I desperately want to climb.

"Short," I say with a straight face, eyeing the plane of his abdomen. "And preferably with a little more meat on his bones."

He runs his hand through his dark hair, flipping the long strands behind his shoulders. It's hard to miss the flex of his muscles, the way his veins rise from his biceps from the heat. "You must be sorry to have stumbled upon the likes of me, then," he says.

"You're not much to snack on." My burning feet cannot bear the stillness much longer. Brushing the sand from my skin and shifting my feet to ease the pain, I peer around him to scan for the escort. I don't have time for games. I'm here for a job. The quicker I find the prince and marry him off to Odissa, the sooner I can check it off my list, earn my freedom, and get out of this hell.

"And you're nothing like what I expected." He's grinning at me, those green eyes dancing with a triumphant flame.

Grunting, I spin on my heels, heading off in the direction of the keep. The male follows me, and for a few heartbeats, I pretend not to notice. But then he starts kicking up sand as he walks, the hot grains spraying against the backs of my legs.

"Look, pretty lord, I'm in the middle of something," I snap, turning to face him again.

He raises his hands, flashing me with a brilliant white smile. My heart squeezes in my chest, and I rub at the spot, trying to push the knotted feeling away.

"I'm headed this way," he says, gesturing to the palace ahead of us. "I kind of live here."

"Oh," I say. Another high-born jackass stating the obvious. "Congratulations."

His laughter is thick and bubbling. Steady, deep. Interesting. Warm. *Dammit.*

I pick up the pace of my skip-hop routine, focusing on getting away from this male as efficiently as possible. But his long legs propel him much faster than mine do, and my land legs are more out of shape than I expected. I couldn't outrun him if I wanted to.

I wave my hand in a general left direction. "Walk over there, please."

He chuckles, sticking close. "Is that what you're doing? Walking?"

I ignore him, just as he ignores my request. I get the impression we are playing a game, and somehow, he's winning.

He takes my silence as encouragement to keep talking. "But that would leave you alone, my lady. Unprotected. Who knows what dangers lurk on this beach."

The beach is wide and blank, void of all life but me and this annoyingly attractive male. I size him up. He's muscular, but he's cocky and likely overconfident in a fight. I bet on a good day I could take him.

But this is not a good day, so I keep walking. We've nearly reached the walled city's shadow. My burning skin cries out for relief.

"Would you like me to carry you? It seems your feet are bothering you."

I stumble over the suggestion, missing a step. I careen forward, the hot sand rising to meet me. *Fuck.* Limbs flailing, I screech, all my nerves screaming in anticipation of my entire body touching that burning sand.

Suddenly, his hand snakes around my waist, lifting me out of free-fall as if I'm a wimpy rope. I'm tucked against his solid abdomen, legs hook over his forearm, and my bare ass greets the breeze.

And maybe it's the heat. The embarrassment. Exhaustion. Or maybe it's the annoyingly persistent nature of this noble male and his inability to leave me alone. But at his touch, I lose my last ounce of control. My spines, sharp and thin, tear through his flesh.

Chapter Ten

SOREN

She's magnificent.

This odd, feisty princess of the deep is intelligent, brave, and—gods above—she's *funny*. Even now, as she hops in a quickening pace through the sand, her legs flailing as if on fire, she's the most beautiful creature I've ever seen. I bite my tongue to keep from laughing. She's nothing like the stuffy, power-hungry princesses I've met. And deep in my gut, I have a feeling my mother finally hit the mark.

"Would you like me to carry you?" I ask in a calm, unprovoking tone. "It seems your feet are bothering you."

At my words, she trips over her feet, careening in a face-plant toward the ground—right for a rogue patch of prickerweed. Instinct propels me. I scoop her legs, and her smooth skin brushes mine. For the second time today, I'm aware of her lack of clothing. I glance down—just for a moment—and instantly I'm hard at the sight of her small, round breasts, those pink nipples puckering under my attention.

Then the pain hits me. It starts as a burning, sharp and hot along my ribs. Then the tearing, the slickness of blood dripping down my side. The female in my arms—moments before helpless and hopping—has sprouted a fan of thin, black spines, armoring the length of her forearm, and just raked them across my abdomen. My blood stains her skin. She glares at me with wide purple eyes. Her mouth parts in a snarl, revealing two wicked fangs.

My first instinct is to drop her on her ass and cater to my wound. But then she says, "Let me go," and flashes those fangs, and I tighten my grip.

If these spines are some Abyssal trait, I cannot ruin my future marriage by reacting poorly now. For all I know, it could be a mating ritual to stab your betrothed. Mentally, I curse myself for not paying more attention to my Abyssal customs tutor.

I clench my teeth, grinding my molars hard to redirect the pain. "Neat trick." I limp toward the keep, pain flaring up my side with each step. "Who taught you that one?"

She frowns at me, wriggling in my arms as if she might escape my grip. Her legs kick to no avail. Those wicked spines flex in and out of hidden sheaths beneath her skin.

"No one taught me," she says finally.

"Does the king have them too? Your sisters?"

Her brow furrows, revealing a dimple so soft and contradictory to the sharpness of the rest of her. She chews on her bottom lip, silent again.

"That's all right," I say. "You'll warm up to me eventually."

"Planning on sticking around?"

I laugh and shake my head at the suggestion. As if I have a choice not to. Where this morning that same idea filled me with dread, my heart is light and easy now. Maybe my destiny won't be so terrible after all, if it means spending a life unpacking the mystery of her.

The gate is close now. I can make out the shapes of the soldiers standing guard—more than usual. They clump together, ten of them. The housekeeper, Clio, stands among them, next to an unamused Captain Nara.

Relief washes over me at the sight of my friend unharmed, followed quickly by confusion. If Nara is here, then why would the princess have been left alone...?

And then I spot her: a tall, silver-haired female, dressed in an elaborate darksteel chest piece, standing with the erect posture of a royal, the rounded ears of magical blood. Nara calls out a greeting, and the female turns. Her eyes are a piercing shade of blue, nearly white, and she locks her gaze with mine. There it is, in her pale eyes—the appetite of a princess.

My stomach turns over, and my nausea returns. The female in my arms—my wicked little dancer—is not my betrothed. All the joy and anticipation slips from my body like water down a drain.

The female squirms again, trying to wiggle free. This time, I set her upright without a word. With the corner of her loincloth, she wipes my blood off her arm and steps away from me.

"Thank you," she mutters.

"What are you?" I whisper, more to myself than anything. If the silver siren is the real princess, then this Abyssal female must be her special escort, a personal guard perhaps, or a handmaid.

The female, smoothing her spines into their sheath with the flat of her palm, stiffens.

"Enna, darling, come join us," says the silver siren, stretching out her hand. "Clio was just about to give us a tour, if you're done making..." She eyes me again, her gaze snagging on my bleeding side. "...friends."

Three things happen at once. First, the housekeeper rushes forward, having spotted my injury. Clio flutters her hands and fusses, procuring a towel from her bottomless apron pouch.

At the same time, the captain chuckles. "Your Highness, allow me to introduce Prince Soren, crown prince of the Kingdom of Coral."

And in my head, I hear the echo of the female's name, meaning *the edge of a sword*. A wicked name for my wicked beach dancer.

Enna. Enna. It feels like gritting teeth.

Chapter Eleven

ENNA

I sliced the fucking Coral Prince.

The world tightens around me, and with it, my throat. If I thought the air on the beach was dry, it's nothing compared to what I'm inhaling now. I can hardly breathe. Like a fish out of water, my mouth gapes and closes, gapes and closes, trying to pull oxygen from nowhere.

Since meeting him, I have flirted with him, insulted him, ignored him, scolded him, and then stabbed him. This male who is apparently the fucking *Coral Prince*.

My cheeks flush with heat. I haven't been in this kingdom for a day, and I've already fucked up the mission.

The housekeeper fusses over his wound. He stands there with a crooked smile, watching me.

"A pleasure to meet you, my prince," says Odissa, her voice thick and sweet. She straightens from her curtsy and flashes him a brilliant smile. Guilt teases my thoughts, sour and unwelcome. Would the owner of this corpse have said the same? Would she have been pleased to meet him, given the chance?

The prince catches Odissa's hand and lifts her fingers to his mouth, kissing them lightly. "Pleasure," he says, wincing as Clio inspects his wounds.

Odissa's gaze flicks between the prince and me, her lips tightening into a thin line.

"Enna?" Odissa whispers, her voice tight with control. "What is the meaning of this?"

My stomach twists, and I feel sick. *What* are you, he asked me, not *who*. A subtle difference, but I read the meaning enough—I'm nothing but a monster.

I step away from the male, eager to retreat before I make a fool of myself. I scan the environment, searching for concrete details to calm my racing heart.

Odissa gives me a once-over and curls her upper lip. "You're covered in sand."

The entrance gate creaks on its hinges, closing with a metal clatter. I glance around. The prince and the captain are gone.

"Your Highness could have waited for me," I snap, swatting at my legs to dispel some of it. It's a harsh thing to say to a princess, and I regret my slip immediately, if only for our remaining audience.

The middle-aged housekeeper stands next to Odissa with her hands folded in front of her. Two fluttering ear fins frame her expressive blue face. She's much prettier than the mermaids of the

Abyss, and I blink, transfixed by the contrast. Her large, golden eyes study me in return, lingering on my loincloth.

I fidget with the fabric, wondering if it may be inappropriate. While Odissa wears the travel skirt and darksteel chest piece her borrowed body came with, my breasts hang bare, decorated only by sand where it clings to my sweat.

The housekeeper frowns. "Your Highness, would you like me to fetch some... more appropriate clothing for your attendant... before or after we get you settled in your room?"

Odissa takes one look at my loincloth and widens her eyes in feigned surprise. Neither of us thought this through clearly. "Now, certainly, Clio," she says to the mermaid. "We seem to have left our manners in the deep."

Clio sizes me up again, and this time, her gaze snags on my breasts. I square my jaw and lift my chin, daring her to continue her scrutiny. In the Drink, clothing is either a liability or a luxury, and I cannot afford either.

Clio snaps her fingers at the nearest guard. "Fetch our lady something to wear."

The guard bows, then disappears through the gate, soon returning with a beaded contraption. Clio takes it, shakes it into the correct positioning, then holds it out for me. The strands hang in complicated loops, threaded with bits of shell and glittering stones. I narrow my eyes. Where do I even begin with this thing?

With a sigh, she gestures for my hand. "May I?" she asks, offering a flat palm. I place my hand in hers, and she lifts my arm, threading it through an opening in the knots. She ties the band around my neck, then maneuvers the piece until it drapes just so, two small white shells hiding the peaks of my nipples.

"That's better, my lady," she says.

"Thank you, Clio," Odissa says, smiling. "You are too kind."

"Now, it is my duty and my pleasure to welcome you to the Kingdom of Coral, and to our spectacular city of Aquisa. If you'll follow me inside, I'll get you situated with your accommodations."

Odissa sidles closer to me. I can sense anger emanating from my master in waves. "Did you stab him?"

I pretend to be engrossed in readjusting my new garment.

"Enna," Odissa whispers. "For goddess's sake, pull your shit together."

As Clio leads us through the gilded gate, I force my hands to hang limply at my sides and place one foot in front of the other. She turns back to us with a whirl and a clap of her hands. "Let's get you settled in."

Odissa follows Clio through the gate, but my feet stay glued to the path. The lump in my throat hardens as I stare up at the keep looming over us. What the fuck was I thinking, coming here?

I could refuse to enter that golden gate. I could turn around. I could swim back to the Abyss and crawl into my cramped hole in the comfort of the dark and frigid, compressing waters. Figure out what exactly Tephra means to do with a lost soul who's broken a blood oath. The goddess may find me favorable. It could be easy.

I take a hesitant step toward the ocean, feeling its pull. Leaning into it. Wanting it.

"Miss?" Clio is still standing at the gate, gesturing for me to approach the palace.

I blink, surprised by the tears brimming in my eyes. One rolls down my cheek, cool against my scorched skin.

"Are you coming?"

I take a jagged breath and nod. Finish the job. The reward is everything I've dreamed of, and as much as I loathe Odissa, she needs my help. Without my Voice, she will certainly fail.

I'm not about to break my oath over a silly prince.

Chapter Twelve

Enna

The inside of the palace resembles the outside—white-washed floors and walls, lofty ceilings supported by large, smooth pillars of white stone. Marble statues of royal males line the hallways, each one depicting their two-legged forms. We follow Clio up a twisting white staircase, and I wonder if the Kingdom of Coral has been named incorrectly. I don't see any color here, other than the servants who flit around quietly on bare feet, dressed in crisp white leathers.

I soak in the brilliance of the servants' colorful skin—pinks, blues, greens, yellows, purples—some patterned with swirls and dots and stripes. Most of the mermaids have broad, fanning ears and soft, round faces. Sharp teeth, but no fangs. None of them are translucent or grotesque. None have pincers or extra legs. Their beauty is foreign compared to the mermaids of Vespyr, yet their presence is the only familiar thing I've found within these white-washed halls.

Reaching the top, Clio steers us down a hallway, stopping before a door. She digs in her apron for a key, which, to my horror, is delicately carved from more white marble. The latch clicks open and the door swings inward.

Odissa sighs and rushes into the room, giggling. "Oh, it's *lovely*! Thank you, dear Clio."

Goddess, where did she learn to *giggle*?

Expecting another white-washed room, I pause as the visual vomit of turquoise and coral assaults me. The room smells of sand and sun and sickly-sweet florals, and I gag a little, noting the open windows. Sheer curtains frame each one, lifting in the sea breeze.

Sunlight spills through, warming the rich pink rugs and the mammoth bed centered against the far wall. An excessive number of colored pillows perch on the mattress, the entire thing looking much too soft to sleep on. I would be afraid I'd sink into it, swallowed whole by fabrics and stuffing, never to emerge again.

I move to the window, surveying my escape routes. Odissa's room is situated on the right side of the palace, opposite of where we entered—which was south, I suppose. Next to this window, a floral vine twists up a column of stone, the tendril ending with a three-foot jump to the next balcony down. Far below, the pebbled path meanders through the inner walls of Aquisa, leading to the gate and the sea beyond.

Odissa squeals with piercing glee. She performs a weird little dance and giggles yet again as she buries her face into the sleeve of something pink.

"Isn't this glorious?" Odissa exclaims.

"I'm glad Your Highness is pleased with the accommodations," Clio says.

"Yes, very much." Odissa runs her hands along the large copper bathtub, frowning. "Where will my handmaid be staying? I do not see adjoining quarters."

Clio shuffles on her feet. "Well, Your Highness, this is an unusual situation. Your handmaid is a siren, is she not?" She turns to look at me, shrugging apologetically. "We usually treat our magic-wielders with the utmost respect they are due, but because of her role, we thought the servant quarters would be appropriate, if her ladyship is prepared to keep them company."

It'd be nice to have my own space, away from Odissa. In my time with her, she's never let me sleep alone. I'm *too valuable an asset*, she says.

"Fetch a cot for my handmaid," Odissa orders. "Enna will sleep in my quarters. I prefer to keep her close, you understand?"

Clio hesitates. "Your Highness, I encourage you to reconsider. It would be most improper for an attendant to *share* your quarters."

"She'll sleep here," Odissa presses, her fists tightening around the pink fabric.

Clio tips her head, then smiles tightly. "As you wish, Your Highness. The prince has invited you to a sunset dinner on the terrace. I'll come to retrieve you beforehand. And in the meantime, might I suggest a relaxing bath after a long journey?"

Odissa releases her grip on the fabric, smoothing out the wrinkles. "That is an excellent idea, Clio, thank you."

Two pairs of eyes flick toward me. I stare at the tub perched on four knobby legs, unsure where to begin with the task.

With a sigh, Clio approaches the tub. She twists both handles and water gushes out, filling the basin. Her fingers trail in the stream, testing the temperature until the water begins to steam. "There," she says, stepping back. "That should get you started."

I flash her a smile in gratitude, and she nods curtly before retreating from the room. "Call if you need anything else, Your Highness."

The door closes, sealing us in.

The room grows silent, save for the sound of water splashing into the tub. An assortment of vials sits beside the tub, labeled with various floral patterns. I frown. "Do you want...?" I pick one up, studying the pink label. *Rose.* I sniff it, then snort, offended by the smell. "Ugh."

Odissa snatches the bottle from my hand, pouring its contents into the bathwater. When the water nears the top of the basin, I turn the knobs in the opposite direction that Clio showed me, proud of myself when the water stops.

Odissa peels off her undergarments and drops them on the floor, dipping her fingers into the water. She hums with pleasure and closes her eyes. "Everything here is so warm," she whispers, smiling. Then she leans over the water and inhales the strong fragrance. "Goddess, can you believe my luck?"

As she slides into the water, her legs snap together, shifting into her silver, glittering tail. She sighs, leaning her head back until the water laps at her chin. After a moment, she peels open one eye to glare at me. "Sponge me."

I look around the room, finding one in the basket next to the fragrance oils. I drop it into the water. The sponge bobs, wobbling on the ripples.

"Have you never given a bath before?" She sneers, eyeing the sponge.

"Have you ever had a bath before?" I snap.

I could slap the look off her face. If we were in Vespyr, I might do it. Instead, I slap the water, sloshing it over the edge. "Look, *princess*," I hiss. "Nobody's watching. Do not fuck with me."

Odissa lifts her lip, revealing smooth, round teeth where sharp points used to be.

"I'm here to Voice for you, to fulfill my oath. Not to scrub your ass with a sponge."

"You agreed to help me, whatever the request," she says, nudging the sponge closer to me and closing her eyes. "Or don't you remember our bargain? Now, scrub." When I still don't move, she says, "What if Clio comes back to find me scrubbing myself? I'm sure she'd find that rather *inappropriate*."

Annoyed, I snatch the sponge, yank her arm up, and begin scrubbing at her skin in harsh circles. She doesn't even flinch. My master smiles and leans her head on the back of the tub, settling in while I attempt to rip her skin off scale by scale.

"Good girl," she says. "Now, tell me about my prince. Since you obviously met him first."

"I didn't know he was *your* prince."

I wring the sponge with too much force as the prince's face flashes in my mind, bright and handsome, his mouth curved into that flirty smile. Warmth spreads over my face. I duck to hide my reaction from the death-dealer, scrubbing at her tail.

"Tell me about him."

"He's tall," I start, wracking my brain for positive adjectives to describe the male. "Broad shouldered. Handsome? By most standards." Also pushy. Cocky. Doesn't know when to leave a girl alone. *Kind eyes.* My breath hitches.

"Yes, I can see all that for myself. But what was he *like*? Was he aggressive? Will he be difficult to seduce?"

I shrug. "Not aggressive, not really. He yelped like a pup when my spines brushed him."

Odissa frowns. "So he's a soft male playing future king."

"Seems so. That should make this easier." I consider his rock-solid abdomen pressing against me, his strong arm wrapping possessively around my waist, pulling me close, and my stomach flips over. The prince was anything but *soft*.

I shove the thought deep, locking it away.

"Excellent," she says, sighing. "I can work with this."

Finished cleaning her tail, I let the sponge float in the water. "Done," I say, wiping my hands on a towel, noting the distinct pinkness that's crept over my skin. I poke the back of my hand. It's warm to the touch.

She rises from the bath, swinging her tail over the edge to dry. After a few moments, her bones shift and her tail splits down the middle, leaving a naked Odissa standing in a puddle.

There's a knock at the door, and I nearly jump out of my skin.

"It's Clio," the housekeeper announces. "I've found Your Ladyship some clothing."

Odissa gasps, covering the puckered scar on her ribs with her hand. I shove a towel in her direction, and she wraps it around herself as the door creaks open.

Clio enters carrying a pile of white fabric, which she sets on the dressing table before addressing me, "I hope you find the skirts comfortable. Most of my staff prefer them. There's a pouch in the waist belt where you can fold and store them for easier transition."

I wrinkle my nose, holding up the fabric and gaping at the sheer amount of it. Why I should need more than the loincloth between my legs, I'll never know. The skirt ties around my waist, overlapping in the front. I strap a knife to my calf, each thigh, then adjust the fabric to cover them, skipping the undergarments. The hem of the skirt brushes the tops of my bare feet.

"Certainly, you don't need all those weapons to perform your duties. Corals are peaceful people, my lady, and there are plenty of guards stationed around the palace to ensure the safety of Her Highness."

I turn to the mermaid, sizing her up. She's soft and stocky, her face plump with the nourishment of a royal servant. The longer I stare, the more her ears quiver.

"Apologies, my lady," Clio stammers. "One more thing." She fishes out a pair of white leather gloves from her apron. "Put these on," she says. "You'll need them at dinner."

"At dinner?"

I tug the gloves over my hands, securing them up to my elbows and grimacing at the tight fit against my claws.

"Yes, my lady. To keep those Abyssal spines of yours under control. You will accompany the princess to dinner tonight, no?"

Odissa coughs, barely covering her snicker.

"You look great," Clio says with a note of warmth, nodding toward the full-length mirror.

Softness greets me, my sharp edges drowning in white fabric. My deep purple eyes are tired, skin sunken, and cheekbones hollow. Both my face and arms are a vivid pink. When I touch my cheek, it's feverishly warm. My short black hair, uneven from the last cut of my blade, sticks out in the dry air. I smooth it against my head, but it perks back up.

Sighing, I lift the skirt to study my slender, weak legs, still wobbly. I'm fast and agile in water, but on land I'm ineffective. Clumsy. I drop the skirt, so I don't have to look at them.

Clio stifles a chuckle. "You look lovely, my lady," she says, and I can't tell whether she's lying or not. "Your Highness, please choose whatever you wish from your wardrobe. We've selected our best pieces for you, and I hope you find our fashion to your liking."

Odissa thanks Clio and rifles through the wardrobe's garish offerings while she clutches the towel tightly around her.

"I'll be back when it's time for dinner," the housekeeper says. But then she eyes the tub full of water. With pursed lips, she crosses the room, reaches into it, and pulls the plug.

Chapter Thirteen

SOREN

The royal council chamber, a small, gaudy room, perches atop the palace's west wing, squarely in line of the evening sun. The soft chatter of vendors in the streets drift up through the open window behind me, mixing with the crash of waves against the shore. Humidity glazes everything in a soft sheen. There's no evening breeze to relieve the sweat clinging to my forehead.

A squat table with thick, pillared legs stands in the middle of the room. Its stone surface bears the topography of the six kingdoms of Adria. The map sweats with moisture, dew pooling in the grooves. Six gilded chairs surround the table—each occupied by an overdressed council member, with the exception of the spot opposite mine, where the queen should be. My mother is late. Again.

I straighten, wincing as pain flares in my side where the handmaid's spines raked me earlier. The healers worked their magic on it this afternoon, but a residual sting lingers beneath the skin. I scrape over the spot repeatedly, slowly, so as to not draw too much attention from the council. But they're not watching me.

Even as I bore my gaze into the side of Lord Ruven's face, studying the soft skin that jiggles under his chin with each animated sentence, the minister of foreign affairs does not turn to look. He whispers to Lady Myrrh next to him, the only female member of the royal council aside from my mother. The mermaid chuckles, tugging absently at a stray curl of her graying hair.

Lord Varik avoids my gaze, studying a tapestry behind me, no doubt still offended over my rejection of his daughter. Beside him Lord Almar, a quiet old priest with a curling mustache, props his head on his fist, sleeping.

I might as well be invisible.

I deepen my scratch, digging my nails into the silk. If I weren't in the company of the council, I would have removed this shirt, searched my skin for the point of irritation, and scratched it to my heart's content. What did that handmaid do to get under my scales? Is she poisonous? Is this some dark-dweller magic I have yet to learn? And why in the six pools of hell does the princess need a handmaid like *that*? The more I dwell on it, the more the sting intensifies.

Inhaling deeply, I recite my to-do list and relax in the knowledge that I'm down to my last two events with required attendance today: this meeting, followed by dinner with the princess. I just need to sit here, assert my presence, try not to scratch myself to death, and then leave.

The door clicks open. My mother breezes in, aiming for the velvet chair at the head of the table. The council straightens their posture, their whispers sucked into stiff silence. Lord Almar snorts awake. She lifts her gaze and nods a greeting.

"The prince and I have a dinner to attend, a guest to welcome, and a wedding to plan," says the queen. "Whatever you must say, make it quick."

The council looks to Lady Myrrh, her violet face suddenly as blank as the moon. She smooths her hair, then clears her throat. "This council expresses concern about the princess. Your proposal was rather hasty, and we have a few questions for you, Your Majesty."

The queen raises her eyebrow. "Does the council mistrust my judgment in selecting a suitor for my son?"

"No, Your Majesty. We just—" Lady Myrrh inhales deeply, steadying herself. The queen's gaze grows colder by the second. "She's Abyssal. And we have some concerns about, well—" Lady Myrrh trails off, searching the room for help.

Lord Varik smacks the table. Lady Myrrh flinches, then nods at him to take over.

"What is the crown's verdict on the latest suitor? Is she a worthy match?" he asks.

"The crown has not yet decided, Lord Varik. I expect we will learn more at dinner tonight," the queen says calmly.

"Not yet decided? Just a few days ago, the crown had plenty of opinions on a certain match *within* this court, did it not?"

"I rejected your proposal, Lord Varik," I remind him rather bluntly. "Do not waste time asking again."

The treasurer slides his eelish eyes to me and scowls. I keep my face neutral, passive. The corner of my eye begins to quiver, and my side flares once more, itching for my attention.

With a grunt, Lord Varik turns to address my mother directly.

"Your Majesty, if I may, the crown prince does not seem to be taking his duties seriously. Lines of suitors at his door, perfectly amiable females, and has he courted even one? No! My daughter is more than worthy to sit on that throne."

My mother stirs in her chair, flicking her fingers in a dismissive wave. "The prince may be... overly selective. But we have our reasons for being so."

"Fact is, we need a royal match." Lord Ruven touches the hooked tip of his large nose and sniffs, his mouth maintaining his permanent scowl. "The coffers will run out, Lord Varik, if we do not secure an alliance with another kingdom. The Kingdom of Frost has no match to offer, at least one capable of producing an heir with our prince. The Kingdom of Sands has their heads buried in their namesake. The Brine is more interested in chasing cloudwhales than aligning with anyone. And Estuary is, well, stubborn as ever."

"But the Abyss is abhorrent," Lady Myrrh protests. "They're nasty, debaucherous dark-dwellers. The Abyss does not get along with this kingdom. Have we tried reaching out to the Brine one more time? They're so pleasant and happy, and I hear their princess Nahla is lovely. Nice, happy face. That's what this kingdom needs." She smiles, as if demonstrating for the council what happiness looks like.

Lord Ruven waves his hand. "The Brine remains unreachable, my lady. What difference does it make if the dark-dweller looks unpleasant, if her brother is rich and the only king in all of Adria willing to bargain? The past is the past. Let's leave it there. If the Abyss is willing to look past the incident with the dredgebeasts, then we should let them."

"Then the prince should marry her and be done with it. He speaks of me wasting his time, when he's rejected the past five suitors, all of excellent character. How many is too many?" The council shifts uneasily at Lord Varik's remark, looking to me for my response.

Seven suitors—beautiful and quiet, but power-hungry—and not one of them fit to be my queen.

As my silence stretches, Lady Myrrh pipes up. "The princess does seem an excellent match, and our prince deserves the best. But we don't know what type of manners they're cultivating down in the deep."

"Stubborn, racist bloodfish. The lot of them," grumbles Lord Almar.

"The prince must get to know her, make sure she's the type of queen this kingdom needs. That's what the courtship is for," says Lady Myrrh. "If her character is less than worthy, time will tell."

"And what time do we have to tell?" Lord Varik clenches his fist on the table.

"We've waited this long for a suitable match. What's one more moon cycle? Our prince needs a proper courtship."

By all means, my lady, tell me again what it is I need. I lean back in my chair, folding my arms over my chest. If Lady Myrrh is intent on speaking on my behalf, I'm no longer needed here. I should skip right to dinner.

While the council is distracted, I slip my finger under the hem of my shirt, leaning forward on the table to cover my movement. I graze my bare skin, fingering each scale along my abdomen, until—there.

At the lower edge of my ribs, the sting flares from beneath a hardened scale. I lift the edge of the scale and press into the stinging flesh, right on the mark. The relief is instant and all-consuming. My eyelids briefly flutter closed.

"I'm inclined to agree with Lord Varik," Lord Ruven says. "A courtship would be pageantry. Apologies for the bluntness, Your Majesty, but it must be stated—your son has no other choice. We have one heir, one chance, and no way of producing another."

"Watch your tongue," I spit, "lest you upset your precious heir." My father is dead; I know I have no choice but to marry and inherit my ancestral throne. I do not need this reminder of my duty. My position has been made abundantly clear since my gills first fluttered. But that does not mean the council can walk all over my wishes. I have been clear in my expectations of my match; I will accept nothing less than perfection, by my own definition.

As the council murmurs apologies and honorariums for my dead father, I grit my teeth, gnawing on my response before it spits out in a near-growl. "I will not marry a female I do not know thoroughly. I've met her only once."

This excites Lady Myrrh much more than I hoped. "So you have met her! Delightful. Tell me, did she have fangs? A barbed tail? Tentacles?"

"We're putting a dark-dweller on our throne, letting her into our keep, and you're worried about what she *looks* like?" Lord Varik sneers.

"Certainly. Abyssals can be terrifying creatures indeed. Imagine, the next princess running around with claws!"

Lord Ruven scowls. "Won't marry a female he doesn't know. Bah! The prince can get to know her after his wedding. He has denied his fair share of suitable matches. This one's a royal magic-wielder, at least. I say, skip the courtship and send them down the aisle before he can back out of another match."

I keep my gaze firmly on Lady Myrrh, ignoring Lord Ruven's remark. "No tentacles that I could see, Lady Myrrh." *Just a wicked handmaid in the wings.*

"The future of this kingdom depends on a reasonable partnership between our prince and his bride," the queen cautions. "These things cannot be rushed. A standard courtship will be adequate."

"Is she beautiful, Your Highness?" asks Lady Myrrh.

Lord Ruven sighs loudly, for once echoing my thoughts. "This is a waste of time."

My mother speaks before I can unclench my jaw. "She's as we hoped—the picture of grace and poise. Quiet and polite. She's beautiful."

"Lord Ruven is right," says the queen. "We don't have many options. This Abyssal Princess is the best choice we have. From the captain's early reports, the princess is showing good character, and that is what should matter to this council."

Lord Varik leans forward, his scowl deepening by the minute. "Did we not gather this information before the princess arrived? What of the informants?"

Lord Ruven narrows his eyes. "They were… lost to the Drink, I'm afraid."

"And how many troops might Captain Nara spare to fetch them?" asks Lord Varik.

"For certain death by dredgebeast, my lord? She will not risk it again."

Lady Myrrh chimes in, "Might be worth the risk, if they have crucial information. They should be able to handle a little fish in the dark. Perhaps they forgot which way was up. I hear it's hard to tell down there."

"Big fish. With teeth twice around the size of you, my lady. Or are you forgetting our history?" Lord Ruven's eyes sparkle with mischief.

A cacophony of complaints rise like a tidal wave. Their voices crash over the room, loud and churning, growing in restlessness and spite. Until finally, Lord Almar rises from his chair. "There is another way."

The entire meeting, the old priest has slouched in his chair as he followed the conversation. He twirls the gray curl of his mustache between two fingers. The scales on the back of my neck lift, an eerie feeling settling over my shoulders. He scans the room, meeting each frozen gaze before continuing.

"To ensure her character. An old way, one used many times by our ancestors before us," he says. "We have the pendant."

In the bowels of this palace, locked behind a door guarded with magic, Queen Amura's pendant rests, untouched for centuries.

King Eero forged the pendant for his queen and laced it with dark magic at the dawn of the kingdom to ensure her safety. One only needs to speak in the pendant's presence, and anyone less than benevolent toward its wearer succumbs to a gruesome penalty.

When hysteria swam rampant under the rule of my great-great grandfather, the pendant's magic was abused, and the entire kingdom faced its judgment. Many merfolk who opposed the Mad King fell to the effects of its magic, until the population dwindled to all but nothing. It took my family three generations to rebuild what we lost, but we were never quite the same again.

"That's barbaric," Lady Myrrh protests.

"We locked that necklace up for a reason, or don't you remember, Lord Almar?" Lord Ruven shakes his head, muttering, "What a mess."

"Less barbaric than a princess with fangs, my lady?" Lord Varik pins her with a look, and she narrows her eyes. "Let's get it over with, then. Send a guard to bring her in now!"

"A bloody, miserable mess," Lord Ruven grumbles. "Are you going to clean it up, Lord Varik?"

Lord Varik frowns. "We'll fetch the housekeeper."

"And if we insult the dark-dwellers?" Lady Myrrh's bottom lip quivers. "That pendant has a bad reputation with the other kingdoms. This council must consider the military repercussions if we wrongly accuse their princess. They'll see it as a threat, a breach of trust. We would lose the match. We'd have a hoard of highly trained dredgebeasts at our gate."

"Aye," says Lord Ruven. "And lose access to their darksteel mines."

A wry smile plays on my lips. "Not to mention I'd need another suitor."

The council grows quiet as they absorb my comment. The queen shifts in her seat, folding her hands onto the table.

Lord Almar smiles, lopsidedly. "Mister Hugo took the liberty to fetch it for me this morning. Just in case."

My attendant steps forward from the shadowy corners of the room, carrying a velvet pouch. He reaches into the bag, pulling out the golden chain of the necklace. From the chain swings the whitesteel shell, simple and seemingly harmless.

The council holds its breath, no one daring to speak in its presence while it touches Hugo's skin. He places it on the table before me.

Wispy remnants of King Eero's ancient magic shroud the surface of the shell, hissing softly as they swirl around the metal.

Lord Almar looks to me. "Your Highness, I encourage you to consider. For the good of the kingdom."

"We need not make this decision in haste," the queen cautions. "I am confident in the value of my selection. The princess is already here and settled. Why not give her the chance to prove her character first, as you said, Lady Myrrh."

Murmurs of approval ripple around the table. My mother looks to me with expectation. "What do you think, Your Highness?"

Using the pendant would risk an attack from the Abyss, and my mother knows that. She will avoid it at all costs. I must choose now between my desire for a love match—a queen suitable not just for the throne but for me—and the good of my kingdom.

Like a fish between a rock and the net, I have only one way out: to accept my fate and see where I end up.

As I fold my arms across my chest, my thumb brushes the bottom of my rib. The stinging returns, dull and throbbing. I flex my hand, aching to reach for the spot, to dig once more under that scale and pluck the feeling out. Instead, I stare at the sweating map in the middle of the table, tracing the carvings with my gaze.

Whether I marry the princess now, as Lord Ruven wishes, or in one more cycle of the moon, it no longer matters, not with Amura's pendant on the table. Accepting the princess is my sole, remaining option. Before my mind's eye, my future narrows into a singular, straight current.

My heart squeezes tightly, its last thumping protest to the inevitable. Am I really giving up this easily?

"What do you think?" my mother prods.

I scoop the necklace into its protective velvet pouch and tuck it into my pocket. Then I grunt, pushing out of my chair. "I think it is time for dinner."

Chapter Fourteen

SOREN

I'VE PLOWED THROUGH MY duties since daybreak. My body screams for respite, and, for what I hope is the last time today, I once again find my ass in an uncomfortable chair. The white arches of the dining room's ceiling blur and twist together, their crisp lines suddenly as unstable as the waves outside the windows. The long table stretches before me, awaiting the arrival of its guests—much too long for three simple chairs.

My face is hot. I dab the sweat from my forehead with a napkin, then pinch my nose, using the new pain to refocus. A set of white plates nest before me on the table. Three forks to the left, two spoons and a knife to the right. A knife with a sharp edge, much like the tip of a fang, long and seductive, glinting in the light.

"Your Majesty?" Hugo's voice sharpens my focus. He stands at the windows, holding a stack of parchment. My mother stands with him, frowning at the distant horizon.

"Clio has made her initial report?" She snaps her fingers. "Tell me what more we have learned of our guests since their arrival."

"Your Majesty, her report was as we expected."

"And you think I have time to read it word for word?" She returns her gaze to the window. "Come now."

"Princess Aris arrived without Abyssal military support, as requested, per our agreement with the king." He flips a page and squints, dragging his finger over the paper so as to not miss anything important. "She did bring a handmaid with her, which shouldn't be an issue according to Clio, because she's not exactly military, but she is a bit—"

"Oh?"

"The handmaid is—" Hugo shuffles the papers, searching for the answer.

"Siren," I fill in, lifting the knife and angling it to catch the light. The mystery of her will surely become the talk of Aquisa, replacing my name in the beach gossip. Who is she? Why would a magic-wielder choose to become a handmaid? And why can't she seem to walk straight? My wicked dancer, ruffling the gills of the entire kingdom.

Not mine.

"Yes, Your Highness, so it seems."

My mother turns to Hugo. "This is the Abyss. Are we truly surprised by that? Tell me, Hugo, is there anything interesting in that report?"

"Nothing unexpected, Your Majesty. She's pleasant. Poised. Royal."

I set down the knife, adjusting it to lay perfectly parallel with the spoon.

The queen shakes her head, clearing the distant look in her eyes. "Excellent. Soren, you must woo her properly. You'll be wed on the full moon, and you can finally take your seat on the throne. Now, wouldn't that be nice." She smiles at me. The expression is the closest thing to affection I've seen her muster in my life.

I chew on my bottom lip to contain my smirk. "You believe I do not know how to woo her properly?"

Hugo hides his smile by busying himself with a crooked vase of flowers.

My mother's glare burns with a command to *obey*. I lift my goblet and take a long pull.

"I'm well aware of my duty, Your Majesty. And after that council meeting, you certainly need not remind me of it."

With a clamor of metal, the doors open, and our guests wander in. My mother softens her glare into a sudden picture of matronly welcome.

The Abyssal Princess, clean and swathed in dripping pink silks, enters. Her silver hair coils in a thick tower, adorned with shells, flowers, and a string of pearls to match the pattern of her chest piece. She bows to me, lifting the fabric of her skirts to reveal a pair of soft white feet. When she smiles, her teeth are round and smooth.

Rising from my seat, I bow at my waist. "Welcome, Your Highness," I say.

My mother smiles warmly. "Yes, indeed," she says, extending her arms. "Come. Let's have a look at you."

Aris glides forward, revealing the pale figure lurking in the doorway.

The wild female from the beach is fully clothed in clean, white skirts and a simple chest piece. Her hair still sticks up at all angles, which someone has attempted to tame with a tie around her head, holding her bangs away from her sharp face. She steps forward on unsteady feet, raising her hand to shield her eyes from the bright light of the crystal chandelier. The way her lips pucker in disgust—it suddenly makes me want to cut the damn thing from the ceiling. Her gaze sweeps the room, pausing on me briefly. Her mouth twitches, one dark eyebrow arching up, as those deep purple eyes hook into my soul. The eyes of a predator. Sweat pricks the back of my neck, and that godsdamn itch begins anew.

"Beautiful, darling," my mother says. "Now turn for me."

Aris spins slowly, her skirts swishing around her feet. She lifts her chin and straightens her posture with the smallest of adjustments, falling into a poise. She finishes her spin and curtsies.

"Our fashion suits you. Don't you think so, Soren?"

"Certainly," I say, stepping closer, and her pale blue gaze lands on me. She smiles sweetly, the white of her cheeks staining pink at my compliment.

"Thank you, Your Highness. You are too kind."

By the end of this moon cycle, if all goes well, this beautiful stranger will become my wife. I know the part I am to play—I've been practicing for this role my entire life. So I smile in return and take her hand, lifting her soft fingers to my lips.

I sneak a glance at the handmaid, who's watching me with curved lips. *Is she disgusted?* Her eyes smolder. Instead of avoiding my stare, she meets it head-on and cocks her chin. *Wild thing.*

Heat floods through me, and I tear my gaze away.

I kiss the princess's hand, and I feel nothing. No zing. No excitement. My heart races, but not from touching her.

Lord Ruven's comment echoes in my mind: *it's all just a pageantry.*

How anticlimactic this day has been. To go from courting the hopping, carefree princess I thought I met on the beach to this stoic, careful alternative; it's enough to sour my appetite.

Disappointment sits heavy and bitter on the back of my tongue, and I swallow it down with the last of my boyish hopes. I shouldn't be surprised. I entertained for far too long the hope of loving my wife. A guppy's fantasy. This is a business arrangement. Nothing more.

Aris's hand is cold to the touch, stiff and impersonal, as if she's already become the statue in the hallway of our future. I guide her to her seat at the table, pull out the chair for her, and she glides into her place.

Chapter Fifteen

ENNA

My master is an excellent actress. In the hour prior, she drilled herself in endless pacing practice, forcing her new body to respond to her commands.

The royals take to her well enough; they ogle her with smug admiration and a hint of surprise as the fake-Aris parades with the prince across the room to her chair. But Odissa is tired. After hours of practicing, she won't be able to hold her body that tight for long. As she slides into her seat, her ankle catches clumsily on the leg of the chair. Her hands shake as she bunches her skirts and twists them to cover her feet. She adjusts her chest piece, ensuring the metal covers the scar between her ribs.

The prince takes the seat across from Odissa, while the queen assumes her position at the head of the table. A slim, tall merman moves to stand behind the prince, hands folded neatly. I stand behind the princess's chair, ready to assist should she need me.

Servants whisk into the room, carrying golden platters brimming with fresh fruits, reedgrass, breads, and fish. The savory scent wafts through the air, thick and inviting, and my stomach grumbles. The queen lifts her fork, and the three of them begin their meal.

"I hope your journey was pleasant, Your Highness," the queen says.

"Oh, yes," Odissa replies, her voice extra thick with sweetness. "I've never been out of the Abyss, so the fleetwhales were a lovely surprise. What gentle creatures."

The prince nods, taking a bite of fish. Juice from the flesh slips through his lips, trickling down his chin. He wipes his face with a napkin.

My stomach gurgles again, and I calculate when I ate my last meal. Two sleeps ago? Before the attack on the princess? I stare at the back of Odissa's head, focusing intently on the silver curls of her hair, the intricate weaving of shell and pearl—anything to take my mind off the discomfort in my stomach. I flex my toes against the floor to keep from wavering on my feet.

Odissa reaches for a bowl of steaming liquid. Chunks of cooked fish float inside, mixed with flecks of greenery. She captures a piece of meat on her spoon, lifts it to her mouth, and hisses quietly, dropping her spoon with a clatter. Droplets of broth stain the tablecloth around the discarded spoon. All heads swivel toward her, and a deep shade of pink crawls up the back of her neck, tinting the tips of her ears.

I tense, scanning the room in a quick assessment for danger. My spines lift from their sheaths, pressing against the insides of Clio's leather gloves. The queen pauses with her fork half-lifted to her mouth. She stares at Odissa with surprise.

Soren smiles, his eyes warm with concern. He reaches to twist the spoon upright and slides it back across the table toward Odissa.

"Apologies," Odissa whispers. The practiced steadiness of her voice cracks, letting in a hint of her Vespyr gravel. "I wasn't expecting the heat." Odissa must have sensed it, too because she coughs quietly, and then takes a long sip of water.

The queen smirks. "You must not have soup in your court."

"Oh, we have soup, Your Majesty," Odissa says. "It's just cold." She sets the bowl aside.

That's news to me. In the short time I spent in my father's house in Dredgemaw, before I became a killer, not once did we eat this dish she calls soup.

The prince grunts, and Odissa's head lifts at the sound. He dips his spoon into his own bowl of soup, then raises it to his lips. Slowly, he blows, rippling the liquid with his breath before taking the spoon into his mouth. He swallows without pain.

Carefully, Odissa copies him, blowing on the soup before trying another bite. When she swallows easily, the prince smiles.

"Good, isn't it?" he says.

"Yes, Your Highness. It's much better warm."

Thank the goddess for the prince. I relax, letting my spines fall flat into my skin once more.

"Soren, darling," the queen says, "have you extended your invitation yet?"

"I'm sure you're exhausted from your trip," he says. "I expect you'll need a day or so to recover. But when you're ready, I'd love to give you a tour of the kingdom."

"That sounds lovely, Your Highness. Thank you," Odissa says. "I am feeling rested enough. I wonder if you might show me the sunrise tomorrow. I saw the sun today for the first time, but I hear the morning colors are a delight to see."

"That's the first item on our itinerary." He smiles at Odissa, studying her face. Then, so fast I could have imagined it, his gaze slips up to me then back again.

"Chaperoned, of course," he adds. "I wouldn't dare part you from the attention of your handmaiden, Your Highness."

Odissa nods. "We'd be delighted to join you."

"It's settled then," the queen says. She claps her hands, and another round of servants hurry into the room, carrying plates of yellow cake.

I sway on my feet as my hunger rattles once again. With two careful fingers, I steady myself against the back of Odissa's chair.

"Do you sing, sweet girl?" the queen says, brandishing her fork and scooping a bite of cake into her mouth. "I'm exceedingly curious how the Voice works for you. Each siren's magic is different, but I've heard you have different flavors in the Abyss. It's different than ours, no?"

Odissa smooths the fabric of her skirts, then lifts her face to meet the queen's assessing gaze. "I'm quite tired from my journey, Your Majesty. I'll admit I'm not at my best this evening."

The queen's eyes narrow. "I see," she says. "Of course."

Dread twists my gut. Odissa must not fail to impress the queen tonight. This whole ruse rests on her ability to woo the entire court, not just the prince. And blind as he may be to her shortcomings, the queen is astute.

Odissa's hand slips from her lap, twisting around the back of her chair. She curls her finger toward me.

"I suppose I could sing a little something for you, Your Majesty," she says.

I inhale, steadying my nerves. With the threads of my energy, I tap into the warmth in my belly. My magic purrs, coiling around my consciousness, and I coax it into obedience, focusing my intent. We need something small, but meaningful. Something to soothe the queen without draining me to the floor.

I twine my fingers with Odissa's, our grasp curling together where the queen cannot see. I squeeze her hand, and Odissa lifts her other hand to the table, a ready conduit.

My tune is soft and sweet, my lips firmly closed as Odissa parts hers. The purple lightning sparks from Odissa's fingers, surging into the air in a display of light. My energy drains quickly. My hunger echoes against the hollow reaches of my stomach. With a final flourish, the sparks fall to the table, dispelling on impact, and I cut the spell. I release my grip on Odissa's fingers, and she flattens her palm to the table.

The queen nods. "A little light show. How fascinating," she says.

Odissa dips her head, the side of her cheeks tugging up into a smile.

The prince watches her with a mirroring smile. "Thank you. That was beautiful."

I waver on my feet, vision darkening. If we don't leave this room soon, I might pass out on the floor. My finger finds a curl of Odissa's hair, and I tug hard.

"The night is getting late," she says, stiffening in her seat. "And I am exhausted from my travels. I wish to retire."

"Of course," says the prince. "I'll see you tomorrow morning, for our sunrise."

We exit the room in a painfully slow procession. Odissa curtsies, waves, dawdles across the room, until finally we pass through the gilded doorway and into the hall.

When the door shuts, I lean heavily against it, panting. Odissa studies my face from a careful distance. She tugs at the string of beads around her neck, as if it's too tight. "Thank you," she manages, voice strained with the effort of her small kindness.

"You can thank me with a hearty dinner."

Chapter Sixteen

ENNA

"Well, they haven't killed me yet," Odissa says, draping herself over the plush pink bed to hang her head off one end. A pile of discarded hairpins scatter across the marble floor beneath her long, silver tresses. She points to the ceiling and smiles. "Do you think someone painted that by hand?"

The mural in question is as elaborate and colorful as the rest of the room, but half as interesting as the plate of roasted wrigglefish in my lap. I stuff two of them into my mouth at once, groaning as the burned, smokey flavor rushes over my tongue.

"Why the fuck do they bother cooking it?" I say around the dry flesh. It's not raw, but it'll have to do. I close my eyes and lean my head against the window, stretching my legs out across the open sill. The fish bones crunch between my teeth with a satisfying snap.

After a few more chews, the roasted meat is not as bland as I thought it would be, its flavor finally coaxed out of hiding. The chef seasoned it with some sort of dried seaweed, and the saltiness hits just right. I slide the fish around my mouth, coating each of my taste buds before swallowing.

"You're disgusting," Odissa says, wrinkling her perfect, borrowed nose.

"Nobody's watching but you."

She sniffs. "I'm a princess."

I slide another fish between my lips and crunch on it. "Hardly."

"Like you could do any better."

I shrug. *Crunch.* "Probably not, but I could at least sing for myself."

Odissa frowns, eyeing my dinner plate. "The food helps though, right? I can't say I ever paid attention to how your magic works."

I pause my chewing to study her. Is Odissa trying to be nice? What the fuck does she want?

"Yeah, it helps. And sleep." The more energy I have in my body, the better control I have over my magic. However much energy it would take me to do the task without magic, that's how much it costs to use the Voice.

"And if you run out? Of energy?"

Crunch. I chew slowly, waiting for her request to drop. "I collapse, like I did in the Drink. Rather inconvenient, really. I almost passed out right there in the dining room."

"Well, fuck," she whispers. "That was a close one."

"You're a princess, Odissa. You shouldn't curse." I wrinkle my nose in much the same way she did when I slurped my dinner.

She snorts. "Nobody's listening but you."

"What do you want, Odissa?"

"I'm just being nice. Can I not be nice to you?"

I ignore her and set the empty plate aside, my stomach uncomfortably full. I lay a lazy hand over the bulge of my belly, relishing the rare feeling of plenty. I can't remember the last time I ate that much food—cooked or not.

A cool night breeze wafts in through the windows, brushing across my cheeks and chilling the sweat on my forehead, and I turn to face it gratefully.

The night sky reminds me of the Drink, a thick black expanse dotted with pricks of green and blue light. The stars collect and swirl in intricate patterns, in much the same way the glowmites sometimes dance. The only difference is Audrina, the moon: a large, shining orb suspended in a thick black sky as if by invisible strings. A wisp of cloud covers her face, the only disruption to an otherwise brilliant sky. Her light shimmers on the waves below, white and wild as the frothing surf.

I've never seen the moon before—I've only heard stories from travelers in the Hissing Bloodfish—and she's more marvelous than I could have imagined. I like her much better than the sun.

"I've figured out my plan," Odissa says, finally giving up on her kindness charade. "I'm going to seduce the prince tomorrow, on this tour. That's your cue to leave."

I glare at her, annoyed that she is making any sound at all. She stares at the ceiling, tracing the mural's figures in the air with her outstretched finger.

"Sex is the quickest way to win a male. I'll seduce him well enough, but he might need privacy before he's open to it. You were right. He's soft."

"No problem. I wouldn't want to see that anyway."

I shift against the wall, angling my ass to locate a more comfortable position on the sill.

"I'm serious. No meddling, no comments. Zip. Just leave," Odissa sniffs. Her hand drops into her lap, and she rolls on the bed to stare at me.

"Goddess, Odissa. It's like you want an audience. Just give me the signal, and I'm gone."

"I just want us to be on the same wavelength here."

"I'm here, Odissa. At your eternal service." I tilt my head in a mocking bow.

Odissa rolls back to stare at the ceiling. "I'm going to make good on my word, Enna. Once this is all done, I won't ask anything of you again. I'll free you from your oath."

I want to believe her. I want to trust that she's good for her word. But I've killed for this mermaid 2,747 times now, and not once has she followed through—not when it means an inconvenience for her. And I've been nothing but convenient since we met.

I crawl my way to a makeshift bed on the floor, the cushion barely more comfortable than the marble beneath. The sheet, the same sickly pink as everything else in this room, clings as I try to settle.

"That's it?" Odissa huffs. "You're done with me? No 'Good job, Odissa, on your first big day!' or 'Thanks for your generosity'?"

Her stare tingles on the side of my face, but I ignore her. I lie flat on my back and stare at the ceiling as the sponge slowly loses its tension and my bones sink through it to the cold, hard floor beneath. The sheet clings to me like water on a fish. I flex my toes, dragging my big toe along the fabric, testing its gravity. With a soft flutter of wind, it lifts then settles around my legs, an extra layer of silken skin.

She finally rolls on her bed, facing away from me.

I tear the sheet away from my body, exposing myself to the sticky night air as I wait for sleep to fold me into its soothing darkness.

But sleep doesn't come easily. Sound rustles through the room in quiet whispers: the breeze on the gossamer curtains, the endless crashing of waves on the beach beyond. Odissa shifts on her bed, snuggling deeper into the pillows. I grit my teeth at the sound of her comfort, despising her for it. Even in sleep, she's keeping up the act, pretending she's some sweet little thing, pink and pure. The Odissa I know is anything but.

In the light of the surface moon, Odissa's borrowed body looks nothing like the death-dealer I met in the Drink. In this body, she is soft. Pretty. Gone are her wicked, sharp teeth. Gone are her tentacles, her barbs, her glowing gelatinous head. Her siren face nests in a satin pillow, long lashes dusting the crests of her rosy cheeks. Plump lips part to let out the rhythmic breath of deep slumber. Inside that borrowed husk, she is still the mermaid who raised me—who taught me the way of killing.

With a grunt, I rise from the mattress. My bare feet meet the sweating marble floor, and I pad quietly to the chamber door.

If I cannot sleep, I can walk. I can walk until the uneven rhythm of my land legs rocks me to sleep, or until I collapse on the floor—whichever comes first.

Chapter Seventeen

ENNA

THE PALACE SWEATS AT night. The air hangs in a blanket over the cold stone floor. The walls drip with condensation, leaving puddles on the marble. Even as my skin prickles with its own sweat, the stone saps the heat from my feet until my toes are numb rocks. I weave through the winding corridors, hoping the careful pace will lull my brain into a false sense of safety.

Each turn brings me into another hallway, lined with sconces of dancing flame. The palace echoes and groans around me. I walk with raised awareness, ears straining for sounds of danger. In the Drink, everything is a shadow. I could not see the darkness there; darkness just was. Here, it moves and dances in slithering phantoms, lurking in the corners and shifting as I pass.

It's silly to think the shadows would pursue me. They're just reflections of the light; they cannot hurt me. Even so, I cast a glance over my shoulder, watching them, making sure they do not make any sudden movements.

My father's house has corridors like this, passageways that wind through the bowels of his water-tight mansion, connecting rooms, holding nothing but thick tapestry and flame, where the *lesser beings* roam free in the night. After my father and his family climbed into their cushioned beds, I haunted the halls, floating from room to room. It was the only time I could be truly alone, where no one looked at me and frowned.

I liked the library the best, for it was the room my father's family used the least. They kept it unheated. The chill from the water outside seeped through the walls, and ice webbed across the ceiling. Dust clung to the shelves, dripping from the corners on strings of glowmite silk. It smelled of ancient history, of buried knowledge. I fell asleep in there often, the thin stone tablet of a book resting on my chest as its magical visions danced through my mind, until the maid discovered me in the morning.

Lost in my thoughts, I almost bump into Clio, her mouth parted in the aftermath of a question. How did I miss her? My senses strain with overload.

I'm losing my fucking mind.

I cross my arms, suddenly feeling the chill. I sway on my feet, the exhaustion washing over me in a wave. "Um, hello."

The housekeeper's mouth lifts in a wry smile. "Can I help you find something, my lady? A glass of water, or perhaps your room? You look a bit lost."

"I was just—" I bite my lip. Do I really expect this strange female to understand my predicament?

Clio's ears swivel, rotating on their axis. "Just wandering late at night?"

"Library?" I blurt the first word that comes to mind. When she studies my face, I nod, as if that's what I've been looking for all along. "Her Highness requested a bit of light reading."

Odissa would never be caught dead with a book, but my heart brightens at the thought. Given Coral's fondness for gold foiling and expensive artwork, this palace must have a nice library. Maybe I could sleep there.

Convinced, Clio gestures for me to follow. "This way, then." She leads me back the way I came, then turns right. I do my best to memorize the path, but my tired brain struggles to keep up. We pass more sconces, more empty halls strung with fabric, art, and flame, then into a large foyer framing two large doors. The detail on the door is elaborate and curving, like waves rolling on the beach. Clio grasps the two golden handles and hauls it open with a grunt.

"Here we are," she says, waving me inside.

My breath hitches. Three stout staircases reach four levels high in a display of disjointed marble curlicues. The bottom stair starts in the middle of the floor and curls to the left. The second stair connects to the third floor, its base hanging freely like a guppy clinging to a ledge. And the third stair rotates in a slow spiral, suspended mid-air by an invisible string.

The ceiling is a shrunken speck above them, dangling a glass chandelier high overhead, casting the room in a million sparkles of light. Tall rows of shelves form labyrinthine paths through the room, lined with the colorful edges of books. So many books.

Hundreds of books suspend mid-air, the flat stone tablets floating toward various shelves. They wriggle and nestle themselves into the open slots. A low hum permeates the room, spinning a soft melody of magic, emanating from an elderly siren who occupies the front desk. A cloud of white curly hair forms a halo around her face. Glasses perch on her round nose, framing a pair of brown eyes half-obscured by her drooping eyelids. Her mouth parts, letting a soft rhythmic breath pass in and out, maintaining her spell even in her sleepy haze.

"Pearl can help you find a book for Her Highness. Don't dawdle too long, my lady. We do have that sunrise appointment with the prince."

The librarian stirs at the sound of Clio's voice. With a snort, her head snaps up, her eyes flaring wide. Swinging the book she held between pinched fingers, she narrowly avoids shattering the teacup on her desk. Her spell cuts off, and the floating books clatter to the floor. I flinch, waiting for the third stair to fall from severed magic, but it continues its smooth rotation without a hitch. How odd.

Clio leaves me standing before the desk. The librarian rakes her eyes over me from head to toe.

"Oh, Your Highness!" Pearl's voice rattles with age. She lays a hand on the desk, pushing herself out of her chair to bow at me.

"No, no." I hurry to correct her. "Just her handmaid."

Pearl completes her bow anyway, tottering on her feet. She hinges at the waist, and her spine cracks in a symphony of pops. "Well, you look like an Abyssal Princess to me, sweetfish." She smiles. "Mmm, that face. Just lovely. Like the star in my romance novel." She gestures with her book. "But she's from the Brine. Can't say I've read about an Abyssal before."

"It's just Enna." Heat stains my cheeks. "Please sit. I can find my way, certainly."

Pearl waves off my concern, moving from behind the desk. "Nonsense. I'm already up."

She's short. The top of her white hair hardly reaches my chin. I wonder if this is how the prince felt when he walked next to me on the beach today. She clears her throat and begins to hum softly, and the books rise, resuming their slow procession to the shelves.

"No, really, Pearl. Just point me to the romance section, and I'll be on my way."

With a jerk of her head, she leads me into the labyrinth of shelves, ignoring my request. I follow, eager to find a place to rest. If I can get the librarian to leave me alone, I could easily curl up at the base of one of these shelves. The floor is clear and cold; nothing I haven't slept on before.

She points out the sections as we pass: self-help, cooking, mythology, science. At the bottom of the staircase, she pauses, frowns a moment, and then taps the railing two times with her hand. The stair trembles, groaning like a dredgebeast, and with a creak of stone, it swivels. The top of the stair curls, rearranging to curve to the right. With a final groan, it stills.

Pearl slaps the railing again. "Atta boy," she says with a twinkle in her eyes. "Didn't want to take the long way 'round."

I test the first step, questioning its stability, but the stairs do not shift again. Pearl's hand clutches the railing, and she huffs the whole way up, her wobbly knees knocking together.

"It's an old spell Queen Amura requested. Mischievous little thing, she was."

The name strikes a bell, but I cannot quite place it. When I don't answer, she chuckles. "I shouldn't expect you to know that. Our first queen, she was. And she loved this place most of all."

She grips the railing as she hoists herself up another step. Slow but steady, she makes the climb, and we arrive at the top.

The second floor looks much the same as the first. More tall shelves. More floating books. I duck my head as one floats past, aimed for a shelf somewhere behind me. I spot a dark section tucked in the far corner. A whitesteel gate seals the entrance to a shadowed room full of thick tomes. I squint into the darkness, then take a step toward it.

Pearl cuts me off with a wave of her hand. "That's the royal section. Off-limits, I'm afraid. Which is a pity, really. I'd love to get my hands on some of those old books. Now, the romance is just over here." I follow her, casting a long, curious glance over my shoulder. The darkness beckons me; the only room in this palace that's dark enough for me to sleep in.

"What's Her Highness looking for? Contemporary siren romance? Historical? A little dark and kinky, maybe?" The librarian stands in the romance section, plucking tablets from the shelves and tucking them against her stomach.

A smile tugs up the corner of my mouth as she smirks. I like this female. Something about her feels like a home I've never had. "I think I can manage from here, thank you."

She hands me the growing stack of books. "Alrighty," she says. "Well, give me a shout if you need anything. It's just you and me in here, so I'm sure I'll hear you if you holler. The stairs should stay put till you're done, don't you worry." Shooting a wink at me, she waddles back toward the stairs.

Already, I am at ease. Putting the books back, I trail my fingers along the spines, closing my eyes to inhale their warm scent. They smell of stone, sun, and salt. Nothing like the cold tomes in my father's house.

My finger catches on a spine, and my thumb traces the engraving of the title: *A Siren's Handbook for Keeping House in the Drink.*

What's an Abyssal how-to guide doing among the romance novels? I should show it to Pearl. She'll know where it goes. I take it from the shelf and tap the tablet's surface, activating its stored memory. In my mind, visions of the Drink dance in full color as the narrator states a stilted welcome, then begins relaying the steps to seal a watertight door properly.

Nostalgia hits me like a blast of cold water. Suddenly, I'm reeling backward in time. My body shrinks, reality spins, and I'm a guppy hiding in my father's library, restless and unable to sleep.

I recognize this moment, the smell of the room. Stale. Like the sea has stopped her gills.

I don't want to see this. Not again.

Sound rises from the hallway, and I flinch, powerless to stop what comes next—a scuffle, a scream, then silence.

I'm ten years old, and my father is dead.

Chapter Eighteen

ENNA

Memory is a funny thing.

I don't remember what I did with the book lying on my chest, or if I remembered to extinguish its magic. I don't know why in that moment I thought of my mother—a Vespyr mermaid I'd never once met.

But I remember the scent of blood. My father's blood. The tang of iron and salt hung in the air. I walked to the door with a pounding heart and peered out of the room. As if I could save him if I just *looked*. But my father, the strongest magic-wielder I knew, was already dead.

Odissa hunched over his body in the hallway, blood gleaming on her hands. A sloppy killer. She lumbered toward me on two legs and, before I could slam the door, lifted me by my throat. His blood smeared my skin, and I kicked my feet.

Odissa pressed her knife against my neck and sneered. Her eyes flicked over my body, snagging on the features that signaled my heritage—my pale white skin, long black hair, and rounded ears. "You're his, aren't you?"

I was, but only in name. My father never wanted me. I was a worthless magic-wielder and a wimpy mermaid. But he'd kept me, given me a place in his court. The future he gave me slipped through my fingers, slick as the blood on her hands.

Odissa killed him, and I was next.

I couldn't find the words to answer her question. I hung limply in her grip, petrified, as I memorized the face of my would-be killer.

"What's your name?" she pressed, and the knife cut deeper. Warm blood dribbled down my neck.

"Valomir," I gasped, as if that name could save me here.

"He already got his dues." She patted an empty pouch on her hip. "And I'll get mine, don't you worry. My client might even pay extra. For you."

"Just kill me and be done with it, death-dealer. You'd be doing the Drink a favor."

I squeezed my eyes shut and waited for the slice. It was better that way—to die young. I was empty and alone, with no prospects, no protector, and the curse of my long siren life stretching eerily before me.

"Got a death wish, do ya? Not every day I meet a Dredgemaw brat who doesn't want to live."

The knife's pressure lessened.

"Do it," I spat.

With narrow fingers, she reached for my face, pinching my skin. She prodded my cheek, my neck, my arm. When she reached my wrist, my spines flared in warning, slicing the tip of her thumb. She hissed and sucked the blood.

"You're the half-blood bastard." She smiled wickedly, revealing rows of pointy teeth. "Look at you, young thing—cowering, alone, ready to die. Tell me, what would your mother think of this?"

I never met my mother. She was a vicious, greedy mermaid from Vespyr, who my father vowed was his worst mistake.

"You are Enna, no?"

I nodded, and she lowered me to the floor. The mermaid was older than me, but not by much. Her skin was a translucent blue, marbled with lighter flecks. From her forehead sprouted her jelly bell, the sack of gelatinous skin shriveling slightly in the air. The barbed tips of her tentacles swished around her knobby pair of legs, flicking side to side.

"You know my mother?" Hope, burning and growing, ate at my insides.

Odissa threw back her head and laughed. The sound was like gravel caught between teeth. "Know her? Sweetfish, she hired me. I'll take you to her myself."

Even then, something about Odissa didn't sit right. But her words stirred the empty chasm of my stomach, awakening something deep and terrifying. Like an animal rising from its slumber, hope stretched and yawned, ready to feed.

With a brush of her hand, she flicked her tentacles over her shoulder and sauntered down the dark hallway.

I should have walked away, should have just let her go. I should have seen it then, the hungry look in her eyes, the way she looked at me like I was the cinnamon cake on my father's table, the kind he never liked to share.

But instead, I stared into the waning dark and asked, "You're not going to kill me?"

She glanced back, a coy smile playing on her lips. "No, darling. I just saved your life. Why would I kill you now?"

Her blue eyes become brown. Sharp face softens, darkens. Round ears. A cloud of white hair. Warm hands brush my cheeks.

"Heavens, child," a raspy voice says. "Now why would I want to kill you? For fainting on my floor? Bah. Happens to the best of us. Trust me, I'd know."

Pearl holds my face between her palms, frowning. I blink away the memory. But it refuses to clear. I'm halfway here, in this library, and halfway stuck in the Drink.

I followed Odissa without question, out of my father's mansion, and crossed the Drink with a glowing, gelatinous head to light my way. We found my mother's body long dead in Vespyr, and without a second thought, Odissa asked me for my first kill. She saved my life, she said. I owed her a favor.

"It was too easy," I whisper, and Pearl taps my cheek twice.

"Let's get you to bed, hmm? Up we go."

I'm slouched against a bookshelf, I realize too late, and with a heaving squat and pop of bones, Pearl lifts me from the floor.

I lean on her for a moment. She wraps her arm around my hips and pats me there—three strong swats. "There you go now," she says. "Right as the tide."

My heart is a flutter of chaos. My throat is tight. And for *fuck's* sake, I'm wide awake. I shake my head as panic grips me. Will I ever sleep tonight?

"Thanks, Pearl," I choke. "But I've got to go."

I leave her there, puzzled, as I bolt down the steps two at a time, not even pausing to see if they shift.

I need air.

I need water.

And I'm not going to find it inside these walls.

Chapter Nineteen

SOREN

My clothes cling to my sweaty skin like I've rolled in hot sugar. Audrina has passed her peak in the sky, and I should be dead to the world by now. Sleep evades me. The arcing filigree of my ceiling spirals under my gaze, and the lines morph into watchful eyes. *Hopping feet.*

I groan and roll out of bed. This female—she is *not* my princess. I should be thinking of Aris. But when I recall the princess's face, my mind goes blank.

I strip off my nightclothes and fold them neatly. A saltwater pool concaves into my chamber floor, steam rising from the calm waters within. Sinking beneath the surface, I let the slow beat of water in my ears drown the noise in my head.

My gills flutter, their easy tempo soon disrupted as the handmaid's face reappears. Seawater drips from her wet hair. A droplet follows the slope of her dark eyebrow past deep purple eyes. It traces the planes of her sharp face and slips into the fold of her plump, pale lips. Lips that part to reveal an impressive set of fangs and a soft, pink tongue.

And then comes her voice, rich and haunting: *Seen enough, my lord?*

I reopen one eye. The smooth stone wall of my bathing pool greets my irritated gaze. I roll my shoulders, willing the tension to leave me, banishing the intrusive thought.

I flutter my tail and ease into a slow lap around the pool. A thin, black spine rising from sunburned skin, wicked and dripping in blood. My cock hardens within its sheath.

Enough. I hoist myself up onto the pool's edge and scan my bedchambers for disorder. The door is closed. The windows, closed. My bed remains a mess of sweaty sheets. My desk is untouched. My clothes lay folded where I left them.

Everything is in order.

I transition quickly into my two-legged form and wrap a towel around my hips, then pad on damp feet to the patio door. It's unlocked, but that's not unusual. My bedchamber is on the top level. Only a highly trained acrobat could scale these smooth walls.

The air is humid, but my wet skin pricks with chill. The moon casts a weary haze as the waves crash in steady rhythm. The city of Aquisa slumbers, cocooned in a warm glow of lamplight. It's too late for mind games.

I lean against the cool stone of my balcony, strung like a lyre. One touch, one glance from her now would bring me to climax. The strength of my attraction is sickening. My stomach twists into knots thinking about her. And she's not even mine.

Gods, for the moment I thought she *was*, I was ready to submit to my fate. I would have dropped to my knees and worshipped her for the sheer *joy* of being bound to an equal. My cock swells against the towel, and I hiss, pressing myself against the railing. The pressure sends a flood of electricity through my nerves, and I groan, grinding again.

It's not enough to ease the tightness in my soul. I drop the towel, and my cock bobs free, hard at the thought of her. *Just a few strokes.* To rid the memory of Enna, my almost-queen, and then I'll get myself under control. I grasp my shaft and pump.

Gods above.

My thumb slides from the base to the tip, coating the soft flesh with the droplet that formed in anticipated release. I clench my teeth as pleasure ripples through me.

That was two. My quota met, I grunt in frustration, holding my swollen cock. But then, out of the corner of my eye, a white shape appears on the beach. A female walking in the moonlight. She's not hopping now, but I'd recognize the sway of those hips anywhere, the spikes of black hair. My wicked dancer. My personal demon has come to torture me in my moment of weakness, as if I'd summoned her with my thoughts.

"What are you up to, Wicked?" I whisper, narrowing my eyes as I watch her. Did she not experience enough of that beach this afternoon?

She pauses at the waterline, stripping her chest piece, then her skirts. The clothing drops to the sand in a heap, revealing that scanty loincloth beneath. She gathers it in her hands, folding it into a pouch on her belt.

That *ass*. I tighten my grip on my shaft and moan. What I would do to have her here, bent over this balcony. The ways I would punish her for making me lose control.

Growling, I thrust into my hand, watching those hips and her round, bare ass. She dips her toe into the water, testing it, then plunges into the sea. The waves swallow her, finally, and I can no longer see her.

My palm is slick with pleasure, and I slip in and out, picturing her mouth, her wicked, dangerous mouth. I wonder how it would feel to have those lips slide around my cock. I want to punish her. For her words today. Her brutal defiance of me. How dare she not tell me who she was?

Did she think it was funny?

I tighten my grip and thrust, losing myself to the angry pace. Again. Again. I bend over, caving in to my need. My cock glistens with sweat and pre-cum. I'm losing control. I cannot stop. My anger builds, and with it, pleasure blooms.

This is so wrong.

I search the waterline for any sight of her. I need to see her. To watch her while I come.

Her head breaks through the water, and with a flick of her black tail, she floats on her back. Relief floods through me, and my cock jerks at the sight of her.

She's not mine.

But I wish she was. With a final stroke, my balls tighten, and I climax, panting, my cum shooting into the night air in thick ropes. I can't remember the last time I came that hard.

I stare, shame burning my ears. Why did I do that? Why couldn't I control myself?

Enna's hands reach skyward then, as if grasping the face of the moon. She opens her mouth and screams without a sound.

The scales along my skin rise. My feet stay glued to the patio, suddenly unable to move. I watch her, floating in her raw emotion, and my heart softens.

She turns and dives into the water, skipping in long, graceful arcs toward the shrunken beach. When she reaches one of the boulders jutting through the surface, she crawls upon it and curls into a tight ball. Her tail shifts into legs, and she stills.

I wait for her to move. To scream. To look up and spot me watching her, at least. Can she sense what I've done?

The handmaid only curls into a ball on the boulder, and I regret it's not my bed.

Chapter Twenty

ENNA

I DRAG A COMB through the tangles of Odissa's hair. I woke before dawn to prepare her for the day, and by the time we reach the rendezvous for the morning's kingdom tour, my limbs are limp seaweed.

I roll my shoulder, and a sharp pain stings between my shoulder blades. My body feels like it has been repeatedly pounded against a rock. My sleep on the boulder last night was anything but restful, after all.

Clio waits for us on the beach, a lacey parasol tucked under her armpit. When she asks me if I slept well last night, I nod and give her my best impersonation of a smile.

On the beach, Odissa paces slowly in a thin pink skirt, frowning at the waves and digging trenches in the sand.

The sun peeks above the horizon, staining the sky with color, first a pale gray, then purple, then pink. I squint into the sky, already missing the dark blanket of night. The merchants in Vespyr lied to me, the little fuckers. The sun isn't a green ball of glowmites, and I'm no longer interested in its burning rays.

"Is the prince usually late for appointments?" Odissa asks.

"Not usually, Your Highness," Clio says.

She resumes her pace, making three more passes before the gate finally opens and the prince walks through, followed by Hugo. The prince's movement is efficient, each step sure and solid. He towers over the merman next to him. His eyes burn through me, as if trying to persuade me with the fierceness of their glare. The skin beneath his eyes is swollen with lack of sleep. With a quick flick of his gaze, he studies me up and down, snagging on my leather gloves before landing again on my eyes. I raise my chin to meet his glare.

The prince is angry. I can see it in the flex of his jaw.

Clio clears her throat. "Welcome, Your Highness."

The prince blinks, breaking our spell. He bows to Odissa, who curtsies in response. "Your Highness," he greets her. Then he tips his head toward me.

"My lady," he says. The anger vanishes, replaced with a sudden calm. "I trust you slept well?"

"Pleasantly well." Odissa's voice drips with cultivated sweetness.

The question was for the princess, but his eyes have not left my face. I consider the rock I slept on and shudder. The corner of his mouth twitches, as if somehow, he knows something I do not.

I look away, searching for anything to draw my attention from the handsome male looking at me how a dredgebeast looks at a meal.

Dammit, Enna, focus.

"And you, my prince?" Odissa says, drawing the prince's attention.

His appraisal finally slides to Odissa, and my body relaxes at the passing of his gaze.

He inclines his head. "I slept very well, thank you. So well in fact, that it seems I am late for our sunrise. My apologies. I am usually more punctual than my behavior this morning would suggest."

Odissa laughs. "You missed a beautiful show," she says. "The clouds were like paints in the sky."

"Lovely. And which was your favorite color?"

"The pink, of course."

"Excellent choice. Shall we begin our tour, Aris?" He offers her the crook of his elbow, and Odissa curls her hand around his bicep. "May I call you that, Your Highness? We are to be married by the full moon."

She giggles, then flutters a hand in front of her lips to cover it up. "Aris would be wonderful, Prince Soren."

He smiles. "Just Soren, then." He tugs his elbow and guides her toward the surf. Even if this is all one giant lie, they make a lovely pair.

***

My arm burns with the weight of the parasol. I clench my teeth with every step, fantasizing about floating in the icy embrace of the Drink. The air grows more humid as the morning progresses, moisture sticking to my skin in an uncomfortable layer of sweat and salt. To our left, the ocean churns restlessly, the bright blue waters reflecting the hot sun.

Odissa remains under the shade of the parasol, while the prince strolls next to her, seemingly unaffected by the heat. I'll never understand Coral merfolk's fascination with walking in circles through hot sand.

They make a perfect picture together. Where he is beastly, she is poised. Where she is eager, he is composed. They each complement the other like two sides of the same royal coin. Except, she's not a royal.

Odissa flirts with him ceaselessly. He points out a bird, and she giggles, grasping his arm tighter. He notes the shape of a cloud, and she throws her head to the sky, exclaiming endless praise. A few times, she feigns tripping just to have him catch her. He obliges, keeping her on course as we walk the perimeter of the city walls, but not once does he look at her lustfully. Never does he pause to sweep her into an all-consuming kiss or offer a piece of jewelry to secure the marriage arrangement with the finality Odissa so desperately needs.

Tephra, pluck out my eyes and save me from this second-hand embarrassment.

The prince steers us inside the city walls, parading through the spiraling streets. Odissa stops to peruse vendors' booths, delighting in the shiny trinkets. The vendors smile at her and offer her free samples of fruit and wine, which she accepts with exaggerated happiness.

The prince greets every noble family he meets, introducing the Abyssal Princess. The distrust in the nobles' eyes quickly dissipates and they bow, kissing the back of Odissa's hand profusely. She basks in the attention while the prince stands there. When they ask if she's the future Coral Queen, he simply smiles and asks them if they've yet received their invitation to the royal wedding.

As the sun reaches its peak in the sky, musicians wander into the streets, tapping out melodies on whitesteel drums and singing lilting Voiceless tunes. One merman sits under the awning of a small, stone abode, wearing a broad-brimmed straw hat to keep the sun from his face. His blue hands skirt expertly over the flat, whitesteel surface, his fingers tapping on random spots to create an eerily joyful melody.

"Enna," Odissa says, irritated. "Come shade me."

I smile at the merman and touch my hidden gills, bowing my head. His music stutters as he loses the beat, and he stands from his seat to bow. "Magic-wielder," he says, beaming at me. "You honor me."

I step back, bewildered. "You make beautiful music," I say, for lack of anything better, and hurry after Odissa with the parasol.

Soon, sweat soaks my scalp. My black hair is hot to the touch, and my eyes struggle to filter the strong light. My parasol arm droops, my muscles nearing the end of their use.

"Tell me, Soren," Odissa says, tugging him away from the crowd of observers. I scurry after her, keeping the shade above her head. "Are sunsets as romantic as sunrises? I would very much like it if you showed me one. Alone." Her voice dips low on the last word and she looks up at him through blinking eyelashes.

He looks at her mouth, then averts his gaze. The parasol drops, managing to both clock Odissa on the head and clip the prince on his cheek before it lands in the sand.

Odissa yelps, whirling on me with a gaping mouth, rubbing the spot on her head. The prince touches his face, his gaze sliding to me for the first time since this morning's awkward encounter.

"Apologies, Your Highnesses." I duck to retrieve the parasol.

"Are you okay, my lady?" the prince says. His face scrunches in concern. I frown at him, hating him for his kindness. I like it better when he's angry with me. At least, I'm used to that emotion.

"We can transition to the underwater districts, if you prefer." He extends his hand, as if to lift me from the street.

I stare at his extended hand. If *I* prefer? If we traded places—if he wandered into the dark waters of *my* territory—he wouldn't last until his first sleep, whereas I'm doing just fine in his. I don't need his pity, and I don't need his help.

"It's not my tour," I say, refusing his hand and pushing off the ground. I brush the sand from my skirts.

"She's fine," Odissa insists. "Let's keep going, please." She grabs the prince's hand, tugging him down the street.

But when she steps away, Prince Soren stays still, and their hands fall apart. Slowly, he reaches for me, cupping my upper arm. I stiffen, holding my breath, as his thumb hovers over my skin.

"Don't touch me," I whisper. My voice sounds unconvincing and weak to my own ears. My spines react, pressing against the constricting glove.

He eyes the gloves. "You won't sting me today, will you?" His thumb floats closer, nearly grazing my skin.

"No," I say. "Your Clio made sure of that."

He smiles, meeting my gaze. His hand is soft against my skin, kind and careful. Slowly, he presses his warm thumb into my skin. My skin flashes from pink to white and back to pink.

He shakes his head. "We should get out of the sun," he says. "I should have checked on you sooner." His voice drops to nearly a whisper, breath dusting my ear. "Deepest apologies, my lady."

His thumb strokes my arm once more, and then it's over. He plucks the parasol from under my armpit and pushes it open, casting a shadow over my head. With his knuckle, he nudges the small of my back, guiding me to the sea.

Chapter Twenty-One

SOREN

THE REEF IS A short swim from the shore, and we welcome the water as a respite from the sun. Sprouting our tails, we glide over the dwellings that cluster around the base of Aquisa's sandbar. A few mermaids poke their heads out of their holes, their bright faces darkened by the shadow of our bellies.

I lead Aris and her handmaid to my favorite part of the reef. Aris twirls in the water, swimming in the most inefficient manner possible so that her silver hair fans out like a cloud. Her hair is pretty, and I suspect she wants me to tell her so. I hold my tongue to avoid the squeal of delight that would undoubtedly come if I gave in to her wishes.

Reedgrass sways in the low current, carpeting the floor of the Coral Gardens. Lush corals and vibrant fish surround us in a symphony of color. The attendants clip and gather ingredients for the kitchen, silently drifting away as we approach. The garden district is usually a tourist favorite, and Aris is reacting as I predicted: loudly.

She giggles in that ragged, rolling manner of hers—unexpectedly rough for a princess—and flashes me what must be her hundredth smile since this morning.

The princess is all too easy to impress. I could point to a pile of bird shit and call it my *favorite*, and she would squeal like a screamerfish, clamp her hand around my arm, and proclaim it the prettiest shit she's ever seen.

During our beach stroll, I pointed out the most boring features of the landscape, checking her reaction. I spotted my *favorite* species of crab, my *favorite* boulder, my *favorite* empty stretch of sand. When the tenth crab crawled across our path and Aris squealed with delight, I had to close my eyes to keep them from rolling.

Where did my mother find her? Is she really Abyssal? Aris acts just like every other female in my court, and I'm utterly bored of her already. They're all the same—each suitor puts on their own interpretation of my preference, assuming I want a pretty little plaything. Aris is no different. When I look into her eyes, I find a frigid void, hungry not for me but for the power I hold.

I need a queen—strong, fierce, and powerful in her own right. My court is needy; my council, childish. My crown is tainted with years of royals ending in tragedy. My kingdom would eat alive anyone less than a goddess in the flesh. My mother has faired well enough, but only at the expense of her emotional capacity.

So, Aris, unfortunately, might just have to do.

A snapperfish slithers out of its hiding spot, latching onto a passing wrigglefish. The snapperfish twists into a brutal roll, its sharp teeth tearing chunks of pink flesh, clouding the water with blood and sand. Aris curls into my side, as if frightened by the display. The soft tendrils of her tail tickle my own, intertwining and making it difficult to swim.

Enna pushes past us, darting after the flesh, while the snapperfish gorges on the rest of its meal. She snatches the meat from the water and slurps it up.

Aris shrieks again, snuggling closer. Her hand tightens around my arm. Enna glances back at us, smirking. She slides a pink tongue over her fangs. Aris relaxes her grip on my arm, and I grunt as my blood rushes back into the area.

Enna twists over, ignoring us, and uses her hands to push herself over a rock. Her black scales provide a stark contrast with the color around her, somehow reflecting every glittering hue in the brilliant light. I watch her slip through the water, mesmerized by the slick turns of her body.

While the handmaid is a clumsy totter on land, in the water, she is lithe and graceful as a pearlshark. How can Enna be both the female who hopped ridiculously on the beach and this creature of wicked efficiency in front of me now? I study her movements intently, as if the explanation might reveal itself with just a few more moments of scientific observation.

She studies the fish and coral, frowning. Her small fingers pluck a lushfruit, and she pinches it between her claws, the juice spurting into the water. Discarding the peel, she glides to the next crop, running her fingers through the green tendrils with that same snarl twisting her lip.

I frown at the reedgrass, trying to see it through her eyes. She frowns at it, discards it, yet it's beautiful to me.

"What do you think?" I ask, aiming my question at Enna.

"It's lovely, Soren," answers Aris, once again appearing at my elbow. Her hair tickles my skin. Then her fingers trace my arm, following the pattern of scales that circle my bicep.

Enna meets my gaze. She holds another lushfruit between her fingers. This time, instead of squishing it, she opens her mouth and slowly lowers the fruit inside. Her tongue slips out, welcoming the fruit. Her teeth break the seal, and the red juice floods her throat. She closes her lips, blinks, and turns away from me.

Wicked thing.

My cock hardens in its sheath, pressing against the thin concealing membrane. This female cannot be giving me a *reaction*—not again. Growling, I twist away from the princess to hide the bulging evidence of my distraction.

Aris mirrors my movement, twisting to end up face-to-face with me against the corals. She chuckles, placing her hand flat against my chest. Her silver tail slips against mine, nudging my sheath. I growl again as her touch feeds the fire in my veins. *Dammit*. Her pale eyes lock on mine, her lips drooping into a seductive pout. One hand trails down my bicep, now curling around my wrist, pressing me into the corals.

"Here?" She giggles. "Your Highness is so *bold*." Her teeth graze my earlobe.

Behind the princess, Enna treads, staring at us with flashing eyes. From her arms rise those sharp, black spines. Her tail whips restlessly back and forth, as if moving without command. When Aris dips in to nibble along my neck, Enna's gills flare. She pins me with her glare, those eyes burning a path to the back of my skull.

Aris drifts into my line of vision, obscuring the handmaid from my view. She eyes my lips and palms my cheek with her warm hand. Her nose slides against mine. "Would you like a kiss, my prince? A wedding night preview, perhaps?"

I stretch my neck, peering around her, aching for another glimpse of the handmaid's face—for my scientific study. One moment, she'd been calm; the next, those spines rose, ready to slice. What triggered her so? I scan the waters behind Aris's head, finding them empty. Nothing but a splattering of bubbles. *She's gone.*

Aris perceives the change in my libido, sliding her tail against me. She withdraws, frowning. "Your Highness?"

And there it is again—that look in her eyes. She does not see me, does not want *me*. This is all just a game to her, a play for my throne.

The garden fish swim lazy circles around us, nibbling lushfruit from Aris's hair.

I force myself to swallow the lump in my throat. Aris doesn't have the barbed teeth of a clingerfish, but she doesn't need them. It's her fingers that won't leave my skin, always trailing up and down my arm as if she's searching for the best place to dig in.

"Our marriage is just pageantry, Aris," I say. "You don't have to play when no one is watching."

Her hand pauses, fingers lingering over the hollow of my throat.

"Yes, I suppose so," she says. "But what a show we could put on with a little practice. Don't you want to play the part well?" She smiles, slipping closer. Her hand trails lower, stopping above my beating heart. She strokes my skin softly, her smile sinking the longer I hesitate to answer.

I wrap my hand around hers, squeezing it, then removing it from my chest. "I'm looking for the real thing."

"The real thing?" She drops her hand, her face cold as stone. "I see you, Soren. You and I, we are the same. The real thing was never likely for royals like us."

"We are not the same."

"We could get there, eventually." Her eyes flash with hope, and I feel sorry for the female. Even if it's all a game, she's an excellent actress.

"Perhaps."

"What's the harm in a little practice?" She presses forward until her breasts brush against my chest, her nipples hard through her soft mesh covering. Then her hand is on my chest again, tracing the planes of my stomach.

I remove it from my skin. "No need." I squeeze her hand until she flinches. "You're already playing your part perfectly."

She tugs her hand, trying to free herself from my grip. I tighten my hold, enraged. The more time I spend alone with her, the deeper she'll sink her teeth. I'll need a sharp knife to pry this one loose.

"Go ahead," I say. "Sing yourself out of this." My anger flares, stirring the magic within me. I want her to push back against me, to show me her strength, her wit. My queen needs to be strong, not some coy little clinger.

But she just treads water, refusing to fight. Her eyes narrow, the blue freezing into pools of ice. "I don't have to," she says coolly. She looks past my shoulder, at the mermaids who hover there, murmuring quietly as they watch our exchange.

Magic stirs, wild and hungry. She wants my power? So be it.

My vision darkens. The hold on my magic snaps. I shout, wordless but full of Voice. With the sharp note, tendrils of my magic snake out from my hands, slicing through the garden. The dismembered bodies of fish sink to the reedgrass, littering the water with blood and bones. Snapperfish slither out of their holes, lapping up the unexpected snack.

Aris finally removes her hand from my chest. "Shall we play again tomorrow?" she asks, that coy smile still on her face.

Drained of my energy, I frown at her. Was I not clear? I do not wish to see her again unless I'm required to by duty.

It takes every ounce of my control to keep my tone even as I lean in and whisper, "If this is pageantry, Princess, I don't like the part you're playing."

Chapter Twenty-Two

ENNA

CLIO TUCKS A PIN into the mass of white fabric around Odissa's hips and takes a step back, surveying her with pursed lips. A row of pins clamped between Clio's sharp teeth wiggles with the movement of her mouth. She moves them to the side to speak. "That should do it. I'll have these adjustments made, and your gown will be all set."

Odissa stares into the gilded mirror, catching my eye. She grins at me, smoothing her hands down the front of her wedding dress. "Don't you love it?" Odissa gushes.

It's garish. Fabric droops in swooping tucks from a band around her waist, sprawling onto the floor so it appears she's floating in a puddle of silk. How she will walk in the thing without falling on her face, I have no idea. And it'll likely be me behind her, gathering up the excess in a not-too-tight wad so she can make it to the dais.

Despite this kingdom knowing nothing about her, the dress is very Odissa. Excessive, ridiculous, and hard to miss.

"It suits you," I offer.

Clio removes the pins from her mouth, stabbing them into a cushion on the dressing table. "You're as pretty as a sunfish, Your Highness. Don't you worry. Now, about your ball gowns. We'll get those situated next, but that shouldn't take as long now that we have your exact size. Are we thinking pink? Gold, perhaps?"

Odissa looks as confused as I feel. "Gowns? As in more than one? His Highness is so generous."

"You are the future queen. The crown wishes for you to look your best during your wedding week," Clio explains as she works to unlace the back of Odissa's gown.

"And these pink dresses in my closet. Will they not do? I'd hate to inconvenience the crown." The bodice freed, Odissa slinks out of the gossamer sleeves.

"Gods, no! It's a Coral tradition, Your Highness. You'll need a new gown for each night."

"Each?" The dress sinks to the floor like an emptied husk. I offer Odissa my hand, and she takes it, stepping out of the silken entrapment.

The housekeeper gathers the dress, careful to avoid the pins. She straightens slowly, holding the lump of fabric, and studies Odissa's face. "Yes, Your Highness. Five nights, five gowns." Clio's eyes narrow. "Surely, you learned of our traditions in your studies?"

"Yes, of course."

"I'll just fetch a bit more fabric for your selections, then." The housekeeper casts one last look at Odissa, pausing with her hand on the doorknob. Odissa gives her a polite nod. Clio stays still, staring, as the silence stretches.

Sweat prickles the back of my neck. What does this female want?

Finally, she walks out the door with the wedding dress. Wordlessly, I offer Odissa a silk robe, and she slips into it.

"Fuck," she says. "Dancing?" Scowling, she slouches out of her royal posture.

Odissa buries her face in her hands, shaking her head. "Fuck me. I can hardly control this corpse as it is. Now I have to dance with it? I couldn't dance in my old skin!"

"You're a shit dancer, Odissa." The only time I've seen her dance was during an infiltration scheme in the Abyssal court. The target was a magic-wielder who frequented a gambling bar in the royal city, and he had a thing for mermaid females, which meant our usual plan wouldn't work.

Odissa glares at me. "Thanks for that. As if you're any better."

Lord Valomir was adamant that all his offspring could present themselves well in the public eye. And that included me, his half-blood bastard. He drilled dancing, posture, and manners into me, until my feet bled.

"I'm better than a twitchy gelfish, yes. You cannot do your... arm movement thing... at a royal ball without blowing our cover."

She demonstrates the move, lifting her arms above her head and swinging them from the hinge of her elbow. "This one?"

"Fuck no." I take her hands and maneuver her into the correct position. "I'll teach you."

Tephra, please let this court know how to waltz.

I place her hand on my shoulder and tuck mine on the small of her back. The princess's body is taller than mine, but it's the only plan we have. "I'll be the prince." I demonstrate the rhythm with my feet, raising onto the ball of my foot, then dropping for the downbeat. "Now, we count to three. Down-up-up. Down-up-up."

Odissa watches my feet with wide eyes, then attempts to mimic my movements. Her toes slam into mine, stubbing both of our toes. I grunt to keep from cursing her out. We try again. And again. Odissa stubs my toes two more times, then elbows me in the ribs. Her arms are stiff as rocks.

"You're off beat, Odissa. Count to three as you move. If you're not saying a number, don't move your fucking foot."

"Watch your tone with me, pet."

I snarl, my temper flaring.

She peers down her thin, perfect nose. "I know how to count."

"It's just the feet we need to fix, then. And the stiff arms. And the lack of effortless, royal ease."

"That's a lot to track at once."

"It's like floating in a current. Let your body be swept away by the beat. You don't force your body to follow rigidly. It's a feeling."

Her arms turn heavy and soft on my shoulders, sagging like reed-grass. This is impossible.

"We're fucked." Odissa will attend five of these fucking balls, dance like the unhinged death-dealer she is, and Tephra will have her dessert.

She growls, grabbing my shoulders and shoving me away. Her nails dig into my skin, scraping flesh. I stumble two steps back. "It's too much to keep track of at once," she snaps.

"Says the brain behind this fucked-up operation," I mumble.

She huffs, throwing her hands in frustration. "Can't you just puppeteer me through this shit with your Voice?"

I shake my head. "I'd have to be touching you, or my light will attract attention. That's not going to go well in a ballroom. I can think of at least one royal who would notice if you had a clinger."

Odissa sets her jaw, then lifts onto the balls of her feet. She counts to three, stumbling by the first number. "These damn legs don't work for me." She eyes my legs with searing envy. "I don't know how you do it. No gel. No flexibility. You'd think it'd be easier with only two appendages to control, but goddess, it's not. I want my body back."

I storm toward her, grabbing the thin material of her chemise. She needs a fucking reality check, and I'm about to give her one. "It's rotting in Tephra's big belly, and unless you'd like to join it, I suggest you focus."

Somewhere behind her, the doorknob turns.

Odissa's eyes light with flame. Her palm connects with my cheek, hard. I release her shirt as the pain registers. I'm suddenly back in my father's ballroom, cradling my sore face as he leered at me.

Clio gasps, and the pink cloth in her hands slaps to the floor.

"Ah, there you are, Clio, darling." Odissa's face fixes into her perfect, wan smile. Clio bends slowly, retrieving the fabric without a word.

Chapter Twenty-Three

ENNA

IN THE ABYSS, THERE is only darkness. When I was tired, I slept. When I felt rested, I stirred. When I killed, I counted each throat. Time seemed nonexistent there.

Here, it is a slow, plodding thing, and yet it is also fleeting. Fast. I wait for the sun to rise, for the tides to roll, for the moon to change—and then suddenly, Audrina has changed, under my careful watching. How long does it take for a small sliver of her face to fill in? How many sleeps? How many rises?

The prince does not offer another tour. In the days that follow, we hardly see him. Busy with kingdom concerns, he announces at dinner. He receives his meals in his rooms, too busy even for dinner with his mother and his betrothed. And there are only so many things Odissa can say to the queen over a plate of charred sweetfish.

After seven sleeps of nothing to do but slather myself with reed-grass to heal my sunburn, attempt to teach a death-dealer to dance, and repeatedly brush Odissa's hair, I tire of the waiting.

"The goddess said he's a slippery catch," Odissa reminds me, running her fingers through her long, silk hair. "He'll call on me soon."

When I ask her again what happened in the gardens, she just smirks and says, "Oh, you know what happened, chum-brain." But as the week progresses, she starts to look worried.

I take to wandering the palace at night, exploring every twisting inch of its marble guts. Maybe there's a secret hidden here, some piece I've been missing.

Every assignment, I've made sure to be in control of the situation, not some sidekick playing parlor tricks. Even if Odissa comes up with the plan, the execution is my game. But this is so far out of my depth. I can't decipher the rules. I *will not* die for this shit.

If Odissa wins the heart of the prince in the end, fantastic—they certainly deserve each other—but a deal is a deal. I cannot keep betting my life on her success. My service ends the moment the bargain is sealed.

As if sensing my betrayal, the familiar icy grip of dark magic wraps around my neck—my blood oath unfulfilled. I shove at it with my thoughts. *I'm not ruining her success,* I tell the magic, *I'm just... ensuring my own.*

This blood oath will end soon enough, and I'll be completely on my own.

I'll be poor, but I'll be free.

I trace the sweating walls, aimlessly following the swirls of pink caught within the marble. Moisture licks my fingers. I press onward, following the curve of the wall to a staircase. I climb it on numb feet, hand caressing the gilded railing with disgust. These Corals have so much wealth, they carve their handrails from solid gold. With the edge of my claw, I scratch at the metal and smile when it leaves a mark. It'll be my secret; here, in the darkened stairwell, I could slowly taint the varnish of grandeur one handrail at a time.

Goddess, even the screws are made of gold. I loosen the fastening, twisting the screw free. One of these would buy a free round of drinks for every patron at the Hissing Bloodfish, every day for a week. A quick scan of the railing tells me there's more than that here.

My mind reels as I climb the stairs, snicking a screw here and there and slipping them into the pouch strapped to my inner thigh. Three. Five. Ten. How many might I take before I'm discovered? I glance over my shoulder, scanning the open space for signs of observers. Just then, a drip of water releases from the ceiling and splatters onto my shoulder. I flinch at the sudden chill. Shaking the paranoia away, I grasp the edge of the wall and peer out of the stairwell into a long, narrow hallway.

A guard stands at the end of the corridor, his face lit by a lone lamp. His eyes glaze with boredom, staring into the darkness between us. The walls are void of options for looting—no art, no gold. I must be on the top floor—aside from the one chamber door and the window at the end, the only way in or out is through this stairwell.

I study him carefully. His shoulders sag with exhaustion. His weight shifts entirely onto his left leg, hip cocked, as he leans his weight onto the trident in his hands. His cheeks are plump with a rich diet; a favored guard, then, for a favored post. This room must be important.

Curiosity gnaws too fiercely for me to ignore. Humming, I send sparks out the window. The guard grunts, his attention shifting. He shuffles to the sill, leaning out into the night.

Silently, I slip down the hall, passing behind him. I extinguish the sconce, and the hallways falls into darkness. I blink, clicking my night vision into place. He turns from the window, then creeps toward the sconce with searching, sweeping footsteps. He raps against the metal with his fist.

"Damn thing," he mutters. He fishes in his pocket, retrieving a piece of flint, and he strikes it with a spray of sparks. With another quick hum, I suck the sparks away, absorbing their energy. The guard grumbles.

I dig my claw into the lock, unlatching it easily, and press inside. The door closes moments before the sconce reignites. The orange glow flickers through the gap in the threshold, and I pause flat against the wall, as I wait for him to knock or trigger an alarm.

The room is empty. A large bed sits untouched to the left, dripping with dark velvet. A desk stands in the corner, the books and parchment organized with precision. Centered in the room, a bathing pool glitters in the low light. Two doors open onto a patio with a stone balcony framing the ocean view.

The obviously masculine presence, the careful precision of the organization, the scent that hangs heavy in the air—this must be the prince's chambers. It's the same smell that clung to his chest when I met him on the beach: salt, sun, and driftwood. I haven't scented him in days, but my heart still flutters in recognition, and my eyelids droop as I greedily inhale.

On the other side of the door, the guard shuffles and grunts but otherwise remains silent. I'm in the clear.

The prince is filthy rich; I'm sure to find something of worth in here. I search the desk first, tracing my finger over the rough spines of his books. I pick one up and ignite its contents—a mess of numbers dances through my head. I place it back on the stack, careful to align the edges.

Next, I slide open a drawer, only to see thin writing bones and jars of ink. The next holds blank parchment. The third drawer is locked. I jiggle the latch and slide it open. A velvet pouch sits in the drawer. Odd thing to keep in a locked drawer.

Outside, the wind gusts, and the patio door sways on its hinges. I flinch at the sound and hold my breath. When nothing further happens, I pluck up the pouch and open it. Inside is a golden chain, a single pendant hanging in the shape of a spiralfish shell. I twist the chain in the dim light, salivating over the way the light dances on its perfect curves.

I should put it back. Lock the drawer. Decide my escape route before the guard—or the prince—comes to check the chamber.

But I've never cared much for should. I slip the necklace over my head, the corners of my mouth lifting at the perfect fit. The shell settles heavy against my breastbone. Where it touches my skin, the pendant warms, glowing with golden light. I clamp my hand over it, the pendant suddenly hot to the touch. Panicked, I remove the necklace and drop it into its pouch, and the light fades.

Forget the golden screws. If this mission fails, I could get good money for this in the Vespyr markets, and I'm not stupid enough to turn down a solid back-up plan.

My ears prick with awareness. Water stirs, a rogue wave lapping at the marble pool.

My stomach flips over, and I drop the pouch back into its drawer. I didn't notice the discrete pile of clothing next to the pool or the slight waft of steam rising from the water. Rookie mistakes. Deep in the pool, settled near the bottom, a dark, masculine shape hangs limply, his dark green tail swishing.

The chamber door is too far away, and the guard is likely leaning against the other side of it. I scan the patio for an easy escape. Vines cling to the palace, but this room is in the upper level. If the vines don't hold, I'll plummet into the streets far below.

As the water churns and the dark shape floats closer to the surface, I shove the drawer shut and sprint to the patio, leaping onto the vine. It holds my weight, thank the goddess. I dig my claws into the woody tendrils, finding purchase for my feet within the roots.

I check the distance to the next balcony down—manageable, but it's going to hurt—and tug my foot. The roots curl around my ankle, digging into my skin. I yank, but my foot does not budge.

The prince's head breaks the surface of the water, water streaming from his thick curls. He pads across the room, a white towel wrapped loosely around his hips.

He approaches his desk. Did I leave that drawer ajar? He stands there calmly, his back turned to me, and checks something on top of his desk. I closed that drawer. I'm sure of it.

Twisting, I attempt to dislodge my foot from the vine. Pain sears up my leg, and I hiss in frustration. Will I have to gnaw my own foot off? Or hang here until he goes to sleep?

He moves toward the balcony, stepping into the light of the moon. I twist the vine into the wall to shield myself, peering through the leaves. Thorns pierce my skin, tangle in my hair. A bit of blood trickles down my ankle. I hold my breath in fear of alerting him to my presence, praying to Tephra this vine holds my weight.

The silver light glistens on his wet skin, enhancing the sparkle of the green scales that scatter across his arms, his chest, and the sharp valley between his abdominal muscles.

The prince leans against the marble banister and surveys the royal city below. His face isn't stern and fierce. It's soft—a expression of kindness utterly foreign to me. Aching. Emotion plays across his features like reflected light, varied in hue and flavor.

His brow knits, his mouth set in a hard line, like he's figuring out a difficult puzzle. He rubs a spot on his ribs, his fingers pressing deep into the skin.

"Where are you, Wicked?" he whispers. After a moment of searching the beach, he sighs and returns to his room, pulling the towel free of his waist.

The towel drops.

I glimpse two cheeks of his round, muscular ass before I tear my gaze away, yank my ankle free at last, and climb down the vine. If Odissa succeeds in her bargain and becomes the permanent Queen of Coral, maybe I'll stick around—play handmaid a while longer—if only for the proximity to her sad, pretty king.

Chapter Twenty-Four

SOREN

THE PRINCESS HAS INFILTRATED my palace. I cannot go anywhere during daylight hours without catching a whisper of her, a glimpse of her. Ever since our understanding in the gardens, I've avoided her at all costs. Still, she's there. Always there. She's at my dinner table, walking my beach, her wicked handmaid stalking after her with that damned parasol. She's flirting with the guards outside my door, begging for admittance.

What more does she want from me? Affection? I'll marry this female, irritating and power-hungry as she is, because it's in the best interest of my kingdom. The least she can do is leave me to mourn the last few weeks of my freedom in peace.

As the moon rises, I straighten at my desk, stack the ledgers neatly, and roll the soreness from my shoulders. All the wedding affairs are paid for, the schedule decided, and the invitations sent. In two weeks' time, Audrina will bloom in her fullness, and the door to my future will close to resounding applause.

I stretch my arms over my head, and my spine cracks in a symphony of relief. As has become my habit, I reach for my ribs next, swiping my thumb over the spot where the itchy scale used to be. In the past few days, the sting has finally subsided, but I still trace the scale, reveling in the loss of its familiar ache.

But the stretch is not enough; my body craves movement. I should go for a walk—the princess won't be out this late in the evening, and I could use the exercise. I've been skipping my sparring sessions with Nara, simply to avoid the possibility of running into Aris on the way to the ring.

My stomach growls, reminding me of my untouched dinner. Perhaps I'll swing by the kitchen for a late-night snack. I nod at the guard, and he returns the gesture.

No sign of the princess.

In the lower hallway, two figures stand around the bend, effectively blocking my only pathway to the kitchen wing beyond. I press myself against the wall to hear the conversation.

"She's like a silver cloud, lovely and delicate. Just what this kingdom needs," Lady Myrrh's bubbling soprano drifts to me.

Lord Varik's voice comes in response, thick with irony. "I see you have yet to uncover the princess's fangs?"

Even if the princess isn't here in body, she's here in name. I cannot seem to escape her.

"Bah," Lady Myrrh huffs. "These things aren't all about appearances, you know."

"No, of course not, my lady," the treasurer chides. "Not when she appears like... What was it you said? A silver cloud? How quaint."

The lady makes a squeal of protest, and I peer around the edge of the wall. The two council members stand in the middle of the hallway, facing each other with crossed arms. Her back to me, Lady Myrrh rattling the beads of her chest piece with nervous hands while the lord towers over her, his face plastered with his signature eelish sneer.

There's space behind Lady Myrrh, just enough for me to sneak past. If luck serves me well, they will continue their argument without notice, and I can be on my way. Lord Varik may spot me, but he'll let me go without incident. It's the lady I must be careful of.

Hunger gnaws at my stomach, sharp and demanding. With a sigh, I step around the corner.

Before I can take three steps, Lady Myrrh turns to greet me with an emphatic curtsy. "Oh, Your Highness!" Her hair bobs, a stray curl falling into her eyes. She brushes it away, quickly tucking it behind her pointed ear.

I nod to her politely and greet her by name, continuing my brisk pace. But as I pass, she raises her voice to a level not easy to ignore.

"I was just saying to Lord Varik how exquisite the princess looked in her day gown on the beach this afternoon. What a treasure you've found! Thank the gods, I don't think we'll need to use that pendant, after all. I don't know what Lord Almar was thinking. Wretched old thing."

"Princess Aris is indeed lovely. I am glad you are pleased, my lady." I step away, signaling my departure with another curt nod. She catches my arm.

"How go the wedding plans?" she pries. "I've been thinking, it'd be lovely to have flowers for the ball." A waft of her scent floods my nose—thick and floral, like roses too long in the sun.

Lord Varik chuckles darkly. "The prince is busy, my lady. Do not worry him with such things."

I stare at her hand on my wrist, curling around my bare skin. Her palm is sweaty and warm. "Silver, do you think? And white? To match the princess's aura."

"The traditional color is pink," I say on instinct. A pity, that. As abundant as it is in my kingdom's decor, I've never cared much for the color. Except for the particular shade of pink that stained the handmaid's cheeks the day I met her—when I thought she was mine.

An odd sensation flutters in my stomach when I recall those sun-stained cheeks. I haven't seen Enna at a close distance since the garden incident, and I—

I shake my head to clear the thought. It can't be that I miss her. Can it? Twisting my wrist, I gently dislodge from Lady Myrrh's grip.

The lady blinks, as if broken from a trance, and steps back. "White and pink, then."

"Sounds perfect. Lady Myrrh, if you could arrange with the florists to bring these ideas to life, I cannot wait to see what you come up with." Once more, I step toward my exit.

The councilwoman splutters. "Pardon, Your Highness. Me?"

"Yes. You are the minister of entertainment, no? And you have an eye for beauty. I'd love to see how your vision transforms the throne room for the upcoming ball."

Her brows furrow as if suddenly calculating difficult math. "It would be an honor," she says finally.

"Excellent." Another step toward the kitchen.

Lord Varik snorts. "Assigning tasks to the council directly, are we? Your mother would never—"

I'm two paces past the council member, yet I whirl to face him. "My wishes have the weight of an order from the crown, do they not?"

He meets my gaze with lifted chin, his top lip twitching with a repressed snarl. Anger burns in his small, yellow eyes, but I refuse to look away. I stare deep into the depths of his gaze until I'm cutting through their golden tides with efficient control.

With a grunt, Lord Varik flicks his eyes away in reluctant submission. "Of course, Your Highness. I simply meant that we are quite busy. I'm sure Lady Myrrh will need to arrange her schedule to accommodate your request."

"Which is not a problem, at all, Your Highness." She flutters her hand, as if that demonstrates her flexibility.

"Well, you both seem to have plenty of time to gossip in the hallway after sundown. Tell me, Lord Varik, what have you been working on?"

He narrows his eyes. "A personal project to ensure the continued success of this kingdom."

"Is that so?"

The treasurer doesn't respond, only pins me with another glare. I play his game for a few moments longer before pushing past him with a curt "goodnight" to Lady Myrrh.

As I round the next bend, at the edge of my hearing, I catch his grumbling tone, muttering under his breath.

"Oh, lighten up, Lord Varik." Lady Myrrh giggles. "Look at our prince. He's simply mad for her. I could see it on his face, plain as sand, when I suggested flowers to match her aura. The prince was blushing!"

I touch my cheek, feeling the residual heat. I'm blushing?

"Don't get too invested in those flowers, my lady. He will walk out on this one, first chance he gets. Mark my word."

"Hush now. That is a male in love, if ever I saw one. And I am an excellent judge of these things."

I cannot keep hiding in my room. I have a kingdom to run, a council to manage. This wedding business? I've worked too hard to secure the future of my kingdom to let it be run by eels like Varik.

Chapter Twenty-Five

ENNA

The palace holds plenty of secrets—the golden screws, for one. The library stairs. The magically locked door in the lowest level. The budding romance between the guard outside the prince's door and a sullen garden maid. My favorite secret, though, is the hidden pool in the kitchen pantry.

In the cramped closet of a room, carved into the floor, is a deep channel full of sea water. If I dive through the channel and follow it to its depth, it leads into the fishery. Surrounded by steep coral walls and a net over the top, the open-water enclosure brims with fish. Large, juicy fish. And the best secret of all—no one guards the door.

I've wandered into the kitchen many times now, under the guise of needing supplies for the princess. If I catch the staff in a busy moment, they shrug at me and shoo me off to fetch the supplies from the closet myself.

If I appear for the dinner rush, by the time I emerge, hours later, dripping wet, they've wrapped up their chores and closed the kitchen.

Odissa takes her meals in her room now, too, since the prince no longer joins us. Tonight, I pause before the kitchen door, listening to gauge the mood of the staff.

The scent hits me first, as it always does, wafting beneath the door, warm and thick. It's ridiculous how the Corals cook a perfect piece of flesh, but damn does it smell good. My stomach gurgles with a painful twist, and I rub my hand over my belly, soothing it.

"Soon," I whisper to it.

The lock isn't difficult—a snick of my claw and I'm pushing the slab of wood open, creeping through the minimal opening and slipping into the fray.

The kitchen is a flurry of activity. Mermaids flutter from counter to counter, chopping vegetables and barking orders. A large stone counter stretches in a wide U, framing a stocky center island.

The closet is in the back corner of the room. I mumble something to a servant about needing more seaweed. She grunts at me, jerking her head toward the door.

I slip into the closet without further notice. Shelves line the walls, displaying baskets and bins overflowing with fruits, kelps, and corals. The pool sits in the middle, and I remove my dressing skirts, shoving them into an empty crate. I dive into the water eagerly, welcoming the sensation as the water swallows me.

The channel opens into the fishery, and a panicked school of wrigglefish greet me with their pink, curling bodies. I snatch one in my claws, greedily slurping it into my mouth. I chase them through the fishery, a predator set loose on a guppy's buffet.

I hunt a sweetfish next. It eyes me with bulging eyes, darting for the nearest cover. The water is bare, cleared for easy fishing. They cannot escape me, and they cannot outswim me. I smack my tail in a burst of speed and sink my teeth into the sweetfish's neck, tearing free a chunk of the sweet, sweet meat. The carcass flops and sinks, and I scoop it from the water, hefting its weight. I settle happily into the sandy floor, plucking pieces of meat from my prize until my stomach swells.

The fiery evening light filters through the surface above, painting the sea in a wash of color. The sunsets here are beautiful, but I much prefer them from beneath the waves. I nestle in the sand, watching as the hues fade from orange to red to the navy of nightfall.

I return to the entryway to complete the last task on my agenda. Beneath the lip of the channel, I've hidden my leather pouch, full of my stolen treasures. Here, Odissa will never find it.

I dig into the sand, retrieving the pouch, and heft its weight in my hand. My collection is growing steadily—golden screws, silverware, gems, jewelry, candlesticks—anything that might fetch a good price on the market. What I really want is that magical necklace hidden in the prince's desk. Tonight, I add two gold coins to my pouch, and it'll have to do. How much I'll need to secure a life on my own once Odissa sets me free, I don't know. The Kingdom of Frost is a mystery to me. All I know is it's cold and secluded in the northern reaches of the sea, and the merfolk there tend to be just as icy as their seascape. My kind of company.

The pouch safely buried, I ascend through the channel and crawl out of the hole onto my dripping pair of legs. As I'm wrapping my skirts around my waist, I hear voices in the kitchen.

It's past nightfall. Usually, the kitchen staff has cleared the room by now. I peek around the doorframe into the kitchen, and my stomach drops to the floor.

There, lounging against the wide, center counter with his back facing me is the Coral Prince, chatting with the royal chef.

A dim fire burns in the white-stone oven set into the far wall. Its flames crackle and pop as they heat a spitted fish. The royal chef stands in front of the cooking fire, rotating the spit with a large, speckled hand.

The prince gestures at the rotating fish, and the muscles along his back flex with the movement. For the second time in a matter of weeks, I find myself staring at the prince's fine ass.

The chef removes the fish from the fire, handing the spit to the prince. This is my chance. I move with as much grace and stealth as my legs can muster, but before I can reach the exit, my foot connects with something hard on the floor. I glance down in horror as a rogue vegetable launches from its sentient place on the floor into the prince's rear end. With a dull thud, the vegetable bounces off his ass cheek, the muscle rippling as it rejects the accidental missile.

Ignoring all my instincts to hit the floor or dash to the door, my body freezes in utter embarrassment—never before have I been so clumsy in a stealth mission. Heat burns my face as the prince turns, brow furrowed, spit in hand. His eyes widen, taking in every inch of me at once. The charred fish slips slowly down the stick.

We both freeze, as if waiting for something to explode. Waiting for *me* to explode, I realize a moment later. I open my mouth to offer some sort of excuse, but my tongue is dry. All that comes out is a pathetic puff of air.

"Chef, I think I've found your mystery fish-eater," he says. His voice is playful. He eyes my wet hair, my damp skirts. "The kitchen has been having troubles maintaining inventory. Do you know anything about a dozen missing sweetfish, Wicked?"

"If you mean to spit me next, Your Highness, I'll gut you where you stand." I suck in a breath. That was hardly appropriate. *Where the fuck is my filter?*

And what did he call me? Wicked? My spines bristle beneath my gloves.

He chuckles. "With what, that potato?"

"I'm sure I could figure it out," I mumble. Embarrassment washes over me once again, red-hot and angry. I fight the urge to stare down at my feet, to funnel my anger into my toes. I hold his searching gaze, lifting my chin to hide the shame.

"Are we not feeding you enough?" His face softens, brow knitting with concern. He gestures, and the chef bends to retrieve a raw fish from a basket beneath the counter, laying it onto the stone worksurface.

"I'm getting plenty to eat, thank you," I say.

"Straight from the fishery." He smiles, and the firelight glints off his teeth. "Something wrong with my chef's cooking?"

The chef glares at me from behind the prince, cleaning his knife on a wet towel.

"No. I just prefer it less…" I eye the fish on the prince's spit. He lifts it to his mouth and sinks his teeth into the burned flesh. I swallow my disgust. "Cooked."

He chews around the bite thoughtfully. "Less cooked," he repeats, swallowing.

The chef threads another spit through the flesh of the uncooked fish, then stokes the fire.

"Hold on there, chef," the prince says. "The lady said *less* cooked."

"You want me to just, lightly roast it, my lady?" the chef suggests.

I shake my head. "If that one's for me, I'd eat it just like that. No fire."

"I can cook that for you, if you'd like." The chef frowns.

"Goddess, no. You've already ruined that one." I nod at the prince's half-eaten fish. The prince smiles around his next bite.

"Criticize my cooking without trying it, I see." As he speaks, he slaps the raw fish onto the counter in front of me. "Go on, then."

After removing my glove so as to not stain it, I dig into the juicy flesh. My teeth sink in deep, ripping and tearing through the soft fibers. Sweetness floods my mouth, and my eyes roll back a little. A moan escapes before I can reign it in.

The prince's green eyes study my every move.

"Never thought I'd see a siren ask for raw meat." The chef scratches his fingers through his short hair. "Is that a dark-dweller thing?"

I pause my frenzy for a moment. Blood dribbles down my chin, and I lick it away with a swipe of my tongue. For effect, I flex my spines, lifting them from their sheaths. "You sun-drenchers could eat it raw, too, if you tried."

"Sun-drenchers, eh?" The chef chuckles. "I suppose that's true."

I suck the skeleton into my mouth, snapping the bones. The final swallow slips down my throat, and I lean onto the counter, pinching up the morsels I missed.

"What would you say to another field trip?" The prince sets his finished spit on the counter, leaning next to me. His shoulder brushes mine, the ghost of a touch. "I know of an excellent little place in the reef districts. I'm sure we could persuade their kitchen to produce something even fresh enough for you, Wicked. My treat."

His eyes swim with a look I haven't seen in years. My throat tightens, and I swallow with difficulty. A fishbone wedged sideways, likely; nothing at all to do with the way the prince is looking at me. Or the way his eyes drop to my lips. He leans closer. His breath skitters across my face, and I lean into the warmth.

My eyelids droop. The prince has an intoxicating pair of lips. I've never studied them this closely before. The smooth slope of them, their gentle curve—

Odissa's voice floats to the front of my mind: *help me win the prince's heart, and you'll swim free.*

I freeze. I shouldn't be here, not with *him*. "I'm sure Her Highness would appreciate another outing with you," I say, speaking around the bone in my throat. "I'm happy to chaperone. If there's raw fish."

The prince straightens from the counter, morphing before my eyes from the relaxed male once again into the stiff royal I'm used to seeing. "Of course, my lady," he says. "I'll see what can be arranged."

Chapter Twenty-Six

SOREN

The handmaid plagues my dreams all night. I watch her, endlessly, as she devours creature after creature alive, until the blood runs thick down her chin. She smiles at me, her fangs long and glinting. Then she saunters toward me, those bright purple eyes sharp. When she reaches me, she sinks her teeth into my neck—and I don't move. I don't protest. I stand there, completely calm, and I let her have her feast.

Sitting in my mother's calling room, I touch my neck, tracing the place Enna's teeth marked me in my dreams. The soft floral scent of the room sticks in my mouth, drying my tongue. Clio busies herself with displays of fabric and flowers, her long blue fingers pinching and prodding the practice wedding arrangements. A broad table brims with decorations I couldn't care less about.

The queen stands in the center of the room in what is to be her gown for my wedding ball, while a slew of maids fuss over her with measuring string and pins.

"These are the flowers Lady Myrrh suggests for the arrangements. What do you think, Your Majesty?" Clio asks, lifting a flower for the queen to sample.

The bright pink bloom nearly brushes the queen's nose. She shifts away from it, frowning. "Too faint a smell. And the color is wrong," she says. "Don't you think so, Soren?"

I lean my shoulder against the wall, feigning interest. "I have no opinion on the color of a flower," I say. "But your gown looks lovely, Mother. Should I have mine done to match?"

The handmaids titter at my comment. A few of them blush. One pricks my mother with a pin and receives a swat on her wrist from the irritated queen.

"Funny, Soren. But you'll be in white. Your suit has already been ordered."

Just as well. I cannot stand the color pink.

The dream resurfaces, Enna's mouth hungry and wide, her pink tongue licking my blood from her fangs. I shake my head, clearing my thoughts. I shouldn't be dwelling on it. If last night's incident in the kitchen didn't make things clear enough, the handmaid's grip on my attention is dangerous. I'm unbalanced. Out of control.

I shouldn't be asking her out to dinner. I shouldn't be dreaming of her or considering the color of her tongue.

Enna is the attendant of my betrothed. My betrothed, who, once queen, will likely still want to keep her close. I see no reason for Aris to send away her one memento from home.

Which means my beach dancer will be around a while. I flex my jaw at the thought. How many nights will I dream of her wicked mouth? How many days will I spend trying to banish her image from my waking thoughts?

"Soren?" My mother's voice penetrates my uncomfortable reverie. My eyes focus on the new bloom Clio twirls in front of my face, a softer shade of coral more in line with the traditional colors of our kingdom.

"Looks nice," I say.

The queen pins me with a look. "That settles it," she says. "Miss Clio, be a dear and show us the fabric for the aisle drapes."

The housekeeper retrieves several swaths of ivory fabric from the chest on the floor and drapes them over each of her arms. She holds them out for my mother to test their texture.

The queen studies each one intently. "Too dull," she says of the first one. She picks at the fabric with a long fingernail. "This quality has certainly suffered of late. Make a note to investigate the modiste's supply chain. This won't do."

"No need," I say, pushing off my perch on the wall. "The modiste is likely suffering from the broadkelp shortage, Your Majesty." I pinch the fabric between my fingers, noting its roughness. "The Kingdom of Estuary has been low on its quota for the past season. Our beloved modiste would appreciate some grace, no?"

The queen inclines her head, eyes shining. "I stand corrected. Well done, my prince. You've been attentive."

I grunt, re-crossing my arms. "Mother, if you have this all sorted, I will trust your opinions and take my leave."

"Your wedding is in a week, Soren. Do you not wish to have a say?"

Where is the time going? If I had a say, there wouldn't be a wedding. I would take the throne without a queen at my side, then take my time finding a love match with which to continue the royal line.

She frowns at my silence, then says to Clio, "I believe we are ready for your report."

The handmaids remove my mother's gown and shuffle out of the room, leaving us alone with the housekeeper.

"I've discovered some interesting things, Your Majesty," Clio says. "I'm not sure if you consider them *suspicious,* as you asked me to watch out for, but I find them... confusing."

"Waste not the time of the crown, Clio. Spit it out if you have something to report." The queen's voice is sharp and cutting.

Clio hides her flinch behind a gentle cough. "I'm not familiar with Abyssal customs, Your Majesty. So it may just be a cultural difference. But the princess absolutely insists that her magic-wielding handmaid give her baths personally. She will not allow one of our own maids to come near her. Not to bathe her, not to dress her."

The queen considers Clio's suggestion. "Is there something wrong with her form? She is beautiful from what I've seen, but underneath, perhaps?"

"I'm not sure, Your Majesty. I've only ever seen her in a towel."

"Could be harmless modesty but please continue your observation of this matter. What else?"

"She's receiving private dance lessons."

"And?"

"From her handmaid," Clio says, and my ears prick with interest. "The handmaid is a good dancer, but the princess, well. I've seen better. And then she—"

I break my silence. "You ladies mean to say you've been spending your time digging up dirt on my betrothed instead of more important matters?"

My mother tilts her head. "And what could be more important than getting to know the future queen? Tell me, Soren, what have you learned from your time with her?"

I learned all I needed to know in the first two days I spent with her. Aris is as I knew she would be, lustful and vain, but she's pleasant enough to appease the kingdom. This is not the answer my mother is looking for, so I keep quiet as I search for a better excuse.

"Your Majesty, if I may—"

The queen raises her hand, and Clio snaps her mouth shut.

"Have you been spending time with her *at all*?" My mother's glare is accusing, all-knowing.

"Not much, no."

"This kingdom depends on you to do your duty, Soren. I have found you a match. You must secure it. And if you do not think the match is *worthy*, we must be sure of it. Am I clear?"

"Then do as Lord Almar suggested. Bring out that damned necklace and see if she bleeds."

My suggestion lands in a silent room. Clio stiffens, her eyes narrowing. My mother's mouth presses into a firm line.

"I will not resort to Lord Almar's archaic measures when you have spent the past two weeks avoiding her," the queen says.

She's right. I've been avoiding my duty in favor of preserving my sanity.

"You'll be pleased to hear I'm taking her out to dinner tonight," I say, flexing my jaw to relieve the tension. I'd already been meaning to ask Aris officially, since I promised Enna I would.

"Excellent." The queen brightens. "Then you can investigate Clio's claims. The wedding festivities begin in less than a week, Soren. See if you can uncover a few secrets lest we make an embarrassment of this kingdom."

What would the wicked handmaid look like, sitting in my favorite tavern, a little ale in her veins, surrounded by platters of raw meat? Would she smile at me again?

Chapter Twenty-Seven

ENNA

Odissa grips my throat, pinning me against her chamber wall. I gasp as my eyes refocus. Round white teeth clench in front of my nose, her breath spilling over my face.

I struggle against her, but I'm half-awake and weary from my late-night wandering, and she's grown in her strength. All I can manage is a few pathetic kicks, connecting with nothing but air.

"Talk," she demands, squeezing. The curtains are out of reach, lit by the morning sun. I eye the chair next to her, and she frowns, kicking it out of the way.

With her other hand, she reaches behind me, unsheathing my knives one by one and tossing them across the room. One punctures the soft bedcover, and tufts of feathers scatter into the air.

"Talk," she says again, pressing harder.

I cough against her hand, and my voice strains. "Hard to talk, like this." Hard to use magic, either. I focus my intent, pushing a zap of lighting through my throat. Odissa's hair statics, lifting from her scalp, but it's all I can manage.

She throws me to the floor. I hit the marble hard, and pain sears through my aching body. "I heard you were with the prince last night. Alone in the kitchen. Explain."

She pins a piece of my skirt to the ground with her foot. I reach for my waist belt, lifting the attachment point with fumbling fingers. She snarls and kicks my elbow. Pain explodes.

"*Fuck*, Odissa! That's going to leave a mark."

"Your gloves will cover it," she says. "Ensure my every success. That is the oath you made. Have you forgotten the price if I fail?"

I glare up at her, hugging my arm to my chest.

"I don't know about you, but becoming Tephra's breakfast doesn't sound like a beach walk to me."

"And lying to an entire foreign court is, what? By comparison." My voice rasps.

"She speaks!" Odissa narrows her eyes. "I haven't talked to the prince in two weeks. *Two fucking weeks*, and you're having a late night pow-wow with him in the kitchen."

"I was hungry. Late-night snack, nothing more." My throat burns as I push my words through it. I cough, spitting blood onto the floor—dark against clean white.

She pouts. "Aw, the little pet is starving." She pinches my cheek, testing the fat that's accumulated there since our arrival. "Have you so easily forgotten the Drink? That I'm the one who got us out? And this is the thanks you give me. Perhaps this isn't your last job. Perhaps I keep you forever. Is that what you want?"

I bare my fangs, disguising the despair that twists in my stomach.

"He wants to take you out, Odissa. He mentioned a restaurant with a fancy menu in the reef districts. By the *goddess*, calm down."

I cough again. Too many words, that time. More blood sprays onto the marble. I push onto my hands and knees, slowly retrieving my knives under her scrutiny. When I stand and remove the blade from her coverlet, feathers spill out of the gash.

Odissa crosses her arms. "You could have just said that."

I sheath each knife, resting my hand on the hilt of my father's dagger briefly before I hide it beneath my skirts. "Yeah, well. Your hand was on my fucking throat." We match our glares, both hating each other and needing each other all at once.

"You need a better game plan," I say.

"Fine. What move would you play next?"

"You could start by being a little more..." I narrow my eyes. "Attractive. Personality wise. It's not just your looks that will win him over. He's a prince with honor. You tried to fuck him, and he didn't talk to you for two weeks, Odissa. You're after his heart, not his cock."

She flinches. "And what do you know about winning someone over? You have the personality of a prickerfish."

I smile, sliding a finger up the length of my spines. It may be true, but the prince did ask for my opinion of the tavern first—a detail I conveniently left out of my tale.

Chapter Twenty-Eight

ENNA

On the way to the tavern, I give the prince and Odissa a wide berth, hanging back with the watchful group of guards.

He guides us into the underwater districts and, just as before, Odissa clings to him like a horny bloodfish.

At the reef's edge, a large cave structure extends above the waterline. We follow a narrow channel, surfacing inside the heart of a cavern. Stalagmites surge up from the stone floor to support scattered tabletops, each surrounded by chattering merfolk. The room is packed to its gills. Noisy.

I haul myself into the humid cave air, my tail splits into a wobbly pair of legs, and I step onto the smooth stone floor. I watch the patrons closely, waiting for the tension to arise. In Vespyr, there's always a tavern fight. But it doesn't come. The merfolk laugh and toast their ale. When they notice the royals, many pause and touch their gills.

The prince points to an empty table at the back of the room. "There's our spot. You ladies get settled in while I grab us some drinks from the bar."

He brushes the small of Odissa's back, and she leans into it, resting her head momentarily on his shoulder. "You're leaving me alone?"

He smiles at her. "I'm sure your handmaid will protect you." His gaze lifts to meet mine, and he whispers, "Won't you, Wicked?"

I nod, heat skittering across my neck, and cross to the table he indicated. Odissa follows quietly, and we settle into chairs across from each other.

"What the fuck was that?" she hisses. "Wicked?"

"It's nothing, Your Highness." I shrug, avoiding her gaze. After a beat of silence, she huffs her retreat.

Beside us, two mermen play a game of Stones, placing them in intricate patterns on a lined stone board. A large male twirls a whiskered spine dripping from his top lip. With a crooked smile, he slaps down a black stone, then leans back in his seat and guffaws. The sound rises above the chatter of the room.

It was a good move. In my father's house, I would sneak in a game of Stones with the butler.

"Oy!" calls the waitress, who carries five foaming mugs of ale in one hand. With the other, she hands another patron their bill. "Shut it down, Krass."

Krass's laugh grows louder, and the waitress shakes her head, smiling.

His opponent, a smaller male with two round eyes too big for his face, frowns at the table. His antennae twitch, peeking through a mop of gray hair. He places a small white stone. Krass stops laughing, squinting at the board. With a growl and a swipe of his large fist, the board clatters to the floor. The pebbles scatter, landing at Odissa's feet.

She kicks the stones away with a sour expression. She mutters to herself, pinching the bridge of her nose and closing her eyes.

"Apologies, my ladies," says Krass, stooping to retrieve the pebbles.

Odissa looks pointedly at the ceiling and moves her foot out of his reach.

I hop from my chair and scoop up the few stones that landed near me and hold them out for Krass. He accepts them with a deep bow, touching his hidden gills with two fingers.

I drop the stones into his large blue hands. "Next time, don't leave your left flank so open," I whisper. "It was a fair move, you know."

"Thank you, my lady," he rumbles, his pointy smile spreading wide. "Truly."

"Don't mention it," I say, returning to my seat.

Odissa pins me with a glare as the males return to their game.

I raise my eyebrow at her. "Something chewing your fins?"

She shakes her head. Prince Soren arrives with three mugs of ale and a plate of seaweed crisps balancing on top. He slides into the chair between us and distributes the mugs.

"Ladies," he says, tipping his head.

"How kind of Your Highness," Odissa purrs. She lifts a mug to her lips, the foam clinging to her upper lip.

He takes a long pull from his own mug. With every bob of his throat, he sucks down the liquid in rapid rhythm, draining the liquid in a few gulps. Then, he licks the foam from his lips.

Odissa watches him, her eyes widening with each gulp.

He plucks a crisp from the plate and crunches it between his teeth. "This is my favorite spot," he says, glancing at her.

She forces a smile. "Oh, really?" she says, taking in the room. Her eyes dart between the tables, snagging on Krass, who leans in our direction with interest, and swivels his large ears.

The prince tips his mug, studying the bottom of it with disappointment. He signals the waitress.

A small band has taken post at the far end of the cavern, coaxing a lilting tune from their stringed instruments. Mermaids spiral in a free-flowing dance, laughing and carrying their mugs of ale to the dance floor, amber liquid sloshing onto the stone floor.

Odissa flexes her jaw. "What a lovely place."

"You think so?" He leans across the table, studying her face intently.

Next to us, Krass belches loudly, thumping his fist onto his table repeatedly. His opponent snickers as he places a white stone.

Odissa flicks her eyes to the game. Her lips quiver as she holds them in a smile. "Of course," she says. She reaches for the prince's hand, smoothing the back with her thumb.

I guzzle my liquid. It's smooth against the back of my throat, and I close my eyes, letting it slide into my gullet. I soon reach the bottom of my mug, too, seeking the buzz. But this ale is weak, and I've spent a lifetime building my tolerance.

"I think the palace kitchen does a fine job, as well," she hedges. "That cake on our first night was to die for, don't you agree?"

He flips his hand and catches her thumb between his fingers, giving it a squeeze before releasing.

"Oh yes, the royal chefs are fantastic. But sometimes, I fancy a good meal away from the pomp of palace life." He leans in close, whispering now. "Don't tell the chef, but the food here is better."

He places another crisp between his teeth, offering a second to Odissa. She pinches it between her fingers.

"Try it. You might like it."

She places the crisp in her mouth and chews, swallowing slowly.

"Excellent," he says. "I figured it'd be nice to relax away from the palace for a while, get to know the people. Have an ale." He nods at the approaching waitress. "Or two."

The waitress delivers the next round of ales with two plates of roasted wrigglefish and one plate raw. The prince slides the uncooked meal to me. "For you, my lady. I know you like it raw."

I reach for the fish eagerly, tearing into the meat.

With a flourish, he skewers a piece of roasted fish with his fork, then lifts it to his mouth. Seasoning dribbles down his chin. His red tongue swipes out and collects the juice.

I glance down at my plate, ignoring the warmth spiraling through my stomach at the sight of his tongue.

Odissa eyes my meal with longing, pinching her fork between her fingers, angling it to stab efficiently at the roasted flesh on her plate.

She gulps down some ale to chase the charred fish. "What do you like about this place?"

He leans back in his chair, the picture of a male at ease. A lopsided grin spreads across his face, and his eyes light up. A stray curl falls across his forehead, caught in a ray of lamplight.

"It feels real," he says. "Every now and then, I like to come here and remind myself that there's more to this world than marble walls and elaborate feasting." He waves a hand to the room. "I'm sure you understand. Palace life can be constricting."

"Yes," she says. "Of course."

Odissa takes another long drag of her ale, finishing it with gentle flourish. I tear another piece of meat with my teeth. Odissa's fork connects with an empty spot on her plate, grating in an unpleasant shriek. She frowns at it, blinking rapidly as her cheeks stain pink.

"You okay there?" the prince asks.

Odissa stabs again, this time successfully snagging a bite. She chews slowly, her eyes slightly unfocused.

Shit.

"Your Highness?" I say, lightly touching her hand.

"Hmm?" She opens her eyes to glare at me, her gaze watery. While Odissa could easily keep up with me at the bar in Vespyr, there's no telling what the limit is for her borrowed body. We may have found it already.

The prince is staring at us, those green eyes sharply focused.

Odissa glances down at her plate, searching for something. "Oh, goddess," she whispers, attempting to stab with her fork once more. I squeeze her wrist, removing the weapon from her grip.

"Does Her Highness usually get drunk this easily?" He moves his fork out of her reach.

I shrug, studying her face. Odissa's forehead prickles with sweat. She reaches for her mug, tilting it to peer into its empty well. I panic under the prince's watchful gaze. When Odissa drinks too much, she gets sobby and prone to spilling her guts, and I can think of at least one secret this prince can never know.

"I'm out of the drink," Odissa says. Then, to my horror, she laughs to herself. "Out of the Drink!"

I snatch the mug from her hand.

She pouts, then scrabbles her hands across the table to grasp onto his wrist. "Your Highness. *Soren*, darling. I require the ladies' room. As it seems, my handmaid is... too drunk to accompany me, would you do me"—she hiccups—"the honor?" She blinks her eyes rapidly, drawing attention to her fluttering eyelashes.

"Of course," he says, lifting his hand. I wait for him to stand up and escort her, but he stays firmly planted in his seat. Footsteps approach, and the guard moves to stand behind Odissa. "Please assist Her Highness."

Her lips tighten, but she nods and stands. She pins me with a watery look. "No more ale for you," she says, hiccupping again.

I show her my sharp fangs, but she's not as impressed with them as I am. With a sigh, I push up from my seat. I should assist her, make sure she doesn't spill her guts to the guard in the ladies' room.

But the prince leans over the table, reaching out to stop me. "Enna," he says. My heart flutters at the sound of my name falling from his lips. "Stay."

Chapter Twenty-Nine

SOREN

Enna can hold her drink much better than the princess. She stares at me with narrowed eyes, scowling.

I'm determined to crack her hardened shell, to draw out my wicked dancer I met on the beach. "How's the fish?" I ask.

Her mouth curls up, and I stare at her lips, willing them to curve the rest of the way into a smile. But she doesn't smile. She just shrugs and says, "Better than the chef's."

"And the ale? You don't seem to be affected much."

"It's fine. Oddly chuggable," she says, tapping the side of her mug. "I've never drunk it without a straw before."

I choke on my drink, caught off guard. "A straw?"

She rolls her eyes. "That was explosive," she says, swiping her hand across her cheek.

"Ah. I got you, didn't I?"

"Seems you might benefit from a straw, Your Highness."

I fold my arms and lean onto the table. "How does that work?"

"The straw? You put your mouth on it and suck."

My face warms, and I'm suddenly aware of the curve of her mouth, the way she pauses with her lips in the shape of an *O*, demonstrating the action on dry air.

"I'm not in need of a lesson," I say, my voice coming out akin to a growl.

"Aren't you, though?"

My cock shifts, awakened by the thoughts of that mouth sucking on a straw. "No." I clench my jaw, resisting the urge to adjust myself. How did we get here? I wrack my brain for an alternative conversation—anything but this one—even as I lean onto the table, arms crossed, dipping my head to get a better look.

"Tell me, pretty prince. Why the sudden outing? After two weeks of silence, you show up, ready to woo my princess."

Gods above. Any conversation but that. I buy time for my response, taking a long pull of my ale before answering. "I've been busy preparing for the wedding."

Her eyebrow arches, unconvinced. "By taking dinner in your room?"

"I'm poring over ledgers, sniffing an inordinate number of flowers, keeping my council in line…" Is that the end of my list already?

"Yet you have time to visit the kitchen after hours and time for long steam baths, but you don't have time for Aris. If my princess has done something to offend you, I'd have you tell me."

Her eyebrow stays raised, mocking me with its perfect, dark arch. At the base of her eyebrow, just at the corner of her eye, there's a jagged scar. When had a knife been that close to her eye? And why had the Abyssal royal healer not attended to her better?

I push my questions aside, focusing on a more pressing matter: "How do you know about my baths?"

Enna leans closer. "Has she offended you?"

"No."

"Then, would you please spend more time with her? She's peeling my scales."

There's that humor I met on the beach, that sparkle of mischief in her eyes. I can't help the smile on my lips. "No."

Her mouth opens, then shuts. She shoots me a puzzled look.

"I don't much like her," I admit.

She takes this in slowly. Her gaze shifts from mischief to a deep, unfathomable sadness. "Then send us away," she says.

"I can't do that."

She blinks slowly, her dark lashes brushing the tops of her cheeks. When she looks up, I catch a flash of fear. I don't like it, not in her, not in the eyes of this female—this fearless, brave, mystery of mine.

"I *won't* do that. You have a place here." My voice rumbles low in my chest and my stomach squeezes into a tight knot.

She shrugs. "Until I don't."

My hands itch to touch her, to comfort her. To brush that fear away. Instead, I pinch the bridge of my nose. "Has she always been like... this?"

"You're going to have to elaborate, before I put words in your mouth that shouldn't be there."

"Persistent?"

Enna's laughter bursts across her face like the morning sun, brilliant against a once-gray sky. "Clingy?"

I chuckle, drinking in the sight of her. "I wasn't going to say it."

"She and I, we... grew up together. She practically ra—she's the closest thing I have to a sister."

"You have no siblings?"

"My parents were not a happy match." As quickly as it appeared, her smile fades, and I miss it already.

"We have that in common, then," I say.

She nods. "I saw your father's statue in the hallway. You look like him."

My throat tightens. "Do they miss you while you're so far away?"

"My father was a sick, twisted siren, and now he is dead." She shrugs, as if relaying the state of the weather. "I never knew my mother."

"And that's when you joined the royal court service?"

"Something like that," she says.

"It's a whole other world down there in the deep, I can't imagine. What do you miss the most?"

I'm asking too many questions. I should stop this silliness now. Should place a barrier, should retreat. Lean away at least. But I can't do any of that; I'm drunk on her words, eager for another glimpse into the world she came from.

"I miss the darkness. And the cold."

I shudder at the thought of a life without the sun. Ugh.

"I can't sleep here. Your kingdom is too bright, too hot. Even when I close my eyes, I can see the light. Nothing is dark here. And it's all warm. Like swimming in piss water."

I laugh. "We're always swimming in piss water."

Her eyebrows shoot up. "Yes. But at least the piss water down there is recognizable for what it is. You swim through it, and you know."

"Isn't that worse? To know? I rather like not knowing." A complete lie. I'm obsessed with unpuzzling her.

She frowns again. The skin of her brow puckers into a tight *V*.

"No," she says finally. "Because if it's dredgebeast piss, then you have a heads up."

"Are there many dredgebeasts?"

"Only in the Drink."

"And you've swum in their piss."

She nods. "Many times. I'm glad I did. Gave me enough warning to stop the bastards."

I close my eyes, greeted suddenly by the beasts depicted in the throne room mural. Their lithe, strong bodies covered in spines, with four broad paddle fins, each the size of a boulder. Their large, snapping teeth; I imagine a small black-tailed form weaving through them. A throbbing ache pulses in my head, and suddenly I cannot see straight.

"Tell me you didn't fight it," I growl.

"Stunned him." Pride rings clearly in her voice.

My blood should not boil at the mere thought of harm coming to her. This female irks me to no end. She's sharp and unrefined. She questions everything I say. She has demonstrated disdain for the culture I come from. She refuses to submit to my authority. She haunts my waking dreams.

"How?"

She flashes a lopsided smile, the tips of her fangs glinting in the dimming light of the tavern. "It's my best secret, pretty prince. What right do you have to uncover it?"

My cheeks warm. I reach for her gloved wrist, needing to touch her. The warning bells peel loudly in my head—the forbidden nature of the touch, the danger of the consequence—and yet my fingers move. They encircle and tighten. The leather of her gloves slides under my touch. Her pulse quickens beneath my thumb.

The leather shreds in an instant as rows of wicked spines rise and slice through the sleeves. She hisses, tugging against my grip. We stare where my fingers encircle her wrist, our shaking breaths intermingling. The noise of the room fades, as if she and I are the only ones here.

With my other hand, I place a knuckle at the base of her spines, stroking upward. They quiver under my touch. I reach the tip of one, gently touching the point. My skin pricks.

"Ah," I say, as a droplet of blood blossoms. "I remember these wicked things well."

The spines flex again, as if deciding whether to flare or retreat.

"I'm willing to bet the dredgebeast is not your only secret," I murmur, swiping my thumb up the line of the next spine. "Who are you?"

Our gazes lock. I stare into the depths of a soul more mysterious than I've ever known. I search her gaze, and, with an odd squeeze of my heart, I realize it's void of the very thing I'm looking for—that burning lust for power. Instead, deep-seated pain molds into crafted defiance.

Slowly, her spines lower into the invisible sheaths beneath her soft skin. When I reach the crest of her elbow, she flinches. Her arm bends, revealing the mottled purple of a nasty bruise. *Fresh.*

She swallows a whimper, but not before I can hear her pain.

"Who did this to you?" I whisper.

"Your Highness, please," she whispers, pulling once more against my hold on her wrist.

"Tell me who."

"I handled it," she says, her voice reaching me through the cloud of my anger, sounding distant.

If I was hot before, now, I am an inferno. My vision blackens around the edges. Magic burns in my stomach, begging for release, pressing against the fractures in my control.

The sound of the room returns with a chattering force, and the soft padding of the princess's footsteps filter through.

I peel my fingers away, blinking out of my trance. I settle back into my chair and lift my mug of ale.

Aris stumbles into her seat, her hair freshly dripping with seawater. She notes the fresh mug of ale and eyes it warily. Then her eyes shift to the shredded remnants of Enna's gloves. She frowns.

"Thank you for the meal, Your Highness," she says. "I think I should return to the palace. This establishment has no ladies' room, would you believe it?"

"Oh, really? I'm sorry to have misled you, Your Highness. I hope you did not struggle to find it."

Aris giggles, still drunk.

I grind my teeth, trying and failing to detach myself from the intensity of the last few moments alone with Enna. Even now, I know it will be fruitless. An evening with her did not cure me of her wiles, did not solve the mystery of her, as I foolishly hoped.

No, it made me want to spend more time with her. And that's a dangerous thing for a crown prince to want.

Chapter Thirty

SOREN

I STORM DOWN THE hallway toward my bedchamber, the soft slap of my bare feet echoing through the empty space. My hands flex and close inadvertently at my sides, moving of their own volition.

I did my duty. I fed the princess, talked with her, and delivered her to her chamber. Mentally, I check the task off my list. But emotionally? My heart squeezes painfully, brimming with a feeling I'm terrified to name.

Why was I letting the handmaid get under my scales? Why couldn't I just leave her alone? I could have easily escorted Aris into the surrounding waters, bonded with her over the awkwardness of the tavern's bathroom arrangement. Instead, I had deliberately chosen to leave her to discover that bit of reef district culture for herself, knowing it would buy me time with her handmaid.

In my mind's eye, Enna's purple eyes flash once more, holding my gaze with unwavering intensity.

I round the corner, and at the end of the hallway, Captain Nara leans against the wall next to my chamber door, sharpening the tines of her trident. She eyes me with a smirk, as if she knows she's the last person I want to see right now.

"Greetings," she says. "Looks like I'm on guard duty tonight."

I cross my arms, slowly resuming my walk.

"The captain doing the work of a lesser soldier? I'm honored."

She rolls her eyes. "Count yourself lucky, I wanted a change of scenery tonight." She gestures broadly to the white-washed walls and endless stretches of marble. With her red stripes, she's the most colorful thing in the room, and that's not saying much.

I stop across from her, leaning against the wall in a mirrored position. "You discharged him, didn't you?"

She smiles. "Guilty."

"What for?"

"He was sleeping on the job."

The familiar throb of my headache pricks at the side of my temple. "Why do they always fall asleep, Nara?"

She tests the sharpness of each tine of her trident with a gloved finger, then inspects the soft white leather for punctures. "It's entirely your fault your sex life is uninteresting, you know."

"Yet here I am, arriving at high tide after spending the evening at the tavern with my betrothed."

"And you delivered her to her rooms just now, I assume?" She glances down the hallway, empty of any pursuing females. "Pity. You could use a good fuck."

I grunt and nod toward my door. "Just unlock it, Nara. Please."

She smirks, fishing for the right key. "That princess is a fine royal specimen. Are you trying?"

"I took her to the bar tonight. She got drunk."

"Very romantic."

I run my hand over the back of my neck, massaging the knot that's forming. I roll my shoulder to ease the tension. "She came onto me, at the beginning of all this, but I turned her down."

Nara pauses with the key in hand. "I assume you're telling me because you want to know what I think. So here it is." She looks over her shoulder to glare at me. "This is your future wife, no?"

"Yes. Yes, she is."

"Then you're an idiot."

"I'll be marrying her in six days, but *gods*, Nara. She's—" I wave my hand, trying to pull the words from thin air.

"Gorgeous? Rich? Super polite? Hardly ever says anything wrong? Has perfect hips for bearing all your royal bloodline guppies?"

"Thank you," I say. "That's not the word I was looking for."

She drops the key on the floor and kicks it down the hallway. It slides to the far wall, where it settles with a dull clink.

"All right," she says. "Talk to me. I'm not getting that key until you say what's on your mind. And by the way you look right now, you're not walking for it."

She's right. The exhaustion of this moon cycle is seeping into my body. I'm nearly swaying on my feet.

"Aris has that look in her eyes," I say, leaning against the wall. "I figured that out the day I met her."

"The one where she looks at you and just sees your throne?"

I nod.

"Ah. You were hoping it'd be different with a princess, no? Someone already used to the power."

"Are my standards really that high?"

She sighs. "Probably. You may be a hopeless romantic, Soren, but you're still the prince. Have you ever had a choice?"

I close my eyes. "No."

"If you did have a choice, what would you be looking for?"

"Someone worthy. Not some pretty thing to... gods, what was it you said? Bear my royal guppies?" I flex my jaw. "I want an Amura to my Eero. Someone intelligent. Interesting. Challenging."

It's my best secret, pretty prince. What right do you have to uncover it?

When Enna's voice sneaks to the front of my mind, I suck in my lip and gnaw on it.

"And Aris is boring, then?"

"She's less interesting than a pile of sand. Hell, her handmaid is more interesting than she is." I open my eyes.

Nara sucks air into her cheeks, then blows it out. "Ah. Your little beach dancer."

Aside from the captain, Enna may just be the one female that doesn't have that *look* in her eyes. And she's funny. Stunningly beautiful. Smart. Quirky. Unpredictable. *Interesting*. A witty conversationalist who's unafraid to fight with me.

I shouldn't be thinking about her so much. She's a handmaid; I'm a prince. Anything more would be impossible. Inappropriate. Not to mention those poisonous Abyssal spines and set of fangs. Her *claws*. Gods, what would those feel like running down my back? Would she draw blood? Would they leave me itching, too?

And yet, warmth churns deep in my gut, and I bring her face back to the forefront of my mind once again. There's something I cannot pin down, despite my scientific study of her. And after an entire evening with her, I'm no closer to finding my answer.

I'm not even sure what my question is anymore.

"Never mind," I say and nod toward the key. "I need to sleep."

Nara levels me with a look, her amber eyes worried. "All right, but only because you look like you've been hit by a fleetwhale."

She retrieves the key and lets me into my room. I walk into the cool air of my bedchamber and sigh. "Nara?"

"Hmm?"

I smile over my shoulder. "Thanks."

She touches her hidden gills in the sign of respect and dips her head, closing the door. "Get some sleep."

Chapter Thirty-One

ENNA

I FLINCH AWAKE, WILDLY snuffing out the remnants of my dream. My skin is sweat-soaked, sand clinging to me after tossing and turning all night. After another sleepless night of wandering the keep, I'd curled up on the beach next to these rocks instead of on top of them. Turns out to have been a shit idea.

I shake out my hair, flinging sand. Growling, I drag my claws over my scalp. The sting sharpens my focus, distracting me from my greatest discomfort—the pool of wetness between my thighs.

I've never had a sex dream in my life. I've had plenty of sex, but it's never been good enough to filter into my dreams.

Last night, I had three, and they all starred the cocky Coral Prince as he took me three different ways—across that tavern table, then in his bathtub, then again on the goddessdamn kitchen floor.

Had it been the ale? I didn't even get drunk. The conversation, perhaps? I knew it'd been a bad idea, sitting alone with him like that. I should have gone with Odissa to relieve herself. That would have prevented any and all sex dreams for the rest of my life.

Fuck. I squint up at the sky. The sun is a sickening pink, the color of Prince Soren's tongue as it dragged down my neck. I clench my thighs as another thrill flutters through my core.

I lurch to my feet and march to meet the surf. A quick swim should cool me off, put these thoughts to rest.

But the water is already piss-warm. The currents caress my sensitive folds, and I can only stand it for long enough to clear the sand from my hair. I burst through the surface and stomp back onto the beach, shivering and quivering with irritation.

This is ridiculous.

I unsheathe a dagger, testing its weight. Dragging a breath in through my nose, I settle into my fighting stance. My enemy appears before my mind's eye—a wispy figure for now—and I form his body and weapon, leaving his face blank. Already, he looks too much like the prince. Too large and looming.

I attack my imaginary opponent, slashing the air where his arm would be. My attack feels off balance, too quick in the dry air. I hiss, digging my toes into the sand to root myself. I slash, dodge, and whirl to kick his stomach. He bowls over, and I slice through his throat.

I tilt my head left, then right, popping the tension from my muscles. Already, blood is flowing hotter in my veins. The dream crawls into the back of my mind where it belongs. Good fucking riddance.

I repeat the exercise until I'm a blur of muscle and movement. I have no room for thought.

Then I hear his laugh, that dark, satisfying baritone, and I freeze. My imagined enemy dissipates. I shake my head—the laugh must be left over from my dream. I shove down the intrusive thought with an inhale and settle back into my stance.

"Am I interrupting?" the prince says.

I blink, and he's there, a lopsided grin on his face.

"Yes."

He's in a cotton shirt today, robe-like and loose. The fabric ripples in the breeze, caressing his muscled chest. He clutches a whitesteel trident.

When his gaze clashes with mine, my heart leaps into my throat. His lips curve, and once again, I'm thinking of those lips dragging down my neck, those white teeth grazing my nipple. I shake my head to clear the thought.

"Excellent," he says, untying his shirt.

It parts to reveal the broad expanse of his stomach, his chest. A speckled pattern of emerald green scales covers his skin, congregating in a trail leading to the deep V of his hips. His shoulders rotate, broader and stronger than I'd imagined last night. The linen pants barely cling to his hip bones, obscuring the rest of him from view.

I swallow hard, willing the fluttering in my core to stop. I'm already fucked. The prince runs a hand loosely through his hair, and my own scalp cries out for the same touch.

His gaze lingers on my form a second too long, his eyes sparkling. "Do you have a thing against our fashion?"

I look down at myself, noting, once again, that I'm wearing nothing but my loincloth. My chest piece is discarded in the pit where I slept last night, having torn it off in my sleep.

"Clio can get you some workout clothing, I'm sure." He gestures to his pants, and I can't miss the strength of those thighs visible through the thin fabric.

"Too restrictive," I spit.

The prince crouches into a fighting stance, tossing the handle of his trident lightly from palm to palm. The tines are curved and sharp, with a wicked serrated point in the center. The golden staff laces with curling white detail, the spiraled shell crest etched in the steel. I eye it with longing. It's the prettiest weapon I've seen, and it'd make a lovely addition to my personal collection. If I had the room.

"Can't say I'm surprised you have a knife," he says. "It suits you somehow."

I should stop him before he learns more of my secrets, before he pushes me to reveal my whole self. But my blood is boiling, and my body screams for a fight. I cannot release it on shadows alone, and lucky or not, the prince is the only one around to volunteer.

"Contact or blood?" I ask, circling him slowly in the sand.

Gripping his trident firmly in his right hand, his legs tense in the tell of a lunge. Before he can connect, I sidestep without breaking my stride. He skitters through the sand.

"Contact," he growls. "Can't have the princess asking questions, can we, Wicked?" He rotates the staff again, readjusting his grip on the handle. If he's not careful, I'll knock his fancy fork out of thin air.

The prince's face twists tighter the longer we circle in our silly game. I sneer.

His patience cracks, and he comes for me again. I see it coming before he moves, but I allow him the satisfaction of getting close. I duck swiftly, bending low and coming up under his arms. I slide the flat of my blade against his ribs, nicking a green scale. Blood oozes from the seam.

He rolls his shoulders, ignoring the cut as we dance back apart.

"One, zero," I say.

"I said contact." He spits into the sand.

I shrug. "I'm getting bored."

A wicked smile curls his lips. "I can fix that," he says, his voice dropping into a deep rumble.

He stalks toward me, his jaw set in determination, and I blink to clear the sudden image from my dream. Except it's not my dream version of the prince wearing this expression. He's here in the flesh, sauntering across the sand and looking at me like I'm a freshly roasted seaweed crisp.

My spines flex, lifting in warning.

"You want to make this more interesting?" he purrs.

I swallow against the lump in my throat and take a step back, meeting the edge of a boulder. I brace a hand on its surface as I rake my eyes up and down his body, enjoying the sight of this male despite myself.

His shadow covers me until I can see nothing, feel nothing, but the nearness of his towering, muscled body before the morning sun. I feign a faint and he leans in, touching his forehead to the rock above my head, framing me with his hands. He inhales deeply and hums, the deep sound reverberating through my bones.

His lips part, releasing a warm breath that spills over my forehead. The curve of his bottom lip is begging to be bitten.

"You like to get under my scales, don't you, Wicked?" he whispers, as if he thinks he's won.

I lift my knee, jabbing it between his legs. He grunts, bending low. I twist the trident from his hand and land a punch to his gut. He drops to the sand. Before he can recover, I squat over him, holding his weapon to his neck. He stares up at me with wide green eyes, the cocky little fuck.

"Two, zero," I whisper, staking his fork into the sand beside his ear, and stand. "Again."

His hand wraps around my ankle, yanking me back to the ground. I kick at his face, but he ducks, reaching for my other ankle.

I hiss, trying to aim a solid kick to his jaw.

He grunts, but he doesn't let me go. We clash again, kicking and clawing, slashing and parrying.

Soon, our bodies enter the smooth rhythm of battle. The knot of tension in my stomach fades with every lunge and duck, the embarrassment of my dream evaporating with my sweat.

He's a surprisingly well-matched partner. Where I'm quick and evasive, he plows forward. Where he's strong and forceful, I'm lithe and precise. But he's not as predictable as I thought. He throws in the occasional quick dodge or graceful twist to keep me guessing.

He may be smart, but he's too confident for his own good. So I play dirty, trailing my fingers down his spine, tracing the sweat beading there. His skin ripples and flexes wherever I touch. He turns to watch me and fumbles his footwork, and I hook my foot around his ankle. An elbow to his back sends him tumbling forward, and he grunts, once more falling in the sand.

I lay the flat of my blade against his neck, laughter bubbling behind my lips. "Seven, zero."

He grips my wrist, leaning into my knife. His gaze is liquid fire, and a grin spreads across his face. The pretty prince has a death wish, so I press harder with my knife.

"No," he growls, his Voice menacing. Energy snakes out in green ribbons of light, wrapping around my wrists. He yanks me off him, sending my knife flying into the sand.

"Release me!" I sing, my own magic surging forth, meeting his magic where it holds my wrists captive. With one quick note, my lightning slices through his control and dispels the green light.

I roll through the sand, scooping up my knife and landing in a crouch.

The prince stands, swaggering toward me with that grin. His magic curls around his arms, twists around his legs, and expands around him into green mist.

"So, you *are* Voiced," he says, triumphant.

This is one giant mistake. I shouldn't be fighting him, shouldn't be showing him all my tricks at once. I've been careful to maintain my handmaid identity up until this point, but that careful disguise is cracking by the second.

Never have I fought an opponent with both song and blade. He's already seen too much. Why not have a little fun?

The prince whispers under his breath, sending his magic snaking toward me. It wraps around my stomach, and before I can react, he lifts me into the air.

Impressive.

I struggle in his grip, every inch of my skin lighting up with the Voice. I push the light outward from my body, pressing against his restraint. He tightens his grip, pressing back. I clench my gut, bare my fangs. His eyes glow the same color as his magic, focused on me with bright green intensity. The pressure of his magic increases, pushing back my boundaries.

We lock gazes, two raging infernos.

Energy spirals out of my stomach at a steady rate, giving me a few minutes until it runs dry. I shift my arms within his restraint, grasping the hilt of the dagger strapped to my hip.

"One, seven," he says, smiling.

I mirror his smile, letting him think he's won. The moment the pressure of his magic wobbles, I unsheathe the knife and hurl it past his ear. The blade slices off a stray lock of his hair.

His magic releases completely, and I land on my feet, diving for the knife. He reaches for me, but I'm quicker, and within seconds, my blade presses flat to his ribs.

"Eight, zero."

He groans. "Why can't I best you?"

He bends to pick up the curl of his hair, weighing it in his hand while he pins me with a glare.

"Because you're a royal playing with knives and magic. And I'm a..." I trail off, cursing myself for the near slip.

He frowns. "You're a what?"

I shake my head, sheathing my knife. "I'm a wicked handmaid, late for her morning duties, Your Highness."

"Stay," he says, his voice rumbling with authority.

I bare my fangs.

"Please," he says, reaching for me with a hesitant hand. I eye it, my heart pumping furiously the closer he draws. He cups my cheek gently, rubbing a soft thumb over my cheekbone. His hand is warm and soft, and I lean into it, closing my eyes.

"What are you?" he whispers, the echo of his question the day we met. "Just a handmaid? I think not, my lady, my wicked dancer." His other hand comes up to cup my face, and he holds me in place. "Enna."

My pulse quickens at the sound of my name on his lips. I try to pull away, but he maintains his hold.

"You have the Voice, and a strong one at that. You fight better than the Coral Captain. You sprout spines when you're angry, and you have the face of a moon goddess."

His thumb continues to trace the crest of my cheek. "Beautiful."

I open my eyes to stare at him, finding his gaze burning with heat.

"I'm convinced you're not a handmaid at all," he says. My stomach flips over, twisting into a painful knot. "You're some sort of Abyssal warrior in disguise."

My mouth parts involuntarily as the rebuttal stirs my tongue, but I snap it shut just as fast. If I'm quiet, he can't learn the full truth, or at least what's left of it.

"I see I've hit the mark." He smiles. "Are you here to kill me, then? Is this all some elaborate ruse?"

"No," I say. Too quickly. This cannot be happening. We were so close, and I've just ruined everything. Today is the day everything crumbles, all thanks to a silly dream.

That damn dream lit me on fire, and I couldn't contain it. I couldn't control myself. And now, I'm ruining the assignment spectacularly.

"I don't care what you are, Enna. I don't care why you're here." He pulls at me, tugging me closer. "Those eyes," he whispers, his breath warming my face. "They've haunted me since the moment we met."

His fingers trail down my neck, my shoulders. Slowly. My scales rise in the wake of his touch.

"I shouldn't want you. Everything about you screams off-limits." He passes over my forearms, coaxing a slight lift of my spines. "I can't have you. Tell me I can't have you, Enna, and I'll walk away."

I will my heart to slow. I will my skin to extinguish the blaze that ignites repeatedly under his touch. My lips part, but the words stick in my throat.

His hands slide around my hips, gripping me. "Say something, Wicked."

"I don't know what you want me to say, Your Highness." My voice wavers.

"Soren," he corrects me. "Please."

"That's inappropriate, Your Highness."

"What if I don't want to be appropriate with you, Wicked?" His voice is hoarse, as if the words choked him on their way out.

"Then walk away." My careful control crumbles in an instant. I drag my claws over his knuckles. The heat between us ignites, threatening to swallow me whole.

"You'll be the death of me," he declares, lifting me into his arms.

And I, shoving aside all my internal warnings, hook my legs around him and hold on tightly.

Chapter Thirty-Two

SOREN

I'VE NEVER CRAVED ANYTHING as I do Enna. My forbidden, irresistible mystery. I can't have her. *Shouldn't.* Yet my desire for her consumes me with a raging fire. As crown prince, I shouldn't want this feral little thing, this brutal fighting machine, the handmaid to my betrothed royal match. But the passion in my gut threatens to explode.

Her skin blooms under my touch, warm currents of her electricity rising to the surface beneath my hands as I trace the valley of her spine and the undersides of her thighs. Her breath hitches, and my control snaps.

Impulsively, I grab her, pressing her soft skin as I lift her into my arms. Her legs wrap around my hips, settling in perfectly, like she was made to fit here. Her bare breasts press against my chest, and she shivers as she brushes her hardening nipples, side to side, across my scales that gather on my sternum.

I groan, tucking my face into her neck, and thank the gods for Enna's dislike of Coral fashion. My lips find her flesh, suckling, kissing, licking. I can't get enough of her taste—this electric sweetness. Her claws slide through my hair, and I roll my hips into her. She whimpers in response, needy and desperate, the tension melting from her body in my embrace.

I lift my chin in time to see the pleasure flash in her eyes. Her mouth opens in a gasp, those wicked fangs glinting in the sun, stark white against the wet chasm of her throat.

Gods above.

I bite down on her collarbone, then smooth the spot with my tongue. She presses down harder on my cock, rocking her hips. But two can play that game. I flex my cock, stiffening under her as my balls tighten with need. She moans as she feels me grow beneath her.

"That's it, Wicked," I whisper, nipping her earlobe. "You want me too."

She hisses, tilting her head back to expose more of her neck. "Pretend to know what I'm thinking one more time, pretty prince, and I'll slit your throat."

I walk her toward the rocks, my vision blurring as she runs her fingers through my hair. Claws on my scalp. Fingers on my neck. Twisting in my hair, yanking, demanding. Her lips find my forehead, decorating me with sweet yet urgent kisses. I duck behind the closest boulder and press her against its ledge. She squeezes her legs tighter, hands rushing to untie the strings of my pants and the belt of her loincloth. With one hand firmly on her tight ass, I slip out of my trousers, cock springing free, and I slide the fabric beneath her for a more comfortable seat on the rock.

She's glorious. Her hair sticks out in its usual crazy angles, full of sand and reedgrass. Her lip pouts, glistening with want. And those eyes—*gods, those eyes*. Like two purple stars, brilliant in color against the pale white of her skin. She devours me with them, even as I'm devouring her, like she cannot get enough of *me*.

Her eyes trail down my chest, landing on my cock. Under her appraising gaze, it strains to its full length. She swallows, eyes widening, and I swell with male pride. Her cunt blooms before me, swollen and wet. My mouth waters, craving the taste of her, even as my hands flex, reaching, trailing my knuckle up through those slick folds. She trembles around me, and I nudge her swollen clit.

"Fuck," she moans.

That dirty mouth needs to be punished. Right along with the rest of her.

I tuck my thumb inside her warmth as I weave my free hand into the hair at her neck and yank, tilting her face to meet mine. Her mouth parts, plump and ready for me. Her eyes darken with hunger.

I capture her lips. Her mouth is cool as the Abyss: ice to the heat that boils in my veins. Our lips move in a frenzied rhythm, and I slip my tongue between those deadly fangs.

My thumb flexes inside of her, massaging. She flexes around me, bucking her hips, breaking our kiss in a shuddering moan.

Her long, pointed claws dig into my shoulders, dragging me closer. The spines on her arms flex in and out as pricks of purple light flicker across her skin. I slip my thumb out of her and tug her closer, right where I need her. My cock slides against the wetness between her legs. She adjusts her position on the rock ledge, maneuvering to align herself.

Her eyes pop open, staring up at me with ecstasy. She slowly drags her sweet pussy along the hard length of my cock. "F-fuck," she whimpers. "I'm going to—" The spines on her arms quiver with her effort.

I grab her chin, tilting her face to meet my gaze. "I want to see your eyes when you come on my cock."

Her lip trembles, and she nods. I lift her higher, angling my cock to meet her entrance. She thrusts, dragging my tip through her wetness. Pleasure zings through me.

I'm not going to last long with her like this. Pressing through her opening, I sheathe myself inside her, and *gods*. She's tight. The walls of her cunt ripple around me to accommodate my size.

I drink in the sight of her expression, the soft underside of her usual hard shell. Her cheeks flush with pink from heat and exertion. Her eyelids droop, then widen, as if she's struggling to keep them in place. She throws her head back, eyes closing, and grips my arms with her claws.

"That's my wicked girl," I growl. Enna has shattered my control, taken it hostage. My body is her weapon, wielded for her pleasure. I have no choice but to rock into her, diving into her warmth.

My lips return to her neck, licking where her gills lay dormant beneath her skin. Her legs clamp around me. Her claws slide over my scalp, the soft pain pricking me to heightened awareness.

She shouldn't turn me on so much—her spines, her fangs, her claws, signs of her hostile kingdom heritage should have sent me running back to my chamber. But they just make me want her more. I crave her danger like my gills crave the water.

I'm not going to last much longer. I slow my pace, moving in a deep, forceful rhythm.

"Look at me, Enna."

Her eyes open, finding mine. "Yes," she whispers.

I lean in closer, sucking her earlobe between my teeth. "Say my name. Tell me who's fucking you good and deep."

She rolls her hips, glancing away. I snarl, pounding into her, ramping my pace, as her warmth swallows me whole. I snake my arm between her back and the rock, cushioning her from the impact. She cannot escape me now. Pleasure builds deep in my stomach. Our skin slaps together, louder than the crashing waves.

"Say it," I hiss. I need to hear my name on her lips.

"Say what, Your Highness?" She's mocking me, even as I'm lost in her. Even as my spirit spirals boundlessly into oblivion, tethered to the sand by her alone.

I lean back, glaring at her as I withdraw my cock until just the tip remains inside. She wiggles, trying to lure me back in.

"Wrong answer, Wicked."

Grasping my shaft, I drag the tip of my cock through her warmth, teasing her once again. Evidence of my own arousal seeps from the end, mixing with her slickness. I rub my cock against her clit. Her legs spasm around me, and she moans.

"Please," she begs. "*Soren*, please."

"That's better."

I drive my cock home, slipping inside her easily, now. Her walls clamp down tight, hurtling me toward the peak of my pleasure. Enna shrieks as the orgasm rocks through her.

"Soren," she screams again, the sweetest sound I've heard in my life. "*Soren!*"

I cannot contain my pleasure any longer. My balls squeeze, and I come. My seed spurts inside her in thick, hot streams, and her name repeats endlessly on my lips.

Enna yanks my hair, pulling me down for a deep kiss. Our tongues fight for territory as she claims my mouth and I hers. The tide batters against the rocks, a stray wave caressing the tops of my feet.

Someone's throat clears on the other side of the rock. "Your Highness?" Hugo's voice comes loudly.

I clamp a hand over Enna's wet mouth to quiet her moans. Our eyes lock, hers suddenly full of fire. I raise an eyebrow in warning. She sinks her teeth into my hand, and I hiss in pain.

"Forgive me for interrupting your"—Hugo clears his throat again—"morning spar, but this cannot wait."

Wicked removes her teeth, licking the remnants of my blood across those fangs. My beautiful monster. She plants her hand flat on my chest, drops her legs, and shoves me away, arranging her features back into her signature look of apathy. Her rejection stings worse than her spines.

"Wait," I whisper, reaching for her arm.

Those spines flare, in warning this time, and the brightness in her eyes snuffs out. She takes a step away from me.

"I'll find you later. At the ball tonight." I step after her, and she lifts her chin defiantly.

"And what would the princess think?" She glances at my deflating cock, and I follow her gaze. My skin is slick with the evidence of her pleasure. She's left her mark.

When I look up, she's gone.

I sink against the rock, sucking in deep breaths to steady my pounding heart. I have no time to look for her, no matter how much each cell in my body screams at me to find her and claim her again. Even now, mere moments later, she slips out of my grasp.

"My prince, I implore you to answer me," Hugo says, irritation straining his manners.

Gritting my teeth, I pull on my pants, adjust myself, and emerge from behind the rock. Hugo stands there, holding up my discarded shirt and trident. I take the shirt wordlessly, slipping my arms through the sleeves.

"Deepest apologies, Your Highness. Her Majesty insisted you see her right away. When you didn't return from your sparring session with the captain on time, well…" He clucks his tongue, taking in my disheveled appearance.

I tie my shirt, then decide better of it, letting the material hang loose. Hugo lifts a quizzical brow.

"Her Majesty is impatient and should wait until breakfast to see me. As usual."

"I'm only the messenger, Your Highness." He turns toward the gate. "You're lucky it was me and not someone with a higher propensity for gossip. The captain did not seem to know what I was talking about."

I pray to the gods Nara will forgive me, but I don't regret my choice. Not for a moment. I'd trade a thousand mornings in the ring to spar with Enna again.

We walk to the gate in silence, our irritation clashing between us like waves battering a stubborn cliff.

Hugo clears his throat again.

"Got something in your throat, Hugo?" I snap.

"No, Your Highness. Just wanted to say. Whoever it was with you behind the rock, I'd advise you to cut ties now. I have a feeling the princess doesn't take kindly to competition."

I rub the tightness in my chest, but the pressure refuses to dissipate. "What rock, Hugo?" I say. "You said you have no propensity for gossip."

He chuckles. "Quite right, Your Highness."

My stomach churns, flipping itself over again and again. I'm pissed. The fight, the magic, the sex—none of it eased my tension. None of it cured my want for Enna. I can still taste her on my lips. My hands tingle in the absence of her touch.

I may never want to be cured of her.

Chapter Thirty-Three

ENNA

I HIDE BEHIND THE rocks until the prince disappears through the city gate. As his broad shoulders shift with each step, I repeat my mantra again: *just because it's pretty, doesn't mean it's mine.*

The gates close, cutting off my view. Only then do I tear my gaze from him and lean against the boulder, my heart still drumming like a damn rattlefish.

It was just sex. Sure, it was lusty, heated sex unlike anything I've experienced before, but still—just sex. In Vespyr, random hate sex with strangers is the best way to pass the time. Under the cover of darkness, a warm body is a warm body, and even a half-blood like me can meet her needs. That's all this was; two people with needs expressing them in the heat of the moment. I shouldn't be reacting this way.

Just because it's pretty...

I cut the mantra short. This sex was different; I feel it deep in my bones. But acknowledging the consequence has me spiraling. I replay the scene in my mind, my body tingling with the ghost of his touch. He'd taken me roughly, but with the utmost care. He'd shoved me against the rocks, but took a moment to make sure I was comfortable. I melt just thinking about it. No one has ever taken care of me like that before, and I'm afraid the prince has ruined me for anyone else.

Prince *Soren*. His name clouds out the formal moniker of his station, attaching new meaning and flavor to his presence in my mind. It was Soren who placed that fabric beneath my ass, arranged it so as to not damage my skin as he pounded into me with his cock. It was Soren who whispered my name into my hair, his tone sweet as sugar, like he was worshiping a goddess. Soren who brought me to the pinnacle of the best orgasm of my life; Soren who left me here, aching and wanting for more.

I try to take a step forward, but my knees shake and wobble, and I collapse against the rock.

He has unbalanced me, and I may never be stable again.

With a laborious breath, I push off the boulder. The tides slosh around my feet, a reminder of the passing time. I need to get back to Odissa before she notices my prolonged absence. I fasten my chest piece, reattach my belt, and secure my skirts to conceal my knives beneath. With a quick pass of the fabric, I wipe myself clean of my arousal. Like it never even happened.

Just because it's pretty...

"Doesn't mean it's mine," I finish under my breath, shaking my head.

This interaction with Soren—the prince—will be a mere blip in my existence; a mistake at best. I will not let myself be bested by a naked male on a beach, not when my life hangs in the balance, tied to the fate of him choosing another. I need Odissa to win her bargain, as quickly as possible. Only then will I be free of this blood oath that binds me, only then can I escape this horrid place, rich and deliciously alone.

That's what I want.

Ignoring the ache in my chest, I trudge forward. My muscles scream in protest. My core flutters with the remnants of my orgasm, crying out for more, more. More! I grit my teeth and take another wobbling step. The hole in my chest widens, gnawing with hunger for something I've long forgotten. It stings of rejection, hurts like hope, and I lock the emotion away before I can remember its name.

Avoiding the gate, I scale the wall. My claws dig into stone, satisfying and sure. I land with a kick of dust, and then I'm sprinting up the spiraling hill to the palace. With each step, I pin a nail on my feelings, securing it tight.

I am a goddessdamn death-dealer from the Drink, and I don't have time for silly things like feelings and future kings and pretty, pretty dicks.

Right?

Chapter Thirty-Four

ENNA

WHAT I SHOULD DO is march up to Odissa's bedchamber, draw her bath, brush her hair, and help her get dressed for the ball. But the thought of seeing her twists my stomach into a tight knot.

A guard flings open the door to the palace, and the breeze of it brushes my neck, lifting my hair. A shiver wracks me from head to toe.

Goddess, how long will this last?

I trace the curve of my neck where his lips had been moments ago. My skin prickles beneath my own touch, keeping the memory of him alive. My spines quiver in their sheaths. *What if this never goes away?*

A crowd of Coral mermaids crowd stand in a loose line outside the throne room door. The subjects dress in their best robes, carrying tokens of gratitude for the royal family inside. They murmur to themselves. A few turn my way, taking me with curious glances. The captain of the royal guard, Nara, stands at the door. Her maroon eyes flick to me, widening slightly. I drop my hand from my neck.

The guard behind me grunts, no doubt irritated at me for blocking the entrance. I mutter something about the princess needing another book and turn toward the library. The captain's gaze warms the back of my neck as I rush down the hall.

The library's ornate doors groan as I pull on the handle. Pearl sits at the desk, chatting with a patron. She tugs her hands through her cloud of white hair as she talks. She glances at me as I enter and winks.

The library is busy today. It's bustling with mermaids ambling through the shelves on all four levels of the room. Some gather in groups, chatting softly. Others hold tablets, their hands hovering over the glowing engraved surfaces. The soft hum of magic fills the air. A few of them look up at the sound of the door. Their eyes drop to my toes, then back up again.

My heart leaps into my mouth, pulsing anxiously. I came here to get away, not to perform etiquette for strangers. I dip my head politely and weave through the shelves, aiming for the center stairwell. Maybe the higher levels are less populated. When I reach the railing, it senses my intent. As soon as my hand touches the stone, the stairwell creaks and swivels, reattaching to the right side of the room.

Mermaids stir at the sound, watching me as I ascend quietly. *Darkest hell.* So much for being ambiguous. The railing is soft under my touch, sending a zing of pleasure up my arm.

The second floor is less populated. Merfolk chat in the history section. A merman plucks books from the romance section, his feathery ears twitching. He taps the surface of his tablet, and the embedded magic glows. He smiles as the book begins to play.

From the back corner, the royal section beckons. I eye its shadows with longing. In there, I could find respite. No one would disturb me once I got past the lock.

The group is far enough away not to notice, but the lone merman is within sight of the darkened corner. I sneak past him, while he sits on the floor, curling up with the book. He closes his eyes.

I hug the far wall, ducking behind a shelf as I study the lock. An iron gate stretches across the opening to the room, fastened shut with a complicated lock and chain. The gaps in the bars are too narrow to fit through.

I should just leave; head back to Odissa and help her prepare for today's festivities. Tonight's ball is a crucial step in maintaining our ruse. But my heart won't stop its rapid rhythm. My stomach turns in endless somersaults. If I face Odissa now, I know I'll crack.

If Hugo hadn't shown up, I'd still be on that beach, blissfully receiving the prince's skillful cock. My core flutters at the thought, the memory of Soren imprinted in places not apt to forget him. *Soren.* My thoughts caress his name, liking the way it sounds as it echoes through my restless mind.

Of all the things I've done for Odissa, this assignment is the most absurd. I'm three weeks into the job and no one is dead—minus the original princess—and I'm not drowning in blood. I've hardly touched my knives. And I just fucked a prince against some rocks on a public beach. If anything, I should be glad for the change of pace.

The thrusting, skin-slapping pace. *Goddess, help me.*

I need time. I need darkness. I need quiet. And this room is the only place in the palace that may give that to me.

So I study the lock. I send a path of electricity through the metal, tracing it through the internal gears. Satisfied, I wedge my claw into the mechanism and twist. The lock pops open. I drag open the gate and slip into the cool, dark room.

It smells faintly of the Abyss. Cold and crisp, with a hint of iron. Shelves line the small space, the ceiling low but not enough to hit my head. I dip into the far corner, where passersby won't spot me. I snatch a few books from a shelf, taking them with me as I settle on the floor, hugging my knees to my chest. I rest my chin on my knees and close my eyes, inhaling the scent of the room. It's not quite the same, but it's the closest thing I've found to smelling like home.

I count my breaths as they filter through my nose. Ten. Twenty. Slowly, my heart gives up its restless rhythm. My stomach settles. My muscles loosen.

I pick up a book and settle in for some light perusing. The inscription on the surface scrawls in a hurried hand, denoting the diary of Amura. Pearl said the first queen, Amura, was a lady of secrets. A queen after my own heart. I swipe my hand over the surface of the first tablet to activate its stored memories.

The narrator's voice fills my head with a sweet, melodic tone. *Today, Eero chased the beasts into the deep. They will not come back, now. He says the reef is safe. We will make a home here.*

The first image shows a young mermaid female swimming in a dead reef. Her soft pink features are the only bright spot among the white-washed corals.

A siren male wields a trident, his gills fluttering with the exertion of a fight. They wear the battle gear of the ancients, hard shells strapped around their breasts and shoulders, hardly strong enough to cover their weak points in a serious fight.

A scattering of mermaid soldiers swim behind them, picking through the debris with grim expressions. They're battle-worn, trailing fresh blood through the water.

It's hard to believe we beat them. There were so many of those beasts and so few of us. But Eero is a great leader, and he will be king someday.

The male, Eero, approaches Amura, with a grin stretching his cheeks. There's a fresh cut on his cheek, slicing through his right eyebrow. His jaw is strong and sharp, flexing as he watches the female. He has bright green eyes. Golden brown skin. Long dark hair tied with a strip of leather. It's a striking resemblance to—

I twitch my fingers, skipping the scene. I have no interest in Coral history, particularly the part of their history that banished the dredgebeasts to the Drink—to *my* home waters. If the beasts didn't lurk in the inky depths, life in the Drink wouldn't be so hard. The mermaids wouldn't be relegated to living in Vespyr, away from the wealth and stability of the royal siren city. I wouldn't have become a death-dealer. I wouldn't be here, hiding in a forbidden closet, avoiding the very mermaid who taught me how to survive.

...will build a palace for me, where our family will reign forever. We found the perfect spot, warm and sunny. Our people are tired of swimming. We are ready to settle, dig our toes into the sand...

The next scene shows Eero standing on a blank sandbar, hands outstretched, as the beach ripples under his invisible magic. Large white stones sprout from the sand, twisting skyward, forming the spires and curls of a marble structure. Amura lounges in the sand with a pile of lushfruit, admiring the backside of her mate. One hand drapes across her rounded stomach, full of her future young.

This isn't an easy read. I flit through the scenes, increasingly aware of the sheer power this King Eero possessed. Who the fuck is this male? Over the next few scenes, Eero builds the entire Coral palace, carves out the reef districts, erects the defensive wall. A few sirens join him, donating their magic, but they tire easily. Eero is like a god among them, with energy that doesn't drain.

No wonder the Abyss didn't fight back when he unleashed the dredgebeasts on us. We cowered in the darkness and let it happen. What would have been the alternative? Fighting a male like this?

Heart pounding, I skip forward, unsure what I'm looking for, if not an excuse to burn this whole palace down. I'm about to give up on the diary when the voice says:

...he says it's a gift for our coronation day. A charm so that no one will hurt me again.

I pause the image, zooming in on the necklace dangling from Amura's hand. I've seen it before, hiding in a velvet pouch. The pendant mimics the shape of a spiralfish shell, curling into a tight point in the center. When Amura slips the chain over her head, the shell rests against her sternum, glowing softly.

"This will keep you safe from those who intend you harm." The king cups her face, brushing his thumb over the crest of her flushing cheek. *"I almost lost you. I will not do it again. I'd see this whole sea perish before I let anything place a finger on you."*

"How does it work?"

The king smiles, a near copy of his descendant's lopsided grin. *"They must speak only one word to you, the slightest of sounds, and if they intend you harm, my magic will consume them body and soul."*

"But you're speaking to me now. Do you not intend me harm, my king?"

Eero's eyes darken. Amura reaches for the king, tugging his chin into an emphatic kiss.

I drop the book with a clatter, severing its connection.

That necklace—if it's a weapon of mass destruction—what the *fuck* is it doing in Soren's desk?

Chapter Thirty-Five

SOREN

The queen's nails rap on the breakfast table, the only sound in the dining room. She sits with her spine straight, chin held high—her favorite posture for intimidation. She parts her mouth as if to speak, then closes it. It's a game we play often, and whoever speaks first loses.

I'm not falling for it. I lift my teacup slowly, taking a sip of the steeped lushfruit.

Our game requires every ounce of my self-control this morning, and after my morning with Enna, my reserves are dwindling. I don't want to be here, sipping tea as the silence stretches. I could have stayed behind those rocks, buried deep inside her. The unbridled shriek as she came still echoes in my mind—beautiful and feral. My cock stirs, summoned by the memory.

I blow on the tea; my mother's lips tighten. I take another sip.

I know I crossed the line this morning. I shouldn't have joined Enna in her sparring practice. I shouldn't have been watching her from my balcony to begin with—shouldn't have grabbed my trident, thrown Nara's name as an excuse to my guard, and marched down there with the intention to rile her. To get under her scales as much as she gets under mine.

I took it too far. Her touch, her fire; I couldn't help myself. And now my body is wrought with tension. Part of me screams to fall back in line and do my duty. The other, louder, part wants to leave this kingdom, to dive into the waves and escape into a world of color and muted sound, with Enna by my side. Away from Aquisa, we could be just two sirens in the sea, leaving the pressures of the crown. The thought is both warming and terrifying.

Impossible. Yet tantalizing, nonetheless.

My mother lifts her own cup of tea, her eyes glinting as she watches me over the rim.

"I need you to hold court again today," she says, finally. *Game over.* My mouth twitches in victory.

"And that's the news that interrupted my morning?"

Hugo shifts behind me, his clothing brushing together in a whisper of disapproval, but he says nothing.

"You're upset," she states.

Upset is not the right word. Tense, maybe. Pissed, definitely. I'm frustrated by the beautiful handmaiden—no, highly skilled royal shadow-guard—who slipped through my fingers moments ago, leaving me alone to deal with the consequences.

My mother resumes her anxious tapping on the table, keeping time with the pace of my chewing.

"I'm not upset," I say, jaw tensed. "Is everything in order for this evening's ball? The wedding? Would you not rather me gallivant around the palace straightening vases and picking ribbons than sitting in court today?"

The rapping ceases. Her first finger curls mid-rhythm, hovering above the table like a claw. She flexes her hand, pressing it flat against the wood.

"I understand the pressure you are under, but I did not expect you to crack so easily."

I clench my teeth. "Apologies, Your Majesty."

"Fill in your cracks, Soren, lest the princess finds them."

The tension stretches me to the brink of my resistance, ready to snap. I inhale slowly, then blow my next words out in a whisper. "I am not cracking, Mother."

"And yet, here you are, despite all my counsel, still wishing for a love match," she says, lifting her tea once more. "Are you not?"

My skin itches under the intensity as she studies my face. Can she see the sweat on my brow? The row of Enna's teeth marks along my collarbone?

"Your father did not choose me for love, you know." She withdraws her gaze, peering into her teacup, her bottom lip quivering with the last word. "This kingdom teetered on the precipice of uproar. Your father needed a queen. He had a love match in mind, yes, but she was not suitable. *I* was." Her steely gaze meets mine. "There are no love matches when you're a royal. Love will break you, Soren, and that is a weakness this crown cannot afford."

I avoid her gaze, unsettled by the sudden anger there, and glance out the window. The waves lap at the stones beneath the eastern terrace. For ages, the tides have followed their predetermined course.

The moon pulls, and the tides answer. Any resistance leads to the same end: one way or another, the waves always crash on the shore.

"Is that why he broke?" I whisper. "Because he had a love match, and it wasn't you?"

The image of my future focuses with clarity—Aris by my side in the light of day, Enna in my sheets at night. Is that what I want? To end up like my father, driven mad by the circumstances he created for himself?

"You're marrying your best match. This princess will do just fine for you."

I may have started our game in the winning position, but over the course of the past few minutes, my mother snatched the victory from under my feet. I craft my retreating remark carefully.

"Aris is a perfect match, Mother, thank you," I say. The words taste like paper on my tongue.

"Good. I wouldn't settle for anything less for you, Soren. You know that."

Her teacup clinks as she sets it into the saucer. "I will finish the arrangements for the ball this evening. You will have an excellent ball, my prince. Don't you worry about that."

"I'm sure it will be splendid, thanks to your expertise."

"If you hold court, that will lessen my burden."

I nod, smiling politely. "Of course."

Chapter Thirty-Six

ENNA

I'VE ADOPTED A NEW mantra: If I kill Odissa now, I'm as good as dead.

I chant it in my head as I wait for her to approve the temperature of her bathwater.

A dead princess in this court would raise suspicion, and I'd be suspect. It's much easier to hide a body in the Drink—not so much in the upper rooms of a marble palace stranded in the air, where blood doesn't dissipate but pools, thick and obvious.

I could drag her into the kitchen closet, feed her to the fishery. But the chef sees everything, and he's friends with the prince. Soren might not like me so much if I murder his future wife—again—even if she is a lying, conniving bitch. I'd be executed on the spot. Is that better or worse than facing the goddess of death?

If I kill Odissa now, I'm as good as dead.

Clio flutters about near Odissa's wardrobe, the housekeeper's presence in the room the only reason for our civility this morning. If she wasn't here, I wouldn't be kneeling on the hard floor, pouring rose oil into water.

But if I can't kill Odissa, what I *should* do is run, make a break for the Frost Kingdom and live off the price I'd get for the collection of treasures I've hidden in the fishery. Leave Odissa here to die at the hands of the Eater of Souls, should she fail. And she will fail if I stay here, because I just fucked the one thing that'll save her from Tephra's teeth.

The magic of my oath seizes my throat, and I cough against its grip. *I'm helping her!* I scream at it. *She cannot succeed if I stay.* The pressure doesn't lessen, only spreads, until my entire body numbs with ice.

Odissa runs her hands through the bathwater.

"Too cold," she says. Two minutes ago, the water had been too hot, and I'd drained half the tub, adjusted the heat on the faucet, and refilled the giant basin.

If we didn't have an audience, I would shove this rose oil up her entitled, stolen ass. But because we have an audience, we must perform.

I press my nails into my palm to keep from ripping out her little silver throat. With numb fingers, I turn the knob for the hot water only. Soon, steam fills the air, swirling between us. The water level laps dangerously high at the rim of the tub. If she gets in now, she will surely overflow it. I reverse the knob, testing the water myself. If this isn't fucking perfect, I don't know what else to do.

She frowns at my work, noting the water level, then touches the surface of the water gingerly. I stare at her, waiting for a response.

"That will do," she snaps.

I wait, watching her fingers skim along the surface in figure eights. She clears her throat. "It's too full."

I count to three, watching her squirm in her borrowed skin, before I unplug the drain and let some water out.

"Good, good. That's good," she says, flopping her hand at me like a fish with a death wish.

It'd be easier to leave, arguably, than sticking out this assignment for Tephra knows what reason at this point. Am I really that terrified of the consequences of breaking my blood oath? After a life spent dealing in the death of others, the thought of my own death shouldn't strike fear into my heart.

I need more time to get my treasure in order, yes—if I am to survive on my own, I want to be set—but that isn't the whole truth.

As the thought crosses my mind, I already know why I've stayed this long. It has to do with a certain Coral Prince and his capacity to make me feel alive. Free. When I'm with him, I can forget for a moment who I am, where I come from. The terrible things I've done to get here.

Odissa disrobes and sinks into the tub. Then, she signals for me to begin scrubbing. I soap the sponge and push it across her wet skin in rough, efficient circles, eager to complete the task. I dunk her soapy arm to rinse it and move on to the next.

"Don't forget to get between my fins this time," she says, flicking her tail in my face, perfectly clean and barnacle-free. I flash her my best grimace as I thread the sponge between her fins.

"Does Your Highness have a preference of hue for this evening?" Clio calls out from next to the wardrobe. She lifts a few skirts, displaying them for Odissa.

Odissa studies the options, tapping the base of her chin. "The pink one, of course. It is the prince's favorite color." Though that hardly narrows the selection; with the exception of her wedding gown, all of Odissa's new dresses are pink.

Clio smiles. "Certainly. Perhaps the darker shade of pink? I know we do not have much for the deeper tones of your court. But it is your marriage ball, after all, and I'm sure your brother, His Majesty, would like to see you in the Abyssal colors one last time. Would he not?"

Clio pinches the hem of a dark magenta dress, lifting it from the array of silks.

I see the moment Clio's words sink in—the corner of Odissa's jaw flexes, her teeth clamping shut.

The Abyssal King is on his way, and when he gets here, he will meet his sister, mysteriously lacking the ten guards he sent with her, and a handmaid he never *authorized*.

"Yes, of course," Odissa says. "Has my brother arrived?"

Her gaze slides to meet mine, and I read in her eyes the same panic that now grips my chest.

"We expect him in time for this evening's ball." Clio pulls the dress from the wardrobe and spreads the skirts across her arms. "This is the darkest color we have. Not quite pink, not quite black, but somewhere in between, no?"

Odissa's knuckles whiten around the edge of the tub. "That's perfect," she says. "Enna, would you be a dear and help me out of this bath? I've had quite enough."

With numb fingers, I wrap a towel around her.

She clears her throat, touching the puckered scar on her rib. "Thank you."

"Tonight's ball will be splendid, Your Highness. We're endlessly grateful to have found you, Princess, and we're holding nothing back. Extravagance is an understatement." Clio grins, draping the dress across the coverlet.

I edge toward the window, pretending to straighten the drapes, then scan the waterline for signs of movement. It's low tide. The sun glints off the sand with dizzying heat. My forehead sweats just from looking at it.

A group of guards stand in wait on the shoreline, facing toward the sea. I recognize the coil of Captain Nara's tight red bun, the stiff posture of her back. She lifts her trident, slamming it into the sand. The guards snap to attention, focused on the sea.

Slowly, an entourage of figures clad in darksteel lifts from the waves. They crawl onto the sand, fingers digging into white crumbs. They drag themselves forward as their gray tails snap and split, then rise on two legs.

I scan their faces, panic rising, for the soldier I never killed in the deep. Did he escape the dredgebeast? Did he tell the king what transpired?

The Coral guards hinge at the waist, bowing to the newcomers. They produce several parasols, shading the Abyssal troop from view like an armored beetle.

This isn't right. The Abyssal King wasn't supposed to come. King Rion is known for his aloofness, his proclivity for the darkness and his hatred for the surface. It's said he emerged from the deep only once in his hundred years and promptly retreated, shrieking, due to the sun.

If the princess's king brother is here in the flesh, expecting to find the real Aris—or worse, her killer—what chance do we have of pulling off this gig? As fat a chance as a bloodfish caught in the den of a dredgebeast, that's what. My avenue for escaping this assignment alive narrows by the moment.

Across the room, Clio chatters to herself, now busy straightening the pins and brushes on Odissa's vanity table. Her eyes meet mine in the mirror, narrowing.

Carefully, I tie the ribbon around the curtain, tucking it into position next to the window.

"Princess," I whisper, voice strained. "This ribbon deserves your attention."

Odissa frowns, tucking the towel around her breasts, and quietly joins me. She follows my gaze to the Abyssal entourage crossing the beach, and her face pales.

"Clio, dearest," she says sweetly, "I wonder if you might fetch me a glass of ice water from the kitchen."

Clio obliges and leaves the room. When the door clicks shut, Odissa lets out a whooshing breath.

"Fuck," she groans.

"Fuck is right."

"Rion was supposed to stay in the deep. He never leaves. Not for anything. I'm surprised he's even here."

"Maybe our soldier friend from the Drink made it back home safe and sound."

Her eyes flash at the unstated threat in my words. "And that's my fucking fault? You're the killer. I'm the brains. You had one job to do, Enna."

I bite my tongue. Now's not the time to remind her of her blunder in the Drink, the real reason that wounded soldier survived.

Odissa crosses her arms. "You saw *him*? You saw the king just now?" She peers outside. Below, the promenade of parasols has barely moved. One of the darksteel figures produces a thin stone for the captain to read.

"The prince likes me well enough, and he's desperate for a wife. Soren will vouch for me."

If that was true, would Soren have ravished me like he did this morning? If the prince liked Odissa at all, wouldn't he be ravishing her instead? And, more importantly, if I *want* Odissa to succeed, if I *want* my freedom, why am I standing between them?

"His opinion is the one that matters, in the end, as it's through him I get my throne. What's a little family drama to stand in my way? I'll simply have Soren order the king away. Uninvite him to the festivities. We parted on bad terms, and I refuse to see my brother's face. That'll do nicely."

It's a shaky plan, but it might work. As long as I'm not the one to deliver her message.

"Wait a minute," Odissa whispers, leaning out the window. She narrows her eyes at the troop. "Look, the guards are leaving!"

The darksteel figures turn back to the ocean, leaving a frowning captain in the sand.

Odissa throws her head back, beaming. "Oh, thank the fucking goddess. It's not him."

Her words reach me through a haze of panic. On the beach, the captain reads the message on the stone. She shakes her head, then stashes it in her belt before marching back toward the keep.

"Guess the dredgebeast ate that soldier after all." Odissa sighs. "I was about to worry." Odissa crosses the room, lifting the dress from the bed. She holds it against her chest and tests the length of it.

If this was a stroke of luck, then why do I feel so sick?

I lean against the wall, studying the former death-dealer as she spins into a sloppy waltz and counts the beats in a whisper. She misses a step, then skitters to catch up—a mistake any royal would surely notice.

The Abyssal King may have passed on his invitation, but Odissa is not in the clear. Not even a well-placed spell from me could smooth those dancing feet, and especially not when I'll be playing watchful handmaid in the corner of the room.

And there's this matter of Soren's secret weapon. What does he intend to do with it?

Sickness churns in my stomach. *Me.* I'm untrustworthy as they come, and if Soren finds out my role in this mess...

Odissa trips again, covering it up with a twist as she returns to lay the dress on the bed. "You'll accompany me on the dance floor," she says. "I'll need you at hand."

"So I can fix your footwork?"

"Precisely."

She will fail. It's as inevitable as the tides. The goddess will come to collect her dues on the full moon—five days from now. Odissa will become the goddess's lunch, I will have broken my oath, and Soren will know the truth of it all.

Even on the off chance she succeeds, Odissa will never set me free. Never. She's selfish and malicious and has never had my best interest in mind. *Or...*

My mind caresses the thought of the necklace. Would it work for me, I wonder, if I wore it? What might happen when Odissa spoke?

For a moment, I imagine her writhing in pain at the hands of an ancient spell. It would be torturous for her, from what I've learned of Eero's character. Odissa would eventually perish, but not after a due punishment for threatening the wearer of Eero's mighty gift.

My scalp prickles. Is this what I want?

I shake my head, clearing the thought as quickly as it comes. No. It's too risky. I don't want her dead; I just want to be free of her. If I want to experience freedom before I die, even if only for a few days, I should leave. Tonight.

My heart aches, an escape plan already forming. I'll take my leave at high tide, when the guests are drunk and the waves are close. If I'm going to die, I'd rather be in the sea when the moment comes.

"And what is a handmaid supposed to wear to a royal ball?"

Odissa eyes the wardrobe, turning to me with a wry smile. "I'm sure Clio would love to help you find something suitable."

Chapter Thirty-Seven

SOREN

"Hugo, I need you to distract me."

My attendant rifles through the formal attire in my wardrobe. He turns to catch my gaze in the mirror.

"And from what event could Your Highness possibly need a distraction?" His eyebrow lifts, then flattens, and he turns back to his work. "Was holding court that unbearable today? Or perhaps my prince is having second thoughts about his upcoming marriage."

Court had been unbearable, though thankfully this time void of more marriage proposals. I grimace, kneading the soreness from my lower back. "Says the male without a propensity for gossip."

He pulls two garments from the wardrobe. "It's not gossip if I'm discussing it with my prince directly. Now, what does His Highness think of these?"

I eye the white leather pants and light blue silk shirt, the constricting staples of Coral male two-legged fashion. The pants will be uncomfortably tight. If a certain mysterious shadow-guard is in attendance tonight, the entire court will get a view of my attraction to her.

"Looks good enough."

"His Highness is avoiding the question," Hugo says as he dresses me.

"You're not good at distractions," I mutter.

"I've known you your whole life. I've watched you grow from a carefree guppy sneaking out to play in the reefs into this"—his eyes flick over me—"carefully chiseled image of the crown. That little guppy, so full of light? I'm afraid you've snuffed him out."

"That little guppy wasn't ready to be king."

"You hold the weight of a kingdom on your shoulders, and you do it well, Your Highness, because you must. Your mother has been grooming you for the throne for the past decade, even more so since your father's death three years ago. You are ready," Hugo insists in a gentle tone, finishing buttoning my shirt.

Even before I marked my third decade and came of age to inherit the throne, my mother shoveled more and more responsibilities into my lap. "I'm more than ready," I growl.

"Yes. And yet here you are, on the eve of your wedding day, tangling with a female behind the rocks and asking me for a distraction."

I tug at the collar once more. Anger flares at his implication that Enna is some random female, a simple means of escaping my duties. I bite my tongue to keep my retort unspoken.

"I do not think His Highness can afford any more distractions," Hugo says. "Do you?"

"This morning didn't feel like a distraction. It felt like freedom."

"Ah." Hugo pinches the bridge of his nose. "Your father said much the same thing to me once."

I swallow, the familiar hole in my chest reopening at the mention of him. "And what advice did you give him?"

Sadness swims in his soft blue gaze as he whispers, "I didn't. I should have said something, but I didn't."

"What do you wish you'd told him, then?"

"Your father needed more freedom in his life."

"Hugo, you dirty fish," I say, clapping him on the shoulder.

The male shrugs, then chuckles softly. "Will your *freedom* be in attendance at the ball tonight?" His eyes sparkle with mischief as he picks up a comb and begins tugging it through my wet curls.

My stomach flutters, a school of guppies battering against the walls of my gut. Surely, Enna will be there.

"I hope so," I breathe, and the admission lifts a weight from my chest.

The Grand Hall crowds with merfolk nobility, each stuffed into tight, colorful garments as they twirl and dance to the pluck of a string band. As I make my way to the queen on her throne, I scan the crowd, searching for a pale streak of white skin, a mess of black hair. Finding none, I push down my disappointment and greet my mother.

"Lovely ball," I say to her. It's true; the evidence of my mother's efforts fills the room with vibrant color. Large bouquets of flowers post in each corner. Garlands of pink roses drip from the ceiling and twine around the marble pillars, the proof of Lady Myrrh's vision filling the room with their soft fragrance. The hall's perimeter lines with rows of tables with food and drink, attracting clumps of laughing guests as they pick at the delicacies.

"She's not here yet," my mother whispers, "but don't upset yourself. If she takes much longer, I'll send the captain to fetch her. A princess should be on time. Even if her brother couldn't bother to show."

I catch a glimpse of her scowl before she hides it behind her careful mask. "You expected Rion to show up?"

"I'm not sure what I expected. An appearance, perhaps? This is the beginning of an alliance, after all."

"At least he sent a note."

"The disrespect, after what we're doing for his kingdom." My mother sighs. "I'm signaling the captain."

Nara stands near the punch bowl, helping herself to a scoop of the frothy pink juice. With a lopsided grin on her face, she hands the drink to a female guard, their hands brushing in the exchange.

"The captain is occupied," I say, smiling to myself.

Just then, the crowd stirs as a guard announces the arrival of the Abyssal Princess. The music lurches to a stop, and the broad sea of faces turns toward the gilded doors, each one lifting to stare as the princess enters the hall.

Aris is a vision in deep pink. She blushes from the crowd's attention and curtsies with a coy smile. Her gaze finds mine, burning with hunger. Even as my scales prick in warning, my mouth moves into an answering smile. I rise from my chair with stiff limbs and march down the steps. The crowd parts around me, clearing a path to the princess.

And then, from the shadows of the doorway, Enna steps into the room, and all breath sucks out of my lungs, leaving me dry and wanting. The silver silk clings to her skin like moonlight on soft waters—but looking at her isn't enough to soothe the ache in my chest. My hands flex at my sides, anxious again to touch, to claim, knowing I cannot have her. Not here. My pace quickens involuntarily, and I force my body into submission as I approach the princess.

"You look lovely," I breathe.

Aris giggles before me, dropping into a curtsy, but my gaze still rests on her attendant. Enna's eyes swim with emotion—distant, then sad, then angry. They transform from quiet lavender pools into burning, hot flames, and I flinch at the intensity. She flicks her gaze to Aris, who stoops before me, and my cheeks warm with embarrassment. I extend my hand to the princess, and she takes it, returning to her full height.

The crowd erupts into applause, and the musicians strike a joyful tune. Aris sidles close, looping her hand around the crook of my elbow to anchor me to her side. She gazes up at me with sparkling eyes. "Ready to whisk me off my feet, my prince?" she says, turning us toward the dance floor.

I follow her numbly to fulfill my duty, mentally calculating the minimum number of dances to meet the appropriate quota for a betrothed royal couple. Just one would be a slight on her honor; five would be tempting mine. An unhappy three, then.

We settle into a waltz, spinning across the dance floor. She clings to me, her feet barely brushing the ground. With every turn, I scan the room, locating Enna's position among the faces. If I cannot have her in my arms, I can at least keep her in my sight.

And my heart aches, knowing that will never be enough for me.

Chapter Thirty-Eight

Enna

As the prince dances with Odissa, I skirt the edge of the room, blending into the shadows. My dress is thin and hugs my curves, but the skirt is loose enough to hide the pouch I've strapped to my thigh.

I scan the room, assessing my targets. A male stands by the drinks, leering over a smaller female, his wrist clad in a gold chain bracelet encrusted with diamonds. He eyes the female's lips and whispers something. She takes a sip of her drink and searches for a quick exit. Resolved, I slip through the crowd toward him, snagging a drink for myself on my way. I pour half of it onto a pink bouquet. I bump his elbow, disturbing his balance and drawing his attention. He turns abruptly, glaring at me with a curled lip. I blush and dip my head, locating the position of his bracelet.

"Pardon me, my lord," I say, gesturing at my nearly empty drink. "I dunno what they put in this drink, but it tastes like *magic*."

Those eelish eyes lock onto my face, and he smiles. "Lord Varik, at your service. The pardon is mine, my lady," he says, and his voice sounds exactly as I expect—slimy and dark, like he belongs in Vespyr.

With a snick of my claw, I unhook the bracelet, tucking it swiftly into the slit in my skirt. I make eye contact with the female and smile. "Oh, there you are, darling," I say. "I wonder if I might have your opinion on which dress I should wear to the wedding." I loop my gloved hand around her arm, and she comes away quickly.

We scurry from the table, arm in arm. She squeezes my hand once we reach a safe distance.

"Thank you," she whispers.

"I'll leave you here." I nod to the door at the back corner of the room. "There's your nearest exit, if you need it," I say, then slip away before she can say anything more or ask my name.

I secure my next three targets with similar ease, and within the first three songs, I've collected another bracelet, a ring, and a set of diamond hairpins. In a matter of an hour, I've collected more than I have after three weeks of sleepless wandering. This should be enough to get me started once I reach the Frost border. And if Odissa happens to marry the prince by then, I'll already be established in my new life of freedom.

Satisfied, I tuck against a wall to watch the dancers. Odissa and Soren finish a spin as the music fades. His hands rest on the small of her back, large and strong against her frame. Through the thin silk dress shirt, I can see the mounds of muscle, and my spines rise against the gloves, remembering how those muscles felt this morning as they wrapped around me instead of her.

Look away, Enna. The ceiling hosts a vast frieze in its circular peak. Dredgebeasts lurk at the edges, dark finned shadows with teeth, contrasting the vivid depiction of Coral history. Colors shift in gilded highlights as the dancers move below, garments spiraling and reflecting under the gaze of their ancestors.

I eye the exit. There's a narrow corridor that runs behind the ballroom, winding away from the heart of the palace. A right turn would lead me past the kitchen, where I could snag a snack for the journey. Then it's a quick leap through a window, scaling the soft side of the building, and out into the streets.

Soren stands at the drink table, now. *Goddess,* is he everywhere I look? Is there no escape from him? I absorb the sight of him, allowing myself one last look. He smiles and thanks the servant, then lifts the punch to his mouth. His perfect mouth parts, touching the pink foam, and my own lips tingle, crying out for his kiss.

The door handle twists easily, opening into the dark corridor beyond. My chest squeezes with guilt, and I glance over my shoulder.

With a deep breath, I slip into the hallway and run into a wall of warm flesh, clad in leather and hardened with whitesteel.

"Going somewhere, dark-dweller?" Maroon eyes glow in the darkness, set within a red and white striped face. Her mouth curls into a smile.

Chapter Thirty-Nine

SOREN

THE BAND PLAYS MY mother's favorite tune, and I settle into the easy rhythm of dance with her, grateful for the reprieve. Sometime during the second song, I lost sight of Enna. Last I saw her, she was sipping punch at the drink table and chatting with Lord Varik. But now, she's gone.

Aris is occupied, thank the gods. Lord Varik has taken her off my hands, and for a sweet moment in time, I am absolved of her voice in my ear.

"Kind of you to share." My mother spins into my arms, and I catch her, leading her into an arcing circle step. She nods toward the dance floor. "Tell me, son. Have you ever seen a waltz quite like that?"

I follow her gaze to the strange duo. He spins her quickly, much faster than I did, adding a new flair to the usual steps for this song. Aris grips his arms, skirts fanning out, her face tight.

"It's an Abyssal thing."

Mother clicks her tongue. "Look more closely, Soren. Watch her feet."

Under the sprawl of her skirts, her feet stutter, adding beats out of pace with the music. Her heels stay lifted from the floor, never sinking to catch the downbeat. With the next turn, her ankle rolls, and she falls into the treasurer's broad chest.

"Looks like she's tired," I say. "Poor thing."

As we turn again, I scan the far wall and finally spot my missing piece. Enna surveys the dance, hugging the far wall. Her posture is composed and easy, her gaze sharp and focused. My mother's hand squeezes mine, snagging my attention. "Soren," she urges. "She cannot dance. How can that be so?"

We rotate, and the princess returns to my view. Lord Varik straightens his dance partner, his mouth visibly working to avoid a frown. Aris clutches his arms and blushes. It is odd, a princess without knowledge of a waltz. Even during the quickstep, she clung to me with the grip of a visefish, leaning on my lead to guide her through.

"Have you thought more of the pendant?"

To be honest, I haven't thought much about the damned thing since I locked it in my desk.

"No," I say. "What of it?"

"Use it."

"Mother, this is your match. Do you rescind your good judgment, just because the princess can't dance?"

"Yes, I do. We cannot risk falling victim to a ruse." Her fingernails drum into the back of my neck. "Something isn't right with that female."

"The pendant is too risky. I could dismiss her quietly."

"What if she has malicious intent? I will not lose you, Soren, not if I can prevent it."

We turn in silence as we consider our predicament. My mother speaks again, hurried and hushed, "Maybe the king wants her out of his fins. There have been rumors of illegitimate royal offspring in the deep. Abyssals hate mixing blood. Perhaps, she's one of them."

"And if you're wrong? If she's harmless?"

My mother hesitates, her precise footwork stuttering half a beat.

"What are you hiding?" I whisper.

"Clio saw something, and I'm concerned the princess is…"

"Spit it out, Mother. We don't have time for games."

Her fingers press into my back with increasing pressure. "Aris brutally struck her handmaiden."

I halt our dance. "What?"

"It was in private, during their dance lessons. She struck her cheek. Clio said the girl's face turned red from the impact."

"I need a drink." With a quick bow, I leave my mother to handle the whispering crowd. Let them watch. Blood pounding in my ears, I push through.

Aris will pay for hurting her. I'd drain the sea before I let her touch Enna again.

Enna. Where is she?

I snatch a drink from the table, sipping the foam as I scan the crowd. I ache to hold her, to soothe her, to kiss her where it hurts. But Enna is gone once again. My frustration deepens. My list of duties for the night is complete, save one: find my missing shadow-guard. And when I do, she will never leave my sight again.

A small hand slips around my bicep, and I flex my jaw, bracing for Aris's nauseating voice.

"I was starting to worry you'd met your quota for dancing tonight," she says.

She struck Enna with these hands. It takes all my self-control not to slice clean through her wrist.

I extricate myself from her hold on my arm. "I have other duties to attend to."

"Too busy for your future wife? This doesn't bode well for us. We'll be married in five days. Tell me, will you avoid me then?" There, in her eyes, flashes that familiar lust for power.

At first, I categorized that look as one of a younger princess eager for a throne of her own. But with my mother's words weighing my mind, I study her with a new lens.

She trails her fingers across my chest, smoothing the silk of my shirt. Her touch is gentle. But the look in her eyes—that's a feeling I'll never shake.

I lean in close to her ear. "Tell me, Aris. Did you strike her?"

She throws her head back, crooning as if I just told the most ridiculous joke. "Darling, I haven't the slightest clue what you're talking about."

"The bruise on her elbow. It's from you." I curl my fingers around her wrist, and she notes my grip with a flick of her gaze.

"Look at me."

"She's still working out her land legs. Poor thing never learned to walk straight."

"As a royal handmaid?"

Aris squares her jaw. *Liar.*

I could end her now. Wrap my hands around her throat. Shake her till she admits her fault. Till she screams, as I imagine Enna screamed when Aris struck her face.

But I am the crown prince, and we have an audience. I cannot confront her. Not now.

I release my grip on her wrist.

The scales at the nape of my neck prickle with awareness. I turn away from her, catching a glimpse of a silver skirt, nearly hidden in the dark shadows of a doorway. Enna peers into the room, her gaze assessing me. Her eyes shine in the darkness like beckoning beams, inviting me to a chase.

Found her. The satisfaction of it warms me from head to toe, then twists with a pang of irritation. Why is she over there and not here with me?

And why, when I take a step toward her, does she flinch and drop her gaze? Enna retreats into the shadows, once more slipping out of my sight.

My wicked dancer is afraid of *me*? I will not have it.

Chapter Forty

Enna

"You're not gonna stab me just for standing here, are you?" the captain says, blocking my path. She straightens the armor piece I knocked askew. "That's a little uncalled for."

I release my grip on the dagger. "I don't know what you're talking about."

"Really." Her eyes flick to my skirts.

I step forward, inching around her toward the hallway that will lead once and for all to my freedom. I don't have time for this. "If you'll excuse me."

She plants her trident, effectively cutting off my escape route. "I don't think I will," she says. "You are Enna, no? The princess's handmaid. Or is it shadow-guard?"

"And you are...?" I feign ignorance, even though I know who she is. My exit plan snaps into place—this corridor winds toward the kitchen, passing a first-level window. From there, I can make the jump to the streets.

Captain Nara shrugs. "A girl who knows things."

"I see."

"If I let you leave now, the prince will have my ass on a pike." She twirls the trident. "I'm not inclined to let that happen."

I stop the trident's spin, and the captain raises her brow.

"Let me pass. This is highly classified."

"Mm," she says. "Tell me, was your mission on the beach this morning highly classified, too?"

The tips of my ears burn. I lift my lip, revealing my fangs. "That *is* a hot trick," she says, chuckling. "Soren is so fucked."

My skin crawls with irritation. Who the fuck does this female think she is and why is she familiar with the prince? Against the barrier of my gloves, my spines flex. With a quick flick of my eyes, I assess her weak points—the soft pocket of her armpit, the exposed stretch of her neck.

"I wouldn't do that, if I were you. I may not bite as hard as you, but trust me, the prince would not be happy if you tried to dispose of me."

"And what makes you think I care what he thinks?"

"Oh, honey," she says. Her mouth curves into a mocking frown. "He mentioned you last night, after your little tavern episode. At first, I thought nothing of it, but today, I took a closer look. Caught up with my good friend, Hugo, and we put some pieces together. You and Soren are like magnets—no matter how far you cross the room, you orientate to each other, seek each other out."

I shake my head. "You're mistaken," I whisper. What does this complete stranger know about how I feel? Those feelings are gone. I've shoved them into the Abyss, next to every other fight I couldn't win.

"See for yourself," she says, nodding through the crack in the door. I follow her gaze, squinting into the bright light of the ballroom. The prince stands at the drink table, arguing with Odissa. A frown twists his handsome face, his brow furrowed in concentration. She smiles at the forming crowd.

"Every time he's done performing his duty with her, he searches the room for you. He's been doing it all evening."

As I open my mouth to deny the captain's claim, her hand lifts into view, pointing. "Wait," she says.

Soren sips on his drink and then, as if pulled by an invisible thread, his head turns, and his gaze locks onto mine.

My breath releases in a whoosh, like he's knifed me in the gut with those piercing green orbs flooding with an emotion I refuse to name, and the world tilts on its axis. I steady myself against the doorframe, dark spots pricking the edge of my vision.

"I need some fresh air." I stumble away from the door, and the captain steps to the side. The empty hallway stretches before me without obstacle. I trace my escape route down the corridor, around the bend. When I reach the open window, I pause, leaning against the marble frame, and peer into the night. A warm breeze brushes my cheeks. Audrina's face is nearly full—in five days' time, she'll flourish, and Tephra will come to claim her dues.

And I won't be here to watch.

The spiraling streets are empty. I lean further out the window, checking the distance to the ground below. The jump might hurt, but it won't be enough to break me. The waves roll in, battering the walls of the keep one after the other, and still I'm glued to the floor like some indecisive guppy. I've dreamed of leaving Odissa every night since I met her, but now, faced with the chance to do just that, I'm not ready to go.

Just then, I hear the soft slapping of bare feet approaching. My ears strain, listening to the shift of weight—heavy, large feet, likely male. I take a step back, eyeing the window. Regardless of the male's intentions, I cannot be seen. But in my hesitation, I didn't properly prepare for my escape. I need to remove my dress, adjust my pouch to hang from my waist for ease of transformation, both actions that take up valuable time in this scenario.

I press against the wall, slipping into a shadow beside the window, hoping the darkness will conceal me. I wrap my fingers around the bone hilt, warm from the heat between my legs.

I plant my feet. First, I'll debilitate this unfortunately lost noble, then I'll leave. Already, my blood warms, eager for the violence—I've missed this.

Not a kill, I remind myself. *Just a little cut, so the male can't chase me.*

The footsteps near, rounding the corner. And with them, a low baritone humming sound, green curls of magic washing across the floor in sweeping passes.

Soren. I recognize his Voice instantly.

One tendril of his Voice lifts, and the rounded form of the tip tilts to the side. I hold my breath, and on the intake of air, the tendril snaps straight, shooting across the floor toward me.

I lose every ounce of reason. Panicked, I make a run, summoned from the shadows into the moonlight that streams through the window.

In the darkness of the hall, a pair of green eyes flash with victory. "Odd place to be during a ball, Wicked," he says in a deep voice. The tendril slithers closer, caressing my ankle.

I launch onto the windowsill and judge the angle of my fall seconds before taking the plunge. The ground rises to meet me. I skitter through a soft patch of sand on the smooth stone of the streets. My shoulder collides with a wall and pain flares through me. From the window above me, a growl sounds, then the tendrils slip out of the sill, rushing after me.

Panic seizes my chest, squeezing its cold fingers around my heart. I cannot let Soren catch me. I fear what might happen when he does—he'll confirm the accusations the captain whispered in the hallway.

I may do lust, but I do not do feelings. Especially not ones like attraction or its deadly cousin, love. Love is a beast with wicked claws and teeth that sink deep, and I'm not about to let it snare me now.

I break into a run, calculating my path to the sea.

Chapter Forty-One

SOREN

The farther she runs from me, the more I crave her presence, the more my need intensifies to hold her in my arms. To explain away that fear in her eyes just now. I spent the whole godsdamn evening wishing for her touch, admiring her from a distance, making sure she was safe, and now she's running. Away from *me*.

What did I do?

I follow through the window after her. The moment of freefall piques my adrenaline, and my feet connect with the ground. Before me, Enna sprints down the spiraling streets of the keep, heading toward the sea.

I sever my seeking spell, conserving my energy. She underestimates my determination. She may be faster, but I am powerful and steady, and she won't outrun me for long. There's only so far she can go, and even in the sea, I will find her. I will make this right, whatever it is. An hour ago, I thought I'd lost her. I will not let her out of my sight now. I sprint toward her, muscles warming, legs pumping, thrilling at the chase.

Enna should not be afraid of me. How could she, when I feel as though I might suffocate without her presence in a room? I am irrevocably, inevitably intertwined with her. The princess is a clingerfish on my arm; Enna is the force behind my tides. Where she goes, I follow, and as she curves down the keep, I make good on that promise.

Ahead, Enna darts around the bend in the path, ducking into the vendors' sector. She tests the doors, rattling the knobs. She looks over her shoulder as I turn the corner, her violet eyes catching the light of the moon. She pushes off a locked door, bolting down the street once more.

I round the next bend, nearly running into a loose pile of barrels in the street. Skirting right, I dodge one in time to avoid it rolling into my legs. I grunt, then grin. I've been thinking Aris isn't challenging enough—here's my challenge, and she's toppling a table of wares. Strings of beaded jewelry scatter. I leap over them, feet pounding hard as I push my body faster. The distance between us narrows. The silver tail of her dress flutters in the wind.

At the next turn, she hesitates before an alley that opens to the right. She takes it, tucking out of the main road. Got her! I slow my pace to a jog, ready for the moment she realizes her mistake in taking a dead-end road.

I cluck my tongue, and she flashes a glare at me before dragging her gaze up the wall.

"No way out, Wicked."

Her hands roam over the surface of the wall, caressing the flat stone in much the same way those hands ran over my chest this morning, and a pang of desire stabs through my gut. I approach her slowly, lifting my hands in a gesture of surrender, even as I move to entrap her against the wall.

I will not let her go this time. My hands land on either side of her head, the heat of her body warming my skin through the thin silk of my shirt. If I inch a bit closer, her bottom will brush against my lap. My breath skims across her bare shoulder, the speckle of silver scales lifting at the touch of air.

"You ran from me," I whisper. "Why?" Between two fingers, I catch a stray strand of her hair. Her throat bobs as she swallows.

Then, quicker than I can follow, she launches herself up the side of the wall. Her long, black claws dig into the stone, creaking and scraping until she scales the top. Too late, my hands close around empty air. She squats, peering at me, her expression guarded.

No. She cannot escape me. I will not allow it. I stir my magic, Voicing my intent, aiming for her waist. She tucks and rolls along the wall, evading the threads of magic. With a growl, I send them after her. I snare her middle, pulling her into the air and lowering her slowly. She thrashes in my grip, humming furiously, as her own magic pushes against mine, crackling with light. I press harder. She settles at my feet once more, and I grin.

"There. That wasn't so hard," I say. Sand dusts the crest of her pale cheek. I reach to clear it. "Are you afraid of me, Wicked?"

"Let me go," she whispers.

"If I do, will you run again?"

She snarls, ducking under my arm. I catch the tail of her skirts and yank. Wrapping my arms around her waist, I tuck her body into mine, molding her into the place she fits so effortlessly beneath my chin. Like a missing piece, finally clicking into place.

"There is nowhere you can go that I will not find you, Wicked. Even if you flee to the depths of the sea, I will follow."

Her wild scent fills my nose, intoxicating me, mind and body. I pull her earlobe between my lips, and a shiver pulses through her.

My fingers trail the length of her arm, skimming the satin of her glove. Taking her hand, I place it on my shoulder, tightening my arm around her waist. I find the deep V of her dress, pressing my fingers into the smooth skin of her back. A gasp escapes her. My legs shift, swaying her to an invisible beat.

"What are you doing?" she whispers. Her feet move, hesitant steps on the stone.

"Dancing."

Her hand curls into the hair at the nape of my neck. "Dancing?"

I hum my pleasure, her rough touch sending a zing of desire through my body. "I watched you all night, Wicked. Standing there alone. And all I wanted to do was take you into my arms, just like this."

"There's no music," she says. But she finds the rhythm easily. Our bodies move to the silent music in a perfect synchrony. Her skirt swishes across the stone with a hush of silk, mixing with sand and stone. My fingers trail a lazy pattern on her back, and her scales rise to meet my touch.

"Isn't there?" I murmur, closing my eyes. My heart feels as if it might explode in my chest. I scatter a dozen kisses across her hairline. One for each time I lost sight of her tonight.

I hum a quiet melody to match our dance, the notes rumbling in my chest. It starts soft and unassuming, the ghost of a lullaby.

But when she leans in, her mouth moving against my skin to form a smile, I find my courage. I breathe magic into the tune, catching the echoes of my Voice and weaving them into a rich harmony. Green balls of light lift around us, each orb sustaining a note of the chord.

She gasps, her breath skittering across my scales. I lift our hands, spinning her through the opening. Her skirts flare in a shimmer of silver, wrapping around her legs. With a push of magic, my orbs encircle her, dipping to kiss her skin. She smiles at me, eyes bright beneath the moon. For a moment, I think she might let go, might take the opportunity to run again. My song takes on a melancholy note, stacking in dissonance. But she slips her hand behind my back, fingers grasping the silk of my shirt, tugging me close. I release the spell, and the orbs scatter into glittering dust in the breeze.

"Enna… I cannot fight this any longer. From the moment I saw you hopping across my beach, I've felt a pull deep in my gut. Wherever I turn, wherever I run, it's there, anchoring me to you. Tell me you feel it, too."

"We can't," she whispers, shaking her head. Her nose brushes my chest. "You are going to be king soon, and I'm… I am not fit for you."

I grab her chin and tilt it. Gone is the fear in her eyes, replaced with hesitation.

"Is that what you're worried about? That we don't fit together?" I smirk. "Wicked, I can show you right now how well we fit."

Chapter Forty-Two

Enna

Wicked, I can show you right now how well we fit.

My body relaxes as the dizziness washes over me. He tucks me against his chest, murmuring sweet nothings in my ear. His teeth catch my earlobe and, despite myself, I shiver and wonder where else those teeth might glide next.

His hands slide over my waist, warm through the silk. The fabric slips over my skin, deliciously soft, and my core heats. Too much fabric. Too much space between us. My bottom presses against his erection straining against those goddessdamn leather pants.

What was I doing? Leaving? There's a pouch of stolen Coral goods strapped to my thigh, ready to carry me all the way to the Rime.

No, that can't be right.

"This dress," he moans. "Gods, as soon as you walked in wearing this, I knew I was done."

His fingers rise to trace the deep V neckline, a knuckle slipping beneath the hem and skirting over the swell of my breast, across my collarbone. His thumb rests in the hollow beneath my neck. My pulse pushes angrily against the pressure of him, battering with the strength of my blood, but it's not enough.

"Nervous?"

I push my elbow back into his ribs, and he catches my wrist, clicking his tongue in disapproval. His thumb passes over the silk of my glove, and my spines lift to meet him, the thin membrane of silk stretching. His fingers stroke the tips of my spines, and another rumbling moan escapes his lips. With a quick pinch of his fingers, he slips the glove off.

"Off with these silly things. Don't hide beneath them for my sake," he says, and the other joins the first in the sand below. He brushes the fading marks of my bruise. "You're beautiful."

My spines quiver in their new freedom, glinting in the light of the moon. My spines *are* beautiful—one of my favorite features, right along with my fangs, my claws. I am a wicked beast of the Drink, sharp and cold as the darkness from whence I came. And this prince—somehow—sees their beauty, too.

Soren grips me firmly by the ass, pulling me securely against his lap, and pressing his erection against me with a moan, my name quivering on his lips. The satin of my dress slips between us, soft against my bare skin. I want it gone—off, shredded, I no longer care. His large hand cups my ass and takes hold like I'm the only thing keeping him afloat in a vast drowning sea.

"My little moon goddess," he whispers.

His bulging cock nudges my center, and I moan, dragging myself along its mound, coating my dress with my arousal.

His fingers trace my upper thigh, slipping along the silk. His thumb hooks into the slit, finding my skin in the secret passage to the evidence of my betrayal. If Soren discovers the contents of that pouch, this will all end in an instant, and I'll be cast out for the snapperfish.

I need to distract him.

"You okay, Wicked?" His voice rumbles in my ear, his thumb retreating.

I nod, then rotate back into his arms. My nipples harden into tight buds as my breasts skim over the expanse of his chest. The dark green scales embedded in his skin rise at my touch. His jaw flexes, one singular blood vessel straining against his pretty skin. I run my claws up his arm, then tangle them in the hair at the base of his neck, pulling myself higher. I steal a quick nip on his collarbone. He smells of salt and sun and driftwood. *Delicious.*

"Soren," I breathe, attaching his name to this heat building deep in my stomach, threatening to consume me with flames. "I need you."

Growling, he lifts me up, hoisting my skirts over my legs. I clench my thighs around his hips, using a claw to snip the strap of my pouch. I toss it into the darkness, out of view, just before his hand slides over my bare skin, cresting my cheek and slipping into the pool of heat between.

"Are you not wearing undergarments?" He chuckles. "You wicked thing."

His knuckle swipes through my wetness, nudging my already swollen clit. I gasp, clawing at his shoulders for purchase as I attempt to bring him closer still. He grunts, the tip of his finger swirling over me.

Who is distracting whom, I no longer know.

"You're already an ocean for me," he murmurs. "I could swim in this heat forever."

I claw at his shirt; his skin warm beneath my touch, smooth as the silk he was just wearing. His hair hangs loosely over his shoulders, swinging into his face.

"The pretty prince is all talk, no action." I snap my teeth in his ear.

With a grin, he dips toward the ground. My stomach flips with the shift in gravity, and I cling to him with all my limbs. He lays me flat on my back. I loosen my death grip around his neck.

"I'm going to devour you." He settles between my legs, gripping my thighs as he parts them and lifts me to his mouth. His breath caresses my skin, cool against my heat. "You consume me with your very existence. Now, I will consume you until my name is the only word left on those lips, and you can tell me if that's action enough for you."

Over the swell of my stomach, I watch him as he studies me, his eyes darkening with lust. My core clenches, craving him in the spot only his breath touches. I ache to absorb him into my heat, to pull him inside of me until we can no longer tell where he ends and I begin. I moan, nudging him closer with my knees. And then his tongue seeks my wetness, drinking deep.

I cry out at the rush of pleasure. His tongue laps at my entrance. With every stroke, my need burns hotter.

"Soren," I moan.

He hooks my knees over his broad, muscled shoulders, lifting my bottom fully. My head thumps against the ground, and the stars crackle above my head, as bright and colorful as the pleasure coursing through my core. One of his hands grips each cheek of my ass as I squeeze my legs together, mounting the heat of his mouth. The tip of his nose nudges my pelvic bone, and I grind against it, faster, faster.

Swirling his tongue in a torturous rhythm, he devours me thoroughly, deliciously, just as he promised. With muffled moans, his voice rumbles through me, vibrating and warm.

An all-consuming pleasure swells my stomach. Soren hums deeper until it feels like my entire body might explode from the vibration. Then his teeth are on me, firm and hard, as he sucks my clit with the pressure I need. My orgasm batters me, body and soul—wave after wave crashing in ceaseless rhythm—and I'm sucked in, spit out, left whimpering, and drenched on the shore of my pleasure. If this is what being devoured feels like, I don't want him to ever stop.

Soren doesn't stop.

Green light slithers out of his mouth, slipping across my belly to tease the swollen buds of my nipples. I gasp as the magic passes over me. Soren lifts his head, grinning, evidence of my arousal dribbling from his chin. He swipes his tongue to catch every drop.

Wide-eyed, I stare at him as the magic continues to swirl. Soren twists his magic around my right breast, teasing the tip with excruciating delay until finally it squeezes. A giggle bursts through my lips, and I suck in an embarrassed breath.

Soren crawls over me, caging me with the bars of his forearms. His face is dark before the light of the moon, the silver light streaming through gaps in his hair. White teeth flash into a smile. "Do that again," he says, and my eyelids close as my mind scrambles into mush.

He cups my cheek, drawing my focus back to his face. "Your laugh," he says. "It's beautiful." His touch traces the planes of my face, catching the bottom line of my lip. He leans in close, leaving only a scale's breadth between our lips. "Do it again."

Through the fog of my lust, I prepare a witty response, gasping for breath. "You're gonna have to make me, pretty prince. I don't take orders during sex; I give them."

I crave the weight of his cock, need it inside me, need it filling every inch of me.

His eyes alight with mischief. "Challenge accepted." Humming once more, he ignites his magic, and those soft tendrils slither over my body, slipping, teasing every vulnerable part of me. Green light swirls inside my navel, tugs at my hips, weaves between my toes. I watch the display with a mask of indifference while my ego rears and purrs, enjoying the careful attention. He covers every inch of my body, save the apex of my thighs. The closer the magic slithers to my clit, the more I squirm in anticipation.

He then slips out of the leather cage, cock springing free. The green scales on his chest trail down in a glistening path, clinging to his heavy balls, skittering down the impressive length of his cock. At the crown of him, a ring of larger scales forms a hardened ridge, wet with his wanting.

"Soren," I moan, my mouth watering. "Please."

His magic lashes my clit, worrying the sensitive bud with perfect rhythm. I buck my hips, riding the next wave of pleasure as it rebuilds deep in my stomach.

"That's it, Enna," he purrs. "I'm not done with you." He parts my legs and seats himself between them. "I'll never be done with you." The thick head of his cock presses against my entrance, hard and slick with his own arousal, even as the light continues to play.

It slides inside me, and I shift to accommodate his girth. That ridge of scales drags into my depth, eliciting ripples of my pleasure.

Soren grabs my hips, pushing deeper inside me. Then he launches into a frantic rhythm, thrusting hard and needy. My name spills from his lips, again and again, like a prayer.

I can't help myself. Another giggle bursts through my lips as pleasure wracks through me, and my soul lifts into a joy I've never experienced. I'm floating weightless in a sea of green light. He shudders and bucks. My core clenches around him, the waves of my orgasm carrying me into a sea of bliss.

Finally, the last wave passes and my eyes pop open. His face hovers over me, his hair unkempt, and he chuckles when he sees my expression. "You sure you want to run from this, Enna?"

I blink, steadying my mind as the post-orgasm dizziness settles in. As I study his face, the kindness in his expression, the care in his eyes, a fragile feeling in my chest breaks open, a splinter wriggling loose at last. I look at Soren, and for the first time in my life, I feel seen—not as my father's daughter. Not as an unlucky half-breed, or death-dealer, or trench-scum. Not as handmaid or shadow-guard.

Just me.

And when the familiar fear rises from my gut, poised to protect me, I brush it away. "No," I answer him, matching his smile with one of my own.

Chapter Forty-Three

ENNA

I wake up before dawn feeling overwhelmingly hot. Soren's arm drapes protectively across my stomach, pressing my body deep into the cushioned mattress. Soft down cradles my aching body; sheets tangle around my legs. The darkness is punctured by the light of a lantern outside, its shadows sweeping through the large and ornately decorated room.

As I take inventory of my surroundings, I recognize Soren's bedchamber, complete with the large pool carved into the center of the floor. The memory of last night floods back to me, and my face warms, deliciously happy. I shift my hips, bringing a stretch to the ache in my lower back, and my thighs brush a hard length of skin tucked between them.

I freeze as he shifts beside me and his cock slips further between my legs—hard as a rock even in sleep. My core flares to life at the brush of attention, instantly drenched with longing.

I clench my thighs, trying hard not to move. But the clenching draws his cock right where I need it, nestled against my clit. My stomach tightens at the slightest movement.

Fuck. I grind my teeth, bite my tongue, dig my claws into my palm—anything to distract me from the temptation of riding Soren's dick while he's slumbering. I shift my hips, hoping his cock will slip away, but in the movement, that velvety, ridged tip slides straight through wet heat, and *goddess,* I need it again. Another shift, minute and controlled, and the pleasure builds. Blossoms. If I'm quiet, maybe he won't wake up and discover my ruin.

Memory supplies the backdrop for my fantasy: Soren prowling through the streets of Aquisa, his eyes dark and searching; Soren, pinning me against the stones, his tongue dipping into me, his chin running with my juice; Soren's eyes as they claimed me with a look. *Mine,* he'd growled.

I moan, sliding along the length of his cock and clenching down. Each orgasm has been different with him—from explosive heat to the slow burn of lava. This orgasm blooms. The scent of him lifts from the bed—safe, warm driftwood.

Goddess, what did I just *do*? As the flutters of pleasure fade, I stare at the ceiling.

My gut twists into knots with sharp realization. Soren could still choose Odissa. For all he knows, she is Princess of the Abyss, perfect marriage material. And then that'd make me... what? His favorite concubine?

This is the end, for us. I will not fuck him again.

I had a plan last night; I'd slip into the sea with my stolen goods and swim until I reached the Rime or my blood price claimed me, whichever came first. Instead, I'm lying here, sore in the passing of my latest orgasm from the cock of the male meant for my master. A bag of the treasure I've stolen from his kingdom rests on his desk.

I eye the leather pouch warily, nestled in the silk pool of last night's dress. I have two choices: I can take that treasure and run now, let yesterday's events stain my soul with the sweetness of a one-time thing—okay, a two-time thing—or I can stay and see this through. Whatever *this* is now.

What the fuck am I even doing anymore? Odissa is doomed to fail, and it's all my fault. I shouldn't have just ridden her prince's cock. Not to mention the stolen glances, or yesterday morning on the beach. The conversation at the tavern. The very first moment I met him, topless and sunburned, where he'd looked at me like a fish meeting water after a day in the sun.

The familiar tingle of my blood oath creeps through my veins, poised to pounce. I'm sabotaging the mission.

Beside me, Soren's face is smooth, softened by sleep. The strong, commanding male from last night is gone, replaced by this guppy-like calm. A dark curl splays over his forehead, and I lift my fingers, as if I might tuck the strand behind his ear. My heart squeezes. He sighs, those plump lips parting. His breath brushes my fingers, and I push the curl to rejoin the rest of his dark halo.

What I would give to stay right here, insulated in the protection of his arms. To have him wake up next to me, greet me with kindness in his eyes, press his lips on my forehead. His mouth would spread in a sleepy grin, and he'd say something stupid and cheesy, or call me Wicked for staying the night.

Stay.

I want it badly. I want him more than I've wanted anything in my life. And I cannot have him.

The dark magic solidifies, wrapping itself around my will. I cannot help Odissa succeed if I stay. The magic knows I'll only get in her way.

Lifting his arm from my waist, I tuck it next to his chest before swinging out of the bed. I locate my knife, belt, and chest piece, securing the casual garments around my body.

I turn to leave, but the metal of the locked drawer catches my eye. Is Soren really hiding that deadly necklace in his room? I twist my claw in the lock, slide the drawer open, and take the velvet pouch.

I weigh the necklace for a moment, admiring the shiny metal as it reflects the moonlight in the room. It warms at my touch, the same way it did when Amura wore it around her neck.

Such a small thing, with enough power to wipe out a kingdom.

But what does Soren want with it?

I chew my lip. Soren is too kind to use a weapon like this, not unless there was great cause for it. My blood turns to ice. My scalp prickles with understanding.

He doesn't trust Odissa.

The two weeks of silence after their time alone together, all those dinners he took in his room, his eagerness to deliver her into the hands of other dancers last night. It all clicks into place.

He is suspicious and intends to use the magic in this shell to prove himself right.

I drop the necklace into its pouch, sliding the drawer shut. That's it. I'm out of here. Odissa is royally fucked, and I will not stick around to die for her.

I step toward the balcony, and the blood oath seizes my limbs. I groan quietly, irritated at the magic for its indecision.

Leaving will help her succeed! He will not fall for her if I stay.

The magic doesn't budge. My feet solidify to the floor. I pull at them, grasping each thigh and yanking. Nothing.

Am I helping her, though? If I know about the magical necklace—if I know it might kill Odissa—am I leaving it behind for her to fuck around and find out?

I should take the damn thing with me. Drop it into some crag in the sea where no one will find it again. Or sell it on the black market. It would give Odissa the best shot at her bargain, at least.

I reopen the drawer, snatching the necklace but leaving its pouch, and stow it with the rest of my treasure. The magic eases, appeased by my choice.

Soren snorts from the bed. I jump at the sound. A sleepy hand lifts to rub his nose before it collapses back onto his pillow.

My heart skips a beat. I'm going to miss him, but this is for the best. I'll be dead soon by blood price, and as much as I'd love to spend my final days with his cock tucked between my thighs, I will not risk Odissa discovering our secret. She'd kill him.

My stomach lurches at the thought. If Soren died because of me, I'd never forgive myself.

I hurry to the balcony, slinking down the vine, hardly feeling the prick of it or the scrape of stone as I slide into the streets below. Nothing compares to the pain that tears through my heart, like flesh caught between teeth, slowly ripping apart.

Chapter Forty-Four

SOREN

"Who calls an emergency meeting the morning after a ball?" I yank open each drawer of my desk. I lift the books, set them down. I toss the cushion of my chair to the floor, and it slides to the edge of the room.

"Do you need help, Your Highness?" Hugo twists his fingers, the first time I've ever seen him flustered by my behavior. "The queen does not like to wait."

I'm acting erratic, I know. But the council has demanded my presence, Lord Almar has requested I bring the pendant to the meeting—the pendant that is now *missing*—and Enna is gone.

She's gone.

I can still taste sweet remnants of her cunt on my lips. And still she is not here.

She left her dress sitting in a pile on my desk this morning, taunting me with its emptiness. The shape of her—luminous and perfect—abandoned it, leaving a deflated heap, only good for proof that she was here.

I shouldn't be surprised. I'd been a stupid, hopeful fool to think she would stay until morning. She's slippery as shadows, and I will need to fight to pin her down—and even then, the likelihood of my success is slim. Enna isn't the type to be pinned down. I can't expect her to stand stoically at my side, take orders, and do what she's told. I wouldn't want her to.

What *do* I want from her?

I rub the sleep from my eyes, dragging a hand down my face, flexing the soreness from my jaw.

"Your Highness?"

I drop to the floor, crawling on my hands and knees. The cool marble does nothing to stave my rising panic. "The necklace, Hugo," I growl. "Can't find Amura's godsdamn pendant."

Hugo joins me on the floor, and we crawl around, our hands sweeping out in wide, reaching arcs.

"Can you spell for it? It's naturally warm, is it not?"

I shake my head. "It's an undetectable magic heirloom. I already tried."

"And you're sure it's in this room?"

I slide my hand under the bed, finding nothing but dust. With a grunt, I lift the mattress, toppling it onto the floor.

"And nobody has been in here except for you?" Hugo stands, picking through the obvious pile of silk on my desk.

"Don't touch that," I snap.

Enna was here. What would the Abyssal shadow-guard want with that magical heirloom?

Hugo stiffens, removing his hands from her dress.

I clear my throat. "Apologies," I say, softening my tone. "No one else was here."

"Understood, Your Highness."

I cross the room, stepping out onto the balcony. A waft of roses drift to me on the breeze, and I reach out to touch the twisting tendrils. A broken twig lies among the blooms, the wound fresh and green. I snap it from the vine, twirling it between my fingers with a frown.

A black cloud of dizziness creeps across my vision, and I stagger against the wall. Enna is *different* from the power-hungry females I've courted. Right?

She wouldn't lure me in on a false premise, only to steal from my bedchamber.

She wouldn't.

"We're late for the council meeting, Your Highness. I'll have your room searched later." He holds out the empty velvet pouch, where the necklace should be. "I assume you want to keep this quiet?"

I nod, and he tucks the pouch into his sleeve.

The hallways echo with Enna's absence at every turn as I storm toward the council room. My stomach grumbles, my muscles ache. I lick my lips, and her taste is still there.

Before me, guards scramble to open the doors to the council room in time for me to pass through them. The council members are already in their seats. Each one of them looks tired. Lord Almar is already nodding off. Lord Ruven's eyes are tight. My mother sits at the head of the table, her face shallow with exhaustion.

I eye my empty chair, debating the consequences of standing for this meeting.

My mother lifts her hand. "Sit."

I cross my arms, leaning onto the backrest. "Tell me what's chewing your fins, council. I'm late for breakfast."

The council shifts, their eyes darting to one another. Lady Myrrh clears her throat, a quiet, pitiful cough. "This council is once again concerned—"

Lord Varik barks a laugh. "Oh, let's just get into it. That princess is a fraud."

Lord Ruven grumbles, the minister of foreign affairs leaning back in his chair. He runs a hand over his stiff, gray beard. "Here we go."

Lord Varik glares broadly at the room. "I've never met a princess who cannot dance."

Lady Myrrh twirls a curl of her hair, pulling at the ends. "Disgraceful, certainly!" she huffs. "But nothing a few lessons couldn't fix. Perhaps she just didn't know the steps."

"The housekeeper said the princess's handmaid can dance, and better than her. Something isn't right here. I smell a trap."

I don't like it, the mention of Enna on his sneering lips. I inhale, steadying my nerves.

"You shouldn't have danced with her."

"You had no problem handing her off to me last night." Lord Varik narrows his eyes. "I did what I must, for the good of the kingdom. We cannot blindly give the seat of power to a dark-dweller without a thorough investigation. The past shows they are conniving and wicked; they'll do anything to avenge their history. Our investigation prior to the matter wound up as a snack for a dredge-beast, so I've taken up the task personally."

Lord Ruven's fist meets the tabletop with a dull thud. "We're so close to the wedding. Our prince doesn't need encouragement to drop his betrothed now! We'll hire a music tutor. No big deal."

My mother massages her temple, closing her eyes. "It's not just the dancing, Lord Ruven. I have my doubts. It's also the weakness of her Voice and the extreme reliance on her magic-wielding handmaid." Her eyes flash open. "It's possible I made a mistake."

"Oh, Your Majesty, how could you have known one way or the other?" Lady Myrrh gushes, eager to please.

Lord Varik sneers. "Odd, isn't it, that she has a Voiced handmaid to begin with. What does the princess need such high security for?"

Lady Myrrh pouts. "Poor thing must have needed a friend, coming to a strange kingdom. I see no harm in it."

"Fact is, she's an Abyssal Princess." Lord Ruven's fist remains on the table, knuckles lightening with the force of his grip. "We need the connection to move toward more civil relations with the deep. I say, drop the whole matter and be done with it."

"And risk the security of our kingdom? She might be a threat. An imposter. One of those death-dealers they breed in the dark." Lord Varik scans the room, daring a challenger to speak.

Lady Myrrh gasps, her hands stilling in her hair. "The horror!"

The queen straightens in her chair. "I don't like that I may have misjudged her quality, but I will not willingly walk our only heir into hostile hands. We must consider the possibility of malicious intent."

Lord Almar shifts in his seat and clears his throat. The room stills, all eyes shifting to the old priest.

"Lord Almar, do you have something to share?" says the queen.

The old male smiles. "Mister Hugo?"

Hugo approaches the table, carrying that damn velvet pouch. He sets it onto the table gently enough to make no sound.

Lord Varik mutters under his breath, shrinking away from the pouch. "Barbaric. We already know she cannot be trusted. Why insist on bloodshed? We must dismiss her quietly."

"Would you oust her on the basis of her waltz? This will produce solid proof." Lord Almar's gaze is smooth and cold. "If the Abyss has malicious intentions for our one and only heir, this is the only way to be sure of it."

I stare into the soft folds of the velvet pouch and consider my choices. I could dismiss Aris quietly. A short conversation, and she'd be on her way back to the deep. We'd part on pleasant terms—a poor match of personality, we'd call it. No more wedding. No more Aris. No alliance.

No Enna. I drag a hand over my jaw. That won't do.

"What of the alliance with the Abyss, if we dismiss their princess quietly?" I ask, buying more time for my decision.

Lord Ruven scowls. "Gone. Darksteel mines, influx of gold. All gone. We'd need another match to fortify our strength against the ensuing wrath of the Abyss. And your options are slim, Your Highness. We cannot risk it."

I nod, considering his words. Around me, the council launches into argument, throwing their opinions at me, each one suggesting a way to secure our strength.

If I find the missing pendant, I could use it on Aris, test her intentions toward me with ancient, brutal magic to ease the council's worries. And if she passes the test, the alliance with the Abyss will stand. Enna will remain here, caught in a royal love-triangle, and I'll swim the current of my father before me, unhappy and angry at my fate, unable to love Enna with the open abandon she deserves. Unable to protect her.

Or Aris could fail the pendant's test. I dismiss her publicly, out the Abyssal Kingdom for its subterfuge. There is no alliance, and Enna will...

She can stay here, if she wants to. Why can't she?

"A match to fortify our strength," I repeat to myself. If the Abyss retaliates, we'll need a warrior queen, one who knows the enemy inside and out.

Would Enna side with us, if it came to war? Would she stay, if I asked her to?

I meet my mother's watchful gaze across the table.

I cross my arms, firmly planting my feet. The council notices my movement, and their voices gradually settle down.

The pendant is missing. But the council doesn't need to know that. I scoop up the empty pouch, tucking it into my pocket.

"I'll use it," I state.

Hugo's fingers twitch. Lord Ruven's frown deepens. Lord Varik scowls. Lady Myrrh sighs.

"Excellent," says Lord Almar.

My mother simply raises her eyebrow, waiting for the catch.

Chapter Forty-Five

ENNA

THE WATER PARTS AROUND me like butter softened in the sun, luxurious and warm. I glide through the reef, skimming over the fronds and corals that cling to the rocks beneath me. Anemones dance in my wake. Crustaceans suck their eyes into their shells. My tail cuts the current, and the fish spin, darting out of my path.

I'm doing the right thing. The farther away from Aquisa I swim, the less and less I sense the tug of my blood oath. I cannot turn back now.

The Intercurrent lies at the far edge of the reef, in the open water after the sandbar drops into the sea. Once I reach the current, I'll hitch a ride on a fleetwhale. The drivers rest on top of the whales' great heads, so I'll approach from beneath, tethering to the belt around its waist. It'll be an uncomfortable ride, but it's much faster than swimming to the Frost border alone. And somewhere along my route, I'll drop the necklace into the deep and fulfill my duty to Odissa in the best way I can.

The reef deepens beneath me, sloping toward the ledge. Beyond it, nothing but dark blue expanse awaits me. The pale line of the intercurrent cuts through, the only object of size amidst the stretching monochrome. That old familiar fear ruffles my scales—of my utter insignificance in the wide, open sea.

I pull up short, hovering at the reef's edge. The sea floor bottoms out in a sharp descent. Few fish venture beyond its edge, hugging the rock. A wrigglefish slips around my torso, circling me with a brush of slippery scales. The fish darts away, vanishing among the corals.

Suddenly the colors of the reef are too vibrant. The sweetfish are too pink, the wrigglefish too orange. The reedgrass, brilliant strands of blinding green. My heart aches to behold its beauty, knowing I'll never lay eyes on it again.

I dig my nails into my palms, sharpening my mind with the pain. *Focus, Enna.* This should be simple. I have nothing to worry about, now; no one to give me orders. No one to care for except myself.

This is the freedom I wanted.

With a grunt, I kick my tail again, angling for the stretching Intercurrent. My body is light. Fast. I twist into a spiral, reveling in the way the water lifts my hair, caresses my skin. I'll never have to use my legs again. Never again constrict myself to pointless fashions. I reach behind my neck, and with a slice of my claw, I sever the band securing my chest piece. The top slips from my body, its many strings of beads reaching sunward as it sinks into the blue.

For a moment, the light shifts, and I imagine it's not the top but my ball gown from last night. I swallow, throat tightening.

Did Soren find my dress this morning? Did he wake sad and alone? Did I cause him pain at my leaving, or is he going about his duties as normal?

Pain rips through my chest anew. I flinch, fingering my sternum to locate the injury. But there's nothing there—no bloodfish bite, no stinging nettle. My skin is smooth and unharmed.

I stir my thoughts, searching for something to distract me, something to focus on. But I cannot clear the image of Soren, cradled by the satin pillow. Those long tresses framing his face, softened by slumber. Is he eating breakfast by now? Is he... angry at me?

My throat constricts, and I choke out a sob. My mouth parts in a silent scream, releasing a spray of bubbles. I batter them away with my hand, blinking to clear my vision, but I cannot see. My eyes sting. My throat burns.

No. I will not cry over this. I've made the right choice. This is the best way I can preserve Soren's life. If I could kill Odissa without a blood price, I would. I would do it in a heartbeat, if I knew it would ensure Soren's safety until the full moon.

With four days left in her bargain and the necklace out of her way, Odissa won't have to work hard to convince him to go through with this fucked-up wedding. He's a male of his word, and he will put the needs of his kingdom before his own happiness.

Another sob wracks through me, and I swim blindly toward the rush of water before me.

It's all a fucking lie. There is no alliance with the Abyss. The real princess is dead; I killed her myself. Soren is not marrying some noble female; he's unwittingly hitching himself to a death-dealer in a walking corpse.

What will Odissa do once they're married? Will she really stop at winning his throne? Or will she kill him in his sleep? Will she torture him? Force *him* into a blood oath?

The roar of the Intercurrent drowns my restless thoughts, and I stop short of its edge. The water rushes past, the clouded forms of fleetwhale and mermaids speed by me, caught in its path. I glance down into the blue. My hand inches for the pouch on my hip.

Drop the necklace, then go.

I tread water slowly, barely keeping myself in place. The spray of the current brushes my neck, and my gills flutter to match the restless tempo of my heart.

The shell warms in my grip, humming at the touch of my palm. It vibrates, growing more and more persistent, like a hungry guppy begging for attention.

Odissa will ruin this place from the inside out, and I've left her alone to do it.

Soren grew up here. He knows every inch of coral, recognizes every species of fish. That reef formed him into the kind, dedicated male he is, the great king I know he will be. I trace his domain with my gaze, and my teeth clench against the rising panic.

The necklace heats further. I can sense its appetite for action. For blood. Soren was going to use this weapon on Odissa, I'm sure of it. My blood oath would not have let me get this far unless it was true.

Why the fuck am I stopping him? For my peace of mind for four short days?

I tighten my fist, and the pendant purrs in my grip.

I've always been a pawn in Odissa's game. What if, for once in my life, I did something selfish? If I'm dead at the end of this, why not risk it for something good for a change?

I can't help Odissa woo a sweet, caring male just so she can sink her teeth into his fortune and steal his crown. Not on my watch, not anymore. I've been sabotaging the plan since day one—what's the harm in making it intentional?

I tuck the necklace back into my pouch, turning away from the roaring Intercurrent. With a flick of my tail, I angle toward Aquisa, pumping as fast as I can.

Dark magic descends, angry ice in my veins. It pulls on my limbs as it tries to yank me into submission. I push through, forcing my numbing body to move through the sheer force of my will. Harder. Harder. The magic squeezes until I gasp, vision narrowing into a dark blur.

I must make it back to the shore, before it's too late. I must find Soren, tell him the truth. He deserves to know everything.

Stirring the magic in my belly, I hum a spell to fortify my limbs. Electricity pulses through me, fighting for control of my muscles. My tail thrashes, gaining speed.

Soren may hate me for my role in this, and he may never forgive me. But it doesn't matter.

Because the truth will cost me my life.

Chapter Forty-Six

Soren

Princess Aris sits alone at the breakfast table when my mother and I arrive. Delicate arrangements of food spread along the table, overflowing with fruits and fish and tea cakes. Morning sunlight streams through the open windows, casting the room in a warm glow. Aris turns at my entrance, teacup in hand, her lips still pursed mid-sip.

"Happy wedding week, Your Highness," the queen says, her voice light and sweet. "What a splendid ball last evening. I look forward to another one tonight."

Aris rushes to her feet, dropping into a curtsy. Her head dips heavily, her hair elaborately coiled, save for one strand that's escaped the nest.

No sign of the shadow-guard. I suck in a jagged breath. Did she take the necklace and run?

I ball my hands into fists. Hugo's fingers brush my shoulder in warning. I force the tension from my hands, unfurling each knuckle one by one.

I will not believe it. Enna is simply late.

"Thank you, Your Majesty. We are absolutely delighted by last night's success, aren't we, darling?" Aris's voice rings with an air of falsehood, too sweet. The pageantry plays on.

"Of course." I clear my throat to dispel the knot forming there. "Looking forward to continuing the merriment this evening."

If I cannot find that necklace, I'll be stuck dancing with Aris at a pre-wedding ball every night this week until the full moon. Four days from now.

I slide into my seat beside my mother, avoiding Aris's gaze under the guise of selecting my breakfast. I pile food onto my plate until I run out of space, then pop a lushfruit into my mouth, chewing slowly as an excuse not to talk.

My mother eyes me sideways. With excruciating attention, she straightens the dainty necklace at her collarbone, then eyes me again.

Across the table, Aris plucks obliviously at a piece of cake, stabbing the cinnamon sponge with her fork. Her hand curls around the handle oddly, her knuckles overlapping, and I squint. Odd that a princess wouldn't know how to hold a fork. She lifts the cake to her mouth with a smile, slipping the tines between her lips.

The doors open with a clatter, and I look up to see Enna push through. My heart climbs into my throat at the sight of her—hair dripping wet and wild, those eyes sharp and focused, dressed in nothing but her loin cloth and a knot of reedgrass around her breasts.

She is here.

"Apologies, Your Highnesses," she mutters. "I seem to have overslept this morning."

Water drips from her hair onto the marble floor, splattering in a soft symphony. She moves slowly, testing the weight of each step as she approaches the back of Aris's chair.

Aris stiffens. Her jaw clenches, then grinds as if she needs to chew her words before letting them out.

"Ah, there you are," she says.

"Yes, here I am," Enna chirps, too happy for a casual tone. She's only made it halfway to the table. Her hands twitch at her sides, hanging limply. Her brow furrows. Her gaze meets mine, liquid lava. Something is wrong.

Aris turns. "Come now," she says with a hint of annoyance.

Finally, Enna stops behind Aris, grimacing. With careful fingers, she tucks a stray pin into Aris's hair.

My body lifts, and the legs of my chair scrape loudly on the floor as I stand to my full height. Porcelain clatters as my mother nearly drops her teacup. I ignore her, gesturing to the remaining open seat at the table—the one next to me.

"Please, join us, my lady," I say.

Three pairs of eyes snap to my face—my mother's darken, Aris's flash, Enna's burn with purple flames. In her three weeks here, not once has she joined us for a meal, aside from the tavern. The shadow-guard smiles coyly, stepping around the table carefully until she reaches the open seat. Aris and the queen track her movements like she might explode. I pull out the chair and help Enna into place, signaling for table service. My fingers brush her shoulder, her skin still dewed with seawater. Aris's hand clenches around her fork.

"Good morning," I murmur. I sink into my chair, tasting the words, wishing them into being. Enna came back to me. It *must* be a good morning. I place my hand on her knee.

She stiffens, staring at the back of my hand. I squeeze her knee, soft and reassuring. Whatever is wrong, I will help her get through it. I'm here.

But she doesn't look at me. Her eyes lock on the edge of the table, glazed. She fumbles with the pouch tied to her hip, fingers digging deep into the leather cavity. Her spines lift out of their sheath.

"Soren, darling? Are you quite all right?" I look up to the curious gaze of my betrothed.

Mother taps her spoon on the porcelain edge of her teacup. She frowns at me and fidgets once more with her necklace.

I drop my gaze back to the pouch, to Enna's fingers now pinching a long, golden chain. Slowly, she places the shell pendant into my palm. It warms at my touch.

I close my fingers around the shell. She stole this from my room last night, and by the look in her eyes, she knew exactly what she was doing. Somehow, Enna learned the magic of this necklace and decided to take it for herself.

My knuckles pop from the pressure of my grip around it. Did she use this weapon on my people? What was she doing with it in the reef?

Enna brushes my wrist, her touch soft and timid. I assess her gaze once more. Those purple eyes swim with a chaos of emotions—sadness, confusion, fear—like she might burst any moment.

The corners of her eyes prick with moisture. Her bottom lip quivers, and she mouths, *Please.*

At that word, my anger melts. Enna may be vicious and unpredictable, mysterious and guarded, but she's never struck me as malicious. In her heart, she is good. I can feel it. And she knows Aris better than anyone in the room.

There is no turning back now.

"Aris, darling, I have something for you. A little early wedding present, if you will." I bring the pendant to light. The metal rests against my palm, glowing softly at my touch.

Aris's eyes widen in delight as I hold the necklace out for her admiration. I've only ever heard the rumors of Eero's spell, never seen it in action. What will the pendant do when the princess finally speaks?

While Aris flutters in a show of excitement, Enna's body turns to cold stone. Her hands grip the table, her bare knuckles bone white. The spines in her arms lift, long and wicked.

Aris lets out a delighted gasp. The pendant warms in my hand, and the room holds its breath.

Chapter Forty-Seven

ENNA

Odissa flutters her fingers, peering at the glowing shell in Soren's hand. She grins, locking her gaze with mine.

"It's beautiful, Soren," she says. "A wedding gift? For me?" Her voice is musical, sweet. Loud enough she should be dead.

If this necklace doesn't work soon, I'm going to kill her myself, slide my knife right through that pretty throat, and watch it bleed all over her cinnamon cake.

I clutch the side of the table. My claws dig deep, carving trenches in the wood. Is the necklace a fake? Did I misinterpret that old queen's diary?

Odissa reaches for the necklace, fingers stretching. "I'm ashamed I don't have anything for you—"

Time slows to a spiralfish's crawl as several things happen at once. The shell's glow, soft and golden moments ago, turns an angry shade of red. Odissa's voice gurgles on the word *you*.

She shrieks, and her hand whips up to clutch at her neck. Glass shatters and water slides across the table setting, soaking into the napkins. Her face crumples with agony; her top lip rises into a snarl. Her eyes widen, the blue fire in them extinguishing into a bitter mist. The shriek morphs into a scream, raising the scales on the back of my neck.

The shell begins to hum, its tune an eerie echo of Odissa's screams. The skin of her neck glows brilliant red and begins to smoke. She claws at her throat as she chokes. The smell of cooked flesh burns my nostrils. Her skin bubbles, black boils spreading. She eyes the pendant, eyes feral with fire.

My heart thunders a frantic beat, and I watch in horror as she lunges across the table, crawling through the shattered glass.

"Enna!" Odissa's palm slices on the edge of a shard. "Do something!"

The command compels me to stand; I cannot disobey. The blood oath churns in my veins, seizing control of my body. My chair tips from the force of my movement, clattering to the floor. Blood surges to the tips of my fingers, and my hand lifts, reaching for her against my will.

It's a game of war within my own body, and eventually I'll lose. But I'm not going down without a fight. I pull against the magic, and my fingers curl into a fist.

Odissa shrieks my name again, and a jolt of renewed command tugs every string of my muscles. *Help her.*

I work my jaw, prying it open. With great effort, I swivel my eyes to lock onto hers. I see the moment realization dawns in her gaze: blue fire flickers, then roars.

I smile. "No."

At the sound of my voice, Soren stiffens. He turns to me, searching the side of my face, but I ignore him.

The death-dealer's borrowed mouth snarls. She reaches for Soren, fingers curling into wicked hooks. Dark sores ripple across the backs of her hands in a boiling current. Her skin hisses and curdles. It smells of burning fish.

HELP HER!

The impulse is strong, but I am stronger. I uncurl my toes, flatting my feet against the marble floor. I will *not* obey any longer. I will stand here, watching her dissolve inch by inch, until there's nothing left but a pile of smoking bones.

But Soren slides the necklace into its velvet pouch, out of Odissa's reach, and the hum of magic stops. "I believe that's answer enough, Mother," he says, cool as the Drink.

I shiver, dread twisting through my gut. This isn't right. Why did he stop the spell? Why didn't he finish her?

Odissa's blistered hand closes around thin air. She squats on the table in a puddle of blood, glass, and strewn lushfruit, dozens of scratches along her knees and legs where she crawled through the shards. Her skin is bleeding and blotchy. Odissa clutches her hands to her chest, whimpering. When she coughs, blood splatters.

"You unworthy ratfish," the queen hisses. "Tell me, dark-dweller, were you sent by the king to ruin us? Is that why he's still hiding in the deep out of our reach? Or is this a plot of your own design?"

Several white-clad warriors rush forward, tridents bared. Odissa kicks and screams as the guards drag her by the ankles. She clutches at anything in her reach—the rolls, the lushfruit, the plate. It all falls to the floor with a clatter of glass. They wrestle Odissa off the table, binding her bloody hands behind her back. "Please!" she screams.

"Hold her fast. Let me look at her." The queen places her hand under Odissa's chin, tipping her face to get a better view.

Odissa sets her jaw, speechless.

"Dispose of her. Send her head back to the Abyss, a gift for the king."

"Soren, please! It's not my fault. My father mated with the nanny. My family has always despised me for my blood; that's why the king sent me here, to get me out of their fins. Please, you have to believe me! I mean this crown no harm!"

Soren watches her struggle, his jaw flexing. "But you do wish me harm," he says. "You just proved it."

Soren steps away from me, into the fray. Closer to *her*. My chest tightens. "And yet..."

The guards hesitate, dangling a kicking Odissa between them on their way to the door.

Soren continues, "If intention is her only crime, it's not enough to condemn her to death. She has not acted on it. She may yet change her life's course, given time to think about it. I will not repeat the mistakes of my ancestors."

Fool. He doesn't know Odissa like I do. He cannot afford to let her go.

I lift my hand, stretching for Soren. I must let him know, somehow. But he stands too far away. My legs glue to the floor, caught in the weight of my curse.

The queen shakes her head, her expression softening. "My sweet son," she says. "You've always had a heart for the bottom feeders. It'll be the death of you."

"So be it," he grunts. "Escort the princess to the dungeon. May her time there show her the error of her thoughts. Perhaps we can strike a deal with her brother yet."

This isn't how it was supposed to happen. All of that, and he's letting her live?

The queen smiles at his final words. "As you wish."

"Thank you, Your Highness. You are most compassionate." Odissa dips her head at the prince, then glares about the room, challenging anyone to speak against the prince's order. Her gaze lands on me last. She flicks her eyes to the prince, then back again, those sharp eyes narrowing.

My spines flex from their sheaths as the guards drag her toward the door. Her bargain with Tephra ends in four days, when the full moon peaks. If Odissa walks free of this room, the kingdom will face her wrath. Soren should kill her now, before it's too late.

At my malicious thought, the blood oath seizes my airway. I gasp. My lungs burn. I cough and stumble into the table, grasping at my own neck. I cannot sever its invisible hold. My tongue sits heavy in my mouth, working to form the words against the weight of deep, binding magic.

"Wait." My voice rings like shattered glass. I refuse to look at the prince, even as my scalp prickles with painful awareness of his eyes on my face.

He steps toward me, sliding his arms up my arms. I cup his cheek as his eyes search mine, even as my vision blurs. His skin is soft, smooth. A parting gift.

This is it, then. This is how I die. *So fucking be it.*

I force the words with a choking gasp, "Soren, she's not the real princess. Her name is Odissa, and she's a death-deal—"

Before I can finish, the world descends like a heavy black cloak, smothering me with its embrace. The last thing I see is Soren's eyes, tightening with fear.

Chapter Forty-Eight

SOREN

One moment, Enna is safely in my arms. The next, she is crumpling like paper. Her eyes roll to the back of her head, and she collapses against my chest, twitching like a wrigglefish.

I cry out her name, clutching her close as her body continues to writhe in unnatural angles. "A healer!" I shout. "Call the healer!"

The room explodes into chaos around me. My mother's voice rings with command, and metal clinks as weapons draw. Aris—if that's even her name—screams. Footsteps shuffle in endless, scuttling rhythm.

In my arms, Enna's face grows unnaturally pale, the usual soft pink hue of her skin draining quickly into cold white. I repeat her name until my throat grows sore, and even then, I whisper it with a dry, cracking voice. This cannot be happening. Whatever sick twist of fate this is, I want out. Enna is mine. The death goddess has no right to take her from me. Not now, not this soon. Not until after we've spent centuries fading our scales and hollowing our bones, on the verge of dissolving. Only then will I part from her.

I touch her neck, confirming the fluttering beat of her heart, the passage of her breath. She's still with me, for now. Hands clap my shoulders, then curl around my hands, prying my fingers loose. I growl, the sound rumbling deep in my chest.

"Don't touch her," I say, holding her more tightly. The guard backs away, stuttering something about the healer preparing the wing. "I will take her myself."

I walk forward on numb legs, following the familiar twists of the hallway. The marble walls tilt in a blur of white, and I nearly stumble. Someone catches my elbow, straightens me, then guides me forward. Enna shifts in my arms, her eyes darting in rapid rhythm underneath her eyelids. I increase my pace, flying through the halls as fast as I can without jostling my precious cargo. The crisp, clean scent of the healer's wing floods my nose. The door swings open with a bang, and I'm ushered inside.

A healer points me to the back of the vast, white room. The healing tank lies horizontal on a steel platform; the glass tube clamps to the marble floor with metal straps, open to the air at the top.

I lower Enna into the warm salt water. Her body twists and snaps, clothes tearing, and her legs snap together as they form her slick black tail. Bits of cloth float to the surface of the tank. Her back arches as the water absorbs her weight, suspending her. The healer touches my shoulder, and I step away from the tank.

"We'll take it from here," the healer says. Her eyes are warm as honey. She approaches the tank, beginning to hum a spell. Golden light slips from her mouth, diving into the tank to surround Enna with its tendrils.

    I lean against the wall, watching the magic swirl and kiss Enna's skin. The moment's weight tugs my limbs, and I succumb, sliding down the stone to land on the floor. My head falls into my hands. I sit there, waiting, until my body becomes one with the stone.

Chapter Forty-Nine

ENNA

THE DRINK IS WARMER than I remember. The water, once so bitterly cold to evoke a sharp sense of clarity, now feels thick as soup. My gills struggle to filter the water, sucking in deep pulls but finding no relief from the burning in my chest. The scent is unbearable, acrid in its sting. Eyes firmly closed, I pump my tail but do not move forward, only drag it a small increment up, then down, hanging suspended in the broth of the deep.

I have to get out of here. This is not right. I was in the middle of something important, somewhere far away from here. My mind spins, searching for the thought I've misplaced. It had something to do with Odissa.

I open my eyes. The water is not black, but a thick, brackish green, the color I imagine the inside of a dredgebeast's stomach would be.

I blink my outer lids to clear the fog from my vision, but the haze does not focus, only thickens. I attempt to turn my head, to scan my surroundings for danger, for this certainly is not the Drink. I am out of my element here. Much like my tail, I get nowhere fast. With painful slowness, my neck swivels, and my periphery expands, revealing a white shape: a mermaid skeleton.

The skeleton floats in the murk, its arms limp at its sides. The cavern of its ribs hosts a lone bloodfish, nibbling a rib bone for final scraps. The skull is nearly picked clean, with only a few threads of sinew clinging to its cheek. Awareness prickles the back of my neck, and my spines rise in warning. I am not alone. The skeleton moves, swiveling its head to lock its cavernous eyes on me. Its teeth snap shut with a creak of its jaw, the tail bones stir, and the bloodfish darts away.

I scream at my body to move. My tail is dead weight, my gills fluttering in normal rhythm. The skeleton lurches forward, extending its bony arms. Its fingers grip my neck and yank, towing me through the water.

Through the murk comes a sinister laugh, deep and rumbling and terrifyingly familiar. The water trembles in its wake. Cold fear twists my panic-stricken heart. The laughter morphs into the sound of my name, a dark, gnashing phrase on repeat.

The skeleton speeds forward, the bones of its tail thrashing my scales, cutting deep. Blood clouds the water. In my periphery, dark shapes begin to move. I open my mouth to shout, to spell, anything to get me out of here, but my voice will not sound. A few bubbles escape, popping on my cheeks as I'm dragged through them.

"You have broken your oath, Enna Valomir," Tephra's voice calls again, clearer, louder. "I will take the blood you owe me."

I glance around as best I can, but do not find the goddess. Her voice echoes from every angle, disembodied.

Something rumbles below me, and the water trembles. A dark, colossal shape comes into view, half buried in a garden of bones on the sea floor. Four flat fins protrude from the long, muscular body, paddling the water in the rhythm of sleep.

My spine tingles. A dredgebeast.

"This is how you'll pay my price. No weapons. No magic. Just you and the blood in your veins."

The skeleton that holds me lurches to a stop, and my tail curls up from the sudden change in momentum, slapping me in the face. The sharp edge of my tail slices the top of my cheek, drawing blood. In a thin, swirling tendril, my blood floats into the water, and the beast's nares flare. One great eyelid peels open, the bright yellow orb locking on me. It releases a rumbling groan. Bones crack and snap under its weight as it shuffles, stirring clouds of sand.

Tephra's voice cuts through the water. "Kill the beast, and your life is yours to keep," she says. "Better swim fast, little fish."

As the final word rings out, the thick weight on my body suddenly lifts. I flex my tail, testing it against the murky water. Relief pulses through me for a moment before adrenaline takes control.

With a push of its paddle fins, the beast emerges from the sand. Its other eye pries open, focusing on me. I eye its sharp teeth, each twice my length, and calculate the beast's age accordingly. A mature adult. Female, judging by her size. Two streaks of red run parallel from the crown of her skull down the length of her spine, joining at a single point of her long, whipping tail. Thick, scaled armor coats her body, save for a few small weak points. I locate them quickly—the underside of her gills and fins and a soft palette between her eyes.

I instinctively reach for my knives, connecting only with smooth skin. My waist belt is gone, my knives with it. My pulse thuds in my ears as the nerves settle in; I've stunned a dredgebeast before, but never killed one. Not with my bare hands.

Her mouth opens wide, that great black tongue lifting at the back of her throat. She screeches. The sound blasts a torpedo of current, launching me into a spiral. I backpedal, steadying myself in the stream. The beast lunges. I dodge. The tips of my tail clear the gap in her teeth before her jaw snaps shut.

I swim along her body, forcing her to twist to find me. Keeping close to her scales without touching them, I lead her into a coil. I slip beneath her great fins, scanning for the weak points. There. The socket rotates as she tips right, baring the soft flesh. I sink my claws in deep and rip free a bloody fistful of her meat. She shrieks and snaps, whipping her long neck to find me.

As I dodge her flailing limbs, I plop the piece of meat into my mouth, warm and tender. Goddess, did I miss this taste. I glide to the next fin, then the next, plucking sweet morsels from her flesh. Her blood clouds the murky water.

A hoard of bloodfish rushes the water, following the smell of iron. Their long bodies wriggle as they screech, scenting the sores. One locks its beady eyes on me, opening its large, funneled mouth. Rows of hooked, razor teeth line the channel, spiraling deep into its gullet. The rim of its mouth quivers, sucking in a trail of my blood from the water, and then it lurches for my face.

I catch its neck in my hand, fingers pressing into its gills, and I squeeze it until its eyes pop and the teeth stop moving. I toss the corpse to the writhing mass of its kin and they devour its stringy flesh to the bone. More hooked teeth sink into my tail, tearing my scales.

I swipe at them with my spines, but the teeth sink deeper with every swat of my arm. Some lose their grip, leaving a searing pain, only to be replaced by more teeth, more pain.

One latches onto my hip and sinks its teeth in deeper than I can dislodge without a knife. Its mouth quivers, suctioning tight as it begins to suck my blood. My veins burn as my blood rushes backward, flooding the fish's mouth.

Fuck.

With my thumbs, I dig my claws into its eyes. The creature holds firm, its tail whipping furiously. Above me, the dredgebeast shifts and a screech vibrates the water, ringing in my ears. Gritting through the pain, I grasp the fish by its gills and yank as hard as I can. My flesh tears, caught in its teeth, and still, the fucker won't let me go. I clench my teeth against the searing pain.

The dredgebeast whips her tail, freeing her body momentarily from the feeding mouths. I scramble for her tail, pulling myself up the length of her spine away from the bloodfish hoard. With my claws, I find purchase in her scales. Her neck arches, head swiveling to watch me climb. I'm exposed here on her back, but I dare not venture beneath her belly among the gnashing teeth. She strikes with her mouth, snapping at me. I release and roll, but the edge of her tooth slices deep into my forearm, gouging free a few of my spines. I howl in pain, holding on by the end of my claws. Latched to my side, the bloodfish drinks greedily. My mind grows fuzzy, and the water begins to spin.

The beast tucks her fins, breaking into a dive. Then, she climbs toward the surface, the current sliding over her lithe body. I'm an attachment, dragging in the stream. The pressure of the water batters me, threatening the strength of my grip. I grunt with exertion; my gills flutter nervously along my neck, fighting to filter oxygen. Fear stings like a whetted knife through my beating heart. The dredgebeast is bleeding but strong. My efforts have barely affected her, and here I am, my arm mottled, a gash in my side and face, and my energy reserves depleting from blood loss. I cannot Voice my way out of this. And if I don't survive, I will never see Soren again.

My heart aches at the impending loss of him. Odissa will find a way to ruin him, and my sacrifice will have been for nothing. I cling to the side of the beast and choke out a curse.

Fuck Odissa. Fuck this blood oath. I should have never agreed to help her; it was a chum-brained pursuit from the start.

The dredgebeast stalls in the water, and I fling forward, sliding up the length of its neck. It twists its head and strikes, catching my tail between its teeth. I shriek in pain and try to wrestle free, but her tooth has impaled the membrane of my fin. I cannot break free without ripping the soft tissue. The beast whips her head, and I fly with her, moments away from becoming her snack.

I kick my tail, trying to rip free, but her tongue snakes out, twisting around my waist. The slippery leather of it holds me fast. The bloodfish releases its teeth at last, abandoning me to my fate.

"I'm sorry, Soren," I cry out, my heart palpitating with the pain of my loss. "Soren, Soren, Soren."

Chapter Fifty

SOREN

"She speaks, Your Highness." Someone squeezes my shoulder, and I flinch awake. The healer apologizes for waking me, then gestures toward Enna.

Enna floats in the saltwater tank. Her face is turned toward me, features smooth with sleep. Gills flutter in constant rhythm along her neck. She's been this way for a full day. Her eyes are closed, but her mouth moves now, muttering something I cannot hear. Bubbles stir and lift from her parted lips.

I place my hand on the glass. "What did she say?"

"I'm not sure."

We press our ears against the glass. The tank water thuds with a drowning echo, faintly tuned with the sound of Enna's hushed voice.

"I cannot make it out," says the healer. "But I thought you'd want to know. This is the first sign of progress since we stabilized her this past high tide."

I strain my hearing, but I cannot decipher her words. "What tide is it now?"

"Evening low, Your Highness. You've been asleep for a while. I did not want to disturb you."

I rub the sleep from my face and grunt.

"Her heart rate and breathing are normal. Vital signs look good right now. She seems to be under some sort of magical distress, an internal war in her spirit. I'm afraid there's nothing more we can do but keep her here and react if anything changes."

"She was twitching like a wrigglefish! She collapsed, has been comatose for a full day already, and you're telling me there's nothing wrong with her?" I ball my hands into fists.

"That's right, Your Highness."

It's not the healer's fault, I remind myself with a deep inhale. I just don't understand the nature of her condition. A magical distress? From what? The only magic in that room was mine, ferried through the pendant.

Could this be my fault?

Regret slices through me, sharp and stinging. I was trying to keep her safe, and in my carelessness, I hurt her somehow. I should have warned her. Should have told her to keep quiet.

"I know it's shocking, but we are well equipped here." She smiles. "Get some rest. I'll call you if there's a change."

"No." I press into the side of the tank; the glass warm against my nose. "I will not leave her."

She's alive, at least. And stable for now. Her chest expands and contracts in a steady rhythm. In, out. In, out. I match my breathing with hers, forcing my heart to slow its frantic beating.

Enna will be okay, just as the healer said. She just needs some time, and she'll break out of whatever this is. I have to believe that, before I fall prey to the madness.

A wash of dark color swirls in the water of the tank, darkening my view. Suddenly, Enna's skin splits along her hip, punctured with a hundred small holes. Blood spreads from the wound, flooding the water. I pound the glass with my fists, desperate to touch her, and the healer springs to action, increasing the strength of her spell. She focuses on the emerging wound, but the membrane refuses to knit back. Her spines flare, and one snaps off, dropping to the floor of the tank. The tip of her tail knots and twists, a severed hole the size of my skull splitting the fine membrane.

Chills cover my body as blood fills the tank rapidly. There goes my heart—battering against my rib cage with renewed horror.

The healer shouts for her attendants, and several magic-wielders rush in, dipping their magic into the tank. They surround Enna in a rainbow of colors, their tendrils prodding and stitching and smoothing.

As soon as they fill the wound, the flesh splits open again, refusing to mend.

I reach into the tank, clasping her hand firmly. Her skin is hot, much too hot for her normal icy touch. I squeeze, as if I might imbue my life force into hers. Her fingers twitch, her pinky wrapping around mine.

She's in there, still, my hopping beach dancer. My fighter. Shadow-guard of my heart.

Along her forearms, her spines lift from their sheathes. What I would give to be back on that beach, on the receiving end of those wicked spines. I would let her slice me a million times over. I would deal with that incessant itch for the rest of eternity, if it means she'll make it through.

"Fight, dammit!" I shout at her. "You hear me, Wicked? Whatever this is, you must fight it. You will not leave me."

Chapter Fifty-One

Enna

The dredgebeast's tongue squeezes tighter, pressing the lifeforce from my breaking body. I wriggle against her death grip, to no avail. She pulls hard, and my tail splits, ripping down the seam punctured on her tooth. The pain is sharp and everywhere all at once, but I don't have the energy to scream. A whimper escapes my lips.

You will not leave me.

A chill races down my spine as the words float down from somewhere outside myself. That voice—a deep, rumbling baritone—I would recognize it anywhere. How Soren found me here at the end, I have no idea. Maybe it's my subconscious mind, providing me with a nugget of comfort just before the lights go out.

It's always just been me, hasn't it? I look out for myself. There's no one else, has never been since the day Odissa killed my father. I'm doing it even now. How kind of me.

Dammit, Enna!

The voice is louder now. I must be close to the end.

I suppose this is true to form, dying in the fight for my life. When the beast swallows me whole, it won't be quick, and it won't be painless. I will pass into her belly, where a sea of acid will dissolve my flesh piece by piece. I will scream—if I still can—and no one will hear me but the skeletons in the dredge that lines her gut. No one can save me from this. I am completely alone, here in the moment of my death.

Like bars on a prison cell, the teeth descend, interlocking. The beast closes her jaw.

Her tongue lifts me high, the soft gray flesh of her soft palette closes in. If I was stronger, I might latch on to it with my claws, slice the beast right where it hurts. But my arms are pinned to my sides, and my mind grows weary. The beast has bested me. Let her take her prize.

FIGHT, DAMMIT! I WILL NOT LOSE YOU. YOU HAVE TO FIGHT.

Pressure at my hand, a dull squeeze. My fingers twitch; my pinky extends, wrapping firmly around something soft, warm, solid. Then the words become a Voice, the soft, mournful note vibrating through my bones.

I gasp. Warmth spreads from my stomach and with it a sudden wash of energy. It burns deeper, hotter, a raging inferno now. My arms regain their strength; my claws find purchase on the beast's leather tongue. I rip into it with fervor, and handfuls of her meat fall into the base of her mouth, sticking to her gums. She screeches—the sound penetrating my skull—and the tongue loosens enough for me to wriggle free. I dash for the roof of her mouth, finding the soft cavity behind her palette. My claws sink deep, and my frenzy begins.

Tearing piece after piece, I burrow tooth and claw into her. Her blood floods my mouth, her stench clings to my nose. Bits of her flesh clump in my hair. I swim no longer in water but in the currents of her blood. Still, I dig. My teeth crack through bone. Around me, the beast's body quivers and shakes. I can feel her shaking her head, trying to dislodge the parasite from her skull. She lifts the back of her tongue, swallowing in a sucking vortex. But I hold on tight. With every gash I make, she grows weaker, her fight lessens. Gripping the edge of an artery, I punch through it.

The beast screams, unhinging her jaw, and I'm washed out of her mouth in a tide of blood. Her great head dives toward the sea floor, crashing into the garden of bones. With a final moan, she collapses, dead. The bloodfish explode into a frenzy, attaching to every inch of her fresh meat.

I killed a dredgebeast with my bare hands.

Tephra's chuckle vibrates through the murky water. "Well done, little fish," she says. "Blood for blood, your oath is complete. Swim freely."

Darkness descends in a cloak. I blink, opening my eyes to a bright, white room. Soren's face is the first thing I see, and he's bawling like a complete idiot.

Chapter Fifty-Two

SOREN

The pool of energy in my stomach drains quickly, spiraling out of my mouth as I pull more, more, anything that might save her.

The healer's hand is firm on my shoulder. She says something, a warning maybe, but I cannot hear her.

Enna's little pinky curls tightly around mine, a lifeline in the dark. Her teeth snap together repeatedly, those fangs long and wicked. She shakes her head, body twitching. Her tail kicks, and water sloshes over. The room erupts into chaos. Still, I stay rooted by her side, that little pinky finger holding me in place.

She shrieks and then goes deathly still. Her tail flops back into the tank, hanging limply. "ENNA!" I scream. *No, no, no.* She can't leave me now. Not like this. Not after a fight like that. I will not let her.

I launch off the floor, diving into the tank to join her. The water hits me with a crack as my legs snap together, knitting into my tailfin. My gills sting from the concentration of blood in the water, but I do not care. I wrap my arms around her, pulling her into my chest. As I hum fervently, magic surrounds her, caresses her with green light, and I will her to respond. My own energy reserve hangs by a thread. With one last push, I sever my spell. I clutch her face, willing her awake with all that's left of my soul.

"Soren?" Her voice is soft, barely a whisper. The slippery scales of her tailfin shift, brushing against mine in the water.

My eyes snap open, greeted by her piercing purple gaze.

I brush her cheeks with my thumbs, marveling at the sight of her.

"You're here," I breathe, a scatter of bubbles kissing her face.

"Almost wasn't." She studies me earnestly, reaching with a shaking hand to cup my cheek. "But then I heard your voice. You told me to fight. So I did."

"Looks like you won." I push past the stone of dread sinking in my gut. Where she was or what she was fighting, I have no idea, but I hate knowing she'd been on the brink of death, and I'd been helpless.

"Thanks to you." Her eyes lock on my lips, hunger burning now in her gaze. The tips of her claws curl into my cheek, pricking and pulling me close.

Our lips collide in a heated kiss. She devours me like a savage beast starving for my mouth. I capture her tongue with my lips and suck on it hard. Her responding moan hums through me, sending a zing of pleasure along my spine. She tastes of raw meat and iron.

"I heard you, Soren," she moans into my mouth. "I was all alone and ready to die, and then you called my name."

A shiver vibrates her body, and I break our kiss to stare into her eyes. Her eyes sparkle with emotion, a wild chaos of color I've never seen before.

"I never left your side, Wicked," I whisper. "And I never intend to again. You're mine."

Her cheeks tint pink. She averts her eyes, taking in her surroundings for a moment, and then frowns. "Why the fuck are we swimming in blood?"

Chapter Fifty-Three

ENNA

Soren moves me to his bedchamber, where I pass in and out of sleep, cocooned in the yellow light streaming through his balcony doors. I'm exhausted—body and soul.

My location has caught the attention of Soren's fan club—his scowling mother, Clio, and the smug Captain Nara who stands outside his door. The females leave me to rest, for the most part, but occasionally, while I'm half-awake, the door creaks open and I can feel their gaze on me, studying from afar.

In the night, I wake to a cold wet cloth lying on my forehead. I peel my eyes open to find Clio's soft face, blurry and warm. She combs my hair, pushing sweaty strands out of my eyes before I close them and return to my fever haze.

While I fought the dredgebeast, my body was unconscious for a full day. The healer said I may take another day or two to burn off this fever and recover from the shock of magical trauma. But I don't have two days to lie in bed, not with Audrina nearing her fullness. I need to find out what happened to Odissa, and I need to make sure those bars are thick enough to hold her until Tephra claims her price.

But when I try to stand, the dizziness encroaches. Sharp pain flares in my side, and I press my hand to my stomach. A knotted circular scar puckers my skin, where I'd yanked the bloodfish free.

Soren wraps his strong hands around my waist. His breath is hot in my ear as he whispers calming words, guiding me back into the bed. I resist him, fighting the dizziness to place my feet on the cold marble floor. I cling to his forearm for stability.

"You going somewhere?"

"Where is she?" I need to find Odissa. Just as soon as I can let go of this strong, muscled arm, I'll be on my way. Visions of her squatting on the breakfast table, clutching her neck, skin reddening and boiling as she choked on dark magic. Is she still in pain? Or is she dead by now?

"Aris? Locked in the dungeon, thinking about her mistakes."

Soren's arm tightens around me, but it's my emotions that strangle. I cough against the pressure, fighting the wave of grief and terror as it anoints me with ice. I broke my blood oath. That means I wanted Odissa to fail. I wanted her dead—I still do. Right?

After all she put me through in my life, after all the emotional twisting, the verbal battering, the incessant demanding—I should want her to suffer the worst. What kind of monster kills a male, then takes his orphaned child and trains her to be a death-dealer?

I can see her, clear as water, in my memory, the moment we found my mother. We'd crossed the Drink, with the hope of meeting the mother I thought I'd never see. But she was dead when we arrived. Had been for some time. Odissa simply dragged her body from the cave and tossed it out for the bloodfish. No acknowledgment. No comfort for the grieving guppy. Just a cloud of blood and ripping teeth.

I guess you're stuck with me, now, aren't you? she'd said, almost smug.

Is Odissa thinking about me? My mouth turns metallic, and I relax my jaw.

"Not Aris. Her name is Odissa."

"Right."

I push his arm, trying to take a step forward. My body sways. His other arm steadies my back. *Trapped.* Wasn't I going to leave, after I was free of her? My blood oath no longer holds me here. I owe her nothing now. I will no longer be caged. My claws sink into his skin as I snarl.

"And what is your name?" His voice is playful, but there's a tinge of unease.

"Enna. Enna Valomir."

Soren's lips press against the top of my head. "So that's true, then."

I sway again as the dizziness returns. This time, when he steadies me, I lean into him. His skin is soft, warm, and smells of the sun. I close my eyes, inhaling the closeness of him. Soren scoops me off my feet and settles me back into the bed. My body absorbs into the plush cushion, jostling as he crawls in next to me.

His fingers swipe across my forehead, smoothing my hair. "Someday, you'll tell me the whole story. For now, you must rest."

I fight to keep my eyelids open. "I'm not a handmaid, if that's what you want to know," I mumble.

"I bet you're not a royal shadow-guard either, are you, Enna?"

I shake my head, hair rustling against the pillow. "I've killed a lot of people, Soren. I killed—" But I can't finish it. I can't tell him I killed his real princess. I killed the female he was meant to marry. If I could collect all the blood I've spilled in my lifetime, under Odissa's order, I could overflow his royal bathtub. The thought churns my stomach.

Soren brushes my bottom lip. "I figured as much. You like knives too much."

My eyelids flutter one last time before they close. I brush his chest with my nose. "Why did you bring me here?"

"To keep you safe." He pulls the sheet over me, tucking it gently over my shoulders.

"Why am I not in the dungeon? If you know I'm a killer, isn't that where I belong?"

"You belong right here. With me." His lips touch my forehead. "I told you, I'm not letting you go. Get some rest, Wicked."

I'll try again tomorrow. Once Soren leaves for his princely duties, I'll sneak out of his room and find the dungeon, find where they're keeping Odissa, and I'll tell her I'm free.

Tell her I'm not sorry. My only regret is that she's not already dead.

Chapter Fifty-Four

SOREN

"I've found her, Father. My love match." I watch the curve of his statue's lips until I imagine them twitching, curling into the smile I remember so well.

My father reveals no emotion, his expression preserved for eternity with stern, sightless eyes. I reach for him, curling my fingers around the marble shaft of his royal scepter.

She may be a killer. She's deadly; she has fangs and claws and a penchant for blood. Given the choice, she'd eat all her food wriggling and raw. She hates the sun and the heat, two things my kingdom thrives on. By all accounts, she and I should not make sense together.

But I've listened to enough *should* statements in my life, and I will not add this one to my list. Enna is the only being in the sea who has matched my fire, who has equaled me in her passion, her fight, her intelligence, and her care. If I lose her, I will never forgive myself.

Footsteps echo through the hallway, disturbing my reverie. My mother approaches, skirts hissing across the floor. Her face is hollow and weary. "The captain said you'd be here."

"Did she now?"

She stops at the base of my father's statue, staring up into his stern, marble face. "He was happier than this, wasn't he?"

I grunt. "The mouth is all wrong. Too straight."

"Indeed." She nods to the empty slab of marble next to him. "You'll be there, too, someday."

The unspoken catch drops between us: *but you need a wife first.*

"The council met this morning," she starts after a few moments of silence. "To discuss next steps. You need another suitor. Lord Almar has proposed using the pendant on every eligible female in the sea until we find your queen."

I flinch, recalling the scent of sizzling flesh, the look on Enna's face as she watched her princess boil alive. "I want that thing swallowed by the depths of the sea."

"You know, when you wore that wretched necklace, Aris wasn't the only one who spoke." My mother studies me with knowing eyes.

"Tell them there's no need." I brush my thumb over the marble handle of my father's scepter. "The council will no longer meddle in my marriage prospects. No more arrangements. No more suitors paraded into my court."

"Is this about the handmaid sleeping in your bed?"

I cannot help the grin that spreads across my face, warming me to my toes. "I love her."

"I was afraid of that," she sighs, answering my smile with one of her own. "I just hope you're right about her. Love matches are hard to find and harder to keep."

"I'm right, Mother. I can feel it in my bones."

She cups my arm and squeezes gently. "Then go get her, son. If you say she's worthy, who am I to argue with the king?"

Chapter Fifty-Five

ENNA

The dungeon smells of damp stone and rotting fish, thick and heavy with decay. Water drips from the ceiling, splashing into pools on the cobbled floor. A small rodent skitters across my path, stopping to drink, before screeching and scampering into the dark. I pick my way through the narrow passage. Odissa is held in one of these cells.

Cold water, I can handle. Cold air, however, turns me into a chattering box of teeth. If Odissa is down here, she'll hear me coming before I round the corner.

I clench my jaw to stop the rattling and step over a puddle. The dark path slopes downward steadily, burrowing deep into the bowels of the palace. The further I walk, the stronger the stench grows, mixing with urine. Eventually, the puddles grow larger and deeper until a shallow pool covers the stones. I slosh into the brown water until it reaches my knees, then thighs. My bones snap and rearrange, and I submerge.

I click my inner eyelid shut to keep out the sting of the pungent water. Then the moaning begins. Barred cages line the path, each full of either the remains of mermaids or mermaids on the verge of death. I use my hands to crawl through the shallow water and pull myself down the path until the water deepens enough to swim freely.

A merman slithers to the bars as I pass, reaching with knotted fingers to snatch at my fin. I avoid it, sinking down to his eye level. I wrap my hands around the slime-coated bars to anchor in place.

"Tell me where I can find the newcomer," I whisper. "Abyssal siren, pale white skin." The prisoner glares up at me with hollow eyes. He's unlike any merman I've seen before—his skin is green as reedgrass. Small, withering leaves sprout along his scalp, hanging in unkempt strands. His splotchy tail curls limply on the floor of his cell. What is an Estuary merman doing here?

"A dozen cells that way," he gurgles, nodding down the hall. "The one at the end." He coughs loudly, spewing a cloud of brown bubbles. The force of his movement causes a dead leaf to fall from his scalp, floating aimlessly through the water.

"Thank you," I say, but he doesn't answer.

I count the cells as I approach, formulating my speech. I almost died trying to escape our blood oath, and I refuse to be her puppet any longer. She can spoil in here for all I care, I'll tell her. I won't kill her—that would be too easy. I'll let her rot until tonight's high tide, and when Tephra comes to claim her dues, I'll be right here, watching.

Yeah, that's good.

Odissa's voice filters through the murk before I reach her cell. "I thought I smelled regret. Look who's come to apologize."

She hovers in a cage of metal and stone. Her silver tail treads the dirty water, like a spoon stirring sludge. Her hair is plucked clean of its adornments, hanging now in a long, knotted mess around her face. Her eyes are sunken and dark. The princess's once-pretty face twists into Odissa's signature scowl. Her neck and hands mottle with burned skin, oozing with thick white slime.

"I'm not here to apologize."

Her voice manipulates to mimic my words from that breakfast. "*She's not the real princess, Soren.* Bah! Traitor!" She lunges for the bars of her cage, fingers wrapping around the metal. Her knuckles pale with the pressure of her grip.

I hold my distance, floating just out of her reach. "You were going to hurt him. He needed to know."

Odissa rolls her eyes. "I wasn't. Not right away. I was going to suck him dry, slowly, over the long span of his life."

"And then?"

"You betrayed me, Enna! We had a fucking deal, and you revealed me to the enemy."

"I paid my price. And now, I'll watch you pay yours." I sink to the stone floor, settling in to wait for Tephra to come. "I'm free of you, Odissa."

"I should have killed you." Odissa sneers. "I should have slit your throat, just the same as I did to your fucking scum parents."

"Parents?"

Odissa tips her head up, laughing with a cloud of dirty bubbles. "You never figured it out?"

My mind churns, reeling backward through time. "My mother hired you to kill my father?"

She flashes me a wicked smile. "No."

I replay the sequence of events of that fateful day. Odissa infiltrated my father's house and killed him with a knife to the throat. Instead of killing me, too, she took pity on me. She decided to take me home to meet my mermaid mother, the female who hired the death deal.

"Your cunt mother was running her trap at the tavern, bragging about how she secured a good life for her half-blood daughter. Lord Valomir's littlest pet. She made it too easy."

We found my mother dead in a cave. She'd been dead for days. Realization dawns with a sharp pain in my chest. "You killed her," I whisper, unable to muster more volume.

"You had something I never did. Those looks—you can sneak into places I could never go. The perfect camouflage. I needed you. I needed a stupid little half-breed guppy, someone I could train. Someone I could break." She says this like it's obvious. And maybe it was, all along.

I hear her voice filtering through the haze of memory—*"Once we get your first kill out of the way, you and I will be unstoppable. Just think of the things we could do together. We could dismantle the Abyssal Kingdom, siren by siren; make them grovel in the dark, make them bleed. Would you like that?"*

This life she offered, I knew I would like it very much. The quiet, vulnerable guppy within me cowered with terror as my desire for vengeance grew. It expanded and flexed, stretching to fill every inch of me, suffocating my childish fear. My fingers tingled with new warmth.

"*If I do this, I'd become a—*" Murderer. Monster. The words stung as they cut through my young mind. And still, that feeling inside me stretched and purred, liking the sound of it. I wanted it. Desperately.

Odissa studies me through the bars of her dungeon cage, waiting for my reaction. My magic stirs in my stomach, a weak supply after days in a fever.

"You monster!"

Odissa smirks. "Yes. But there are worse things to be than deadly." She's quoting the same thing she said to me then.

Anger burns hot in my veins. My spines flex out of their sheathes, ready to defend. Or attack. "You robbed an innocent guppy of a better life."

Everything Odissa taught me has been a lie. Since the day I met her twenty years ago, I've been living in an illusion of her careful design.

"Robbed you? I saved your life. I gave you a purpose. You should be thanking me."

Who does this bitch think she is? I draw my blade, lunging for the cage. The bars catch my face, cold and slimy. I thread my arm through the gaps, swiping with my knife.

But Odissa swims to the back of her cage, calm and smug, where I cannot reach her. My blade cuts the water, snaring nothing but a rush of bubbles.

"You'll never be free of me, Enna." Her grin spreads wider. "I'm going to haunt you for the rest of your miserable life."

I grip my knife, pulling my arm back. I turn away from her, swimming up the way I came. I will not stay here all day, drowning in her lies. The water clogs my gills, and my head grows light and weary. I crawl up the stones, gasping as the damp dungeon air fills my lungs and my tail rips in half.

I will never see Odissa again. Tephra will claim her in the night, and I will live on. Tomorrow, I will wake to a sea without her in it, and that will have to be good enough.

Chapter Fifty-Six

SOREN

Enna curls into a fetal position outside my door, lying in a puddle of grime. Water drips from her hair, rolling off her bare skin. Her shoulders tremble, and she hugs her arms to her chest. Her spines flex in and out of their sheathes, a nub appearing where her broken one used to be.

Captain Nara squats beside her, shooting me a panicked look. Her hands hover over Enna, hesitant to touch.

"What happened?" I demand, storming down the hallway.

My newest guard cowers in the corner, looking like someone pissed in his lushfruit tea. Enna is lying in a puddle, and my guard service stands there, supervising her misery. He splutters excuses as I approach. I cut him short with a hand around his neck. His eyes widen under my grip.

"Fetch the servants. My lady requires a warm bath." I crouch beside Nara. "He's discharged."

She nods. "I already told him that."

With the back of my hand, I brush Enna's forehead. She jerks at my touch, her eyes flying open. Shadows dance across her tired face. Her gaze rises to meet mine for a moment, then her eyelids close again.

"Any ideas?" I ask Nara.

The captain sighs. "She hasn't been here long. There's a trail of grime up the stairway. Looks like she crawled here from the dungeon. No signs of injury that I can see."

Enna's mouth curls down at the corners, and my heart aches to see her so unhappy. I lift her to her feet, folding her into my chest. Her skin smells pungent. I inhale again and—"You smell of dead fish."

Nara unlocks my bedchamber door, kicking it open with a promise to keep watch.

I walk Enna gently toward my bathtub. She nuzzles underneath my chin, and my breath hitches. Already I can feel my heart slowing, lulling me into that sense of wholeness whenever she's in my arms.

"She's a monster," she whispers. Her lips brush the skin of my neck. "She always has been. You should have killed her."

"You saw Odissa." I shudder at the image of my Enna, swimming in the gunk of the dungeon.

Servants rush past me, dropping warm stones into the bath, setting out fresh towels, mopping Enna's puddle on the floor. I set her at its edge, shifting her so I can see her face. "Hey, look at me."

Her eyes open, brimming with fresh pain. I stroke her cheek, plowing a clean line through the dirt.

"Let's get you cleaned up. Then you can tell me everything."

She nods slowly.

With a towel, I wipe the grime from her face, her neck, her chest.

"Thank you," she whispers. The towel brushes across her nipples, and they pucker. She sighs and leans against me.

"Do you want to talk about it?" I settle behind her, pulling her into my chest, and work to clean her stomach.

She nods, sucking in a breath, and then her words rush out. Enna recounts her life in the Drink, her miserable guppy phase, then her parents' murder. Odissa and the oath bound in blood. 2,747 kills. How she can remember the face of each one. Then, finally, the deal they made with Tephra.

My pulse quickens. I lift her arm, wiping her clean. Moving the towel down each leg, threading between her toes, I then reach between her thighs.

"Soren, there's one more thing... I killed your princess." She grows still in my arms, waiting for my reaction.

I consider her words for a moment, the impossibility of it all, the violent twists of fate that brought my Enna here, into my arms.

"You killed her," I say, testing the words aloud as the reality sets in—I'm in love with an Abyssal death-dealer.

She straightens in my arms. "I'm sorry," she says, her voice suddenly cold. She leans away from me, ready to stand. "If you no longer want anything to do with me, I understand."

"She didn't deserve to die." I wrap my arm around her waist, pulling her back into my embrace. "And you didn't have a choice."

She shakes her head.

"Tell me, what was she like?"

"You're not mad?"

"Humor me, Wicked."

Enna thinks for a moment. "Gentle. Soft. She didn't even fight me in the end. A real princess, worthy of your hand." Her voice cracks, and she clears her throat.

"I'm sure she was." I trace the curve of her arm, her muscles flexing under my touch. "But that doesn't make you less worthy of me." Her spines lift, and I trail my finger along their sharp edges. I nuzzle into her neck, nipping at the skin that covers her gills. *"Mine."*

She shifts, and her ass presses against my growing erection. I reach around her, unhooking the clasp of her belt and freeing the loincloth.

"Soren," she moans.

"Let's get you clean, Wicked," I whisper into her hair. "Care for a bath?"

She twists in my embrace, and her hands loosen the tie on my shirt. "That depends, Your Highness," she says, a note of humor in her voice. I sigh in relief at the sound of it. "Will you be joining me?"

"Get in the water," I whisper, shoving her. She splashes into the pool, transforming from the plunge. I strip out of my pants and dive in after her.

We circle, devouring each other with our eyes. She traces the walls with skirting fingers. Her black tail flicks lazily, turning her at the corners. I flex my muscles, and her eyes note the movement, missing nothing. I get the sense I'm caught in a cage with a predator.

With each turn around the pool, the world shifts and clicks into place. I understand Enna with clarity. The skillful flex of her fins, the shift of her weight to glide, soundless—each movement with a fluid grace she's mastered over her life in the Drink. Not as a royal handmaid, not as a shadow-guard, but as a lawless killer.

Why does that turn me on?

My cock strains against its scaled sheath, desperate to bury in her heat. Her nostrils flare as she scents my arousal.

"Do you want me, pretty prince?" Her voice drops low, blooming with seduction.

I shudder. "Yes."

With a growl, she launches herself at me. Her fingers knot into my hair. Her mouth meets mine in a battle of tongue and teeth. We ravish each other thoroughly while our gills do the hard work of breathing. We moan in unison as she presses her body against the length of mine. The tips of our tails twine together, soft and smooth. Her scales glides against my hidden sheath and my cock stiffens to attention.

I groan, and she angles herself, teasing me with the touch of her slick slit. In this form, every nerve ending is a live wire.

My cock slips through the thin membrane of my sheath, hard and ready for her. It's longer and thicker in my tail form, curved and coated in hard scales to reach deep inside her. She eyes it with wonder, and her fingers find the velvety tip. She strokes over the scales there, her careful touch a shocking contrast to the fire in her eyes.

Her fangs prick my bottom lip. "Claim me."

I position myself at the entrance of her slit, growing harder when I brush against her heat. She's soft and ready for me, already slick with need. I slip inside, filling her to the brim. Her channel in this form is deep but narrow, and the soft walls clamp down tight around me.

"You're so tight, Wicked. So tight and wet."

She moans, twisting into me so that our tails slide, nudging my cock deeper. Her eyes roll. "*Goddess*, I thought you were huge before," she whispers. Her walls flutter around me, flexing to accommodate my size.

"There is no goddess here," I growl. "Only you, my love, and I intend to worship you."

She whimpers at my words. I kick my tail and rock into her, slow and firm, gradually building my momentum. Her tail wraps around mine, her hands tighten in my hair, and she clutches me as I rock her world.

I take my time worshipping her body. My hands roam her soft skin, tracing the circumference of each scale. I take inventory of every part of her, from the velvety tips of her nipples, the soft underside of her breasts, to the joint of her hip, with a soft, puckered scar where her wound had been. My thumb passes over the spot, and she shivers, tightening her grip on me. I drive into her again and again, until her walls grow unbearably tight. Pleasure builds deep in my belly with every thrust. Then, with a gasp, she clamps down hard. She bursts with a rush of heat, and she writhes against me, milking my own pleasure from me. We come together in waves, steadily crashing against each other until we slow and settle to the bottom of the pool, two limp bodies in a warm sea.

I hook my thumb under her chin and tilt her face. Her eyes are wide and searching, blissed-out. I hum at seeing her so bright, so alive. "I want nothing more than to spend the rest of my life being devoured by you. Slowly, one scale at a time. My heart is yours."

The words flood me with a thrill of pleasure. I stare at her, memorizing every inch of her face. She has sunk her little teeth into me, body and soul, and I never want her to loosen her hold.

And tonight, I will make her my queen.

Chapter Fifty-Seven

ENNA

I tell him everything. I lay my soul, my past, my sins bare. Every bloody detail. And still, he wraps me in a warm towel and holds me close, unafraid of the monster lurking within me. He wraps his arm around my waist, tucking me into his side, and we sit on his balcony to watch the sunset. I'll never deserve him, this kind, cocky prince.

The city below rustles with evening activity. Merfolk strolls the beach. Vendors pack up their booths. Birds chirp from their perches among the abodes, singing one last tribute to the sun.

We sit on a blanket, complete with a dinner spread from the kitchen. The baskets of fruit and bread and plates of fish tempt me with their warm aroma, but my stomach twists in revulsion. Beyond the railing, the faint outline of Audrina's face peeks over the horizon, preparing to ascend.

"Front-row seat," Soren says, nodding to the full moon. He picks up a roll of bread and picks it apart with his fingers.

I tuck my towel tighter around me and hug my knees. Ever since we finished our bath, I've had a sinking feeling in my stomach. The feeling that I've forgotten something, somehow. The breeze lifts the leaves on the twisting vine that climbs the palace wall, and I flinch.

Soren pauses, holding a half-eaten roll. "Something out there?"

I squint at the vine, searching for any unusual movement among the twitching green leaves. A stray petal drops from one of the pink blooms. "Nothing," I say. "Just a funny feeling."

He pulls me close, pressing a kiss to my hair. "She can't hurt you anymore, Enna. She's in the dungeon where she'll rot until high tide, like you said."

I pick a roll and separate the dough. The bread is buttery and warm on my tongue. I chew it slowly, letting the flavor wash through my mouth. "I want to see her die."

"Of course you do, Wicked." Soren chuckles, running a hand through his long, damp hair. "Tell you what. After dinner, we can visit her, and you can taunt her all you like until the goddess shows up."

I smile into my bread. "I'd like that." Earlier today, when I saw her alone, I went soft. I let her get into my head. With Soren at my side, I will be stronger. With my words, I will make her writhe.

"On one condition," Soren adds. "I have something to show you. A detour on our way to watch the shit show."

"It better be good."

I eye him sideways, and a goofy grin plasters his face. "Oh, it will be dazzling."

Whatever that means. We finish off the bread, half the lushfruit, and two whole sweetfish as the sun retreats into darkness.

With our bellies full and hearts warm, we start down the hallway. Soren reaches for my hand, and I thread my fingers through the gaps in his. Our palms brush, and he squeezes my hand. "A perfect fit," he says.

We descend the stairs. Captain Nara rushes around the bend. Her maroon eyes are focused, her mouth set in a hard line. We skirt sideways to avoid a collision, and the mermaid stops short, grasping Soren's arm.

"Your Highness!"

Soren steadies her with a hand to her shoulder. "What's wrong?"

Nara shakes her head. "There's been an accident. She's dead. One of my soldiers found her in a pool of blood. Not ten minutes ago."

Odissa, dead? The scales on my neck tingle. "Show me the body," I say. I won't believe it until I see the corpse, dead and dissolving. This could be an act, a ploy to lure the prince close enough to stab him.

The captain blinks at me in surprise, a smile curling the corners of her mouth.

Soren squeezes my hand. "You sure?"

"I'm not a helpless female, pretty prince." I shoot him a dark look. "Show me the blood."

The captain turns back the way she came and leads us through the darkening corridors. Sconces flicker with low flames, casting long shadows that stretch and dance as we walk past. The palace settles with a deathly silence, as if holding its breath before the scream.

"Clio was near the guest wing," Nara whispers as we ascend the marble staircase.

The sickness in my stomach returns, twisting with renewed intuition. "Clio?" I whisper.

Nara nods. "That's right. Poor thing."

I trail my hand along the golden rail, walking the same path I've followed a hundred times. I can smell the blood from here, sharp and metallic. My pulse flutters in anticipation, loud in my ears.

Nara pushes open the door to the hallway. Odissa's old room is the last door on the right. And outside it, face-first in a pool of blood, the housekeeper lies with a messy gash in her neck. Clio's large blue ears, once fluttering with expression, droop lifelessly onto the floor. Her hand curls into a fist, save one finger, stretching to point toward the door.

She wasn't an awful person. She was annoying and clingy, and she had a bad habit of disapproving everything I did, but she didn't deserve to go like this. My throat tightens the longer I look at her.

How soft I've become.

"Nasty way to go." The captain grunts. "May the gods accept her gladly."

Soren murmurs something similar, his fists balling tightly at his sides.

I kneel next to the housekeeper's body and ruffle through her wound, assessing the nature of the kill. No blade would leave a gash like this. Clio died by tooth and hand. The imprint of the killer's round teeth surrounds the wound. The flesh is ragged and torn.

There's nothing clean about this kill. I lean on my hand for support as I scan the hallway for signs of Odissa. That tricky little bitch. I should have known a cell would never hold her. She may look like a royal on the outside, but at her core, she's just as much death-dealer as I am. And her clock is ticking.

"You're not safe here." I turn to Soren. He stares at the housekeeper with a blank expression.

"It was her, wasn't it?"

I nod, fingering the flesh of Clio's wound. "Odissa is messy. No one else would kill this way."

"Right." The captain lets out a hissing breath. "Your Highness, we must get you to safety."

Chapter Fifty-Eight

SOREN

"Nara, find someone to care for the body. A proper dissolvement."

Nara shoots me an empathetic wince. "Understood, Your Highness, but your safety is my first concern."

"Here I am, in the middle of my own palace, with the two fiercest females in the sea. I'm not worried."

Enna stands, wiping her bloody hands on her clean, white skirt. "There must be somewhere secure for you to hide, Soren. Just for tonight. The danger will pass after high tide. She'll be looking for you until then."

I draw her hands into mine, rubbing my thumbs over the back. Her spines flex in and out, restless. "And for you."

"She only came here for your throne, and now you've taken it away from her. She will kill you, given the chance."

"Neither of you are safe," Nara says. "I'll see what I can do to track her down before then. I cannot allow a killer to run loose through the palace, endangering my staff, just because we think some goddess will descend from the sky."

Enna shakes her head again, so I pinch her chin, stopping the refusal in its tracks. Her jaw clenches under my touch. "I'll track her." She flicks her eyes to the captain. "You're persistent, I'll give you that. But I know Odissa's ticks."

"And leave me alone in a cage? I don't think so, Wicked. If I'm going into hiding, then you're coming with me." I already have a spot in mind. The romance may be ruined for the evening, but I can at least show her the royal vault. I know of a knife or two in there Enna would melt to see. "We can have some fun."

She tugs her jaw out of my grip. "I'm going to find Odissa."

Stubborn female. "You want me to hide? I have the perfect spot in mind, and you're coming with me," I growl, grabbing her by the waist. I sling her over my shoulder and march down the hall. "Nara, we'll be locked in the vault."

"Soren!" Enna snaps. Her hands scrabble against my back, accompanied by her furious grunting. "Soren, let me go!"

I slap my palm onto her plump ass, and she squeaks. My cock hardens at the sound. If she wants to hide out with me, then fine. I rest my hand on her ass, smoothing the sting. She jostles as I reach the stairs, and her panicked words come out in short bursts.

Enna twists her head, sinking her teeth into the skin of my arm. I slap her ass again. If she really wanted to escape, she would. She settles then, her body relaxing under my grip.

We pass a cluster of guards, and they watch us with widening eyes. The hallway darkens, lit only by a few scattered sconces. The air is damp down here, the stone walls carved deep into the floor of the sea. At the end of the tunnel sits a thick, iron door, locked with an intricate magical mechanism.

The siren guard at the door shifts at our approach, avoiding staring too much.

Enna squirms again, and I adjust my grip, slinging her forward into my arms. Her legs wrap around my hips.

"You missed the point," she whispers. "She'll try to kill you. It's what Odissa does when she loses; she takes everyone down with her."

"Not if you have anything to say about it, hmm?" I grip her ass and bend my mouth to her ear. "The way I see it, we're going to go into this room and we're going to hide, just like you want. Because I have a plan for us this evening, and I'm not about to let some killer from the Drink get in our way of a good time. Now tell me, Wicked, are you going to stand in the way?"

Enna shakes her head. My lips brush against her ear, and I exhale. The scales along the back of her neck rise.

"Never ask me to leave you again," I whisper. "As if I could exist without you by my side. As if we could breathe without the same air. I need you like a fish needs water. You are my Audrina, directing the course of my tides. Face it, little thief. You've stolen my heart. Where you go, I go. You can't rid me so easily."

Her eyes melt before me, warm and needy. She tangles her fingers in my hair. "Is this your brilliant hideaway, then? The basement?"

With a growl, I clamp my lips over her wicked mouth, punishing her for not taking this moment seriously. Our tongues slide together, and we feast on each other as if we're starved for weeks. Her nails scrape over my skin, dragging me closer. Her lips taste of passion, hunger, and something darker. I search the wet cavity of her mouth for that darkness, determined to blot it out with my tongue. Her fangs cut the side of my tongue, and my blood swirls in her mouth.

"Soren." She moans my name, her voice still tinged with anxiety. The two should not exist in the same space.

I cup her face. Her lip trembles. I suck it between mine to stop the anxious movement, but when I look to see the effect of my efforts, it continues its restless quiver.

"Come. I have something to show you."

She unfolds herself from my waist and drops to the floor. I take her hand in mine, my heart squeezing in anticipation as we face the door to the royal vault. Inside, she'll have her choice of the royal jewels, and I'll have my queen at last.

"This is better than the basement, Wicked. This is the door to your future and my undoing."

With a steady, ringing Voice, I sing the song of my ancestors. The mechanism on the door unlatches with a grating creak and a thudding boom.

Chapter Fifty-Nine

ENNA

The room brims with jewels in a glittering display of wealth gathered over millennia. Towering marble walls stretch toward a ceiling I can hardly see, each wall carved with thousands of pockets in the rock. Gems and jewelry display within the pockets, arranged with delicate care to highlight each object's best feature in the dim, sparkling light. Weapons line the far wall: a crumbling trident, a diamond-encrusted scythe, and a tantalizing array of polished daggers.

A pedestal sits in the center of the room, lavished in velvet and holding a glass bell jar. Under the jar, the whitesteel shell pendant glints, misting with magic.

Soren grazes my back, tracing the path of my spine, and the flutters subside. He nudges me further into the chamber. "What do you think? See anything you like?"

I eye the daggers in the back of the room and imagine how it would feel to have a collection that large.

Soren follows my gaze and chuckles. He takes my hand to lead me closer. Our palms brush, and my heart leaps into a frenzy. I nearly forget about the knives until we come to a stop at the base of the wall.

"Let me guess which one is your favorite," he says.

We survey the options: kukris and dirks, trailing blades and clips, a hawkbill with a double serrated edge. A needlepoint dagger catches my eye, thin enough to slip through ribs, light enough to avoid drag in the water. The bone hilt carves into the figure of a female. Her tail wraps around the handle, framing a single red jewel.

"This belonged to Amura," Soren says, following my gaze. "She was our first queen and a strong *fighter*." He lifts the knife from its hook and weighs it, then extends it to me. "It's yours."

"Mine?" The red jewel glints in the dim light of the room, taunting and delicious. I reach for the hilt.

Soren folds my fingers around the carved handle, his hand warm against mine. He guides it to my hip, where I attach the leather sheath to my belt. His body presses against my back, and suddenly I am warm all over. The damp chill of the room dissipates until it's just me and his body heat, the brush of his skin against mine. His breath skitters over my shoulder as he bends to kiss my neck.

"Enna," he whispers. His lips trace the slope of my neck, landing in the pocket between my shoulder and collarbone. I lean into him, exposing more of that delicate flesh for him to explore. "I want to—I need to—" He grunts and shakes his head.

"Fish got your tongue?" I tease.

"Not just any fish, Wicked." He laughs. "It's you. You've hooked me so deeply; I fear I may never rip free."

My spines flex, lifting from their sheaths.

"We may be hiding from my uncertain demise, but I meant to bring you here tonight. Here, in the hall of my ancestors, to ask you an important question."

His hands skim the length of my spines, shaking with nerves.

I turn to face him, placing my hand on his chest. He stares down at me with wild, thirsty eyes, as if he's on the brink of dying and I'm his spring of eternal life.

"This dagger is nice, but I was thinking something more..." He turns me around, grasping my shoulders. With a gentle push, he leads me to a wall of jewelry. "Official."

We stop before a cluster of rings, housed in a pocket carved from the white stone wall. Hundreds of rings. Each one nestles in its own velvet bed. The gems glimmer in the dim light—each a different color, different metal. Some large, some small. My mouth waters at the lavishness of them.

Slowly, Soren reaches for one with a shimmering, opal stone, the very same I would have picked for myself. He holds it flat on his palm, the soft curves of the silver band ominous in the dark lighting. He meets my eyes and the corner of his mouth curls into a smile.

Then he settles onto one knee, taking my hand into his. His thumb brushes over my knuckles, and my heart flutters.

When he speaks again, his mouth cherishes every syllable. "Enna, my beautiful darkness. Queen of my heart. I offer you this ring as a token of my devotion. I'd very much like to marry you."

His voice penetrates to the deepest parts of me and tugs on some plug within my heart. All the feelings I've kept locked up tight—hope, joy, love—swirl and rush for the opening. It all trickles out, washing through every dry crevice within me. I'm standing on dry land, here in the bowels of a foreign palace, and I've never felt more saturated.

Soren looks at me expectantly, his thumb tracing the back of my hand. I part my lips, my answer at the ready, and then—

A whispered Voice. Grinding gears. A soft grunt. Slow gliding of leather against stone. My ears prick toward the door. I lock eyes with Soren, his brimming with hope.

"She's here," I whisper.

If Soren wasn't such a goddessdamn beast of a male, I would pick him up myself and carry him out of this room. If Odissa is here, then he needs to be as far away from here as possible, somewhere safe. Where he can disappear until Tephra comes to claim Odissa's soul.

Soren stands, nudging me behind him, placing himself as a barrier between me and the doorway.

Odissa glides into the chamber on silent feet, wreathed in candlelight and holding a bloody trident. Her mottled hand flexes around the long, golden handle, caked in dried blood. Her hair is loose and wild, stained with grime and gore. Behind her, the body of the magic-wielder bleeds on the marble, his eyes wide and glassy.

"This doesn't look like an apology, Enna. I brought you here to help me, and you fucked my prince."

"You're not welcome here, Aris. Or do you prefer Odissa?" Soren spits.

"It seems the fish is out of the net. Unsurprising."

Odissa catalogs his posture—his arm curling protectively around me. My stomach churns as her expression changes from her usual apathy into undiluted rage. She glares at me, as if she might murder me with a single look.

"Oh, this is grand. He thinks he loves you. Ha! YOU!" Odissa's voice is as piercing and cold as the Drink. "Enna Valomir, whatever should I do with you?"

"Speak her name again, and I'll rip out your throat." Soren steps forward, the picture of a predator, with clenched fists.

She cocks her head. "I've always wanted a guardfish. You've trained this one well. Tell me, were you planning to loot him before or after you turn down that heart-warming proposal? Because I can't imagine the trench-scum I know would be in this room for any reason other than the money. That was our original deal, was it not? Help me win the prince's heart and then you can finally run."

"I paid my blood price." My lips curl around the words, snarling. "You didn't win his heart. I did."

"Don't make me kill you, Enna. I have a job to finish."

Bad things usually happen in slow motion: the moment I made my first kill, the moment the dredgebeast impaled me on its tooth.

This moment is no different. Odissa grins from ear to ear, her teeth glinting with yellow flame. Her muscles tense, then bend, then snap. With a whistle of stale wind, the trident spirals across the room, straight for Soren's heart.

Chapter Sixty

SOREN

Enna slams into my side. Her shoulder connects with the hard plane of my ribs and I teeter off balance a split second before the trident whizzes past my face. The tip of the trident grazes my shoulder with a burst of searing pain. Blood sprays my face. Metal clatters as it collides with the wall of knives behind me.

I hit the floor with a grunt. Enna lands next to me, narrowly avoiding several knives now scattered on the floor.

"Soren!" Her hands find my arm, slicking with my blood. I groan, rolling to look at her. Her eyes flood with fear, hurt, anger.

I roll my shoulder and gasp as the pain throbs through the muscles. There's a deep gash missing from my shoulder, a bloody trench carved out by the trident's tine. "Just a scratch," I tell her. "I've had worse." I try to roll my shoulder but cannot. My left arm hangs limply by my side, dead weight. A whimper escapes through my lips as I push off the floor, standing with great effort.

Odissa curses, marching on. Her eyes flash with chaos, darting around the room. She grabs the glass bell jar and hurls it at me with a manic screech. The glass shatters on the floor, the spray of shards slicing across my legs.

I hiss as the blood swells and the residual sting settles in. Enna grasps a knife and takes aim. The blade slices a piece of Odissa's hair, narrowly missing her ear.

"You don't really want me dead, do you? You would have hit me if you did." Odissa pauses, eyeing the cushion where the bell jar had been. With slow, bloody fingers, she picks up the necklace. She eyes me, and with a smile, lifts the necklace above her head.

"No!" My Voice extends with rapid speed, slicing through the air. But I'm too late. As soon as the pendant touches her skin, I cut off the sound with a clack of my teeth. With that necklace on, my magic is more a danger than a useful tool.

Teeth bared, eyes flashing, she zigzags across the room, dodging Enna's flying knives as she tries to reach me. Enna empties her personal arsenal in seconds, but Odissa dodges them all, save a slice on her arm, another across her cheek. Not enough to stop her.

I heft the discarded trident with my good hand, settling into my fighting crouch as Odissa draws near.

"Your heart is mine, princeling," she growls. "And I will take it, dead or alive."

She scoops up one of Enna's knives and hurls it back. The blade lodges into Enna's thigh, and she stumbles.

With a screech and flail of limbs, Odissa launches toward me. I stab with the trident, but she's faster. Like a clingerfish, she latches to my chest and sinks her blunt teeth into my open wound. I bite back a silent scream as the pain sears through me. I whack her with the broad side of the trident, but she stays hooked on, her legs tight around my waist, her hands burrowing into my hair, those teeth biting deeper and deeper into my flesh. I seize her by her scalp and pull until a chunk of her hair releases, blonde and bloody. Still, she clings firmly.

Enna crawls along the floor, dripping blood. She reaches for a discarded dagger, glaring at Odissa with hatred. I turn my body, giving her a better shot. She hurls the knife, striking true. The blade lodges between Odissa's ribs.

I wait for Odissa, now gurgling and spitting blood, to loosen and fall. But she reaches behind her, grasping the hilt of the knife, and dislodges it. She smiles at me as she twists in my arms, trailing the tip of the blade across my chest. She circles my heart, cutting a thin, stinging line.

"Forgot your next line, Soren? Pity. You were never very good at pageantry."

One wrong move, and that blade will sink into its mark. I study the plane of her cheek, weighing the repercussions of an attack on her.

"You could have made this easy, Soren. Painless. But you didn't choose that path, did you? You chose the half-blood traitor."

My fist connects with her cheek with a crack of bone. Her head snaps back and two teeth break free, but the punch seems to have little effect on her resolve. The skin around her eye begins to swell. She coughs and spits the teeth out, tightening her grip with her legs. Her fingers dig into my wound, and I clamp my teeth, eyes stinging with the pain.

My vision swirls, dots of color pricking my line of sight. My chest squeezes in panic as I realize I've lost track of Enna's position in the room.

"Careful, prince. I hold your life in my hands. If you will not love me, you will bleed for me. You will *boil* for me."

Her feet jab into the pit of my knees, and I buckle from the impact. Teetering sideways, I land on my good arm. Odissa pins me to the floor with her knees. The pendant dangles between us, taunting me with its seeking red glow.

"This heart is mine in the name of the goddess. I will carve it out of you if I must," she says. "Tephra said I must win your heart? So be it."

I glare into her cold, hostile eyes. I cannot speak it aloud for Enna to hear my dying confession. Even if I knew this is how it all would end, I would still choose her. Again and again, I choose her. My heart is hers already. What right does Odissa have to it?

I try to suck in a breath, but the air does not come. I kick my legs and twist my torso—anything to wriggle free. But nothing hits my mark. My energy drains by the second; my vision clouds with darkness.

The sting of the blade leaves my skin as she winds up for the stab that will kill me. And in that moment, I feel an overwhelming sense of regret—sorrow for the life I might have led with Enna; mourning all that time I wasted before making her mine.

She would have made a great queen.

Chapter Sixty-One

ENNA

When I was ten, the day before Odissa murdered my father and destroyed my world, he told me to swim away and never come back. He was tired of my mermaid shit, he'd said. Tired of training a worthless half-breed to act like a siren. Tired of seeing me toddle on my wobbly two legs and struggle with my magic. I would never pass in an Abyssal court as the real thing.

He grabbed me by my hair and pulled me close, spitting the words in my face. His breath smelled of liquor. He did not see me, not then. He looked at me and saw *her*. My father was always afraid my mother would find me some day. He feared she'd sink her mermaid claws into me, drag me into the depths, and seduce me into a life of depravity and lust—just as she had done to him.

I didn't listen to him that night when he told me to leave him. I waited for the magic to drain him, waited for him to release his grip, to fall into a stupor in his leather office chair, and I took away his knives, rum, and ropes. I hid them in the garbage chute like I always did.

When he got like that, he wasn't the father I loved. The person who sometimes sat me in his lap and bounced me on his knee, ran his fingers through my long silky hair, telling me far-fetched stories of fighting monsters in the Drink.

Would I have left him, had I known what would come next? I thought I was safe there, hidden from the watchful eye of Vespyr. But the Drink couldn't separate me from the wrath of Vespyr forever. Servants talk, secrets spread, and soon enough, trouble found us.

Odissa found us.

And I watched as everything I knew and loved ended in an instant.

I had no fight in me then, and as Odissa led me across the Drink, I vowed to never be caught weak in love again. I would become the monster my father feared I would be—so hard and loveless that when I visited my memories of him or imagined Odissa dragging her knife across his throat, I could look him in the eye of my memory and feel nothing.

Loving my father ended in pain. My love for him felt like cold and cutting numbness, and I'd tread the icy waters of my grief until the day I stepped onto that beach and Soren began to thaw my frigid heart.

This is not the same love. My love for Soren is all-consuming, brighter, and more beautiful than anything I've ever imagined. And if I lose him now, the sea will boil with the heat of my rage.

Odissa chokes my Soren with her knee. He flails his legs weakly in an attempt to kick her off.

I am no longer that helpless guppy, and I will not run from a fight. I will not hesitate to protect the one I love, for I am no longer alone in this world. My feelings, my safety—they shrink in proportion to a new, clearer focus.

That choked sob, stifled now by the weight of Odissa's knee on his neck, will be the end of her.

I push onto my hands and knees, gritting my teeth through the searing heat as my muscle flexes around the foreign blade buried in my leg. Step by agonizing step, I drag myself across the floor. Odissa lifts the knife in her hand, aiming for Soren's heart, and I attack.

I wrap my body around hers with blunt, barreling force. My legs snake around her hips, my hands around her neck, and I tear her away from him like a bloodfish from my side. The knife clatters to the floor seconds before we hit and roll, scrabbling into a fury of slashing nails and teeth.

Odissa's hand twines in my hair, and she yanks, but I do not release her from my wrath. I find the soft flesh of her face and dig in my claws, drawing deep, bloody gashes. Her blood runs thick and wet, and I revel in the sight of it.

"Back off, Enna," she spits, spraying blood on my face. "You should know better than to get between a death-dealer and her prey."

Her fist connects with my cheek, sending a starburst of pain through my head. I twist to avoid the full impact, and my vision grows fuzzy. Still, I grab her by the neck, curling my fingers. Her pulse flutters manically under my touch. As she coughs, blood drips into her mouth, and she swipes her tongue over her lips, drawing it in.

With an impressive twist of her body, Odissa slips her legs beneath me and kicks. Hard. My claws scrape through the skin of her throat as I'm torn away from her, flung into the air. I land with a half-assed roll, colliding with the wall of weapons. The display rattles, loosening sharp blades. A gilded scepter clatters to the floor, narrowly missing my stomach. The scepter tapers into a sharp point, caging a solid, red jewel. And despite the horror of the moment, despite the stakes at hand if I fail, as I assess its potential for use as a weapon, I grin. That'll work.

I grasp its handle and push from the floor. My wounded leg cries out at the exertion, but I press forward. Heart pounding in my ears, I cross the room. Soren lies moaning on the floor, streaked in blood and mumbling incoherently.

Odissa stalks toward him, drawing close now. A dagger glints in her hand.

I push my leg faster, ignoring the pain. A few more steps and I'll intercept her.

I heft the scepter, just as she leaps for him, knife outstretched. I club her body mid-air. She crashes into the wall with a crunch. Whimpering against the stone, she slumps, her eyes searching the room but seeing nothing. I limp toward her, dragging the tip of the scepter across the floor. It screeches against the marble, the sharp sound mingling with her mewling protests. Her arm twists at an unnatural angle. Blood runs from her many cuts.

As I approach her, she lifts her face and squares her jaw, meeting my gaze with her steely eyes. "Finish it," she spits. "Put me out of my misery."

I raise the scepter, touching the soft part of her throat just beneath her chin. It would be so easy. One final thrust through her soft flesh with a sharp metal pike, and she'd be gone.

Because of her, Soren lies in a pool of blood. I should end her. For him. For my ten-year-old self and the life she robbed from me. Revenge is sweet; avenge is sweeter still.

"What are you waiting for, death-dealer? Quickly now."

My hand twitches around the handle, readying for the final push. I lift her jaw further, exposing her lymph. Swift and easy. As easy as sliding my knife across my target's throat, the day I made my first kill.

My stomach twists into a hard knot, and my anger snuffs out. My fingers slacken. My make-shift club clatters to the floor.

I won't do it.

Odissa trained me to be a killer. She cultivated me into her personal weapon, void of emotion, blind to the beauty of the world. If I kill her now, I'm no better than the monster she created me to be.

She stares up at me, her mouth popping open in surprise. I kick the scepter away from both of us, discarding it like a poison snakefish.

I lean in until our ragged breaths mix. I grip the glowing pendant around her neck and yank. The chain snaps. Its magical glow dims. I throw it away, and the metal clatters across the floor.

I lean close so Odissa can hear every word, and I look her in the eye. "If I kill you, that'd be too easy for you. Too quick." I cup her face. "Who am I to deprive the Eater of Souls from her midnight snack?"

She twists and snaps her teeth. With my knife, I cut a strip of cloth from my skirt, and then I bind her hands and ankles.

Her eyelids flutter shut, and she slouches against the wall. "I should have killed you in the Drink," she wheezes.

The threat contained, my pain rears up and swallows me. I buckle at the knees, landing on all fours with a jolt. My arms wobble, burning as they support my weight.

Soren.

My elbow bends. My hand inches forward. One knee follows. My wounded leg drags behind me, careful to avoid knocking the knife deeper.

Soren.

He cannot be dead. The pain I feel now is nothing to the loss of him. That, I will not survive.

Slowly, I make my way to him, hauling my broken body onto his chest. His ribs expand and collapse in rhythm—shaky, but breathing.

"Soren."

He groans, and his head tips toward me. He opens one eye. With bloody fingers, he digs into his pocket, producing the opal ring. "Enna," he whispers. "You never answered my question."

When the emotion rushes in, I do not push it away. I do not shove it deep. I unlock the cage and let it drown me alive. For if this is what love feels like, I never want to surface again.

I cup his cheek, smudging the splatter of blood away. My chest brims with heat, burning with the strength of my joy to see him alive. Breathing. Making shit jokes.

"My heart is yours, pretty prince," I say, smiling. A fat tear rolls down my nose and splashes onto his face. "Forever."

He slides the ring on my finger, a perfect fit.

Chapter Sixty-Two

ENNA

The captain arrives with reinforcements, whisking into the vault in a clatter of whitesteel armor. Soren and I lie together in a heap on the floor, barely moving.

I turn my head toward the door and squint, a dull ringing in my ear. Weapons lie scattered. Odissa slouches against the wall where I left her, covered in blood. She screeches as the captain walks past, and she flails against her bindings, kicking her feet.

Nara's striped face blurs above me as she kneels, checking my pulse. She barks an order at her men. Feet shuffle.

"About time you got here, Captain," Soren wheezes.

"You're a shit comedian, Your Highness."

I lift my arm, wincing, and grasp the captain's wrist. "Don't kill her," I whisper.

Nara frowns as Odissa screeches again with ear-splitting reverberation. The sound echoes throughout the lofty room in endless dissonance. "You sure about that, my lady?"

I nod. "Wouldn't want to disappoint a death goddess now, would we?"

Nara grunts and shouts another order. The warm, smiling face of a healer hovers over me. The healer sings, and magic flows, wrapping me in a cocoon of light.

Pain sears swiftly through my leg as the fibers of my skin knit together. Soren gasps and twitches. His hand squeezes mine against his blood-soaked chest.

Boom. Jewels rattle and fall from their perch. The walls fracture in long, ragged lines, flakes of stone falling to the floor.

A drop of water lands on my cheek, icy as the Drink.

Boom. Sconces snuff out, plummeting the room into pitch darkness. The air grows metallic in my mouth. A hissing mist descends, coating my exposed skin with pricks of moisture. Another drop of water on my cheek.

The healer hesitates, looking toward the ceiling, and the searing pain of magic lessens.

Water falls. In a hissing stream, it hits the floor with a woosh. I'm submerged instantly. My tail snaps together. My gills sprout from my neck. The current spins, tumbles, and roars in my ears. Daggers and rings and bottles of glass churn in the onslaught, bumping into me.

Soren's hand slips from my grip. I reach for him through the icy water, screaming his name. My voice is drowned out by the furious roar of water.

Somewhere in the room, Odissa's laughter gurgles, rasping, maniacal. "Come and get me!" she shrills.

A haze of purple light flickers at the apex of the ceiling, shining through the dark water. Above me, the waterline nears the ceiling, rising fast. A dark shape moves in front of the light—swirling, thick bands of muscle, lined with glowing suckers. In a vortex of tentacles, the goddess of death descends. Her dark laughter crackles through the water.

Tephra touches down, eerily beautiful in the dim purple light. Her torso perches in the epicenter of the writhing mass of her limbs. One muscular hand rests on her hip. The other brandishes her golden trident. Hungry eyes scan the chaos of the room.

The current subsides, and my body comes to rest on the floor. Guards rush the goddess, tridents bared. With a twitch of her tentacles, Tephra flicks them away. I search for Soren among the confusion, finding him nowhere.

This is it. The goddess's gaze lands on Odissa's slumped figure against the wall. The trident moves, pointing straight at the failed death-dealer.

Odissa's eyes crack open, and she glares up at Tephra, eyeing the large, shiny fork. With great effort, she purses her mouth and spits. The saliva spreads into the water, a gelatinous shape, missing the tine.

Tephra blinks. Her chest rumbles with a chuckle. The water quivers, and the vibration rattles my bones.

There. Across the room, I spot the dull glint of Soren's green tail. I push off the floor and glide, weaving between the scattered weapons and fallen soldiers.

"Odissa, darling, how nice to see you again so soon," Tephra says. The corner of her mouth twitches into an almost-smile. One tentacle slithers out, wrapping around Odissa's waist. The tip of the tentacle tucks under her chin, tilting her face up.

Odissa snarls, wrenching her chin away. "I was sabotaged," she hisses.

I find Soren's hand, and he grips me, pulling me tight to his side. Where my ear presses against his chest, I can hear his heart accelerate.

Tephra clucks her tongue. "Now, now," she says wryly. "We had a bargain. You were to win the heart of a prince, with proof, and did you?" She shakes her great head, her gaze landing for a moment on Soren and me, embracing in the face of the unknown. "Seems not."

"You knew!" Odissa's eyes are full of fire. "You *knew* they had that fucking necklace. You set me up."

Tephra eyes the death-dealer. "And?"

Another tentacle slips out, twining around Soren's tail. Before I can react, he's torn from me again, my hands left grasping nothing but water. Tephra yanks him into the air, dangling him in front of her face. She smiles at him. "Hello, little fish," she says. She touches the tine of her trident to his chest. "The price of your heart is quite high. I wonder what *you* would pay to keep it."

He struggles against her grip, but he's weak and still wounded. The tentacle wraps tightly around him, pinning his arms to his sides. His gaze finds mine, eyes wide and searching in the dark water.

"Leave him out of this," I say, wincing. "Please, Your Darkness. Save your wrath for the one worthy of it."

Tephra turns toward me, narrowing her eyes. I shift to meet her glare, ignoring the pain in my tail, and lift my chin. My spines rise, and my fangs lengthen, pushing through my snarling lips.

Her face lights with a flash of recognition. "Enna, darling!" she says. "You've been quite the wild card in our little ruse, haven't you? My dredgebeast sends its regards." The tentacle nearest me slithers closer, the tip of it caressing my tailfin. I eye it warily. Tephra chuckles, and the water trembles in the wake of her humor. "I do like surprises. They keep things interesting for me. And I'm just *starving* for entertainment these days."

"You cannot have him. If you want him, then bargain with me, Goddess, for his heart is mine."

Tephra does not tolerate weakness, and I do not intend to show her mine.

I will chew through the last inch of tentacle muscle if I must, if it means Soren swims free. I didn't come this far just to lose him in the end.

The goddess considers me for a long, agonizing moment. I tremble under the weight of her gaze, fear gripping me with its icy fingers. I have nothing left to bargain, save my soul.

But if that's what Tephra requires for Soren to swim free, so be it. I look her dead in the eye. The cut on my cheek stings with new vigor. Yet I hold myself tall, ready and willing to accept my fate.

Her lips twitch, then smile. "I'm feeling generous this evening," she says. "Take what is yours."

Tephra's tentacle lowers, releasing Soren. He sinks and comes to rest on the floor. I swim toward him as fast as my screaming muscles will carry me, and soon enough, his hands find mine, pulling me into a trembling embrace.

Odissa growls in protest. "Fuck you both."

Tephra turns on her, raising her trident. "Odissa of Vespyr, you have failed your bargain. Accept your consequence." Her voice booms like thunder. Odissa pales before her, scrabbling and kicking her tail as the trident lowers.

With a squelch of flesh, Tephra stabs her with the golden fork, lifting Odissa's writhing body to meet her parted lips. With a crunch and a gulp, Odissa's screams cut short, and silence settles over the room. Tephra's black tongue swipes over her lips, licking up the remnants of her snack. She hums with pleasure, casts one final look at us, and snaps her fingers.

As quickly as it filled, the room drains of water, and the goddess disappears. The soldiers sink to the floor, flopping their fins until their bones snap and rearrange into legs.

Soren holds me in the descended darkness, the only sound our ragged breathing and the beating of our hearts.

His lips brush the top of my head, as he murmurs, "I would not have parted with you that easily, my queen."

"I like the sound of that," I whisper, my heart warming at the thought. *His queen.* I tilt my face up to meet his, and he rewards me with a kiss, deep and sweet and tainted with blood.

Chapter Sixty-Three

SOREN

ONE WEEK LATER

The doors to the throne room open to reveal a sprawling velvet carpet. Voices murmur and bodies shift, the sounds of an entire kingdom showing up to witness the beginning of a new age. Coral subjects crowd together in the space, the colors of their clothes and scales vibrant against the white-washed walls. Flowers drip from the ceiling in cascading clusters, another of Lady Myrrh's exquisite designs.

"Are Your Highnesses ready?" Hugo says, clapping a hand over my shoulder. He squeezes softly. I turn to catch his gaze, and he smiles at me with tangible warmth.

A tight knot forms in my throat as I look at him. "Thank you, Hugo," I croak. "For getting me to this day."

He squeezes my shoulder once more and releases. "I'm looking forward to seeing you on that throne for good. And you, too, my lady."

Enna squeezes my hand, and I look at her, pulling strength from the affection swimming in her gaze.

"Thank you, sir," she says.

I drink in the look on her face. She's radiant today, glowing from the inside out. Her unruly short hair has been molded into a delicate array of curls on top of her head, woven with beads and diamonds. Her scars have all but faded by now, shrinking into a dreadful memory. *She's here*, I remind myself. *She's mine.*

Since I was a guppy, I'd dreamed of this day, and I'd always hoped it would feel this *right*.

"Are you ready, Your Highness, or are we going to admire your queenie's face all afternoon?" The captain stands at the door, holding it open with a ridiculous grin.

Enna laughs, and I kiss her forehead. "Something like that."

"Off you go now," Hugo says, nudging us forward.

Enna tugs my hand, and we begin our promenade down the aisle. Her white silk skirts trail behind her in a long train, embroidered with silver thread to match my formal jacket.

My mother waits for us at the top of the dais, holding herself in perfect posture behind the wedding ritual items—one large, glass vase and two smaller golden jars. In her hand, she holds the ceremonial orb and scepter of my ancestors, freshly cleaned of blood after the incident in the vault. On a pedestal to the side, cushioned in pink velvet, rest two delicate crowns.

Enna and I ascend the steps, coming to a stop before my mother. She greets us with a smile, looking first to Enna and then to me. She begins the ritual, lifting the two smaller jars, each filled with sand. "The one on the left represents Enna," she says, projecting her voice to fill the room. Enna's sand is black and coarse, reminiscent of the Abyss. The jar of smooth white sand is mine.

"A reminder that we all are from the sand, and to the sand we will return." She holds the jars above her head, tilting her head back and closing her eyes. Her lips move as she begins to Voice the ancient ritual, calling on the gods to bless our union.

Her song is low and urgent, matching the quickening pace of my heart. A presence trails its icy claw up my spine, and I shiver. Black mist hisses out of my mother's mouth, pouring into the room. She continues to incant until the entire dais is covered in a thick black cloud.

Ending the spell, her eyes flash open, and she lowers the jars of sand, handing one to each of us.

Together, we lift them, pouring the contents to mix together in the ancestral vessel. They form a speckled pattern as we empty them into the container. When the last of the sand falls from our jars, my mother reaches for our hands.

She places Enna's hand in mine—rough, scarred. I brush my thumb along the top of her knuckles, and she glances at me—my personal devil. My Wicked.

"Repeat the words of the ritual," my mother says. "To the sand we belong, and to the sand we return."

We repeat the words in unison as my mother wraps a thick, satin ribbon around our wrists. Enna's fingers slip into mine, and I squeeze them, relishing the touch.

"By the power of the gods, I pronounce you joined as one. Kneel to accept these crowns as a symbol of your devotion."

We sink to the floor, settling onto our knees. The bulb of the scepter touches my left, then my right shoulder, and my mother places a crown on my head, then on Enna's. The metal is cold and heavy, and my scalp tingles at the new weight.

My mother grasps our bound wrists, lifting them high for the crowd to witness. The crowd whispers in excitement, voices rustling like the hush of wind through reedgrass.

"Kingdom of Coral, rise and greet your Crown!"

Then the crowd erupts into applause, and a band begins to play a sweet, happy tune. Rose petals shower the dais.

A petal has caught in Enna's hair, delicate pink against her sharp features. She rolls her eyes at it, juts her lip out, and attempts to blow it away with a poorly aimed puff of air. It's the most normal thing I've seen her do, and my stomach flutters.

"Does Her Majesty require assistance?" I say.

"Only if the king is willing," she whispers.

I reach for her, brushing the crest of her cheek, her temple, her forehead, before plucking the petal free.

Her lips match the color of the roses, pink and plump. She parts them under my gaze, and her eyes flood with need. I lean in, inhaling the raw scent of her—a blend of darkness and sunlight—and capture the lips of my queen.

Chapter Sixty-Four

ENNA

THE SAND IS COOL under my feet, lit by the moon. Stars stretch and curl behind Audrina in colorful swaths. A wisp of cloud covers the moon's face, the only disruption to an otherwise brilliant, perfect sky.

I'm reminded of my old home in the Drink—the pricks of light against vast nothingness, small bioluminescent shapes hanging in a black sea. I cannot chase the stars or snap at them with my teeth, but I can watch them endlessly, and if I stare long enough, maybe they'll move.

And maybe, if I stare long enough, the feelings from today's events will sort themselves out. *Queen of Coral*. I still can't believe it. Me. This morning, I woke as a death-dealer; tonight, I'll sleep as a queen. It's more than any half-blood from Vespyr could have dreamed.

High tide has shortened the beach, leaving me a few paces of sand on either side as I circumnavigate the keep's walls. The boulders where we first fucked jut out of the surf now, like smooth molars cresting through the dark gums of the sea. On top of the largest boulder reclines a male shape, his green tail hanging lazily in the foam to keep from shifting. My heart quickens at the sight of him—my husband, my king.

A rogue wave crashes over the rock, spraying him in silver beads of water. His hair drips across his face, water slipping down the strong line of his jaw, the scaled expanse of his chest, before tracing the delicate path my fingers ache to follow.

I dive into the surf, paddling out to meet him. The water holds a touch of chill tonight, the cold season beginning to dip and stir its fingers in the reef. At last, a break from the heat.

A rough knob juts out of the rock, and I grab hold as I tread the waves, eyeing the flick of his tail. In a glittering arc, I spit the seawater from my mouth, spraying Soren's tail.

"For someone who wanted a midnight swim, you are much too grounded," I tease.

Soren's teeth flash in a white smile, catching in the light of the moon. "Is that a challenge?" His muscles flex as he slips into the waves, shoulders rolling, his back a perfect arc. The tip of his tail flicks as it submerges in the waves.

Smiling, I sink beneath the surface, and open my eyes to the colors of the reef. Soren paddles backward, watching me with sparkling eyes. The strong curve of his tail ripples with power.

I glide my body over his, starving for his touch, and our tails slide together. My hands find his hair as his arm wraps around my waist. His mouth nuzzles my throat, nibbling along the sensitive lines of my gills. When he reaches my ear, he whispers, "I want to show you something tonight."

My hands slip down the hard plane of his stomach, my claws catching on the raised edge of his scales. "Oh?"

His chuckle vibrates through me. "How do you feel about graveyards?"

My answering smile spreads on instinct—wide and greedy. "I love them."

"Thought you might. There's a new site nearby." He slips from my embrace, leading the way.

We swim over the shallow reef, bellies skimming the urban sprawl of the homes perched among the coral forest. Fish dart into their holes as our shadows pass over the slumbering city.

The reef soon drops into open water. Soren leads me into the expanse, the proximity of the corals dropping sharply away. He dives, and we follow the slope to the sea floor. There, lying in the sand, rests the skull of a dredgebeast.

The large skull nestles in the sand, mouth still parted to display its rows of sharp, pointed teeth. The rib cage reaches for the surface like curved fingers around empty water, caught dead and grasping. The large bones slope and curl into the sand, disappearing beneath the grains. Small fish lounge by lazily, nibbling the last remnants of its flesh.

"The captain said it showed up a week ago." Soren turns to assess me, and I realize I've stopped swimming. "You okay?"

I stare at the beast, the particular curve of its teeth, and frown. The scales on my neck prickle in recognition.

"Yeah, I'm okay."

I flick my tail, gliding to approach her great skull. I grasp a tooth, sliding my hand over the smooth bone, searching for a crack. The next tooth is smooth, and the next. I round the bottom jaw, searching for the proof I'm sure will be here. My fingers slip into a crevice on the back of her pointed molar, nearly invisible to the casual observer. I trace the fissure in wonder. My tail prickles with memory—the rip of my flesh, the grinding of my claws against the unpierceable enamel.

Soren's arm brushes my waist, bubbles lifting from the stir of his tail. "Isn't it marvelous? I've never seen one up close, and as of last week, there's one here on my reef."

"I imagine it got caught by a predator," I whisper. My spirit shivers for a moment, acknowledging the uncanny with rising spines. Somehow, the Eater of Souls left me a trophy.

I slip away from the jaw, trailing my fingers along the edge of her gum, her nose, finding my way to her giant eye socket, hollowed out by the work of bloodfish. I settle into the hollow cave, resting against the cool bone. Soren joins me, tucking into my side.

"She's beautiful," I say.

"She?" he says. "How do you know?"

I smile. "Because I killed her."

He grips my face, turning me to look him in the eye. His gaze blazes with anger. His jaw flexes, the veins on his forehead lifting from his skin. "When?"

"Remember that time I fainted at breakfast and ended up in the healer's tank?"

His eyes widen. "How did it get here?"

I shrug. "Tephra has a wild imagination. I'm sure she had her reasons. I won my blood price fair as the tides—perhaps she thought to reward me with a trophy."

Soren leans back against the bone, studying the slope of the eye socket. "Caught by a predator." He chuckles. "How'd you do it?"

I lift up my hands and flutter my claws. "With these and a little help from you."

His forehead wrinkles. "Why didn't you tell me sooner?"

"We were too busy fucking."

Soren growls, dragging me on top of him. His tail wraps around mine and his hands slide up my back to twist in my hair. "You're telling me you killed a dredgebeast with your bare hands?"

I nod against the tightness of his grip, my scalp burning. "And teeth," I say, swiping my fangs with the flat of my tongue. "It stood between me and the safety of a certain pretty prince, so I devoured it." His collarbone slopes into a delicious divot beneath his neck, and I trace the line with my claw. "Do you require a demonstration?"

He growls, his sheath barrier rising to meet the slick of my scales. "I require nothing of you, my queen, only your love in return." Our touch is electric, igniting a fire within us even the chilly waters of the night cannot extinguish. He kisses my forehead, my cheek, my nose. "You've stolen my heart, and I have no intentions of escaping your clutches."

His lips press into the dimple on my chin. "Not now," he says. He sucks on my bottom lip. "Not ever."

I could stay here forever, wrapped in the arms of my king—my love, my equal.

As his kiss consumes me, the last internal fetter in my chest loosens and falls.

This is what freedom feels like.

THE OCTOPUSSY'S GARDEN

Spicy scenes and where to find or avoid them:
Chapter Nineteen
Chapter Thirty-Two
Chapter Forty-Two
Chapter Forty-Three (first half)
Chapter Fifty-Six (second half)

ACKNOWLEDGMENTS

First thanks goes to my husband, my real-life book boyfriend. Thanks for showing me the fairytale moments in our every day world. I couldn't do this without you.

Thank you to my ever-supportive family and friends. Special thanks to Mom and Dad, for always believing in me. To my sister for playing mermaids with me in the pool. To my brother for introducing me to my first fantasy book.

To all my writing friends, I owe you a great deal of thanks. To Laura, Laura, and Cait: our critique group is the best thing that's happened to my writing career. I'm so glad we found each other, and I cherish our time together each week! Thank you for helping me get project stabby mermaids into completed book form. To my alpha and beta readers: Hannah, Jenna, Ashley, Emma, and Jane, your feedback was incredible and inspiring, and I'm so grateful for your time and insight. You helped take this book to the next level. To my book club, my college roomies, my sisters of the heart, my Blackberry Winos: Hannah, Susanna, and Kaitlin, you have kept me afloat through many a rocky sea, and I couldn't have done this without your support. To Lexi, Ashley, Jen, Rowan, Jessica, and Alexis, my first readers: I wouldn't have made it this far without your encouragement and enthusiasm for our mutual love of sharing story ideas around the middle school lunch table.

A huge thank you to my wonderful editing team. Christine, your developmental edits took my book baby to depths I didn't think possible. Zainab, you empowered me with your shouty caps, enthusiasm for my work, and your fairy godmother powers to make my words sing. Laura, your eagle eyes saved me from many embarrassing typos.

And finally to you, my reader, for taking a chance on this one, for taking a chance on me. Thank you.

About the Author

When Liesl West was a child, she desperately wanted to be the little mermaid. Maybe it's because she grew up in rural Ohio, USA, without an ocean in sight, but something about the sea has always called to her. It's just too bad she can't swim. She can, however, write dark fantasy mermaid romance featuring strong female characters and their moody, brooding love interests. And for now, that's close enough.

Visit her website www.lieslwest.com to learn more, and find her on social media @authorlieslwest

Stay connected with Liesl. Join her Newsletter:

www.lieslwest.com/links

LEAVE A REVIEW

I hope you enjoyed your time in the Sea of Adria.
Please consider leaving a review on your preferred platform!

CONTENT NOTES

This book is intended for mature audiences and contains the following sensitive content: profanity, violence, explicit sexual intimacy, battle sequences, monsters, knife violence, blood, past death of a parent to murder, past death of a parent to suicide, physical abuse, and emotional abuse. This is dark fantasy but not dark romance; intimate scenes do not contain the violent elements described.

Please read safely. If you have any questions, or you're wondering about the presence of a trigger not listed here, please contact me by email: author@lieslwest.com

Printed in Great Britain
by Amazon